Strange Tales from The Strand

Strange Tales
from
The Strand

Selected and introduced by
Jack Adrian

Foreword by Julian Symons

Oxford   New York
OXFORD UNIVERSITY PRESS
1991

Oxford University Press, Walton Street, Oxford OX2 6DP

Oxford New York Toronto
Delhi Bombay Calcutta Madras Karachi
Petaling Jaya Singapore Hong Kong Tokyo
Nairobi Dar es Salaam Cape Town
Melbourne Auckland
and associated companies in
Berlin Ibadan

Oxford is a trade mark of Oxford University Press

British Library Cataloguing in Publication Data
Data available

Library of Congress Cataloging in Publication Data
Strange tales from the Strand / selected and introduced by Jack Adrian;
foreword by Julian Symons.
p.   cm.
1. Fantastic fiction, English.   2. Horror tales, English.
3. Supernatural—Fiction.   I. Adrian, Jack.   II. Strand magazine
(London, England)
PR1309.F3S7   1991   823'.0873808—dc20   91-21493 CIP
ISBN 0-19-212305-X

Printed in the USA

Dedicated to the Editors
of the
Strand Magazine

H. Greenhough Smith (1891–1930)
Reeves Shaw (1930–1941)
R. J. Minney (1941–1942)
Reginald Pound (1942–1946)
Macdonald Hastings (1946–1950)

Foreword

STRANGE enough, these stories from the *Strand*, and remarkably various. Lord Beden, careering along in his 12 hp Napier at 40 miles an hour rather than the statutory 12 (the year is 1901) crashes into a totally imaginary rival 'kind of motor car' with fatal results. In another motor car story, 'A Sense of the Future', *circa* 1924, the world supply of oil gives out, cars become obsolete, and after three months of turmoil we are back to horse-drawn traffic. The future also looms ominously when a pawnbroker finds he has in stock a camera that takes snaps of it, five, ten, or fifteen years ahead according to where you point the numbered arrow. Elsewhere a newspaper dated 1971 is pushed through a letter-box forty years earlier, a violin plays with nobody plucking the strings because its maker long ago sold his soul to the devil . . .

That gives no more than a hint of the contents in this box of all-sorts. These are stories that breathe strongly of the years when they were written, many of them Victorian or Edwardian, and are none the worse for that. Their strangeness, and occasional horror, have no touch of science fiction—the nearest thing to it is a lizard with a body 'about the bigness of two horses' unwisely wakened from centuries of slumber by a speleologist. A tale by Edgar Wallace, surprisingly about neither crime nor horse racing, tells how the world went blind for five days. Grant Allen contributes a piece about the destruction of London by earthquake. What look at first like ghost stories, by 'Sapper' and W. L. George, turn out to be crimes of a particularly nasty kind. A tale about a plane crash has a climax bearing some resemblance to Agatha Christie's *Ten Little Niggers*. Greenhough Smith, who edited the *Strand* from its beginning for nearly forty years, contributes a slightly dotty version of the 'dead body with no footprints in the surrounding snow, how did it happen?' story at which G. K. Chesterton was so expert. This is one of half-a-dozen stories here that could easily have found a place in Jack Adrian's companion volume of 'detective stories' from the *Strand*.

These are typical *Strand* stories—robust, unpretentious, not pretending to psychological subtlety. Most of them were written with no more serious purpose than to occupy a reader's attention for an hour; yet the best do more than that, leaving echoes in the mind. Hugh Walpole's tale of the hatred felt by unsuccessful Fenwick for lucky Foster shows the darker side of a writer wrongly believed to have produced nothing but work of saccharine sweetness by those who don't know such chilling novels as *Above The Dark Circus* and *Portrait of a Man With Red Hair*. Villiers de l'Isle-Adam's story, a genuine find, savours horror in a way reminiscent of Poe, and W. W. Jacobs's equally horrific piece gains some of its effectiveness from the things deliberately ignored, like the reason for murder. And of course Conan Doyle and E. Nesbit, with whom the collection ends, were never less than expert tellers of tales.

It is indeed the capacity to tell a tale that comes through particularly strongly from the collection. The writers knew what their predominantly male audience wanted, and that they were able to supply it. The zest they felt, the gusto of their writing, is what keeps one turning the pages with enjoyment today.

Julian Symons

Acknowledgements

I should like to express my gratitude to the staff of the Bodleian Library, Oxford—to all those in the Old Library Reading Rooms, the Copying Department, and the Stack, and in particular to R. J. Roberts, Deputy Librarian and Keeper of Printed Books—for all their varied and crucial assistance in the preparation of this volume. I should also like warmly to acknowledge the very generous help given to me by Bob Adey, the late Derek Adley, Mike Ashley, my editor Michael Cox, Roger Ellis, Professor Douglas G. Greene, Eric Korn, Bill Lofts, Tony Medawar, Joke and the late Joe Whitt, as well as Sylvia Hardy and Christopher Rolfe of the H. G. Wells Society and Roger Lancelyn Green of the Arthur Conan Doyle Society.

The full history of the *Strand* was vividly set down by Reginald Pound (the magazine's fourth editor) in *The Strand Magazine: 1891–1950* (1966), a fascinating slice of social and literary history. John Sutherland's *Companion to Victorian Fiction* (1988), too, has been of inestimable value as a source-book.

Contents

Introduction

THE *Strand Magazine*—the monthly budget of stories, features, and interviews, profusely illustrated, which ran from 1891 to 1950—was a child of its time, a mirror of its age, the paradigm upon which a score or more of other monthly magazines modelled themselves and for a time flourished, though none with the extraordinary popularity of their exemplar. The *Strand* was enormously, uniquely, successful.

When the first sixpenny issue appeared it sold out so rapidly it had to be reprinted, and then reprinted again; and then yet again at a 'special reprint' price of a shilling. So popular was this premier number that the second issue was put back nearly three weeks, finally appearing over two months after the first. Altogether something approaching 300,000 copies of that initial issue were printed and sold, a staggering number for the time.

This runaway success was due partly to the canny business sense of the *Strand*'s founder, the publisher George (soon to be Sir George) Newnes. Although the first issue was dated January 1891, and would normally have been on sale in London and the larger provincial cities a few days prior to the first of the month, Newnes decided not simply to push publication forward by a few more days to gain pre-Christmas goodwill, but three whole weeks, fiercely advertising the launch countrywide on billboards, hoardings, through the trade, and, especially, in his own already hugely successful downmarket weekly *Tit-Bits*. The lengthy lead-time together with Newnes' main promotional weapon—the slogan 'A monthly magazine costing sixpence *but worth a shilling*'—created a furore that has rarely been paralleled in the field of periodical publishing.

There were, of course, other monthly magazines to be found in High Street newsagents and on railway station bookstalls in this last decade of the nineteenth century: *London Society*, *Temple Bar*, *Longman's Magazine*, *Cassell's Family Magazine*, *Blackwood's*, *Macmillan's Magazine*, *Belgravia*, the *Cornhill*. All were worthy, all reasonably prosperous; a number had fine literary track-records—the *Cornhill*, market-leader amongst the monthlies, had at one time or another serialized novels by many of the foremost writers of the day, including Wilkie Collins, Trollope, Thackeray, Elizabeth Gaskell, Hardy, and George Eliot; *Temple Bar*, its nearest rival, works by Kingsley, Gissing, Trollope, Mrs Henry Wood; *Cassell's*, newly-famous house-authors such as Stevenson, Quiller-Couch, and Rider Haggard. Yet all now were more or less drab and uninspiring in both content and presentation—especially the latter, since illustrations were rarely to be found breaking up page after page of closely-packed type.

The *Strand* changed all that. Newnes' dream of an illustration, or at least some pictorial or ornamental device, on every page was a technical impossibility in January 1891 (though achieved very soon afterwards); his initial compromise of an illustration at the start of every 'fold' and a less eye-straining typeface was enough of a revolution to be going on with. He also eschewed serials (at least in the first half-decade of the magazine's existence), resolving that each monthly issue should be organically whole: as he said, 'like a book'. He knew, of course, that a powerful serial could act as a hook, forcing the reader to buy the following issue (the sensational serials featured in *Tit-Bits* assured him of that); but, something of a psychologist, he argued that readers might well feel a sense of satisfaction in starting and finishing a periodical with no loose ends hanging over—which, in turn, could be a crucial factor in a new market rapidly gaining in importance for magazine publishers: that of the railway bookstall.

With the rail network now reaching nearly all parts of the country, and six- or seven-hour journeys a long-distance norm, Alice's memorable plaint—'What is the use of a book without pictures . . .?'—struck home. A magazine with interminable columns of unbroken type, or even a 'Yellowback', however thrilling its plot, was far more likely to bring on a headache than relieve the tedium and discomfort of extended travel. Far better to offer the rail-traveller a bright and bustling magazine, plentifully illustrated, with half a dozen complete stories, a number of entertaining articles (on flower arranging, say, the Port of London, and head-hunters in Borneo), a children's corner, and a page of quizzes or photographic curiosities (the biggest tricycle in the world; the youngest engine-driver—4-year-old Hume Gibson Richards, known to his family as 'Buster', of Laramie, Wyoming—on record; the smallest model of Westminster Abbey constructed entirely out of matchsticks). And all for half the price of his rivals.

George Newnes was an entrepreneur in an age of entrepreneurs. Once the *Strand* was established, other publishing moguls stepped in. The firm of Routledge (with Astor money behind it), which had pioneered the Shilling Railway Library 'Yellowback' during the 1850s, and which had probably been hardest hit by this new style of railway reading, brought out the *Pall Mall Magazine* in 1893. Its content, however, was in general as stodgy as its initial boast that it would maintain a 'high and refined literary and artistic standard'. It also suffered from its proprietors' insistence that it should be priced at a shilling. In 1895 the book publishers Ward, Lock put out the *Windsor*, a determinedly middle-class monthly, which remained throughout its rack-life (it expired in 1939) the safest magazine on the market. Arthur Pearson, who had once worked for Newnes then broken away to start *Pearson's Weekly* (a competitor to Newnes' *Tit-Bits* though with a strong science fiction bias), came out with *Pearson's Magazine*, a bright and busy sixpennyworth which, however, never quite became the serious rival Pearson himself intended it to be. Possibly, at the outset, the colour of its cover had something to do with this: a vivid, indeed garish, yellow and with a predominantly Art Nouveau design, it perhaps had in the public mind unfortunate associations with John Lane's already ailing but still notorious *Yellow Book*, then so closely linked with the recent trial of Oscar Wilde, although Wilde had never contributed a line to it (the *Windsor*, too, sported a yellow wrapper, though a rather more feminine, and thus acceptable, shade of lemon-and-lime). Alfred Harmsworth (later Lord Northcliffe) had worked for Newnes as well but, even before Pearson, had left to launch his own weekly compendium of fascinating trivia, *Answers*. His own answer to the *Strand* was *Harmsworth's Magazine* (later—cleverly pre-empting all other publishers who might have wished to utilize street-titles taken from the nation's, and the Empire's, capital—the *London Magazine*). Harmsworth impudently priced his own monthly at 3*d*., thus undercutting the undercutter.

Other general interest monthlies appeared over the years: *Nash's Magazine* (later to merge with the *Pall Mall*), the *National Magazine*,

Hutchinson's; and under the novelist Max Pemberton, *Cassell's Magazine* (originally launched in 1867) underwent a complete facelift in an endeavour to match the new standard set by Newnes's prodigy. Yet none throve as the *Strand* throve; none, indeed, even approached the *Strand*'s initial print-run.

Looking at those very early issues it is at times difficult to see what all the fuss was about. In quality of printing and general presentation the magazine was undeniably different from its predecessors. And it was cheaper. Even so, the featured fiction—upon which Newnes based all his hopes—is by no means enticing. The novelist Grant Allen appears, as does J. Maclaren Cobban; the young E. W. Hornung (later creator of Raffles but then so young, and so unknown, that on his first appearance his initials are misprinted 'S. W.') provided a couple of tales of the Australian Outback; there is an indifferent story by Walter Besant, and one, clearly bought on a second-rights basis, from the American Frank R. Stockton. Stanley J. Weyman, still some years from being the leading, and wealthiest, historical novelist of the time, contributed a competent tale. Otherwise, a good deal of the fiction emanated from the Continent: Pushkin, Prosper Mérimée, Daudet, Lermontov, Henryk Sienkiewicz (later author of *Quo Vadis?*); even the children's stories (within a decade the sole province of the splendid Edith Nesbit) were mainly French, the very first, in that January 1891 issue, from Voltaire.

Yet in less than a year from launch the *Strand* was selling not just 300,000 copies a month but nearly half a million (with an aggregate readership of between two and three million), and was the pre-eminent British monthly periodical.

This sudden surge in circulation at a time when interest would normally have been expected to slacken—new magazines, however pugnacious their promotion, however enticing their content, rarely maintain their initial momentum—was due solely to the enormous success of the series of Sherlock Holmes short stories by Arthur Conan Doyle that began to appear from the July 1891 issue onwards. It would be impossible to exaggerate their popularity, or, indeed, their significance in the history of popular fiction, not only in Britain but worldwide. They were, for the time, unique.

In writing of a private 'consulting' detective—one who had no links with the official force (apart from when he solved their cases for them) and who let it be known that his services were available to the general public—Doyle was creating an entirely new genre (Poe's Dupin, whom Doyle admired, was a dilettante, more akin to Holmes' idle brother Mycroft than to Holmes himself); in making sure that his hero solved his cases by his own powers of observation, and by a deductive reasoning process that could be followed effortlessly not only by his faithful, but far less acute, companion and the scoffing police but, crucially, by the readers themselves, he was presenting a wholly new approach to story-telling; and by placing Holmes at the centre of a series of short stories, complete in themselves but linked cyclically, he was launching a revolutionary new literary form and setting a pattern for detective fiction still in use today, a century later.

It would not be overly fanciful to liken the launch of the *Strand* to the launch of a spacecraft. Newnes' enthusiasm, money, and canny promotional abilities sent the magazine soaring high into the pub-lishing empyrean; publication of the Holmes stories acted as the crucial secondary booster, at almost precisely the moment when the initial thrust was beginning to fail, hurling the *Strand* into safe orbit. And just how safe that orbit was may be gauged from the fact that when Doyle selfishly threw his hero off the edge of the Reichenbach Falls in 1893 (to general consternation: 'You brute!' an outraged correspondent wrote; in London wags tied black mourning bands around their upper arms; and when George Newnes informed an aghast board of directors of Doyle's decision it was as if he were announcing the end of the world) it was too late to do any major damage. By then readers were firmly hooked; the *Strand* was a part of their lives, and by the end of the decade, seven years later, it had almost gained the status of a national institution.

During this first decade of the magazine's existence the notion was fostered in the public mind that George Newnes himself was the man in charge, the man who took the decisions, the man who, every month, signed all the final proofs; it was even proclaimed on the masthead: 'Edited by George Newnes'. In truth the real editor was H. Greenhough Smith, a tall, scholarly individual with pince-nez whose sober looks belied his true personality; in fact Smith had a dry wit and was fond of complicated word-games and fiercely combative poker sessions, during the course of which his pale, routinely expressionless face gave him a distinct advantage.

He was a peerless editor, precisely the right man for the job (there is strong evidence that the *Strand* was originally his brain-child, Newnes taking on the idea and providing the backing, the enthusiasm, and the benefit of his own considerable commercial clout). Smith demanded from his fiction writers pace, colour, and, above all, plot, preferably with a twist in the tail, a sudden and startling upending of the reader's expectations (in this he was guided by his fondness for Maupassant, whom he read in the original; he was, as well, an authority on French verse). Readability went without saying; not everyone had the Conan Doyle touch, but during Smith's 40-year reign as editor remarkably few truly execrable writers appeared in the *Strand*'s pages. This did not mean that Smith liked all he bought; he published a good deal of tosh in his time, and winced at it. But the tosh that he accepted, paid for (always on acceptance, never on publication—a house rule for which a considerable number of hard-pressed writers must have given thanks over the years), and printed was invariably the very best tosh available—whether lush, perfervid romance from Ethel M. Dell, the impossibly glittering opulence of E. Phillips Oppen-heim, or stark, blazing-eyed melodrama from Sapper. Like all great editors, Smith knew his public.

To be sure he had his blind spots. While sultans of the circulating libraries such as Hugh Walpole, Gilbert Frankau, and Warwick Deeping were well represented in the *Strand*'s pages, Galsworthy made few appearances (two stories and some paragraphs on 'How I Broke Into Writing' in the company of other bestsellers of the day); Stanley J. Weyman (a single story in the magazine's first year) and Baroness Orczy (a paragraph or two in one of the *Strand*'s symposia) even fewer; Maurice Hewlett (the hugely popular historical roman-ticist) and Anthony Hope none at all. Since it can hardly have been the case that such writers, or their agents, ignored the *Strand* (which, after all, paid the highest fees of all the monthlies), the only conclusion to be drawn is that Smith himself did not care for their work. Some editorial exclusions seem illogical, even arbitrary. Smith bought any amount of material by Sapper, who was, without question, a bad writer, yet nothing from Sax Rohmer, not much better. But while Sapper may have been a poor stylist he was a fine story-teller; Rohmer was both an inferior writer and a lamentable story-teller.

Smith was keen on humour and promoted most of the leading exponents of the day, including W. W. Jacobs and P. G. Wodehouse, the latter having started his writing career on Newnes' boys' paper *The Captain* and then, as it were, moved across the corridor: from 1906 until 1940 he supplied nearly two hundred short stories to the *Strand* and half a dozen serials. And if he wasn't available there were plenty of sub-Wodehousean (some only just sub) writers—like Denis Mackail, Ian Hay, K. R. G. Browne, and Anthony Armstrong—who were.

If *The Times* was the newspaper of record, the *Strand* was its equivalent in the periodical field. The great and the good clamoured to write for it—even if it was only two hundred words for one of the magazine's famous symposia, such as 'Who Has the Best Time: Man or Woman?', 'What Makes a Joke *Go*?', 'What Types Do Women Like Best?', 'Are Cats Intelligent?' (a resounding 'yes' to that one; other questions were not so readily agreed on)—or be written about in it. In the same issue that saw the initial adventure of Sherlock Holmes there appeared the first in a long-running series of 'Illustrated Interviews': the interviewees included Jules Verne, Rider Haggard, Sir Lawrence Alma-Tadema (whose often *risqué* Roman canvases adorned many a wealthy Edwardian's walls), Cardinal Manning, the lawyer Sir George Lewis (of whom it was said, though not in the interview, that he knew more heinous secrets about the aristocracy than did the Royal Family), W. S. Gilbert, Sir Henry Irving, and Mr Charles Lutwidge Dodgson. All the interviews (uncredited, but in fact carried out by the journalist Harry How, a *Tit-Bits* staffer) were lavishly illustrated with photographic portraits and pictures of the subject's house, interiors and exterior. Smith devised another ingenious method of ingratiating his magazine into the hearts and minds of the highborn and the celebrated: 'Portraits of Celebrities at Different Times of Their Lives' consisted of just that, with an accompanying text that oozed servility.

Other famous men were allowed to be rather more trenchant: throughout the 1930s Winston Churchill (who had first appeared in the *Strand* in 1908, with the serialization of *My African Journey*) wrote prolifically and at times aggressively on a range of topics from 'The Tragic Story of Parnell' to 'The Truth About Hitler'. He also contributed only the second, and as it turned out the last, piece of short fiction he wrote (the first was a *conte cruel* for the *London*

Magazine at the turn of the century), a story based on Shakespeare's *Julius Caesar* and part of a series whose authors included John Buchan and Clemence Dane. The £450 fee he received per article went some way to keeping the wolf from the door during that fraught decade.

The *Strand* had continued publication through the First World War, though, like its rivals, its page-count noticeably shrank. The Second World War was a different matter. With the Germans this time cutting off supplies of paper completely from northern Europe and sinking merchantmen bringing bolts of it from Canada, the magazine drastically slimmed down to eighty editorial pages and a handful of advertisements (in its heyday the advertisements alone had taken up eighty pages). From the October 1941 issue it was reduced to pocket-book dimensions, a size pioneered in the early 1930s by Theo Stephens' delightful gardening monthly *My Garden* and later seized on and made popular by Stefan Lorant with *Men Only* and *Lilliput*, but not one that seemed ideally suited to the magazine that for fifty years had represented not only the very best in popular literary entertainment but, in its own way, Great Britain itself. Circulation contracted with the page-size.

Although the *Strand* never regained its dimensions, it did, from October 1946, under the editorship of the journalist Macdonald Hastings (whose father had contributed humorous fiction in the 1920s), enjoy an Indian summer. Not so much in the fiction department—although Eric Ambler, Simenon, John Dickson Carr, Graham Greene, Nicholas Blake, W. E. Johns, David Footman, and Mgr Ronald Knox all wrote for it (the last with a Holmes pastiche that recaptured some of the essence of the original)—but in the pictorial.

The young artist Robin Jacques was appointed Art Editor and proceeded to fill the pages with his generation's Young Turks: Mervyn Peake, Ronald Searle, Walter Fawkes (later the political cartoonist Trog), Michael Ayrton, and Jacques himself transformed the *Strand* into a bright and bustling, though little, magazine which for a time was the best on the market. Paper costs and distribution charges, however, had trebled; circulation, now down to a paltry 95,000, had not. In February 1950 the last issue went to press. Macdonald Hastings, unconsciously echoing those City wits who, nearly sixty years before, had protested at Conan Doyle's summary execution of their (though not his) detective hero, placed a black band around his arm, signed the final proof, and shut up shop.

During its sixty years the *Strand* was consistently middlebrow. It steered a safe course through the mainly turbulent decades of its existence; it did not threaten, it did not shock; its goal, as seen by its various editors, was not to expose social evils or injustices. It was there (the odd Churchillean thunderbolt apart) solely to entertain. And this it did, its list of contributors constituting a roll-call of the British popular literary establishment.

There were two particular genres at which it excelled: detective fiction and weird fiction. The former is dealt with in this anthology's companion volume, *Detective Stories from the* Strand; here are collected some of the very best 'strange tales' from its pages—not simply ghost stories, but tales of the weird, the wonderful, the bizarre; stories of darkness and dread from some of the finest writers of the past century. Some are known; some, today, wholly unknown. All knew how to entertain.

Jack Adrian
April 1991

I

REVENANTS

For many *Graham Greene* (1904–91) was one of the greatest novelists of the twentieth century, certainly the greatest of his generation. Most of his finest novels contain a hard core of chilly despair, yet at the same time reveal fresh insights into the human condition. 'Greeneland', an instantly recognizable locale, was travelled by many writers after the 1930s, the decade he placed it firmly on the literary map; there are few serious novelists today who have not been touched in one way or another by his influence. A secretive man, he would on occasion twitch aside the curtains covering his very private life; a book-collector, he knew the worth of his own *oeuvre* and took an inordinate delight in making things difficult for those who collected him, producing pre-UK first editions in obscure countries and limited numbers of British first editions which differed in various minor (though to the collector highly significant) ways from the rest of the print-run. There was a streak of interesting malice in him. He was no armchair novelist: in youth and middle-age he obsessively travelled the world for copy, often in the most dangerous circumstances. In old age he pugnaciously challenged official corruption in the south of France; whether or not the story he often told of playing Russian Roulette was true, he was not averse to feasting with panthers. He wrote a handful of macabre stories—psychological terror tales—of which 'All But Empty' contains the very essence of what W. H. Auden epitheticized as 'grahamgreeneish' seediness and fear, as well as a neat final twist.

After winning the prestigious Newdigate Prize with a poem on the life and death of Amy Robsart, *J. B. Harris-Burland* (*fl.* 1903–25) descended from the rarefied heights of literature to the more commercial plains of pulp. He was a prolific supplier of sensational fiction—titles such as *The Curse of Cloud* (1914), *Love, the Criminal* (1907), and *The Secret of Enoch Seal* (1910) largely speak for themselves—to downmarket publishers like Greening and Everett (both of whom went bankrupt, though not on Harris-Burland's account). He also wrote socio-realist novels (*Workers In Darkness*, 1908; *The Financier*, 1906) touching on plutocratic conspiracies, some engaging fantasy-adventures with a 'Lost Race' theme (notably *The Princess Thora*, 1904), and tales of black magic and the weird (*The Gold-Worshippers*, 1906). *The Red Moon* (1923) presciently features a hero who has a 'licence to kill'. 'Lord Beden's Motor' is written in Harris-Burland's most wild-eyed manner.

For much of his career *Hugh Walpole* (1884–1941) vied with John Galsworthy for the title 'Emperor of the Subscription Libraries'; his one surmounting regret was that his rival was honoured by the Nobel Prize committee and not he. Yet although his narratives were skilfully constructed he lacked Galsworthy's insight and moral indignation (especially in the matter of social injustice and inequality) and could never have written so angry a novel as *A Man of Property*. During the latter part of his career he embarked on a series of swashbuckling historical novels almost in the vein of Rafael Sabatini, chronicling the turbulent history of a Lakeland family, the Herrieses, from the eighteenth century to the twentieth. He was also fascinated by psychological, rather than overtly supernatural, horror, writing a number of novels, including *Portrait of a Man With Red Hair* (1925; as a play, first revealing the talents of Charles Laughton) and *Above the Dark Circus* (1931), which exhibit a Hoffmannesque attitude to the macabre. *The Killer and the Slain* (1941, his last completed novel) is a neglected *tour de force* of terror in which the narrator is possessed by the malevolent spirit of a man he murdered (there is some resemblance to Walter de la Mare's *The Return*). 'The Tarn' is a brilliant and claustrophobic tale which displays all of Walpole's talents in this direction.

Rina Ramsay (*fl.* 1915–30) wrote almost exclusively for the women's market, her work more often than not appearing in the superior periodicals of the day, although stories were published too in downmarket story magazines such as the *Grand* (the *Strand*'s all-fiction stable-mate), the *Novel*, and *Storyteller*. A post-war novel, *The*

Step in the House (1926), was a workmanlike thriller. 'Resurgam' was one of her few contributions to the *Strand*, written at a time (the middle of the First World War) when Greenhough Smith, the editor, was experiencing some difficulty in filling his Contents pages with known names and often having to make do with stop-gaps. Some of the new authors were of inferior quality; Ramsay was not one of them.

F. Tennyson Jesse (1888–1958) was a great-niece of Alfred, Lord Tennyson and an incurable writer, earning her living by journalism and novel writing from the age of twenty. Fascinated by murder ('my chief passion', she once remarked) she edited, and supplied penetrating introductions to, a number of volumes in the Hodge Notable British Trials series, including those for Dougal (the Moat Farm murderer), Madeleine Smith, Mrs Rattenbury, and Evans and Christie. She also utilized her wide knowledge of crime and murder in her fiction: 'The Pedlar' is based on the atrocious 1891 Rainhill murders by Frederick Deeming, while her most celebrated novel *A Pin To See The Peepshow* (1934) relies heavily on the Bywaters-Thompson case of 1922. Jesse wrote two series of stories about a female psychic sleuth, Solange Fontaine (who relies on a 'feeling' for evil to solve her cases): the first for the *Premier Magazine* in 1918–19, the second for the *London Magazine* in 1929 (the latter collected in *The Solange Stories*, 1931). Her most striking weird tale was 'Treasure Trove' (1928, concerning the malign power of thirty silver coins dug up in a farmer's field). 'The Railway Carriage', her last Solange story, combines her fascination for the supernatural with her fascination for the banalities of murder.

Beverley Nichols (1898–1983) was a journalist, novelist, and playwright who in his youth won all the glittering prizes (President of the Oxford Union, acclaimed novelist at the age of 23, on companionable terms with Epstein, Churchill, Augustus John, Shaw, and the Asquiths by 25) yet who is best known today, if he is remembered at all, for his books on cats and flower arranging. He ended his career writing soothing bromides for women's magazines, a kind of male Patience Strong (when reviewing one of Nichols' books Graham Greene insisted on picturing him as a 'maiden lady . . . in rather old-fashioned mauve with a whalebone collar').

Nichols had an exaggerated view of his own talent, feeling that in a hundred years his work would be 'on the same shelf as Jane Austen, Mrs Gaskell, Hazlitt and Lewis Carroll', and a vicious streak: after an attacking review from James Agate (a homosexual, as was Nichols) he threatened to reveal the critic's cottaging proclivities to the police. Nichols and Godfrey Winn (of the same sexual inclination and a very slightly better writer) detested each other. Yet he had courage: his book *Cry Havoc!* (1933) is a muscular polemic against war and the war-makers, and during the 1950s, in the face of Home Office harassment of homosexuals in public life, he tried to spur the famous, such as Somerset Maugham and Noel Coward, into declaring their sexuality in a full-page advertisement in *The Times*. 'The Bell' is an unusually powerful little tale, which must surely have had some influence on Robin Maugham's *The Servant*.

All But Empty

Graham Greene

Iᴛ is not often that one finds an empty cinema, but this one I used to frequent in the early 1930s because of its almost invariable, almost total emptiness. I speak only of the afternoons, the heavy grey afternoons of late winter; in the evenings, when the lights went up in the Edgware Road and the naphtha flares, and the peep-shows were crowded, this cinema may have known prosperity. But I doubt it.

It had so little to offer. There was no talkie apparatus, and the silent films it showed did not appeal to the crowd by their excitement or to the connoisseur by their unconscious humour. They were merely banal, drawing-room drama of 1925.

I suspect that the cinema kept open only because the owner could not sell or let the building and he could not afford to close it. I went to it because it was silent, because it was all but empty, and because the girl who sold the tickets had a bright, common, venal prettiness.

One passed out of the Edgware Road and found it in a side street. It was built of boards like a saloon in an American western, and there were no posters. Probably no posters existed of the kind of films it showed. One paid one's money to the girl of whom I spoke, taking an unnecessarily expensive seat in the drab emptiness on the other side of the red velvet curtains, and she would smile, charming and venal, and address one by a name of her own; it was not difficult for her to remember her patrons. She may be there still, but I haven't visited the cinema for a long time now.

I remember I went in one afternoon and found myself quite

alone. There was not even a pianist; blurred metallic music was relayed from a gramophone in the pay-box. I hoped the girl would soon leave her job and come in. I sat almost at the end of a row with one seat free as an indication that I felt like company, but she never came. An elderly man got entangled in the curtain and billowed his way through it and lost himself in the dark. He tried to get past me, though he had the whole cinema to choose from, and brushed my face with a damp beard. Then he sat down in the seat I had left, and there we were, close together in the wide dusty darkness.

The flat figures passed and repassed, their six-year-old gestures as antique as designs on a Greek coin. They were emotional in great white flickering letters, but their emotions were not comic nor to me moving. I was surprised when I heard the old man next me crying to himself—so much to himself and not to me, not a trace of histrionics in those slow, carefully stifled sobs that I felt sorry for him and did not grudge him the seat. I said:

'Can I do anything?'

He may not have heard me, but he spoke: 'I can't hear what they are saying.'

The loneliness of the old man was extreme; no one had warned him that he would find only silent pictures here. I tried to explain, but he did not listen, whispering gently, 'I can't see them.'

I thought that he was blind and asked him where he lived, and when he gave an address in Seymour Terrace, I felt such pity for him that I offered to show him the way to another cinema and then to take him home. It was because we shared a desolation, sitting in the dark and stale air, when all around us people were lighting lamps and making tea and gas fires glowed. But no! He wouldn't move. He said that he always came to this cinema of an evening, and when I said that it was only afternoon, he remarked that afternoon and evening were now to him 'much of a muchness'. I still didn't realize what he was enduring, what worse thing than blindness and age he might be keeping to himself.

Only a hint of it came to me a moment after, when he turned suddenly towards me, brushing my lips with his damp beard, and whispered.

'No one could expect me to see, not after I've seen what I've seen,' and then in a lower voice, talking to himself, 'From ear to ear.'

That startled me because there were only two things he could mean, and I did not believe that he referred to a smile.

'Leave them to it,' he said, 'at the bottom of the stairs. The black-beetles always came out of that crack. Oh, the anger,' and his voice had a long weary *frisson*.

It was extraordinary how he seemed to read my thoughts, because I had already begun to comfort myself with the fact of his age and that he must be recalling something very far away, when he spoke again: 'Not a minute later than this morning. The clock had just struck two and I came down the stairs, and there he was. Oh, I was angry. He was smiling.'

'From ear to ear,' I said lightly, with relief.

'That was later,' he corrected me, and then he startled me by reading out suddenly from the screen the words, 'I love you. I will not let you go.' He laughed and said, 'I can see a little now. But it fades, it fades.'

I was quite sure then that the man was mad, but I did not go. For one thing, I thought that at any moment the girl might come and two people could deal with him more easily than one; for another, stillness seemed safest. So I sat very quietly, staring at the screen and knew that he was weeping again beside me, shivering and weeping and shivering. Among all the obscurities one thing was certain, something had upset him early that morning.

After a while he spoke again so low that his words were lost in the tin blare of the relayed record, but I caught the words 'serpent's tooth' and guessed that he must have been quoting scripture. He did not leave me much longer in doubt, however, of what had happened at the bottom of the stairs, for he said quite casually, his tears forgotten in curiosity:

'I never thought the knife was so sharp. I had forgotten I had had it reground.'

Then he went on speaking, his voice gaining strength and calmness: 'I had just put down the borax for the black-beetles that morning. How could I have guessed? I must have been very angry coming downstairs. The clock struck two, and there he was, smiling at me. I must have sent it to be reground when I had the joint of pork for Sunday dinner. Oh, I was angry when he laughed: the knife trembled. And there the poor body lay with the throat cut from ear to ear,' and hunching up his shoulders and dropping his bearded chin towards his hands, the old man began again to cry.

Then I saw my duty quite plainly. He might be mad and to be pitied, but he was dangerous.

It needed courage to stand up and press by him into the gangway, and then turn the back and be lost in the blind velvet folds of the curtains which would not part, knowing that he might have the knife still with him. I got out into the grey afternoon light at last, and startled the girl in the box with my white face. I opened the door of the kiosk and shut it again behind me with immeasurable relief. He couldn't get at me now.

'The police station,' I called softly into the telephone, afraid that he might hear me where he sat alone in the cinema, and when a voice answered, I said hurriedly, 'That murder in Seymour Terrace this morning.'

The voice at the other end became brisk and interested, telling me to hold the line, and then the seconds drummed away.

All the while I held the receiver I watched the curtain, and presently it began to shake and billow, as if somebody was fumbling for the way out. 'Hurry, hurry,' I called down the telephone, and then as the voice spoke I saw the old man wavering in the gap of the curtain. 'Hurry. The murderer's here,' I called, stumbling over the name of the cinema and so intent on the message I had to convey that I could not take in for a moment the puzzled and puzzling reply: 'We've got the murderer. It's the body that's disappeared.'

Lord Beden's Motor

J. B. Harris-Burland

A HARD man was Ralph Strang, seventh Earl of Beden, seventy years of age on his last birthday, but still upright as a dart, with hair white as snow, but with the devilry of youth still sparkling in his keen dark eyes. He was, indeed, able to follow the hounds with the best of us, and there were few men, even among the youngest and most hot-headed of our riders, who cared to follow him over all the jumps he put his horse at.

When I first came to Upstanway as a doctor I thought it strange that so good a sportsman should be so unpopular. As a rule a man can do pretty well anything in a sporting county so long as he rides straight to hounds. But before I had been in the place a month I attended him after a fall in the hunting-field, and I saw that a man like that would be unpopular even if he gave all his goods to the poor and lived the life of St Francis of Assisi. Not that he was harsh or even unpleasant, but he had the knack of making one feel foolish and uncomfortable, and there was something in the expression of his eyes that made one unable to look him squarely in the face. His manners, indeed, were perfect, and he retained all the old-world courtliness which seems to have been permanently abandoned by this generation, but I could not help feeling that underneath all his politeness and even hospitality lay a solid substratum of contempt.

It was doubtless this impression which had earned him his unpopularity, for I never heard a single one of his enemies lay anything definite to his charge beyond the fact that his elder brother had died in a lunatic asylum, and that Lord Beden was in some vague way held responsible for this unfortunate event.

But it was not until Lord Beden purchased a 12-h.p. 'Napier' motor-car that the villagers really began to consider him possessed of a devil. And certainly his spirit of devilry seemed to have found a worthy plaything in that grey mass of snorting machinery, which went through the lanes like a whirlwind, enveloped in a cloud of dust, and scattering every living thing close back against the hedges as a steamer dashes the waves against the banks of a river. I had often heard people whisper that he bore a charmed life in the hunting-field, and that another and better man would have been killed years ago; and he certainly carried the same spirit of dash and foolhardiness, and also the same good fortune, into a still more dangerous pursuit.

It was the purchase of this car that brought me into closer contact with him. I had had some experience of motors, and he was sufficiently humble to take some instructions from me, and also to let me accompany him on several occasions. At first I drove the car myself, and tried to inculcate a certain amount of caution by example, but after the third lesson he knew as much about it as I did, and, resigning the steering-gear into his hands, I took my place by his side with some misgivings.

I must confess that he handled it splendidly. The man had a wonderful nerve, and when an inch to one side or the other would probably have meant death his keen eye never made a mistake and his hand on the wheel was as steady as a rock. This inspired confidence, and though the strain on my nerves was considerable, I found after a time a certain pleasurable excitement in these rides. And it was excitement, I can tell you. No twelve miles an hour for Lord Beden, no precautionary brakes downhill, no wide curves for corners. He rode, as he did to hounds, straight and fast. Sometimes we had six inches to spare, but never more, and as often as not another half inch would have shot us both out of the car. We always seemed to come round a sharp corner on two wheels. It was certainly exhilarating. But there was something about it I did not quite like. I don't think I was physically afraid, but I recalled certain stories about Lord Beden's mad exploits in the hunting-field; and it almost seemed to me as though he might be purposely riding for a fall.

Then all at once my invitations to ride with him ceased. I thought at first that I had offended him, but I could think of no possible cause of offence; and, besides, his manner towards me had not changed in any way, and I dined with him more than once at Beden Hall, where he was as courteous and irritating as usual. However, he offered no explanation, and I certainly did not intend to ask for one. I watched him narrowly when we talked about the motor, but he made no mystery about his rides. I noticed, however, that he looked older and more careworn, and that his dark eyes burned now with an almost unnatural brilliancy.

I met him two or three times on the road when I was going my rounds in the trap, and he appeared to be driving his machine more furiously and fearlessly than ever. I was almost glad that his invitations had ceased. Strangely enough, I always encountered him on the same road, one which led straight to Oxminster, a town about twenty miles away.

One evening, however, late in August, while I was finishing my dinner in solitude, I heard a familiar hum and rattle along the road in the distance. In less than a minute I saw the flash of bright lamps through my open window and heard the jar of a brake. Then there was a ring at the bell and Lord Beden was announced.

'Good evening, Scott,' he said, taking off his glasses. 'Lovely night, isn't it? Would you care to come for a ride?' He looked very pale, and was covered with dust from head to foot.

'A ride, Lord Beden?' I replied, thoughtfully. 'Well, I hardly know what to say. Will you have some coffee and a cigar?'

He nodded assent and sat down. I poured him out some coffee, and noticed that his hand shook as he raised the cup to his lips. But driving a motor-car at a rapid rate might easily produce this effect. Then I handed him a cigar and lit one myself.

'Rather late for a ride, isn't it?' I said, after a slight pause.

'Not a bit, not a bit,' he answered, hastily. 'It is as bright as day and the roads clear of traffic. Come, it will do you good. We can finish our cigars in the car.'

'Yes,' I replied, thoughtfully, 'or at any rate the draught will finish them for us.'

'Look here, Scott,' he continued, in a lower voice, leaning over the table and looking me straight in the eyes, 'I particularly want you to come. In fact, you *must* come—to oblige me. I want you to see something which I have seen. I am a little doubtful of its actual existence.'

I looked at him sharply. His voice was cold and quiet, but his eyes were certainly a bit too bright. I should say that he was in a state of intense excitement, yet with all his nerves well under control. I laughed a little uneasily.

'Very well, Lord Beden,' I replied, rising from my chair. 'I will come. But you will excuse me saying that you don't look well tonight. I think you are rather overdoing this motor business. It shakes the system up a good deal, you know.'

'I am not well, Scott,' he said. 'But you cannot cure me.'

I said no more, and left the room to put on my glasses and an overcoat.

We set off through the village at about ten miles an hour. It was a glorious night and the moon shone clear in the sky, but I noticed a bank of heavy black clouds in the west, and thought it not unlikely that we should have a thunderstorm. The atmosphere had been suffocating all day, and it was only the motion of the car that created the cool and pleasant breeze which blew against our faces.

When we came to the church we turned sharp to the right on to the Oxminster Road. It ran in a perfectly straight white line for three miles, then it began to wind and ascend the Oxbourne Hills, finally disappearing in the darkness of some woods which extend for nearly five miles over the summit in the direction of Oxminster.

'Where are we going to?' I asked, settling myself firmly in my seat.

'Oxminster,' he replied, rather curtly. 'Please keep your eyes open and tell me if you see anything on the road.'

As he spoke he pulled the lever further towards him and the great machine shot forward with a sudden plunge which would have unseated me if I had not been prepared for something of the sort. We quickly gathered up speed: hedges and trees went past us like a flash; the dust whirled up into the moonlight like a silver cloud, and before five minutes had elapsed we were at the foot of the hills and were tearing up the slope at almost the same terrific pace.

As we ascended the foliage began to thicken and close in upon us on either side; then the moon disappeared, and only our powerful lamps illuminated the darkness ahead of us. The car was a magnificent hill-climber, but the gradient soon became so steep that the pace slackened down to about eight miles an hour. Lord Beden had not spoken a word since he told me where we were going to, but he had kept his eyes steadily fixed on the broad circle of light in front of the car. I began to find the silence and darkness oppressive, and, to say the truth, was not quite comfortable in my own mind about my companion's sanity. I took off my glasses and tried to pierce the darkness on either side. The moon filtered through the trees and made strange shadows in the depths of the woods, but there was nothing else to be seen, and ahead of us there was only a white streak of road disappearing into blackness. Then suddenly my companion let go of the steering-gear with one hand and clutched me by the arm. 'Listen, Scott!' he cried; 'do you hear it?'

I listened attentively, and at first heard nothing but the throb of the motor and a faint rustling among the trees as a slight breeze began to stir through the wood. Then I noticed that the beat of the piston was not quite the same as usual. It sounded jerky and irregular, faint and loud alternately, and I had an idea that it had considerably quickened in speed.

'I hear nothing, Lord Beden,' I replied, 'except that the engine sounds a little erratic. It ought not to make so much fuss over this hill.'

'If you listen more carefully,' he said, 'you will understand. That sound is the beat of two pistons, and one of them is some way off.'

I listened again. He was right. There was certainly another engine throbbing in the distance.

'I cannot see any lights,' I answered, looking first in front of us and then into the darkness behind. 'But it's another motor, I suppose. It does not appear to me to be anything out of the way.'

He did not reply, but replaced his hand on the steering-gear and peered anxiously ahead. I began to feel a bit worried about him. It was strange that he should get so excited about the presence of another motor-car in the neighbourhood. I was not reassured either when, in rearranging the rug about my legs, I touched something hard in his pocket. I passed my fingers lightly over it, and had no doubt whatever that it was a revolver. I began to be sorry I had come. A revolver is not a necessary tool for the proper running of a motor-car.

We were nearly at the top of the hill now, and still in the shadow of the trees. The road here runs for more than a mile along the summit before it begins to descend, and half-way along the level another road crosses it at right angles, leading one way down a steep slope to Little Stanway, and the other along the top of the Oxbourne Hills to Kelston and Rutherton, two small villages some miles away on the edge of the moors.

We had scarcely reached the level when a few heavy drops of rain began to fall, and, looking up, I saw that the moon was no longer visible through the branches overhead. A minute later there was a low roll of thunder in the distance, and for an instant the scenery ahead of us flashed bright and faded into darkness. I turned up the collar of my coat.

The car was now moving almost at full speed, but to my surprise, before we had gone a quarter of a mile, Lord Beden slowed it down and finally brought it to a full stop with the brake. Then he appeared to be listening attentively for something, but the rising wind and pouring rain had begun to make an incessant noise among the trees, and the thunder had become more loud and continuous. I strained my sense of hearing to the utmost, but I could hear nothing beyond the sounds of the elements.

'What is the matter?' I queried, impatiently. 'Are we going to stop here?'

'Yes,' he replied, curtly. 'That is to say, if you have no objection. There is a certain amount of shelter.'

I drew a cigar from my pocket and, after several attempts, managed to light it. To say the truth, I was in hopes that we should go no further. The downward descent, three-quarters of a mile ahead of us, was about one in ten, and I did not feel much inclined to let my companion take me down a hill of that sort.

Then, for a few seconds, the rustling of the wind and pattering of the rain ceased among the trees, and once more I could distinctly hear the thud, thud, thud of an engine. It might have been a motor-car, but it certainly sounded to me more like the noise a traction engine would make. As we listened the sound came nearer and nearer and appeared to be on our left, still some distance down the hill. Then the storm broke out again with fresh fury, and we could hear nothing else. Lord Beden pulled the lever towards him and we ran slowly forward until we were within thirty yards of the cross-roads, when he again brought the machine to a standstill.

The noise had become much louder now, and was even audible above the roar of the wind and rain. It certainly came from somewhere on our left. I looked down through the trees, and thought I saw a faint red glow some way down the hill. Lord Beden saw it too, and pointed to it with a trembling hand.

'Looks like a fire in the wood,' I said, carelessly. I did not very much care what it was.

'Don't be a fool,' he replied, sharply. 'Can't you see it's moving?'

Yes, he was right. It was certainly moving, and in a few seconds it was hidden by a thicker mass of foliage. I did not, however, see anything very noticeable about it. It was evidently coming up the road to our left, and was probably a belated traction engine returning home from the reaping. I was more than ever convinced of my companion's insanity and wished that I was safe at home. I had half a mind to get off the car and walk, but he had by now managed to infect me with some of his own fear and excitement, and I did not quite fancy being left with no swifter mode of progression than my feet.

The thumping sound came nearer and nearer, and, as we heard it more distinctly, was even more suggestive of a traction engine. Then I saw a red light through the trees like the glow of a furnace, and not more than fifty yards away from us. My companion laid his left hand on the lever and stared intently at the corner.

Then a rather peculiar thing happened. Whatever it was that had been lumbering slowly up the hill like a gigantic snail suddenly shot across the road in front of us like a streak of smoke and flame, and through the trees to our right I could see the red glow spinning up the road to Kelston at over thirty miles an hour. Almost simultaneously Lord Beden pulled down the lever and I instinctively clutched the seat with both hands. We shot forward, took the corner with about an inch to spare between us and the ditch, and dashed off along the road in hot pursuit. But the red glow had got at least a quarter of a mile's start, and I could not see what it proceeded from. A flash of lightning, however, showed a dark mass flying before us in a cloud of smoke. It looked something like a large wagon with a chimney sticking out of it, and sparks streamed out of the back of it until they looked like the tail of a comet.

'What the deuce is it?' I said.

'You'll see when we come up to it,' the Earl answered, between his teeth. 'We shall go faster in a few minutes.'

We were, however, going quite fast enough for me, and though I have ridden on many motors since, and occasionally at a greater

speed, I shall never forget that ride along the Kelston Road. The
powerful machine beneath us trembled as though it were going to
fall to pieces, the rain lashed our faces like the thongs of a whip, the
thunder almost deafened us, the lightning first blinded us with its
flashes and then left us in more confusing darkness, and, to crown
all, a dense volume of smoke poured from the machine in front and
hid the light of our own lamps. It would be hard to imagine worse
conditions for a motor ride, and a man who could keep a steady
hand on the steering-gear under circumstances like these was a man
indeed. I should not have cared to try it, even in the daytime. But
Lord Beden's luck was with him still, and we moved as though
guided by some unseen hand.

'You will find a small lever by your side, Scott,' he said, after a
long pause. 'Pull it towards you until it gives a click. It is an
invention of my own.' I found the handle and, following out his
instructions, saw the arc of light from our lamps shoot another fifty
yards ahead, leaving the ground immediately in front of the car in
darkness. We had gained considerably. The light just impinged on
the streaming tail of sparks.

'At last!' my companion muttered. 'He has always had half a
mile's start before, and the oil has given out before I could catch
him. But he cannot escape us now.'

'What is it, Lord Beden?'

'I am glad you see it,' he replied. 'I thought before tonight that it
was a fancy of my brain.'

'Of course I see it,' I said, sharply. 'I am not blind. But what is
it?'

He did not answer, but a flash of lightning showed me his face,
and I did not repeat the question.

Mile after mile we spun along the lonely country road, but never
gaining another inch. We dashed through Kelston like a streak of
light. It was fortunate that all the inhabitants were in bed. Then we
shot out on to a road leading across the open moor, which stretches
from here to the sea, twenty miles away, and I remembered that
eight miles from Kelston there was a deep descent into the valley of
the Stour, and it was scarcely possible that we could escape
destruction. I quickly made up my mind to overpower Lord Beden
and gain control of the machine.

Then we suddenly began to sweep down a long and gentle

gradient, and second after second our speed increased until the arc of light shone on the machine ahead of us, and I could see what manner of thing it was that we pursued.

It was, I suppose, a kind of motor-car, but unlike anything I had ever seen before, and bearing no more resemblance to a modern machine than a bone-shaker of twenty years ago does to the modern 'free-wheel'. It appeared to be built of iron, and was painted a dead black. In the fore-part of the structure a 5 ft. fly-wheel spun round at a terrific speed, and various bars and beams moved rapidly backwards and forwards. The chimney was quite 10 ft. in height, and poured out a dense volume of smoke. On a small platform behind, railed in by a stout iron rail, stood a tall man with his back to us. His dark hair, which must have reached nearly to his shoulders, streamed behind him in the wind. In each hand he grasped a huge lever, and he was apparently gazing steadily into the darkness before him, though it seemed to me that he might just as well have shut his eyes, for the machine had no lamps, and the only light in the whole concern streamed out from the half-open furnace door.

Then, to my amazement, I saw the man take his hands off the levers and coolly proceed to shovel coal into the roaring fire. I held my breath, expecting to see the flying mass of iron shoot off the side of the road and turn head over heels down the sloping grass. But nothing happened. The machine apparently required no guidance, and proceeded on its way as smoothly and swiftly as before.

I took hold of my companion's arm and called his attention to this somewhat strange circumstance. He only laughed.

'Look at the smoke,' he cried. 'That is rather strange too.' I looked up and saw it pouring over our heads in a long straight cloud, but I did not notice anything odd about it, and I said so.

'Can you smell it?' he continued. I sniffed, and noticed for the first time that there had been no smell of smoke at all, though in the earlier part of the journey we had been half blinded with it. I began to feel uncomfortable. There was certainly something unusual about the machine in front of us, and I came to the conclusion that we had had about enough of this kind of sport.

'I think we will go back, Lord Beden,' I remarked, pleasantly, moving one hand towards the lever.

'You will go back to perdition, Scott,' he answered, quietly. 'If you meddle with me we shall be smashed to pieces. We are going forty miles an hour, and if you distract my attention for a single instant I won't answer for the consequences.'

I felt the truth of what he said, and put my hand ostentatiously in my pocket. It was quite evident that I couldn't interfere with him, and equally evident that if we went on as we were going now we should be dashed to pieces. My only hope was that we should speedily accomplish whatever mad purpose Lord Beden had in his mind, although by now I began to think that he had no other object than suicide. The valley of the Stour was only two miles off.

But we had been gaining inch by inch down the slope, and were now not more than thirty yards from the machine in front of us. Showers of sparks whirled into our faces, and I kept one arm before my eyes. I soon found, however, that, for some reason or other, the sparks did not burn my skin, and I was able to resume a more comfortable position and study the occupant of the car.

His figure somehow seemed strangely familiar to me, and I tried hard to recollect where I had seen those square shoulders and long, lean limbs before. I wished I could see the man's face, for I was quite certain that I should recognize it. But he never looked back, and appeared to be absolutely unconscious of our presence so close behind him.

Nearer we crept, and still nearer, until our front wheels were not more than 10 ft. from the platform. The glow of the furnace bathed my companion's face in crimson light, and the figure of the man in front of us stood out like a black demon toiling at the eternal fires.

'Be careful, Lord Beden,' I cried. 'We shall be into it.'

He turned to me with a smile of triumph, and I thought I saw the light of madness in his eyes.

'Do you know what I am going to do?' he said, in a low voice, putting his lips close to my ear. 'I am going to break it to bits. We have a little speed in hand yet, and when we get to the slope of the Stour Valley I shall break the cursed thing to bits.'

'For Heaven's sake,' I cried, 'put the brake on, Lord Beden. Are you mad?' and I gripped him by the arm. He shook my hand off, and I clung to my seat with every muscle of my body strained to the utmost, for as I spoke there was a flash of lightning, and I saw the road dipping, dipping, dipping, and far below the gleam of water among dark trees, and on the height above a large building with many spires and towers. I idly called to mind that it was the Rockshire County Asylum.

Our speed quickened horribly, and the car began to sway from side to side. I saw my companion pull the lever an inch nearer to him and grip the steering-wheel with both hands. Then suddenly the road seemed to fall away beneath us; we sprang off the ground and dropped downward and forward like a stone flung from a precipice. We were going to smash clean through the machine in front of us.

For five seconds I held my breath, only awaiting the awful crash of splintering wood and iron and the shock that would fling us fifty feet from our seats. But we only touched the ground with a sickening thud an inch behind the other machine, and then a wonderful thing happened. We began to slowly pierce the rail and platform in front of us, until the man seemed to be almost touching our feet, and at last I saw his face—a wild, dark face with madness in the eyes, and the face of Lord Beden, as I had seen a portrait of him in Beden Hall taken thirty years ago.

My companion rose on his seat and grappled with his own likeness, but he seemed to be only clutching the air, and neither car nor occupant appeared to have any tangible substance. Steadily and silently we bored our way clean through the machine, inch by inch, foot by foot; through the blazing furnace, through the framework of the boiler, through bolt and bar and stanchion, through whirring fly-wheel and pulsing shaft and piston, until there was nothing beyond us but the dip of the white road, and, looking back, I saw the whole dark mass running behind our back wheels.

Lord Beden was still standing and tearing at the air with his fingers. Our car was running without guidance, and I sprang to the steering-wheel and reversed the lever, but it was too late. We struck something at the side of the road and the whole machine made a leap from the ground. There was a rush of air, an awful shock and crash, and then—darkness!

A week afterwards in the hospital they told me Lord Beden was dead. He had fallen on a large piece of scrap-iron by the roadside, and nearly every bone in his body had been broken. I myself had had a miraculous escape by falling into a thick clump of gorse, and had got off with a broken arm and dislocated collar-bone, but I was not able to get about for two months. I said nothing of what had happened, and the accident required but little explanation. Motor-car accidents are common enough, especially on slopes like that of the Stour Valley.

When I was able to get about, however, I visited the scene of the disaster. A friend of mine, one of the doctors at the County Lunatic Asylum, called for me and drove me over to the place. The smash had occurred nearly half-way down the hillside, close to a ruined shed. The ground was covered with gorse and bracken, but here and there huge pieces of rusty iron were scattered about. Some of them were sharp and brown and ugly, but many were overgrown with creeping convolvulus. They looked as if they had once been parts of some great machine.

'A curious coincidence,' said my companion, as we drove away from the place.

'What do you mean?'

'I have been told,' he continued, 'that thirty years ago this old shed was used by the late Earl's elder brother. He was a mechanical genius, and they say that his efforts to work out some particular invention in a practical form drove him off his head. He was allowed to have this place as a workshop, and, under the supervision of two keepers, worked on his invention till the day of his death. It was thought that perhaps he would recover his reason if he ever accomplished the task. But in some mysterious way his plans were stolen from him no fewer than three times, and after the third time the poor fellow lost heart and destroyed himself. I have heard it whispered by one of my colleagues up yonder that the late Earl was not altogether ignorant of these thefts, but this is probably only gossip. All the fragments of iron you saw lying about were parts of the machine. Heaven knows what it was.'

I did not venture any suggestion on this point, but I think I could have done so.

The Tarn

Hugh Walpole

As Foster moved unconsciously across the room, bent towards the bookcase, and stood leaning forward a little, choosing now one book, now another, with his eye, his host, seeing the muscles of the back of his thin, scraggy neck stand out above his low flannel collar, thought of the ease with which he could squeeze that throat and the pleasure, the triumphant, lustful pleasure, that such an action would give him.

The low white-walled, white-ceilinged room was flooded with the mellow, kindly Lakeland sun. October is a wonderful month in the English Lakes, golden, rich, and perfumed, slow suns moving through apricot-tinted skies to ruby evening glories; the shadows lie then thick about that beautiful country, in dark purple patches, in long web-like patterns of silver gauze, in thick splotches of amber and grey. The clouds pass in galleons across the mountains, now veiling, now revealing, now descending with ghost-like armies to the very breast of the plains, suddenly rising to the softest of blue skies and lying thin in lazy languorous colour.

Fenwick's cottage looked across to Low Fells; on his right, seen through side windows, sprawled the hills above Derwentwater.

Fenwick looked at Foster's back and felt suddenly sick, so that he sat down, veiling his eyes for a moment with his hand. Foster had come up there, come all the way from London, to explain. It was so like Foster to want to explain, to want to put things right. For how many years had he known Foster? Why, for twenty at least, and during all those years Foster had been for ever determined to put things right with everybody. He could not bear to be disliked; he hated that anyone should think ill of him; he wanted everyone to be his friend. That was one reason, perhaps, why Foster had got on so well, had prospered so in his career, one reason, too, why Fenwick had not.

For Fenwick was the opposite of Foster in this. He did not want friends, he certainly did not care that people should like him—that is, people for whom, for one reason or another, he had contempt—and he had contempt for quite a number of people.

Fenwick looked at that long, thin, bending back and felt his knees tremble. Soon Foster would turn round and that high reedy voice would pipe out something about the books. 'What jolly books you have, Fenwick!' How many, many times in the long watches of the night when Fenwick could not sleep had he heard that pipe sounding close there—yes, in the very shadows of his bed! And how many times had Fenwick replied to it: 'I hate you! You are the cause of my failure in life! You have been in my way always. Always, always, always! Patronizing and pretending, and in truth showing others what a poor thing you thought me, how great a failure, how conceited a fool! I know. You can hide nothing from me! I can hear you!'

For twenty years now Foster had been persistently in Fenwick's way. There had been that affair, so long ago now, when Robins had wanted a sub-editor for his wonderful review, the *Parthenon*, and Fenwick had gone to see him and they had had a splendid talk. How magnificently Fenwick had talked that day, with what enthusiasm he had shown Robins (who was blinded by his own conceit, anyway) the kind of paper the *Parthenon* might be, how Robins had caught his own enthusiasm, how he had pushed his fat body about the room, crying: 'Yes, yes, Fenwick—that's fine! That's fine indeed!'—and then how, after all, Foster had got that job.

The paper had only lived for a year or so, it is true, but the connection with it had brought Foster into prominence just as it might have brought Fenwick!

Then five years later there was Fenwick's novel, *The Bitter Aloe*—the novel upon which he had spent three years of blood-and-tears endeavour—and then, in the very same week of publication, Foster brings out *The Circus*, the novel that made his name, although, Heaven knows, the thing was poor enough sentimental trash. You may say that one novel cannot kill another—but can it not? Had not *The Circus* appeared would not that group of London know-alls—that conceited, limited, ignorant, self-satisfied crowd, who nevertheless can do, by their talk, so much to affect a book's good or evil fortunes—have talked about *The Bitter Aloe* and so forced it into prominence? As it was, the book was stillborn and *The Circus* went on its prancing, triumphant way.

After that there had been many occasions—some small, some big—and always in one way or another that thin, scraggy body of Foster's was interfering with Fenwick's happiness.

The thing had become, of course, an obsession with Fenwick. Hiding up there in the heart of the Lakes, with no friends, almost no company, and very little money, he was given too much to brooding over his failure. He *was* a failure and it was not his own fault. How could it be his own fault with his talents and his brilliance? It was the fault of modern life and its lack of culture, the fault of the stupid material mess that made up the intelligences of human beings—and the fault of Foster.

Always Fenwick hoped that Foster would keep away from him. He did not know what he would not do did he see the man. And then one day to his amazement he received a telegram: 'Passing through this way. May I stop with you Monday and Tuesday? Giles Foster.'

Fenwick could scarcely believe his eyes, and then—from curiosity, from cynical contempt, from some deeper, more mysterious motive that he dared not analyse—he had telegraphed 'Come.'

And here the man was. And he had come—would you believe it?—to 'put things right'. He had heard from Hamlin Eddis that 'Fenwick was hurt with him, had some kind of a grievance.'

'I didn't like to feel that, old man, and so I thought I'd just stop by and have it out with you, see what the matter was, and put it right.'

Last night after supper Foster had tried to put it right. Eagerly, his eyes like a good dog's who is asking for a bone that he knows that he thoroughly deserves, he had held out his hand and asked Fenwick to 'say what was up'.

Fenwick simply had said that nothing was up; Hamlin Eddis was a damned fool.

'Oh, I'm glad to hear that!' Foster had cried, springing up out of

his chair and putting his hand on Fenwick's shoulder. 'I'm glad of
that, old man. I couldn't bear for us not to be friends. We've been
friends so long.'

Lord! how Fenwick hated him at that moment!

'What a jolly lot of books you have!' Foster turned round and looked
at Fenwick with eager, gratified eyes. 'Every book here is interesting! I like your arrangement of them too and those open book-
shelves—it always seems to me a shame to shut up books behind
glass!'

Foster came forward and sat down quite close to his host. He
even reached forward and laid his hand on his host's knee. 'Look
here! I'm mentioning it for the last time—positively! But I do want
to make quite certain. There *is* nothing wrong between us, is there,
old man? I know you assured me last night, but I just want——'

Fenwick looked at him and, surveying him, felt suddenly an
exquisite pleasure of hatred. He liked the touch of the man's hand
on his knee; he himself bent forward a little and, thinking how
agreeable it would be to push Foster's eyes in, deep, deep into his
head, crunching them, smashing them to purple, leaving the empty,
staring, bloody sockets, said:

'Why, no. Of course not. I told you last night. What could there
be?'

The hand gripped the knee a little more tightly.

'I *am* so glad! That's splendid! Splendid! I hope you won't think
me ridiculous, but I've always had an affection for you ever since I
can remember. I've always wanted to know you better. I've admired
your talent so greatly. That novel of yours—the—the—the one
about the Aloe——'

'*The Bitter Aloe?*'

'Ah, yes, that was it. That was a splendid book. Pessimistic, of
course, but still fine. It ought to have done better. I remember
thinking so at the time.'

'Yes, it ought to have done better.'

'Your time will come, though. What I say is that good work
always tells in the end.'

'Yes, my time will come.'

The thin, piping voice went on:

'Now, I've had more success than I deserved. Oh, yes, I have.

You can't deny it. I'm not being falsely modest. I mean it. I've got some talent, of course, but not so much as people say. And you! Why, you've got so much *more* than they acknowledge. You have, old man. You have indeed. Only—I do hope you'll forgive my saying this—perhaps you haven't advanced quite as you might have done. Living up here, shut away here, closed in by all these mountains, in this wet climate—always raining—why, you're out of things! You don't see people, don't talk and discover what's really going on. Why, look at me!'

Fenwick turned round and looked at him.

'Now, I have half the year in London, where one gets the best of everything, best talk, best music, best plays, and then I'm three months abroad, Italy or Greece or somewhere, and then three months in the country. Now that's an ideal arrangement. You have everything that way.'

'Italy or Greece or somewhere!'

Something turned in Fenwick's breast, grinding, grinding, grinding. How he had longed, oh, how passionately, for just one week in Greece, two days in Sicily! Sometimes he had thought that he might run to it, but when it had come to the actual counting of the pennies—— And how this fool, this fathead, this self-satisfied, conceited, patronizing——

He got up, looking out at the golden sun.

'What do you say to a walk?' he suggested. 'The sun will last for a good hour yet.'

As soon as the words were out of his lips he felt as though someone else had said them for him. He even turned half-round to see whether anyone else were there. Ever since Foster's arrival on the evening before he had been conscious of this sensation. A walk? Why should he take Foster for a walk, show him his beloved country, point out those curves and lines and hollows, the broad silver shield of Derwentwater, the cloudy purple hills hunched like blankets about the knees of some recumbent giant? Why? It was as though he had turned round to someone behind him and had said, 'You have some further design in this.'

They started out. The road sank abruptly to the lake, then the path ran between trees at the water's edge. Across the lake tones of bright yellow light, crocus hued, rode upon the blue. The hills were dark.

The very way that Foster walked bespoke the man. He was always a little ahead of you, pushing his long, thin body along with little eager jerks as though did he not hurry he would miss something that would be immensely to his advantage. He talked, throwing words over his shoulder to Fenwick as you throw crumbs of bread to a robin.

'Of course I was pleased. Who would not be? After all it's a new prize. They've only been awarding it for a year or two, but it's gratifying—really gratifying—to secure it. When I opened the envelope and found the cheque there—well, you could have knocked me down with a feather. You could, indeed. Of course, a hundred pounds isn't much. But it's the honour——'

Whither were they going? Their destiny was as certain as though they had no free will. Free will? There is no free will. All is Fate. Fenwick suddenly laughed aloud.

Foster stopped.

'Why, what is it?'

'What's what?'

'You laughed.'

'Something amused me.'

Foster slipped his arm through Fenwick's.

'It *is* jolly to be walking along together like this, arm in arm, friends. I'm a sentimental man, I won't deny it. What I say is that life is short and one must love one's fellow-beings or where is one? You live too much alone, old man.' He squeezed Fenwick's arm. 'That's the truth of it.'

It was torture, exquisite heavenly torture. It was wonderful to feel that thin, bony arm pressing against his. Almost you could hear the beating of that other heart. Wonderful to feel that arm and the temptation to take it in your two hands and to bend it and twist it and then to hear the bones crack . . . crack . . . crack . . . Wonderful to feel that temptation rise through one's body like boiling water and yet not to yield to it. For a moment Fenwick's hand touched Foster's. Then he drew himself apart.

'We're at the village. This is the hotel where they all come in the summer. We turn off at the right here. I'll show you my tarn.'

'Your tarn?' asked Foster. 'Forgive my ignorance, but what *is* a tarn exactly?'

'A tarn is a miniature lake, a pool of water lying in the lap of the hill. Very quiet, lovely, silent. Some of them are immensely deep.'

'I should like to see that.'

'It is some little distance—up a rough road. Do you mind?'

'Not a bit. I have long legs.'

'Some of them are immensely deep—unfathomable—nobody touched the bottom—but quiet, like glass, with shadows only——'

'Do you know, Fenwick, but I have always been afraid of water— I've never learnt to swim. I'm afraid to go out of my depth. Isn't that ridiculous? But it is all because at my private school, years ago, when I was a small boy, some big fellows took me and·held me with my head under the water and nearly drowned me. They did indeed. They went further than they meant to. I can see their faces.'

Fenwick considered this. The picture leapt to his mind. He could see the boys—large strong fellows, probably—and this little skinny thing like a frog, their thick hands about his throat, his legs like grey sticks kicking out of the water, their laughter, their sudden sense that something was wrong, the skinny body all flaccid and still——

He drew a deep breath.

Foster was walking beside him now, not ahead of him, as though he were a little afraid and needed reassurance. Indeed the scene had changed. Before and behind them stretched the uphill path, loose with shale and stones. On their right, on a ridge at the foot of the hill, were some quarries, almost deserted, but the more melancholy in the fading afternoon because a little work still continued there, faint sounds came from the gaunt listening chimneys, a stream of water ran and tumbled angrily into a pool below, once and again a black silhouette, like a question-mark, appeared against the darkening hill.

It was a little steep here and Foster puffed and blew.

Fenwick hated him the more for that. So thin and spare, and still he could not keep in condition! They stumbled, keeping below the quarry, on the edge of the running water, now green, now a dirty white-grey, pushing their way along the side of the hill.

Their faces were set now towards Helvellyn. It rounded the cup of hills closing in the base and then sprawling to the right.

'There's the tarn!' Fenwick exclaimed—and then added, 'The sun's not lasting as long as I had expected. It's growing dark already.'

Foster stumbled and caught Fenwick's arm.

'This twilight makes the hills look strange—like living men. I can scarcely see my way.'

'We're alone here,' Fenwick answered. 'Don't you feel the stillness? The men will have left the quarry now and gone home. There is no one in all this place but ourselves. If you watch you will see a strange green light steal down over the hills. It lasts but for a moment and then it is dark.

'Ah, here is my tarn. Do you know how I love this place, Foster? It seems to belong especially to me, just as much as all your work and your glory and fame and success seem to belong to you. I have this and you have that. Perhaps in the end we are even after all. Yes. . . .

'But I feel as though that piece of water belonged to me and I to it, and as though we should never be separated—yes. . . . Isn't it black?

'It is one of the deep ones. No one has ever sounded it. Only Helvellyn knows, and one day I fancy that it will take me, too, into its confidence. Will whisper its secrets——'

Foster sneezed.

'Very nice. Very beautiful, Fenwick. I like your tarn. Charming. And now let's turn back. That is a difficult walk beneath the quarry. It's chilly, too.'

'Do you see that little jetty there?' Fenwick led Foster by the arm. 'Someone built that out into the water. He had a boat there, I suppose. Come and look down. From the end of the little jetty it looks so deep and the mountains seem to close round.'

Fenwick took Foster's arm and led him to the end of the jetty. Indeed, the water looked deep here. Deep and very black. Foster peered down, then he looked up at the hills that did indeed seem to have gathered close around him. He sneezed again.

'I've caught a cold, I am afraid. Let's turn homewards, Fenwick, or we shall never find our way.'

'Home then,' said Fenwick, and his hands closed about the thin, scraggy neck. For the instant the head half turned and two startled, strangely childish eyes stared; then, with a push that was ludicrously simple, the body was impelled forward, there was a sharp cry, a splash, a stir of something white against the swiftly gathering dusk, again and then again, then far-spreading ripples, then silence.

*

The silence extended. Having enwrapped the tarn it spread as though with finger on lip to the already quiescent hills. Fenwick shared in the silence. He luxuriated in it. He did not move at all. He stood there looking upon the inky water of the tarn, his arms folded, a man lost in intensest thought. But he was not thinking. He was only conscious of a warm luxurious relief, a sensuous feeling that was not thought at all.

Foster was gone—that tiresome, prating, conceited, self-satisfied fool! Gone, never to return. The tarn assured him of that. It stared back into Fenwick's face approvingly as though it said: 'You have done well—a clean and necessary job. We have done it together, you and I. I am proud of you.'

He was proud of himself. At last he had done something definite with his life. Thought, eager, active thought, was beginning now to flood his brain. For all these years he had hung around in this place doing nothing but cherish grievances, weak, backboneless—now at last there was action. He drew himself up and looked at the hills. He was proud—and he was cold. He was shivering. He turned up the collar of his coat. Yes, there was the faint green light that always lingered in the shadows of the hills for a brief moment before darkness came. It was growing late. He had better return.

Shivering now so that his teeth chattered, he started off down the path, and then was aware that he did not wish to leave the tarn. The tarn was friendly; the only friend he had in all the world. As he stumbled along in the dark this sense of loneliness grew. He was going home to an empty house. There had been a guest in it last night. Who was it? Why, Foster, of course—Foster with his silly laugh and amiable mediocre eyes. Well, Foster would not be there now. No, he never would be there again.

And suddenly Fenwick started to run. He did not know why, except that, now that he had left the tarn, he was lonely. He wished that he could have stayed there all night, but because he was cold he could not, and so now he was running so that he might be at home with the lights and the familiar furniture—and all the things that he knew to reassure him.

As he ran the shale and stones scattered beneath his feet. They made a tit-tattering noise under him, and someone else seemed to be running too. He stopped, and the other runner also stopped. He breathed in the silence. He was hot now. The perspiration was trickling down his cheeks. He could feel a dribble of it down his back inside his shirt. His knees were pounding. His heart was thumping. And all around him the hills were so amazingly silent, now like indiarubber clouds that you could push in or pull out as you do those indiarubber faces, grey against the night sky of a crystal purple upon whose surface, like the twinkling eyes of boats at sea, stars were now appearing.

His knees steadied, his heart beat less fiercely, and he began to run again. Suddenly he had turned the corner and was out at the hotel. Its lamps were kindly and reassuring. He walked then quietly along the lake-side path, and had it not been for the certainty that someone was treading behind him he would have been comfortable and at his ease. He stopped once or twice and looked back, and once he stopped and called out 'Who's there?' Only the rustling trees answered.

He had the strangest fancy, but his brain was throbbing so fiercely that he could not think, that it was the tarn that was following him, the tarn slipping, sliding along the road, being with him so that he should not be lonely. He could almost hear the tarn whisper in his ear: 'We did that together, and so I do not wish you to bear all the responsibility yourself. I will stay with you, so that you are not lonely.'

He climbed the road towards home, and there were the lights of his house. He heard the gate click behind him as though it were shutting him in. He went into the sitting-room, lighted and ready. There were the books that Foster had admired.

The old woman who looked after him appeared.

'Will you be having some tea, sir?'

'No, thank you, Annie.'

'Will the other gentleman be wanting any?'

'No; the other gentleman is away for the night.'

'Then there will be only one for supper?'

'Yes, only one for supper.'

He sat in the corner of the sofa and fell instantly into a deep slumber.

He woke when the old woman tapped him on the shoulder and told him that supper was served. The room was dark save for the jumping light of two uncertain candles. Those two red candlesticks—how he hated them up there on the mantelpiece! He had always hated them, and now they seemed to him to have something of the quality of Foster's voice—that thin, reedy, piping tone.

He was expecting at every moment that Foster would enter, and yet he knew that he would not. He continued to turn his head towards the door, but it was so dark there that you could not see. The whole room was dark except just there by the fireplace, where the two candlesticks went whining with their miserable twinkling plaint.

He went into the dining-room and sat down to his meal. But he could not eat anything. It was odd—that place by the table where Foster's chair should be. Odd, naked, and made a man feel lonely.

He got up once from the table and went to the window, opened it and looked out. He listened for something. A trickle as of running water, a stir, through the silence, as though some deep pool were filling to the brim. A rustle in the trees, perhaps. An owl hooted. Sharply, as though someone had spoken to him unexpectedly behind his shoulder, he closed the window and looked back, peering under his dark eyebrows into the room.

Later on he went up to bed.

Had he been sleeping, or had he been lying lazily as one does, half-dozing, half-luxuriously not-thinking? He was wide awake now, utterly awake, and his heart was beating with apprehension. It was as though someone had called him by name. He slept always with his window a little open and the blind up. Tonight the moonlight shadowed in sickly fashion the objects in his room. It was not a flood of light nor yet a sharp splash, silvering a square, a circle, throwing the rest into ebony blackness. The light was dim, a little green, perhaps, like the shadow that comes over the hills just before dark.

He stared at the window, and it seemed to him that something moved there. Within, or rather against the green-grey light, something silver-tinted glistened. Fenwick stared. It had the look, exactly, of slipping water.

Slipping water! He listened, his head up, and it seemed to him that from beyond the window he caught the stir of water, not running, but rather welling up and up, gurgling with satisfaction as it filled and filled.

He sat up higher in bed, and then saw that down the wallpaper beneath the window water was undoubtedly trickling. He could see it lurch to the projecting wood of the sill, pause, and then slip, slither down the incline. The odd thing was that it fell so silently.

Beyond the window there was that odd gurgle, but in the room itself absolute silence. Whence could it come? He saw the line of silver rise and fall as the stream on the window-ledge ebbed and flowed.

He must get up and close the window. He drew his legs above the sheets and blankets and looked down.

He shrieked. The floor was covered with a shining film of water. It was rising. As he looked it had covered half the short stumpy legs of the bed. It rose without a wink, a bubble, a break! Over the sill it poured now in a steady flow but soundless. Fenwick sat back in the bed, the clothes gathered to his chin, his eyes blinking, the Adam's apple throbbing like a throttle in his throat.

But he must do something, he must stop this. The water was now level with the seats of the chairs, but still was soundless. Could he but reach the door!

He put down his naked foot, then cried again. The water was icy cold. Suddenly, leaning, staring at its dark unbroken sheen, something seemed to push him forward. He fell. His head, his face was under the icy liquid; it seemed adhesive and in the heart of its ice hot like melting wax. He struggled to his feet. The water was breast-high. He screamed again and again. He could see the looking-glass, the row of books, the picture of Dürer's *Horse*, aloof, impervious. He beat at the water and flakes of it seemed to cling to him like scales of fish, clammy to his touch. He struggled, ploughing his way, towards the door.

The water now was at his neck. Then something had caught him by the ankle. Something held him. He struggled, crying, 'Let me go! Let me go! I tell you to let me go! I hate you! I hate you! I will not come down to you! I will not——'

The water covered his mouth. He felt that someone pushed in his eyeballs with bare knuckles. A cold hand reached up and caught his naked thigh.

In the morning the little maid knocked and, receiving no answer, came in, as was her wont, with his shaving-water. What she saw made her scream. She ran for the gardener.

They took the body with its staring, protruding eyes, its tongue sticking out between the clenched teeth, and laid it on the bed.

The only sign of disorder was an overturned water-jug. A small pool of water stained the carpet.

It was a lovely morning. A twig of ivy idly, in the little breeze, tapped the pane.

Resurgam

Rina Ramsay

I

THE London parson had taken a night off to run down and preach for Stackhouse.

He liked the change. It was like dipping into another world to slip out of his own restless parish into the utterly different atmosphere of this quiet country town. It had struck him most in the pulpit, when the lights went up on the sleepy congregation and he gave out a concluding hymn. How alike they were; all one pattern, all known to each other, all leading the same staid, ordinary lives. What a blessed tonic, his brief sojourn in this placid community.

He puffed out his chest, drinking in the soft night air that was so good to swallow. He was a big man and burly, and the narrow pavement would hardly hold the three of them abreast, so he was walking between the other two down the middle of the darkened street. They passed various worshippers in the glimmer—families, friends, and sweethearts—all of them pausing to say good-night. Such a peaceable little town and so friendly! It struck him again as comical that it should have been Stackhouse and not himself who had had a nervous breakdown last summer.

He burst out chuckling, and then, on the point of sharing his amusement at such an anomaly, was discreet. Those highly strung individuals were so touchy. And Stackhouse did not seem in the humour for chaffing. His mouth was set in an odd line of strained endurance and he hardly spoke. His long, lean, ascetic figure had something monkish about it as he stalked along in his cassock. His eyes were staring into the gloom ahead.

Mrs Stackhouse, on the other side, was making up for her husband's silence. Robinson had had no idea she was such a chattering woman. It began to annoy him. It seemed to him that there was a suggestion of hysteria in her incessant prattle.

Near the vicarage gate they overtook a woman of the charwoman class, and the vicar's wife hailed her with the usual salutation and asked why Bessy had missed Sunday-school. The woman unlatched the gate for them. She had a small child with her, and spoke for its benefit in a mincing tone.

'Bessy's bin a very bad girl, ma'am. She's been telling lies.'

'Oh, dear!' said Mrs Stackhouse, properly scandalized.

'Yes, ma'am; the young monkey! She *will* have it her lady, as used to, sat with her on Sunday night.'

'Oh!' said Mrs Stackhouse again, but swiftly. 'Nonsense, nonsense!'

She whisked through the gate, which clanged after them, leaving the woman outside with the infant, unadmonished, hanging to her skirt with a finger in its mouth. In the light of the hall lamp she glanced furtively at her husband.

'My dear boy!' she said, hurriedly, almost wildly; 'a child of four——!'

Stackhouse dropped his eyes from hers, and lifted his hand with a curious gesture as if he were wiping the sweat from his brow.

Inside the house Mrs Stackhouse fled to the kitchen to hurry that uncomfortable meal called supper, and the two men waited a minute or two by the study fire.

'Awfully good of you to come down, Robinson,' said the vicar. He spoke in a strained voice; there was something in it that sounded like expectation, like some faint hope; but the Londoner, for all his alertness, had not the clue. He noticed, however, that his host's knuckles gleamed white as he gripped hard on the edge of the chimney-piece. These long, weedy men had no stamina, physical or nervous. It must have been his temperament, certainly not his surroundings, that had made Stackhouse go to pieces.

'Good of you to ask me,' he said, politely. 'I love this quiet place. Such a contrast to my parish! You should see us up there, how crowded, quarrelling and fighting. I'm afraid that sea voyage didn't set you up altogether?'

'I thought it had, though,' said Stackhouse, abruptly. 'When I came back——'

He shut his mouth suddenly in the middle of the sentence, but looked hard at his fellow-priest. In his look was wistfulness, and an imminent despair.

'I'd like to ask you something,' he said, 'but—I dare not.' He let go the chimney-piece and led the way into the dining-room, where Mrs Stackhouse was calling them. She was too anxiously hospitable for comfort, bouncing up and down behind her coffee-pot, fussing about the food, and rattling on feverishly; but keeping, the visitor could see, a distracted eye on her husband. There was not much coherence in her prattle, and sometimes she lost the thread of it and looked for a minute helpless. Only at such disconcerting moments could the Londoner, coming to the rescue, get a word in.

Why would the woman insist on talking, and what was she afraid of? Some outbreak of nerves on the part of the silent man? Was it pure hysteria on her part, or was she trying to cover some private fear?

He seized the first opportunity to take his share in the conversation, mildly humorous, but conscious all the while of the peculiar strain in the atmosphere. And then, incidentally, he remembered something.

'By the way,' he said, 'you lucky people, you know all your congregation. Who is the lady who sat in the side aisle alone in the seat next the pillar? A singularly interesting face——'

Mrs Stackhouse started violently.

'Wh—what was she like?' she asked.

'Rather eager and sad,' said Robinson, reflecting, 'but quite a girl. She had a pointed chin, and dark hair, I think, and large, dark eyes—penetrating eyes; and she wore some kind of glittering jewel hung round her neck. It was her troubled expression that struck me first——'

He broke off astonished. For Stackhouse had stood up and was staring at him, gripping the table, leaning over. His look was half incredulous, half unspeakable relief.

'Then,' he said, in a choked voice, 'you, too, saw her. Thank Heaven! I am not mad.'

Mrs Stackhouse hid her face suddenly in her hands and burst into an uncontrollable fit of crying.

The visitor looked from one to the other in real alarm. He could see nothing in his harmless remark to affect them so deeply, or to relax, as it seemed, an intolerable strain.

'I'm afraid——' he began.

Mrs Stackhouse sat up and smiled.

'But we are so thankful to you,' she said, still sobbing. 'Oh, you can't imagine what a relief it is! You're an independent witness—unprejudiced—and you saw her. Oh, you don't know what it means to us. We were both so terrified that his mind was going——'

'Still,' said the Londoner, puzzled, 'I can't see how my mentioning that young lady——'

She interrupted him. Something like awe hushed her excited voice.

'The girl you saw in church,' she said, 'died last year.'

'Impossible!' said Robinson.

Stackhouse—who was with difficulty controlling a nervous tremor that shook him from head to foot, but whose voice was steady—moved to the door.

'Let us go back to the study,' he said, 'and talk it over.'

His whole manner was changed as he stood on the hearthrug looking down on his guest and his wife. He had lost the pathetic hesitation that Robinson had noticed in him that night, and recovered something of his old bearing of priestly pomp. 'Most of us believe in the unseen,' he pronounced; 'but to find what belongs to the other world made visible—brought so close—is a dreadful shock. My wife thought it must be an hallucination; she thought I was going mad—and I, too, grew horribly afraid. You see, I had had that nervous breakdown before, and the doctors sent me away for six months. It looked as if the prescription had failed. We thought that my breakdown must have been the warning of a mental collapse. We—I can't tell you, Robinson, what we suffered. And yet I saw that poor girl, night after night, so plainly——'

'She was *such* a nice girl!' broke in Mrs Stackhouse, in her gasping treble; 'and such a help in the parish. We liked her so much. And, of course, we were getting no letters—the doctors had forbidden it; we had heard nothing whatever till we came home and they told us she had committed suicide soon after we went away. I thought the shock of it had been too much for George. No wonder—such a *good* girl, Mr Robinson. She—she used to sit in that seat with the schoolchildren to keep them quiet. No one could have *dreamt* she could do anything so wicked——'

'Do you mean,' said Robinson, bluntly, 'that I saw a ghost?'

Stackhouse bent his head. His wife shivered suddenly as if she had not till then fully realized what it meant. Her mind had been so possessed by fear for the sanity of her husband; her relief had been too intense.

'I—suppose so,' she said, in an awe-stricken whisper.

There followed a short pause; no sound but the fire crackling and the night wind sighing a little outside the room. Mrs Stackhouse drew in nearer the fender as if she were very cold, and made a little gasp in her throat. The Londoner, looking from one to the other with his kindly, humorous glance, began to talk common sense.

'Of course it's a mistake,' he said. 'The girl I saw in church tonight was real. It can only be some chance likeness—perhaps a relation——'

Stackhouse shook his head.

'No,' he said. 'There's no one like her. Poor girl, poor girl; her spirit cannot rest. God forgive me, there must have been something deadly wrong in my teaching, since it could not keep her from such a dreadful act. Is it strange that she looks reproachful?'

'But haven't you made enquiries?'

'We have not dared to speak of it to a soul!' cried Mrs Stackhouse. 'They would all have believed—as I did—that George was going mad. Oh, can't you see the horrible difficulty? And then——'

'I am not going to have my church made a public show for the rabble,' said Stackhouse, violently. 'I won't have that desecration! Can't you see them crowding here in their thousands, staring, scoffing, profaning a holy place? The newspapers would seize on the tale in a moment! For Heaven's sake, man, hold your tongue.'

He stopped, and again that nervous tremor took him.

'Do you mind telling me the circumstances? Who was this girl?' said the Londoner curious, but stoutly incredulous. 'It certainly wasn't the face of a suicide that I saw——'

'No. It's incomprehensible,' said Stackhouse, trying to recover a sort of calm. 'She was the last person in the world, you would have said. How little we creatures know! She lived with her uncle, a solicitor here, and kept house for him. The uncle is my churchwarden. She was going out shortly to India to be married. There was nothing to worry her.'

'Poor little Kitty!' said Mrs Stackhouse, in a sobbing breath. 'If only we had been there——'

'Yes, she might have confided in us,' said Stackhouse. 'But the priest I left in charge here was a young man, lately ordained; shy, and not observant. And nobody had noticed anything strange about her. Only her uncle said at the inquest that he was afraid she had been a little scared at the idea of her approaching marriage. She had lived in this place all her life, and it was a wrench to leave it; and she had not seen the man for five years. He was afraid she must have been brooding in secret and dreading the journey; and he blamed himself for thinking it only natural a girl should be fluttered at the prospect of such a tremendous step. Poor man, he must have been terribly distressed. One of the jury told me that if they could have found any possible excuse they would have brought it in misadventure, if only to spare his feelings——'

'But she went down to the chemist herself and bought the stuff,' broke in Mrs Stackhouse. 'She told him she wanted it for an old dog that had been run over; she signed the poison book and asked him particularly if it would be painless. Of course, knowing her as he did, he never dreamt——'

'And the dog?' said Robinson.

'There was no dog,' said Stackhouse. 'No one in the house had heard of it. She locked her door as usual at night—she had done it ever since an alarm of burglars in the house years ago; and when they got frightened in the morning and burst it in she was found dead in bed. She had drunk the poison in the lemonade she took up with her every night.'

'And they buried her with a mutilated service!' said Mrs Stackhouse, shuddering.

'Poor girl!' said Stackhouse, and turned away his head.

The London parson broke the distressing silence.

'A very sad case,' he said; 'but aren't you letting it overcome your judgement? Why in this case beyond all others should her unhappy spirit be allowed to haunt the church? I dare say it is just what a miserable soul would wish, sorrowful, self-tormenting—if uncontrolled. But I see no reason why it should be permitted. And assuming it could be, I'm curious to know why she should appear to you and not to her own relation. *He* would have spoken of it, wouldn't he, if she had?'

'Poor man!' said Mrs Stackhouse, with an hysterical laugh that she was unable to check; 'he would have raised the whole neighbourhood.'

'Probably,' said Stackhouse, the grave line of his mouth relaxing, 'but he shut up his house and went away; the loneliness was too much for him. And I hear that on his travels he seems to have come across a sensible woman who took him and married him. Some middle-aged person like himself, who had no ties and was feeling lonely. It's the best that could happen.'

'The blinds were up as I passed the house yesterday,' said Mrs Stackhouse.

'Heavens, Robinson, what's to be done?' burst out Stackhouse. 'Look at us, talking coolly in the face of this horror! I can't stand the thing much longer. Think of it, man! Week after week, there she sits, with her eyes fixed on me——'

'Oh, George, George!' said his wife, shuddering.

Robinson was sorry for them both. Evidently both of them were neurotic, and the tragic circumstance they related had affected them; their highly strung temperaments, acting on each other, had worked them up to a really dangerous pitch. And Stackhouse hadn't enough to do. Perhaps it was worse for him to rust in this quiet parish than to wear himself out with work. The doctors had sent him on a sea voyage, had they? Months of idleness and too much introspection. Fools!

'Look here,' he said, 'you go up and take over my job for a bit, and I'll stop down here and discover something. You'll be giddy at first, but the organization's good, and I've got a regular martinet of a curate. He'll manage you and see you don't kill yourself. And I think Mrs Stackhouse will find my house quite comfortable for a bachelor's. *I* want a holiday badly—and you'll soon shake off this obsession of yours in a London slum.'

Mrs Stackhouse looked up eagerly at her husband. Relief at the great suggestion shone in her eyes.

'It would be cowardly to do that,' said Stackhouse, irresolutely. 'I should feel as if I had deserted a poor soul that needs my help.'

'You're not fit to help anyone in the present state of your nerves,' said his fellow-parson, and clinched the argument like a Jesuit.

'How do you know she wants your help more than mine? Didn't I see her too?'

II

The October sun shone aslant the quiet street as the Revd Mr Robinson marched along it to call on his—or, rather, on Stackhouse's truant churchwarden, Mr Parker. He had a straw hat on and swung his stick.

Personally, he was hugely enjoying his interval of peace, and he had in his pocket a letter from his head curate extolling Stackhouse, who was working like a demon, and looked less ill. It only remained for Robinson to clear up the ghost worry in unmistakable fashion, which ought not to be too hard. He smiled. Odd tricks one's imagination played sometimes! Recollecting Stackhouse's unbalanced asseveration, he had himself experienced a slight thrill as he peered down the glimmering aisle on the following Sunday evening, and saw the same face that had impressed him before, the same dark eyes riveted on him. His robust intellect, that admitted all things to be possible, but few of them expedient, had been a little staggered by the sad intensity—imagination again—of her look. But a very commonplace incident had rescued him from any foolishness; just a little nodding child that had snuggled up against her as she gathered it in her arm.

He told himself that what he had to do was simply to make a few discreet enquiries and get acquainted with the disturbing young woman. He had spoken to the clerk after service, but that ancient worthy had not noticed who was sitting by the pillar; his sight, he explained, was not so good as it might be, with that chancy gas. Happen it was some stranger; folk was a bit shy of sitting that side because of the children fidgeting, and them boys—you couldn't keep them boys quiet! Happen it was a teacher?

Clearly there was no disquieting rumour current, no local gossip; there seemed to be no foundation for any supernatural hypothesis but the overwrought condition of the parson's nerves.

Robinson reached his destination, and pushed open the iron gate. Mr Parker was out, but Mrs Parker was at home, and the caller was marched into the drawing-room.

This was a mixture of ancient middle-class superstition and modern ease. It amused Robinson to compare the two, and even to

track the ancestral album to its lurking-place behind a potted palm.
While he waited he undid the stiff clasp and turned over the pages.
Pity that people had given up that instructive custom of pillorying
different generations for the good of posterity! It was an interesting
study to look back and mark how family traits persisted, how they
cropped up on occasion as ineradicable as weeds. He went through
the book with the keen eye of an anthropologist. There was
something elusive, something distantly familiar running through the
whole collection. He must have met a member of that family at one
time without knowing it. On the very last page he saw her; a
photograph of a girl.

Breaking in on his moment of stupefaction Mrs Parker sailed into
the room, having furbished herself for the occasion with fresh and
violent scent on her handkerchief. A dashing female, with quantities
of blazing yellow hair and round eyes that stared and challenged; a
splendid presence, indeed, in this sober house. But not at all the expected type of a middle-aged comforter. Much more like a firework.

She excused her husband in a high London voice. He was obliged
to be at his office. Everything was in a muddle owing to things
being left so long to the clerks. It really was time they came back,
though how she was to endure this place——! Still, of course, with
a motor——! Dull, did he say? It was simply dreadful. She had
always warned Jimmy that it would be too much for her, but he
had persuaded her at last.

'How lucky for him!' said Robinson, politely. The lady agreed at
once.

'Rather!' she said. 'Poor Jimmy! He must have proposed to me
twenty times in the last two years!'

The accelerated clatter of a tea-tray approached. The bride was
not going to allow her one visitor to escape her. She began moving
things on the table.

'I have just been looking through that album,' said Robinson,
turning it over as carelessly as he could. 'That is a striking
photograph on the last page. I fancy I have seen the original.'

She uttered a little shriek and closed the book.

'Oh!' she said. 'Don't you know? It's Mr Parker's niece who
committed suicide. A shocking thing, wasn't it? Haven't you heard
about it? It was in all the papers!'

Eagerly she plunged into the story. His shocked countenance encouraged her to enlarge. He sat facing her across the gaudy little painted tea-cups ('a wedding present from one of my pals,' she remarked) that surrounded the heavy silver pot.

She poured out the whole history as Robinson had heard it from his fellow-parson, but with amplifications. He heard what a queer temper poor Kitty had, and what a drag on a girl it was to be tied by a long engagement. When a man she hadn't seen for years wrote suddenly wanting her to come out at once and be married, no wonder the poor girl was terrified. Men alter so. He might have taken to drinking, he might even have grown a beard! And she didn't dare to back out of it, because she was a religious girl, and she'd promised; and very likely he needed her bit of money. She wasn't dependent on her uncle—oh, dear, no! Why, that heavy old tea-pot that made your arm ache belonged to her share! And she'd never stirred an inch from home. If Jimmy had had a grain of sense he would have put his foot down and said if the man really wanted her he must come and fetch her. But he didn't think of it, and so— and so—— Well, it must have sent her crazy. Look at her artfulness, making up that story about the dog, when she went out to buy the poison! Wasn't it awful how cunning a person could be, and yet not right in the head, of course!

Her ear-rings tinkled as she shook her head with an air of wisdom. Her eager relation was no more personal than that of anybody retailing the latest sensational case in the papers—except in so far as she possessed the distinction of inside knowledge. There was a certain pride in her glib recital. But she was utterly unaffected by any breath of superstition, any hint of the supernatural hovering.

'Did you know her well?' said Robinson, trying to shake off his strange feeling of mental numbness.

'Oh, my goodness, no!' she said. 'I never saw her. I didn't get engaged to Jimmy till it was all over, and he came up to town more dead than alive, poor fellow, and told me how his circumstances had changed; and I was so sorry for him I just got married to him at once and off we went to Monte Carlo.'

An incongruous picture presented itself to her listener's mind, the spectacle of this splendid person leading a dazed mourner by the scruff of his neck towards consolation. But the flicker of humour passed.

'I should like to meet your husband,' he said. She took, or mistook, him to be severe.

'I'm afraid we have both been naughty,' she said. 'I know we have never been to church, and Mr Parker a churchwarden, too! I used always to call him "the churchwarden" when I wanted to tease him—and he used to get red and say it was a very important office. I must really apologize. And the cook says nobody will call on me till we've appeared at church. I'll *promise* to bring him next Sunday evening. The cook says it used to be his turn to take round the plate at night.'

Eagerly, but with condescension, she gave this undertaking to satisfy the conventions (the cook having omitted to point out the superior social stamp of Morning Service), and effusively she shook hands. Robinson got out of the house and into the empty street. His mind began to work slowly, in jerks, like a jarred machine.

It was the original of that dead girl's photograph he had seen.

Something remarkably like panic shook him. He drew his hand across his forehead and found that it was wet.

By an odd trick of memory his own involuntary gesture reminded him of Stackhouse, who had wiped the sweat from his brow like that when the charwoman complained that her little girl had been telling lies. The insignificant incident, printed unconsciously on his brain, came back to him now with an unearthly meaning. He remembered that baby face, wide-eyed, insistent, too young to explain, too little to understand. And he remembered a sleepy head supported safely within a protecting arm.

'Good Lord!' he said, and his ruddy face was pale.

III

It was a hot, full church, the atmosphere thick with the breath of humanity and the purring gas. Evening service was popular with the multitude, and a wet night had driven all and sundry who would have been taking walks in the lanes to the only alternative. They pushed in, furling their dripping umbrellas and stacking them in the porch, till there was scarcely an inch of room in the middle aisle. And as the organ ceased rumbling and the packed congregation prepared to shout out the opening hymn a small, rabbit-faced man came stealing up the nave.

In his wake, plumed and hatted and scented, advanced Mrs

Parker, making her triumphal entry. Indisputably there was nobody in the church dressed like her. The man ushered her into her place, and took up his own, with a countenance of uneasy rapture, beside this tremendous fine bird he had somehow caged.

Robinson, at the reading-desk, shot one furtive glance at the side aisle and withdrew his eyes. He was conscious of a mixed sensation of relief and of disappointment. His timorous look had travelled along rows of blank, unimportant faces, and seen nothing to send a shock to his sober sense. The appearance, whatever under God's mysterious providence it might be, was not there. He took heart to rate himself inwardly for a pusillanimous yielding to superstition. Obstinately he refused to let his attention wander and pinned his eyes to his book.

The service wore on, chant and psalm, prayer and preaching. He found himself halting unaccountably in the pulpit; the terse, vigorous words he sought for became jumbled in his head. In his struggle to keep the thread of his discourse and be lucid he had to fight a growing horror of expectation, a kind of strange foreknowledge that pressed on him. His eyes searched the dim spaces while his tongue stumbled over platitudes. He tried vainly to pierce the veil of mystery that hung over the darkened church. It was not time yet.

And then the glimmering lights went up.

She was there, in her place by the pillar, with her tragic eyes raised to him and the jewel glittering on her breast. All the other faces around her seemed indistinct, as if she alone were real—and yet the seat had been packed with worshippers standing up finding the places for the concluding hymn. Straight and still she stood among them, and, filled with a sense of impending climax, Robinson found it impossible to turn from gazing and go down the pulpit stairs. He, too, waited, watching, holding his breath, while the organ struck up and the churchwardens began to take the collection under cover of a lusty, long-winded hymn.

All at once, without consciously looking in that direction, he became aware that Mr Parker's place was vacant. He saw the small, rabbit-faced man drawing himself up to be stiff and pompous, carrying out his duty. Row after row he collected gravely, passing down the nave and coming up the side aisle. With a shock that staggered him for a moment the watcher realized that it was Mr

Parker's part to collect on that side of the church. Would nothing happen, or would he, too, be granted the power to see?

The people were swinging through the third verse to an undercurrent of tinkling pennies. Nearer and nearer the man approached. Mechanically the watcher in the pulpit counted. Three more rows—two more—he had nearly reached her, but had made no sign. One more row and then—*crash*! The plate of coins went spinning in all directions. The man lay still where he had dropped on his face.

He did not die immediately. The numbing paralysis took a little time to kill. But he lay like a trodden insect, muttering, muttering. Blank terror was fixed immutably on his face.

It was clear from his own words that he had murdered his niece, but even the doctors did not know how much was intelligent confession and how much the involuntary betrayal of a stricken brain automatically reeling off old thoughts and guarded secrets.

'She'll not have me, she'll not have me; she says I'm not rich enough——'

That was his continual refrain, the fixed idea that had obsessed him, and that found utterance now at intervals, breaking even through the more coherent statements that had been taken down.

'It was all Bill's fault. Why didn't he leave his money to me instead of the girl? If I had it now; if I had it——! That fool of a girl, she thinks of nothing but her lover——'

Only for a moment the muttering voice would pause. Robinson, watching beside him, would speak of the everlasting mercy.

'She'll not have me, she'll not have me; she says I'm not rich enough!' and then, in the monotonous babble that was like a recitation, 'I did it. Draw up the legal documents. Put it down. They called it suicide, that's why she can't forgive me. That's why she came. Look at her, reproaching me with her eyes! Oh, my God, Kitty, take your eyes off me——'

On it went, over and over.

'I sent her to get the poison. I told her the dog had been run over in the street. I said I had shut it in the coach-house and the only merciful thing was to put it out of its pain. I told her to hurry and not to say anything to the servants—they would come bothering round, and they would not understand it was kindness—— And I took it from her and put it into her lemonade on the sideboard. It was so easy. Look at her, look at her, come back to curse me!'

It was not hard to reconstruct the whole sordid story of a weak-minded man's infatuation and greed. It was also wiser, remembering Stackhouse and his horror of letting his church be profaned by a sightseeing crowd, to acquiesce in the public view that it was remorse that had brought on the stroke that killed Kitty's uncle. And so Robinson held his peace.

The Railway Carriage

F. Tennyson Jesse

SOLANGE FONTAINE nearly missed the train that Monday morning. She had been staying at Merchester for the weekend, with that old Colonel Evelyn, whose son she had been the means of saving from the gallows, and the old gentleman had kept on talking, with the pathetic garrulity of age, till the cab-driver had warned her that there was a bare five minutes to get to the station. Luckily, Solange had only a small suitcase, and she ran across the platform to the nearest carriage, wrenched open the door, and jumped in as the cabman flung the case in after her. She handed him his half-crown through the window as the train began to move.

At first, Solange, like anyone who has ever just caught a train at the last moment, leaned back, breathed thankfully, and took no notice of her surroundings. Then, also like everyone else, she looked round with a little smile of self-congratulation on her lips, ready to share with any strangers present that fraction of intimacy which such a happening strikes, like a spark, from one's fellow men.

It was a third-class carriage, with hard seats and varnished wooden doors. Its only other occupant was a woman who was sitting in the far corner. Apparently she had noticed neither Solange's abrupt entry nor her smile. She was an elderly woman, dressed in shabby black, she had no luggage, and she was sitting with her hands—the knotted veiny hands of a working woman—folded together in her lap. She was staring out of the window, and her lips were moving a little, as though she were talking to herself soundlessly.

Solange's smile died a natural death; she looked at herself in the little mirror from her handbag to make sure her hurry had not disturbed the set of her plain little helmet-hat. All was well; she was her usual clear, fine-drawn self, save for an unwonted flush on her pale cheeks, and one loose feather of fair hair that lay against her temple. She tucked it back and put the mirror in her bag again. Her cigarette-case caught her eye as she did so; she took it out, then hesitated, and glanced at the silent woman.

'Do you mind if I smoke?' asked Solange.

The woman drew her eyes away from their blind staring as though by a physical wrench, and looked at her. Something in that gaze struck unpleasantly on Solange's senses, but, as the woman did not seem to have understood her, she repeated her question.

'Eh? Oh, naow. It don't make no matter.'

The woman had a slight Cockney accent, but a surprisingly soft voice for one of her hard, almost wooden appearance. Solange thanked her and took out a cigarette, only to discover that she had no matches and that, as usual, her lighter wouldn't work. She glanced again at the woman, who had reverted to her occupation of staring out of the window. No good asking her for a light. She would just have to wait till someone else got in; the train was due to stop at the junction in another couple of minutes.

The platform was crowded, for it was market day at a neighbouring town, and it seemed that every farmer in the countryside was going in by this train. The carriage in which Solange was, however, being at the tail-end of the train, only one man came towards it and got in. He was a small, insignificant-looking man, with a big grey felt hat pulled right over his ears, and he carried a black bag.

He glanced sharply from Solange to the woman in black as he opened the carriage door and seemed satisfied by what he saw. Before he took his seat he stood for a moment, his bag in his hand, as though uncertain what to do with it. He glanced up at the rack, and even made a movement towards it, then sat down opposite Solange and stowed the bag away between his feet, under the seat. The whistle blew, the guard waved his flag, and the train started off again through the hot, summer countryside.

Solange took out a cigarette and leaned towards him with a smile.

'Will you be so kind as to let me have a match?' she asked. The little man started. He, like the woman in black, seemed oddly abstracted. He stared at her, and then repeated: 'A match? Oh, yes.' He also had an accent, but it was a North-country one, Solange noted. He almost said: 'A match. Oh, yez . . .' Solange began to feel a little impatient. Was the world peopled by the half-dead this fine morning?

He brought out his matchbox pretty smartly, however, and struck a light for her. His gallantry might be a little clumsy, but his movements were noticeably deft and economical, so much so that Solange was struck by the contrast between his stubby fingers and their neat precision of action.

Her cigarette alight, she leaned back, and the little man relapsed into a sort of surly abstraction. The elderly woman continued to stare out of the window at the bleached fields and the dark trees, and the rhythmic movements of the haymakers. The train gathered speed and roared and rattled through the lovely domestic landscape, a landscape with no touch of savagery or wild beauty, but which held in its contented folds the pastoral activities of men for generations past.

It was a run of ten minutes to the next stop—the village before the market town—after which the train would suddenly become converted into an express and pursue its quickened and uninter-rupted way to London.

To Solange, in spite of the lovely country, and of the inoffensive-ness of her fellow-travellers, that ten minutes seemed like one of those curious spaces when time, as we know it, ceases, and an endless period, like a breath held beyond human endurance, is the only measure. Why this should be so, she could not have told. She only knew that she would have given a great deal to be out of that little third-class carriage, to be in a modern corridor train, to be—this, above all—away from her travelling companions. Inoffensive . . .? Obviously . . . then what was wrong—and when had it begun?

The silent wooden woman had struck her with a sense of oddness, but not with any feeling of something definitely wrong. The commonplace little man, with his shaven cheeks and his deft, stubby fingers, had seemed unusual in a way that was not altogether good, but no message of evil such as had so often told her of harm, had knocked upon her senses when he entered the carriage. Yet it was only since he and the old woman had been in it together that she had felt this spiritual unease. Something was wrong between these two human beings—and yet they apparently did not know each other. Neither even knew that the other was in some queer way inimical, each was self-absorbed to the exclusion of the other, the woman in her strange daze of thought that was like a stupor, the man in some stony sort of regret. Sorry—that was the word for him, thought Solange, sorry but stubborn. He wasn't unhappy as the woman was unhappy, only ill at ease, as an animal is ill at ease when it is driven up the road to the slaughter-house.

Solange was glad when the train drew up at a little wayside station. This time their carriage was invaded by four or five men, for the front of the train was already full. Solange felt a curious sense of relief at this influx of other human beings. At least she would not be penned in with the two strange, lost people who had sat silently on the seat opposite her, one at each end, for the last ten minutes. There was only another quarter of an hour to go before the market town was reached, and then, doubtless, everybody would get out and she would have the carriage to herself for the rest of the run to London.

A big red-faced farmer, with side-whiskers, sat beside Solange, and pulled out his pipe, glanced at her, and saw she was smoking herself. She smiled at him, and he grinned back and proceeded to light up.

'That's good, Missis,' he said. 'I don't like to get the ladies' hair full of smoke, but it's hard luck on a man not to have his pipe.'

A thin, dried-up man, who was sitting opposite to the farmer, nodded several times as he proceeded to pack his own pipe with peculiarly evil-looking tobacco.

'That's so,' he agreed. 'I wonder if they let that poor young devil have a last smoke this morning.'

'Sure they did,' said the farmer, authoritatively, 'they always let 'em do what they like. He could 'ave 'ad a bottle of champagne if he'd fancied it.'

'No!' said the other man, in admiring disbelief. 'Is that so?'

'That is so,' asseverated the farmer.

'Well, now, I thought,' said a third man, 'that all they was allowed was an ordinary sort of breakfast—a good one, mind you, eggs and bacon, and anything like that.'

'I heard they was given nothing but brandy in the way of a pick-me-up,' said the thin man, rather encouraged by this contradiction of the farmer on the part of the third man.

'Anything they likes,' repeated the farmer, stubbornly, 'everyone knows that.'

'Suppose they wanted poison, eh?' asked the thin man. 'Something that would do it nice and quick without having to stand on the trap and have their necks broken. Don't tell me they'd give 'em poison.'

The farmer was rather staggered by this novel suggestion. 'Perhaps not poison,' he said, 'but champagne I don't doubt.'

Solange guessed of what they must be speaking. There must have been an execution that morning. She refrained from saying that bromide and four ounces of brandy was the official assuagement for the last agony. The execution must have been at Merchester, and it was not remarkable that she heard nothing of it, for she had been staying with Colonel Evelyn, and such subjects were never mentioned in his house since that dreadful night, which might have been young Charles Evelyn's last. That was why the servants had watched the old Colonel so anxiously and why the local paper had not been forthcoming. . . . The Colonel had been very childish since his son's narrow escape, and it was easy to delude him in little practical matters.

'I don't believe,' said a fourth man, of the black-coat class, perhaps some lawyer's clerk travelling to his work at the market town, 'that they ought ever to have hanged him. It was a cruel shame, that's what it was. After all, it was only circumstantial evidence.'

'That's as good as any other evidence, and better,' said the farmer, stoutly: 'the only other evidence is what folks tells you they've seen, and we have it on the authority of the Bible that all men are liars. Give me circumstances every time, I says, they can't lie nearly as well as a man can.'

'And a man can't lie near as well as a woman,' said the clerk, with a little snigger.

'That's true enough,' said both the other men in chorus.

It suddenly struck Solange as odd that only the newcomers were talking. The little man with the black bag and the woman in the corner were still silent.

'Well,' said the farmer, 'I met young Jackson once or twice, and he seemed to me a decent young fellow enough, not the sort of chap you'd expect to go and cut a man's throat behind his back, as you might say.'

'He did it all right,' said the clerk, 'that's plain enough.'

'They were both after the same woman, weren't they? And t'other man got her. You don't need to look much further than that. There's motive enough for you. Must ha' been fools.'

'Come now,' said the farmer, 'that's not very polite, with ladies present.' He glanced at the silent woman in the corner, but she seemed to have heard nothing. She was no longer staring out of the window, her eyes were closed, and her hands were tightly folded together in her lap, and he looked away from her to Solange.

'I only came over from France on Friday,' she said, 'so I'm afraid I'm very ignorant. Has something—been happening?' She didn't like to say: 'Has there been an execution?' so strongly were the memories of that dreadful morning in Merchester Jail implanted in her consciousness.

'Something happening!' said the farmer, 'I should say so. Why, all Merchester has talked of nothing else for weeks and weeks. A young fellow called Jackson, Timothy Jackson, who served in Jordan's, the corn chandler's at Merchester, was walking out with a young woman who was already tokened a bit above her station—to a young lawyer. Smart fellow, young Ted Emery. My lawyer he was, at least his father's my lawyer,' added the farmer, importantly, 'and one night in a dark lane young Jackson has a row with him and cuts his throat. He was hanged this morning, young Jackson was, in Merchester Jail. People were pretty sorry round about. Tim Jackson was a good fellow, though he was a Londoner. Had to live in the country for his health. He was delicate-looking, white as a girl, but handsome enough if it hadn't been for one of them birthmarks on one cheek. Shaped like a bat's wing, it were, and my old missus allers said it fair gave her a turn to look at. But he was handsome, in spite of it, and this girl took a fancy to him. But he was no match for young Emery, who was one of those smart young fellows who think no end of themselves, and had a motor-bike and a sidecar to take his girl in and all that sort of thing. She was pretty bitter against Tim Jackson at the trial. If you ask me, she had only been amusing herself and would rather have got

Emery than young Jackson. Now she's got neither, and serve her
right, too.'

'Aye, that's right enough,' said the man opposite him.

Solange remembered having read something about the case in the
Continental *Daily Mail* three weeks earlier. Only a short paragraph,
for it had been an ordinary enough crime of jealousy. The judge
had made some scathing remarks as to the method of the murder. It
was 'un-English' to cut a man's throat. It would have been more
English, and consequently better, if he had killed his adversary with
a blow of a club, or his fist. Jackson, being a rather weedy town-
product, had been unable to do this essentially English thing, and
had resorted, in a moment of passion, to a razor. There had been a
struggle, he hadn't crept up to the other man from behind, but
undoubtedly in the course of the struggle he had cut his throat from
behind, getting his arm round his neck and pulling the heavier man
back towards him.

'I hear he confessed,' said the clerk, importantly, 'they were
saying that at our Merchester office this morning, so I was told. It's
my day at Winborough, you know, but they rang me up and told
me just before I left home.'

The whole carriage, still with the exception of the little man with
the black bag and the elderly woman, was agog at this piece of
news.

'Confessed, did he?' said the farmer. 'Oh well, that'll put everybody's mind at rest. It's something to know justice has been done.'

'Justice?' said the man opposite, bitterly. 'Do you call it right to
hang a decent young fellow because a woman had been driving him
crazy? And if it comes to that, I'm not so keen on this capital
punishment business. What right have we got to take life, I should
like to know? I can tell you this, I'd sooner meet a young fellow like
Timothy Jackson than meet the man who hanged him. There's a
fellow I shouldn't like to shake by the hand. That's a dirty trade.'

'Dirty enough,' agreed the farmer, soberly.

The rhythm of the train began to slacken. Winborough was
reached, and the carriage was emptied, but Solange saw, with a
little feeling of dismay, that her original companions were continu-
ing with her to London. She suddenly felt she couldn't bear this
strange atmosphere of which she was conscious as surrounding
them, and she got up to see if she couldn't change her carriage, but

she had left it till too late. For the fourth time since the brief half-hour when she had jumped into the carriage at Merchester, she heard the guard blow his whistle, and the rhythm of the train began to beat upon her senses once more. Now there was no getting away from her strange, dumb companions for an hour and a half. She had to stay with them whether she would or no. It was really an outrage, she thought to herself, that such a thing as a non-corridor train should still exist. This wasn't even a very good train of the old-fashioned type. It ran very bumpily. Perhaps, thought Solange, all the rolling-stock on this line was very old. Then in a flash she realized that something had gone wrong. The train was bumping in a curious fashion, its rattle changed to a roar, a crashing sound broke through the rapidly accelerating conglomeration of other noises, and then the whole world seemed to go mad. The coach reared up, attacked the coach in front like a mad beast, rocked, lurched sideways, and at last came to a standstill, like a leaning tower, poised on its rear end. Solange and her two companions were spilled like rubbish from a shoot, against the door and windows at the bottom end, splintered glass all about them, and the black bag hit Solange full upon the temple . . .

Why did this voice persist in waking her up? She didn't want to wake up, she only wanted to stay in this dark world where she felt numb and sleepy. She tried hard not to listen to the voice, but it went on and on. *Wake up, wake up, wake up* . . . the words beat over and over upon her brain, would let her have no rest. Reluctantly at last she allowed her mind to pay attention. The voice sounded more clearly now, *Wake up, wake up, you must wake up.* The darkness of the world began to be shot with flashes and gleams of light even before she opened her eyes. *Wake up, wake up* . . .

She opened her eyes and slowly realized where she was and what had happened.

'You're all right,' the voice went on, 'but you must get out.' The voice seemed to come from above her head, and rather surprised to find she could move, Solange looked up. She saw the head of a young man, dark against the blinding square of light made by the window of the carriage which was right up above her head. The young man looked down at her as though she were at the bottom of a well, and he were peering in over the rim. She stirred and felt

herself cautiously. Yes . . . she was intact, she could waggle all her
fingers and toes, her back was not broken, she could feel pain where
a sharp angle of splintered coachwork stuck into one thigh. She
looked about her, still dazed by the shock and her senses confused
by the shouts and wails of terrified human beings that came to her
ears. The elderly woman was either unconscious or dead, she was
lying crumpled up, her eyes shut, and a thin skein of blood, where
a splinter of glass had caught her, lying across her face like a
ravelling of red worsted. The commonplace little man was doubled
up, his head sunk sideways on his shoulder, his eyes closed and his
face very pale. His hat had been knocked off, and Solange saw with
a shock of irrational surprise, that, save where it was grey at the
sides, his hair was a bright red. It was one of those stupid and
irrelevant details that strike the mind at such moments of stress.

Solange looked up. There was the face of the young man still
peering in from the top of that strange well into which the railway
carriage had become changed as though by magic.

'Can't you help us out?' she called.

He shook his head. She saw the dark weaving motion of it against
the clear square blue of sky.

'You must wake him up,' he called down to her. 'Shake him,
wake him up.'

Solange managed to stagger to her feet, pushing aside bits of
broken wood that hemmed her in. She looked doubtfully at the
little man crumpled up at her feet. She hardly liked to shake him,
and yet she couldn't climb up the tower that was the up-ended
railway carriage without his help. She put her hand on to his
shoulder and spoke urgently.

'Are you hurt? Oh, do try and do something. We've got to get
out. We've got to get the old woman out. Wake up. Wake up,' and
she did actually begin to shake him, as one shakes someone who is
having a bad dream. Slowly, the commonplace little light eyes
opened and looked at her unintelligently. Then the man moaned a
little, and put up one hand to his head.

'You're all right, you really are,' said Solange, urgently. 'Do see
if you can climb up. There's someone up there who will help you if
you only can.' She glanced up and the young man above her met
her gaze.

'Make him hurry up,' he said, 'there's a fire. Listen.' And Solange, with a pang of pure fear that she never forgot, realized that the crackling sound which she had thought came entirely from breaking woodwork, was really made by the burning of the next coach, perhaps even by the burning of one end of the coach she was in.

'There was petrol in the van,' said the young man, 'and the guard was smoking.'

The little red-haired man now began to feel himself all over, as Solange herself had done.

'I'm a'reet, Miss,' he said, a little unsteadily, 'I'll climb oop and hold down my hand to you.'

He looked round him and saw the woman still lying crumpled up, unconscious, and a worried look came across his face. However, he wasted no words, and began laboriously by the aid of the splintered luggage rack to try and pull himself up to the gaping window above his head. Solange saw, to her disgust, that the young man had gone. She managed to climb on the wreck of the seat, and exerting all her force, gave the little man a leg-up. With a mighty effort he pulled himself through the jagged frame of glass above his head and levered himself out into the air. For one awful moment Solange thought that perhaps he, too, was going to desert her, but he wriggled himself round on the up-ended side of the carriage, and looking down at her, held a hand that was cut and bleeding down towards her.

'Get a grip o' that,' he said.

'I can't,' said Solange. 'I can't leave the old woman. We must get her out somehow.'

The head of the young man came back now, and she saw it behind red-head's shoulder.

'You want a rope,' said the young man, 'make a rope fast round her. Oh, hurry up.'

Solange looked frantically round the shattered compartment. There was not so much as a luggage strap round the little man's black bag, and none round her suitcase. 'Can't you get a rope?' she called up to the little man, 'ask someone for a rope.'

Then the red-headed man spoke, slightly hesitating, in spite of that dreadful crackling that was coming nearer and nearer.

'Ma bag, Miss,' he said, 'ma bag. Tha'll find a rope there.'

Solange seized the little black bag, and struggled with the lock.

'Don't pull it,' called the little man, 'slide it. That's reet.'

The bag gaped open, and Solange saw a rather crumpled night-shirt and a shabby sponge bag.

'Look underneath,' called down the little man.

She plunged in her hand and to her intense thankfulness her fingers met a good, strong rope, that filled up with its coils the whole of the bottom of the bag, as a serpent might have done. She pulled it out. It was amazingly strong, smooth, and flexible. The next moment she saw that it had a running noose at one end that passed through a brass ring. Her mind became very clear and cold. She handled the thing without any distaste. She even thought how convenient the running noose would be.

'Be quick,' urged the young man, who was still peering in behind the flaming red head of that apparently commonplace little man. 'Get her out before she sees what it is.'

Solange worked the noose down over the limp form of the elderly woman, pulled her arms through it so that they hung out helplessly each side, and then flung the free end of the rope upwards. The little man with the red head caught hold of it, and began to pull. Solange heaved with all her strength upon the dead weight of the old lady. She was a very frail old lady, it appeared, now that Solange had her hands upon her, but she was heavy, nevertheless, with the weight of her unconsciousness.

'Be careful. Try not to cut her face any worse,' Solange called up.

The little man seemed amazingly strong as well as deft with his hands. He groaned and sweated, but he pulled the woman up till her head and shoulders were through the window untouched by the jagged frame of glass. Then he clutched her under the arms and pulled her right through the opening.

'Wait a moment, lass,' he called down to Solange. 'I'll have thee out in a jiffy.'

He disappeared, and Solange felt terrifyingly alone. The heat seemed suffocating, the crackling was nearer, and through the roar of escaping steam and the roar of the flames she could still hear faint thin cries from further down the train. She was never so thankful to see anyone in her life as she was to see the red head of the public executioner appear once more above her. He lowered the rope down to her, and she fitted it round her waist, and, taking a good purchase with her hands, kicked her way up the carriage and was in her turn pulled out into safety. The air was fresh and sweet, for the smoke was being blown away in the opposite direction, and for a moment Solange felt, as she stood swaying a little upon the grass at the side of the track, that it was good merely to be alive. Then she looked about her. The train was piled on itself in the most fantastic fashion. The engine lay upon its side. The accident had happened at a level crossing, and already there were motor-cars going backwards and forwards, and people busy at work.

'I reckon they're all out now,' said the little red-headed man, wiping his wet brow with the back of his hand. 'Eh, that was a near thing, lass!'

It dawned on Solange that he was still holding one end of the rope, which was round her waist, as if she were a heifer being led to market, and she suddenly realized, emotionally, as well as with her mind, what it was that had saved her. She began to tear at it with her fingers, feeling as near to hysteria as she had ever felt in her calm, well-ordered life.

'I'll tak' it off, lass,' said the little man, apologetically. 'I was sorry about it. I didn't want you to see it, but there weren't no other way.'

While he was talking he began to ease the rope from about her waist.

'That's why I didn't get in at Merchester. You see, with my red hair, I'm what you might call noticeable like. They drove me from t'jail t'next station.'

He had got the rope off her by now, and was coiling it round his own waist, under his coat. 'Government property nowadays,' he explained as he did so. 'I mun use this again next week.'

'Did the young man help you?' asked Solange. 'Was he helping you with us? It must have been dreadfully heavy work otherwise.'

The little red-headed man stared at her.

'What young man?' he asked.

'The young man who looked in at the carriage window and woke me up. He told me to wake you up. The young man who told us we must have a rope.'

'I'll get one o' they cars to take 'e home, lass,' said the red-headed little man, with a rather worried expression on his face. 'Tha'll be wanting a lay down.'

'But did he?' persisted Solange.

'There weren't no young man that I ever saw or heard of, nowt but you waking me and telling me to get out and get rope. You saved my life, lass. I'd ha burned . . .' and he pointed to the railway carriage which was now a roaring furnace, the flames were pale almost to invisibility in the bright sunlight, but their heat reached Solange where she stood.

'Well, there was a young man,' said Solange, wondering whether red-head had been too confused to notice him, 'and, what's more, it was the young man who woke me up. It was he saved the lot of us.'

She looked about her, and saw the elderly woman lying in the grass some twenty yards away where the little man had dragged her. The young man was kneeling beside her, his head bent down to hers. The woman's eyes were open, and she was looking up into his face with a smile upon her own. She opened her mouth as though to speak but the young man very gently laid his fingers, long, delicate, over-white fingers, against her lips. A little crowd of people, among them two men bearing a stretcher, were approaching the woman. The young man bent a little lower over her, then raised his head and looked across at Solange. She could see his face clearly now in the bright sunlight, it was no longer shadowed as it had been when he was peering down into the railway carriage, and with a pang, half of incredulity, half of pure terror, she saw that he had a port-wine stain, shaped like a bat's wing, lying over one cheek beneath the eye. The stretcher-bearers and their assistants closed in about the woman and began to lift her. Solange ran towards them. She seemed to have lost the young man in the little crowd of people, but she motioned the stretcher-bearers to stay still for a moment, and thinking she might be some relation or friend, they did so.

'Did you see him?' asked Solange, bending over the woman. 'Did you see him?'

The woman smiled at her: 'I saw him,' she said; 'he must have escaped after all. You won't tell anyone, will you?'

'No, no,' said Solange, 'I won't tell anyone.'

'He said it was all right,' said the woman, feebly. 'He said I should meet him this evening. He was always a good boy, was my Tim, though I knew he was marked for misfortune from the moment I first set eyes on that bat's wing on his poor face, but he was always good to his mother. "Don't worry, mother," he's just told me, "it's all right. I'll see you this evening!"'

She closed her eyes and seemed to drift into unconsciousness.

'Where are you taking her?' asked Solange.

'Cottage Hospital, Miss,' said one of the stretcher-bearers. 'It isn't far. Just down the road,' and they set off, carrying their burden carefully over the uneven ground.

The little red-headed man, who had stayed behind to fasten his coat completely over the rope, now came up to Solange.

'I wish I could get a hat,' he complained. He was evidently worried about his conspicuous hair.

'I don't think anybody will notice,' said Solange; 'they've got other things to think about now, you see.'

He jerked his red head towards the disappearing stretcher. 'Who was t'owd lady?' he asked. 'Did tha know her?'

'She was the mother of the young man who saved us,' said Solange.

It was most unreasonable, she concluded later, that she had refused to share the offer of a car up to town with the little red-headed man. After all, he had, under instruction, saved her life, and there were souls evidently capable of resentment and crime but capable also of forgiveness. There was no reason why she shouldn't like to stay with the red-headed man whom Tim Jackson had saved from a death by fire. Nevertheless, Solange was glad to have seen the last of him, and glad also that Mrs Jackson died that evening in the local hospital, without knowing what it was that had been passed over her head and fastened about her body.

The Bell

Beverley Nichols

'WELL, Hugh,' said Mrs Lupton, giving a final pat to the pillow, 'you're sure there's nothing more you want?'

Hugh shook his head, and sighed deeply. 'No, my dear. Nothing.'

'In that case I shall be going. The night's growing wilder, and it's past ten o'clock. Mrs Jenkins will come round from the vicarage in the morning, in plenty of time to give you breakfast. Of course, she won't be able to come permanently, but I can easily spare her till you're settled.' She bent down and gave her brother an affectionate peck. 'Good-night, my dear.'

'Good-night.'

She went to the door and turned off the switch. The room was now illuminated only by the green glow from the reading-lamp. In this light Hugh looked very wan and frail. She hated to leave him all alone like this, but then it wasn't as if he were *ill*, though, of course, his heart had never been strong. It was simply a matter of nerves, and though she loved her brother she did think he was being unreasonable.

She obeyed an impulse to speak her mind.

'Hugh, dear, before I go, *do* try not to take it so badly.'

'I can't help it. Frank was with me for forty years. And I feel as if I'd killed him.'

'That's morbid, Hugh, and you know it.'

'He was going to the village on an errand for me when that car ran over him.'

'What has that got to do with it? The car skidded. It was no more your fault than it was mine. It was an act of God.'

'God moves in a mysterious way.' He frowned. And then . . . 'Of course, if I had wished him to die, nothing could have been more convenient, could it?'

'Wished Frank to die? Frank, of all people? But he was the perfect servant!'

'He was too perfect. He never let me do anything for myself.'

'But, my dear, you never showed the least desire to.'

'Didn't I?' He shifted impatiently on the pillow. 'Didn't I?' he repeated. And then, as though he were speaking to himself. 'Maybe not, in the last fifteen or twenty years. You see, by then, he'd got me.'

'"Got" you?'

'Where he wanted. And that was *there*.' He pressed his thumb on the counterpane; she noticed that his hand was trembling. 'He knew I couldn't move an inch without him. It was like a sort of slavery.'

'Hugh . . . You sound as if you hated him.'

'Do I?' he laughed, but there was little mirth in his voice. 'Perhaps he made me hate myself. If life hadn't been so easy, if I'd had to fend for myself, to do my own thinking, even to do my own packing . . .'

'Well?'

'Things might have been different. I might have had adventures. I might have met people.'

'Do you mean women?'

'Perhaps. Frank was jealous of everyone, you know. He was even jealous of you.' He shrugged his shoulders. 'Anyway, it's all too late now.'

He seemed to have drifted far away. Mrs Lupton's kind face was troubled. She had never seen her brother like this before. But then—now she came to think of it—she had never seen him without Frank. All these years, all their lives, Frank—tall, dark, inscrutable Frank—had been hovering somewhere in the background, handing a drink, drawing the curtains, silently, discreetly, serving and watching. It was as though he were with them at this moment. And then, just as she was reproving herself for such thoughts, her heart seemed to freeze.

For she saw that her brother was reaching for the bell.

It lay just above his head—a little bronze button set into the wall.

He had lifted his hand over his shoulder, and his finger was groping over the wall's surface.

'Hugh!' Her voice rang out sharply. 'What are you doing?'

He blinked and stared at her. His hand fell down again. He smiled sheepishly.

'Old habits die hard,' he muttered.

There was silence, except for the faint ticking of the bedside clock. Then he spoke again.

'I wonder'—it was as though he were speaking to himself—'I wonder how many thousand times I have rung that bell? And always it's been answered. I'd lie back, and count nine. One, two, three, four, five, six, seven, eight—nine. And at exactly nine, I'd hear the swing of the green baize door into the hall. Then, if it were stormy weather, there'd be a little tinkle from the Japanese wind bells, as the draught blew down the passage. After that, there'd be three steps on the marble pavement. Then silence, till he reached the top of the staircase. It always creaked, that top step. Then three more steps, and the door opened . . .'

'Hugh!' Try as she would, Mrs Lupton could not prevent her voice from trembling, for Hugh was staring at the door. 'I simply will not listen to this sort of talk.'

He smiled, and seemed to pull himself together.

'I'm sorry, my dear. I was only reminiscing.'

'Well—they're very unhealthy reminiscences.' She stepped forward and gave him a final peck. 'Tomorrow I shall look for some nice old housekeeper who'll make you forget all about—everything.' She felt a sudden aversion to mentioning Frank's name. 'And now, once again, good-night.'

'Good-night, my dear.'

She went out, shutting the door softly behind her. As she began the descent of the staircase, she gave a sudden start as she trod on the top step; she had never noticed that it creaked before.

The hall was bitterly cold and very dimly lit; the electricity must be running down now that Frank was no longer there to tend the little independent plant. It was incredible, she thought, as she groped for the handle of the front door, how much that man had done for Hugh.

She flung open the doors, and the wind rushed in with such force that she staggered back as though she had been pushed aside by some violent intruder. As she pushed it to again, she heard the tinkle of the Japanese wind bells. They seemed to be laughing at her.

Hugh could not sleep.

He switched off the light—noticing as he did so that the power was growing very faint—and lay back staring into the darkness, making plans.

Now that his sister was gone, he felt a curious exhilaration. Life, which had previously been so safe, so ordered, and—frankly—so *dull*, had suddenly become, through Frank's death, dangerous, chaotic, and exciting. If he went abroad, as he well might, he would not have to stay at the best hotels, as he had always done, for forty years, lest he should risk Frank's disapproval. He would not even have to take a dinner-jacket. He could go where he pleased, stay as long as he liked, be shabby, meet artists, gamblers, adventurers. It was not too late—he was only sixty—he might have ten years of life, even now.

Of course, there would be drawbacks. This house—for example. If he stayed in this house, he would need at least three servants to take Frank's place. A man and his wife, and a gardener as well. But then, why need he stay in this house? Would he ever have stayed in it, if it had not been for Frank? It was far too large, too lonely, too gloomy. But he would never have dared to suggest to Frank that they should move. Frank would have been hurt; he would have taken it as a personal reflection on his service—his perfect, all-absorbing, devoted service.

All that was changed now.

Hugh sat up in bed, and switched on the light once more. Even this little act gave him a sense of freedom, for in the old days he would have hesitated, in case Frank, with that weird sixth sense of his, had seen the light and come to ask if there was anything he wanted.

Hugh lay back, letting his mind drift, enjoying the sensuous pleasure of the warm bed in contrast to the tempestuous night outside. But gradually, perhaps because the room was growing colder and the night more wild, his mood changed. He felt restless, fidgety.

He shifted from one side to another, and now and then he paused, tense and rigid, because he had a curious idea that he had heard a sound, far below. He told himself not to be a fool; the old house was full of sounds on a night like this.

What really worried him was his hand, his right hand; he could not keep it still. It plucked nervously at the blanket, straying hither and thither; it seemed to have an independent life of its own. One would have said that it was searching for something, that it was trying to obey some order that it could not, as yet, understand.

And then, suddenly, Hugh realized that without his knowledge or desire his hand was moving—moving slowly, very slowly, in the direction of the bell.

His eyes were wide with terror, but his hand continued to move, nearer, ever nearer. It was being dragged by an irresistible force; and he noticed that the fingers of this hand were numb and cold, though the rest of his body was warm.

He longed to call for help; his lips moved convulsively; but no words came. By a supreme effort of will he held his arm rigid, digging his fingers into the plaster till he could have cried with pain. But the wall seemed cold and slippery, like ice; inch by inch his fingers slid nearer. And now they were touching the little brass ring round the bell itself, and now they were sliding over it—and now . . . 'O God, give me strength!' . . . his heart cried within him. But no strength came.

Far below came the familiar ring. It seemed to echo all through the empty house, like a voice, calling down the deserted corridors, through the lonely hall, calling for someone who was not there.

Who was not there?

His arm dropped to his side, like a dead thing. His head sank forward; he lay crouched, waiting, like an animal in hiding.

And he began to count nine.

One, two, three—four, five, six—seven . . . eight . . . nine.

He waited. The seconds ticked by. If . . . if . . . anyone were coming . . . surely he would have heard some sound by now?

But there was no sound save the moan of the wind and the fitful lash of the rain on the windows.

A sob of relief escaped him; and though he was trembling violently, he felt the blood surging back into his arm, warming the icy fingers. Slowly he lifted his head, and raised his hand to his eyes, staring at it.

*

It was just an ordinary hand—wrinkled, white, with the gold signet ring on the second finger; yes—it was his own hand—and look! It obeyed his own commands. He had no desire to ring the bell any longer. His eyes filled with tears of gratitude; he even began to laugh.

And then the laugh died in his throat. For in the distance, he heard the swing of the green baize door. And the faint tinkle of the Japanese wind bells.

Silence again. His teeth were clenched in expectation, but not yet had he completely surrendered to the wild beast of terror. A part of his conscious brain was working, trying desperately to comfort him, to tell him that his fears were only creatures of the storm, that a window was open, that the door was swinging in the wind.

'Why this long pause'—his conscious brain demanded—'if anything is below? Why are the seconds again ticking by, with nothing happening?' It was this same conscious brain that supplied the answer.

'Because the thing that is down below is hurt, is wounded—the thing is only dragging itself towards me under a sense of terrible compulsion.'

No sooner had this answer flashed across his mind than the next sound came—the step on the marble pavement—then another, and another—very slowly, as though the thing were dragging its feet in agony.

He was conscious of a sharp pain in his heart. But he knew that at all costs he must get out of bed, and cross the room and himself open the door before the thing that was mounting the stairs could open it. If only he could open the door in time he knew that at last, at the end of his life, he would prove himself the master and not the servant. But if he could not reach it, he knew that the door would be opened by the thing, and that this slavery was on him for ever, beyond the grave.

Gasping, entreating, muttering little prayers, he staggered out of bed. As he did so, the light from the bedside lamp flickered—flickered again—and once again. The electric plant, which Frank had always managed so perfectly, was failing. The room was almost dark.

But there was still time . . . still time. He staggered to the door, and reached for the handle. As he did so, he heard a creak. It was the top step.

He sank to his knees. At that very moment, the light went out. Moaning pitifully, he groped for the handle in the darkness.

As he touched it, it turned very slowly, from the other side.

II

MURDER AND MADNESS

W. W. Jacobs (1863–1943) was one of the writers who ensured the success of the *Strand*: his name, boldly printed on the front cover, guaranteed a satisfactory jump in copies sold. Like those of the romantic thriller writer Dornford Yates (Cecil William Mercer), Jacobs' public and private lives seemed distinctly at odds with his literary persona. An intensely shy man, low-voiced, with a habit of muttering out of the corner of his mouth, once he had the pen between his fingers he was transformed into a comic giant whose yarns of London's teeming dockside—and the crafty, garrulous, or put-upon characters who inhabited its pubs, back-to-backs, and seamen's missions (mainly from the mouth of his narrator-hero, the Nightwatchman, triumphantly characterized on the small screen in the early 1950s by the Cockney actor Wally Patch)—sold in their scores of thousands once translated from the pages of the *Strand* into book form. Jacobs' reputation as the foremost comic writer of his day, however, too often served to obscure his other talent, as a creator of atmosphere and dread in his stories of the macabre. 'The Monkey's Paw', a tale of three wishes that go dreadfully wrong, is his most celebrated excursion into the horror genre (another story, 'The Well', is less well known, though in fact even more impressive). Jacobs now is more or less forgotten as a humorist, though he was an intelligent concocter of plots and had a good ear for deadpan tavern soliloquizing. In the inter-war years he was often compared with his successor as house-humorist on the *Strand*, P. G. Wodehouse, and had some formidable champions, including J. B. Priestley, V. S. Pritchett, and Reginald Pound (the magazine's fourth editor who had little time for Wodehouse, though for Jacobs nothing but the deepest respect). Certainly Wodehouse could never have carried off so artful a combination of farce and terror as Jacobs does in 'His Brother's Keeper'.

The very best short stories of *Sapper* (Herman Cyril McNeile, 1888–1937) are those in which the reader's expectations are neatly, ingeniously, and very swiftly upended in the last sentences, frequently in the final few words. In this he was very nearly peerless. Sapper's most celebrated character was Bulldog Drummond who, according to taste, was either a mighty hero who biffed his way unstoppably through the grandiose schemes for world-domination of evil men (invariably foreigners) or an unspeakable thug whose berserker tendencies ideally qualified him for the post of head-guard in an extermination camp (it might one day be instructive to research the favourite reading-matter of those who flocked to join up as 'stewards' in Oswald Mosley's British Union of Fascists). It is doubtful that Sapper (an unremittingly hearty man who, as his friend and collaborator, the thriller-writer Gerard Fairlie, once admitted 'was not everybody's cup of tea') believed in the supernatural, yet on the odd occasion he revealed a talent for making the flesh creep in some notable weird tales. 'Touch and Go' is less implausible than most of his yarns, and rather more grisly.

W. L. George (1882–1926), too, was by no means a likeable man, although his faults stemmed from frustration and physical pain (he died dreadfully, and slowly, at the early age of 44 of a creeping paralysis, dictating his final novel, *The Ordeal of Monica Mary*, to his wife, the novelist Kathleen Giepel, and secretary, the only two who could make sense of his by then largely unintelligible speech). Born in France of a British father and Jewish mother, George spoke no English until the age of 20; thereafter he had a pronounced Gallic view of life, and accent. Unlike Sapper, he was liberal in outlook, embracing feminism, pacifism, and republicanism; yet his temper was short-fused and he did not suffer fools kindly. His early writings had a sociological bias, both fiction and non-fiction: his first novel, *A Bed of Roses* (1911), was a sympathetic portrait of a prostitute, while his study of the Lever Brothers' philanthropic experiments in Liverpool, *Labour and Housing at Port Sunlight* (1909), was much admired. After working as a journalist for six years George turned to full-time novel writing when *A Bed of Roses* was an instant success, and before he died published twelve novels (three more were issued posthumously); his work in general found critical favour in America, George diligently cultivating American editors.

The Triumph of Gallio (1923), which opens with the arresting line 'I, Holyoake Tarrant, have succeeded in slaying in myself faith in God, in woman, and even in man', is a remarkable study of a towering egotist who goes from rags to riches and then rejects all to return to the gutter, and would bear reprinting. Like much of his work, both short and long, 'Waxworks' (an enticing enough subject for any story-teller worth his salt) is perfectly structured, beginning lightly, ending powerfully.

B. L. Jacot (*fl.* 1925–60) was another writer who aimed his sights deliberately at the American market, carefully customizing his style and his plots to the requirements of the high-paying 'slicks' (the glossy large-circulation periodicals such as *Collier's*, *Saturday Evening Post*, and *Liberty*). He was a prolific short-story writer and a master of the attenuated form. His early work was highly reminiscent of that of P. G. Wodehouse and he wrote numerous stories about an upper-class layabout called the Hon. Winslow Moult (Rugby, Winchester, Harrow; sent down from Balliol). Jacot based his character not on Bertie Wooster but on one of Wodehouse's rather more interesting creations, Stanley Featherstonehaugh Ukridge, who, as his long-suffering friend Corky Corcoran was wont to complain, was 'a blot on Society', and, as the critic Richard Usborne (assistant editor of the *Strand* during the 1940s) has pointed out, is Wodehouse's 'only arrant rogue'. Winslow, cut from the same cloth, is a blackmailer, liar, and sponge on the grand scale whose dialogue is a not unappealing mixture of upper-crust English and hard-boiled Americanese (Jacot was an admirer of the novelist Dashiell Hammett, bestowing the American's surname on one of his own characters, Hammett McCorquodale); his exploits appeared in *Frogs Don't Grow Feathers* (1930, pungently illustrated by the young Leslie Illingworth) and *Winslow Moult* (1934). Jacot tired of comedy in the 1930s and turned to drama, at which he was equally proficient. 'White Spectre', which first appeared in the ante-penultimate issue of the *Strand*, is a tale of tension with a horrifying denouement.

His Brother's Keeper

W. W. Jacobs

Aᴺᴛʜᴏɴʏ Kᴇʟʟᴇʀ, white and dazed, came stumbling out into the small hall and closed the door of his study noiselessly behind him. Only half an hour ago he had entered the room with Henry Martle, and now Martle would never leave it again until he brought him out.

He took out his watch and put it back again without looking at it. He sank into a chair and, trying to still his quivering legs, strove to think. The clock behind the closed door struck nine. He had ten hours; ten hours before the woman who attended to his small house came to start the next day's work.

Ten hours! His mind refused to act. There was so much to be done, so much to be thought of. God! If only he could have the last ten minutes over again and live it differently. If Martle only had not happened to say that it was a sudden visit and that nobody knew of it.

He went into the back room and, going to the sideboard, gulped down half a tumbler of raw whisky. It seemed to him inconceivable that the room should look the same. This pleasant room, with etchings on the walls, and his book, face downwards, just as he had left it to answer Martle's knock. He could hear the knock now, and——

The empty tumbler smashed in his hand, and he caught his breath in a sob. Somebody else was knocking. He stood for a moment quivering, and then, wiping some of the blood from his hand, kicked the pieces of glass aside and stood irresolute. The knocking came again, so loud and insistent that for one horrible moment he fancied it might arouse the thing in the next room. Then he walked to the door and opened it. A short sturdy man, greeting him noisily, stepped into the hall.

'Thought you were dead,' he said, breezily. 'Hallo!'

'Cut myself with a broken glass,' said Keller, in a constrained voice.

'Look here, that wants binding up,' said his friend. 'Got a clean handkerchief?'

He moved towards the door, and was about to turn the handle when Keller flung himself upon him and dragged him back. 'Not there,' he said, thickly. 'Not there.'

'What the devil's the matter?' enquired the visitor, staring.

Keller's mouth worked. 'Somebody in there,' he muttered: 'somebody in there. Come here.'

He pushed him into the back room and in a dazed fashion motioned him to a chair.

'Thanks, rather not,' said the other, stiffly. 'I just came in to smoke a pipe. I didn't know you had visitors. Anyway, I shouldn't eat them. Good night.'

Keller stood staring at him. His friend stared back, then suddenly his eyes twinkled and he smiled roguishly.

'What have you got in there?' he demanded, jerking his thumb towards the study.

Keller shrank back. 'Nothing,' he stammered. 'Nothing— no——'

'Ho, ho!' said the other. 'All right. Don't worry. Mum's the word. You quiet ones are always the worst. Be good.'

He gave him a playful dig in the ribs and went out chuckling. Keller, hardly breathing, watched him to the gate and, closing the door softly, bolted it and returned to the back room.

He steadied his nerves with some more whisky, and strove to steel himself to the task before him. He had got to conquer his horror and remorse, to overcome his dread of the thing in the next room, and put it where no man should ever see it. He, Anthony Keller, a quiet, ordinary citizen, had got to do this thing.

The little clock in the next room struck ten. Nine hours left. With a soft tread he went out at the back door and, unlocking the bicycle-shed, peered in. Plenty of room.

He left the door open and, returning to the house, went to the door of the study. Twice he turned the handle—and softly closed the door again. Suppose when he looked in at Martle, Martle should turn and look at him? He turned the handle suddenly and threw the door open.

Martle was quiet enough. Quiet and peaceful, and, perhaps, a little pitiful. Keller's fear passed, but envy took its place. Martle had got the best of it after all. No horror-haunted life for him; no unavailing despair and fear of the unknown. Keller, looking down at the white face and battered head, thought of the years before him. Or would it be weeks? With a gasp he came back to the need for action, and taking Martle by the shoulders drew him, with heels dragging and scraping, to the shed.

He locked the door and put the key in his pocket. Then he drew a bucket of water from the scullery tap and found some towels. His injured hand was still bleeding, but he regarded it with a sort of cunning satisfaction. It would account for much.

It was a long job, but it was finished at last. He sat down and thought, and then searched round and round the room for the overlooked thing which might be his undoing.

It was nearly midnight, and necessary, unless he wanted to attract the attention of any passing constable, to extinguish or lower the companionable lights. He turned them out swiftly, and, with trembling haste, passed upstairs to his room.

The thought of bed was impossible. He lowered the gas and, dropping into a chair, sat down to wait for day. Erect in the chair, his hands gripping the arms, he sat tense and listening. The quiet house was full of faint sounds, odd creakings, and stealthy rustlings. Suppose the suddenly released spirit of Martle was wandering around the house!

He rose and paced up and down the room, pausing every now and then to listen. He could have sworn that there was something fumbling blindly at the other side of the door, and once, turning sharply, thought that he saw the handle move. Sometimes sitting and sometimes walking, the hours passed until the occasional note of a bird outside announced the approach of day.

In the bright light of day his courage returned, and, dismissing all else from his mind, he thought only of how to escape the consequences of his crime. Inch by inch he examined the room and the hall. Then he went into the garden, and, going round the shed, satisfied himself that no crack or hole existed that might reveal his secret. He walked the length of the garden and looked about him. The nearest house was a hundred yards away, and the bottom of the garden screened by trees. Near the angle of the fence he would dig a shallow trench and over it pile up a rockery of bricks and stones and earth. Once started he could take his time about it, and every day would make him more and more secure. There was an air of solidity and permanency about a rockery that nothing else could give.

He was back in the house when the charwoman arrived, and in a few words told her of his accident of the night before. 'I cleaned up the—the mess as well as I could,' he concluded.

Mrs Howe nodded. 'I'll have a go at it while you're having your breakfast,' she remarked. 'Good job for you, sir, that you ain't one o' them as faints at the sight of blood.'

She brought coffee and bacon into the little back dining-room, and Keller, as he sat drinking his coffee and trying to eat, heard her at work in the study. He pushed away his plate at last, and filling a pipe from which all flavour had departed sat smoking and thinking.

He was interrupted by Mrs Howe. She stood in the doorway with a question which numbed his brain, and for a time arrested speech.

'Eh?' he said at last.

'Key of the bicycle-shed,' repeated the woman, staring at him. 'You had a couple o' my dusters to clean your bicycle with.'

Keller felt in his pockets, thinking, thinking. 'H'mm!' he said at last, 'I'm afraid I've mislaid it. I'll look for it presently.'

Mrs Howe nodded. 'You do look bad,' she said, with an air of concern. 'P'r'aps you hurt yourself more than what you think.'

Keller forced a smile and shook his head, sinking back in his chair as she vanished, and trying to control his quivering limbs.

For a long time he sat inert, listening dully to the movements of Mrs Howe as she bustled to and fro. He heard her washing the step at the back door, and, after that, a rasping, grating noise to which at first he paid but little heed. Then there was a faint, musical chinking as of keys knocking together. *Keys!*

He sprang from his chair like a madman, and dashed to the door. Mrs Howe, with a bunch of odd keys tied on a string, had inserted one in the lock of the bicycle-shed, and was striving to turn it.

'Stop!' cried Keller, in a dreadful voice. 'STOP!'

He snatched the keys from her, and, flinging them from him, stood mouthing dumbly at her. The fear in her eyes recalled him to his senses.

'Spoil the lock,' he muttered, 'spoil the lock. Sorry. I didn't mean to shout. No sleep all night. Neuralgia; 'fraid my nerves are wrong.'

The woman's face relaxed and her eyes softened. 'I saw you weren't yourself as soon as I saw you this morning,' she exclaimed.

She went back into the house, but he thought she eyed him curiously as she passed. She resumed her work, but in a subdued fashion, and, two or three times that morning meeting his eyes, nervously turned away her own. He realized at last that he was behaving in an unusual fashion altogether. In and out of the house, and, in the garden, never far from the shed.

By lunch-time he had regained control of himself. He opened a bottle of beer, and, congratulating Mrs Howe upon the grilling of the chops, went on to speak of her husband and the search for work which had been his only occupation since his marriage ten years before. Some of the fear went out of the woman's eyes—but not all, and it was with obvious relief that she left the room.

For some time after lunch Keller stayed in the dining-room, and that in itself was unusual. Two or three times he got up and resolved, for the sake of appearances, to take a short walk, but the shed held him. He dare not leave it unguarded. With a great effort he summoned up sufficient resolution to take him to the bottom of the garden and start his gruesome task.

He dug roughly, avoiding the shape which might have aroused comment from any chance visitor. The ground was soft and, in spite of his injured hand, he made good progress, breaking off at frequent intervals to listen, or to move aside and obtain an unobstructed view of the shed.

With a short break for tea he went on with his task until he was called in to his simple meal at seven. The manual labour had done him good and his appearance was almost normal. To Mrs Howe he made a casual reference to his afternoon's work and questioned where to obtain the best rock-plants.

With her departure after she had cleared away, fear descended upon him again. The house became uncanny and the shed a place of unspeakable horror. Suppose his nerve failed and he found himself unable to open it! For an hour he paced up and down in the long twilight, waiting for the dark.

It came at last, and, fighting down his fears and nausea, he drew the garden-barrow up to the shed, and took the key from his pocket. He walked to the front gate and looked up and down the silent road. Then he came back and, inserting the key in the lock, opened the door, and, in the light of an electric torch, stood looking down at what he had placed there the night before.

With his ears alert for the slightest sound, he took the inhabitant of the shed by the shoulders, and, dragging it outside, strove to lift it into the barrow. He succeeded at last, and, with the rigid body balanced precariously and the dead face looking up into his, seized the handles and slowly and silently took Martle to the place prepared for him.

He did not leave him for a long time. Not until the earth was piled high above him in a circular mound and a score or two of bricks formed the first beginnings of a rockery. Then he walked slowly up the garden, and, after attending to the shed, locked it up and went indoors.

The disposal of the body gave a certain measure of relief. He would live, with time for repentance, and, perhaps, for forgetting. He washed in the scullery, and then, fearing the shadows upstairs, drew the heavy curtains in the dining-room to shut in the light and settled himself in an easy-chair. He drank until his senses were deadened; his nerves quietened, his aching limbs relaxed, and he fell into a heavy sleep.

He awoke at six, and, staggering to his feet, drew back the curtains and turned out the gas. Then he went upstairs, and after disarranging his bed went to the bathroom. The cold water and a shave, together with a change of linen, did him good. He opened doors and windows, and let the clean sweet air blow through the house. The house which he must continue to inhabit because he dare not leave it. Other people might not share his taste for rockeries.

To the watchful eye of Mrs Howe he appeared to be almost himself again. The key of the shed had turned up, and he smiled as he presented her with her 'precious dusters'. Then he rode off on his bicycle to order slabs of stone and plants from the nearest nurseryman.

He worked more and more leisurely as the days passed, and the rockery grew larger and more solid. Every added stone and plant seemed to increase his security. He ate well, and, to his surprise, slept well; but every morning misery opened his eyes for him.

The garden was no longer a place of quiet recreation; the house, which was part of the legacy that had so delighted him only a year before, was a prison in which he must serve a life-long sentence. He could neither let it nor sell it; other people might alter the garden— and dig. Since the fatal evening he had not looked at a newspaper for fear of reading of Martle's disappearance, and in all that time had not spoken to a friend.

Martle was very quiet. There were no shadows in the house, no furtive noises, no dim shape pattering about the garden by night. Memory was the only thing that assailed him; but it sufficed.

Then the dream came. A dream confused and grotesque, as most dreams are. He dreamt that he was standing by the rockery, in the twilight, when he thought he saw one of the stones move. Other stones followed suit. A big slab near the top came slithering down, and it was apparent that the whole pile of earth and stone was being shaken by some internal force. Something was trying to get out. Then he remembered that he was buried there, and had no business to be standing outside. He must get back. Martle had put him there, and for some reason which he was quite unable to remember he was afraid of Martle. He procured his tools and set to work. It was a long and tedious job and made more difficult by the fact that he was not allowed to make a noise. He dug and dug, but the grave had disappeared. Then suddenly something took hold of him and held him down; down. He could neither move nor cry out.

He awoke with a scream and for a minute or two lay trembling and shaking. Thank God, it was only a dream. The room was full of sunlight, and he could hear Mrs Howe moving about downstairs. Life was good and might yet hold something in store for him.

He lay still for ten minutes, and was about to rise when he heard Mrs Howe running upstairs. Even before her sudden and heavy rapping on the door he scented disaster.

'Mr Keller! Mr Keller!'

'Well?' he said, heavily.

'Your rockery!' gasped the charwoman, 'Your beautiful rockery! All gone!'

'*Gone?*' shouted Keller, springing out of bed and snatching his dressing-gown from the door.

'Pulled all to pieces,' said Mrs Howe, as he opened the door. 'You never see such a mess. All over the place, as if a madman had done it.'

In a mechanical fashion he thrust his feet into slippers and went downstairs. He hurried down the garden, and, waving the woman back, stood looking at the ruin. Stones and earth were indeed all over the place, but the spot that mattered was untouched. He stood gazing and trembling. Who could have done it? Why was it done?

He thought of his dream and the truth burst upon him. No need for his aching back and limbs to remind him. No need to remember the sleep-walking feats of his youth. He knew the culprit now.

'Shall I go for the police?' enquired the voice of Mrs Howe.

Keller turned a stony face upon her. 'No,' he said, slowly. 'I— I'll speak to them about it myself.'

He took up the spade and began the task of reconstruction. He worked for an hour, and then went in to dress and breakfast. For the rest of the day he worked slowly and steadily, so that by evening most of the damage had been repaired. Then he went indoors to face the long night.

Sleep, man's best friend, had become his unrelenting enemy. He made himself coffee on the gas-stove and fought his drowsiness cup by cup. He read and smoked and walked about the room. Bits of his dream, that he had forgotten, came back to him and stayed with him. And ever at the back of his mind was the certainty that he was doomed.

There was only one hope left to him. He would go away for a time. Far enough away to render a visit home in his sleep impossible. And perhaps the change of scene would strengthen him and help his frayed nerves. Afterwards it might be possible to let the house for a time on condition that the garden was not interfered with. It was one risk against another.

He went down the garden as soon as it was light and completed his work. Then he went indoors to breakfast and to announce his plans for sudden departure to Mrs Howe, his white and twitching face amply corroborating his tale of neuralgia and want of sleep.

'Things'll be all right,' said the woman, 'I'll ask the police to keep an eye on the house of a night. I did speak to one last night about them brutes as destroyed the rockery. If they try it again they may get a surprise.'

Keller quivered but made no sign. He went upstairs and packed his bag, and two hours later was in the train on his way to Exeter, where he proposed to stay the night. After that, Cornwall, perhaps.

He secured a room at an hotel and went for a stroll to pass the time before dinner. How happy the people in the streets seemed to be, even the poorest! All free and all sure of their freedom. They could eat and sleep and enjoy the countless trivial things that make up life. Of battle and murder and sudden death they had no thought.

The light and bustle of the dining-room gave him a little comfort. After his lonely nights it was good to know that there were people all around him, that the house would be full of them whilst he slept. He felt that he was beginning a fresh existence. In future he would live amongst a crowd.

It was late when he went upstairs, but he lay awake for a few minutes. A faint sound or two reached him from downstairs, and the movements of somebody in the next room gave him a comfortable feeling of security. With a sigh of content he fell asleep.

He was awakened by a knocking; a knocking which sounded just above the head of his bed and died away almost before he had brushed the sleep from his eyes. He looked around fearfully, and then, lighting his candle, lay listening. The noise was not repeated. He had been dreaming, but he could not remember the substance of his dream. It had been unpleasant, but vague. More than unpleasant, terrifying. Somebody had been shouting at him. *Shouting!*

He fell back with a groan. The faint hopes of the night before died within him. *He* had been shouting and the strange noise came from the occupant of the next room. What had he said? and what had his neighbour heard?

He slept no more. From somewhere below he heard a clock toll the hours, and, tossing in his bed, wondered how many more remained to him.

Day came at last and he descended to breakfast. The hour was early and only two other tables were occupied, from one of which, between mouthfuls, a bluff-looking, elderly man eyed him curiously. He caught Keller's eye at last and spoke.

'Better?' he enquired.

Keller tried to force his quivering lips to a smile.

'Stood it as long as I could,' said the other; 'then I knocked. I thought perhaps you were delirious. Same words over and over again; sounded like "Mockery" and "Mortal", "Mockery" and "Mortal". You must have used them a hundred times.'

Keller finished his coffee, and, lighting a cigarette, went and sat in the lounge. He had made his bid for freedom and failed. He looked up the times of the trains to town and rang for his bill.

He was back in the silent house, upon which, in the fading light of the summer evening, a great stillness seemed to have descended. The atmosphere of horror had gone and left only a sense of abiding peace. All fear had left him, and pain and remorse had gone with it. Serene and tranquil he went into the fatal room, and, opening the window, sat by it, watching the succession of shadowy tableaux that had been his life. Some of it good and some of it bad, but most of it neither good nor bad. A very ordinary life until fate had linked it for all time with that of Martle's. He was a living man bound to a corpse with bonds that could never be severed.

It grew dark and he lit the gas and took a volume of poems from the shelves. Never before had he read with such insight and appreciation. In some odd fashion all his senses seemed to have been sharpened and refined.

He read for an hour, and then, replacing the book, went slowly upstairs. For a long time he lay in bed thinking and trying to analyse the calm and indifference which had overtaken him, and, with the problem still unsolved, fell asleep.

For a time he dreamt, but of pleasant, happy things. He seemed to be filled with a greater content than he had ever known before, a content which did not leave him even when these dreams faded and he found himself back in the old one.

This time, however, it was different. He was still digging, but not in a state of frenzy and horror. He dug because something told him it was his duty to dig, and only by digging could he make reparation. And it was a matter of no surprise to him that Martle stood close by looking on. Not the Martle he had known, nor a bloody and decaying Martle, but one of grave and noble aspect. And there was a look of understanding on his face that nearly made Keller weep.

He went on digging with a sense of companionship such as he had never known before. Then suddenly, without warning, the sun blazed out of the darkness and struck him full in the face. The light was unbearable, and with a wild cry he dropped his spade and clapped his hands over his eyes. The light went, and a voice spoke to him out of the darkness.

He opened his eyes on a dim figure standing a yard or two away.

'Hope I didn't frighten you, sir,' said the voice. 'I called to you once or twice and then I guessed you were doing this in your sleep.'

'In my sleep,' repeated Keller. 'Yes.'

'And a pretty mess you've made of it,' said the constable, with a genial chuckle. 'Lord! to think of you working at it every day and then pulling it down every night. Shouted at you I did, but you wouldn't wake.'

He turned on the flashlight that had dazzled Keller, and surveyed the ruins. Keller stood by, motionless—and waiting.

'Looks like an earthquake,' muttered the constable. He paused, and kept the light directed upon one spot. Then he stooped down and scratched away the earth with his fingers, and tugged. He stood up suddenly and turned the light on Keller, while with the other hand he fumbled in his pocket. He spoke in a voice cold and official.

'Are you coming quietly?' he asked.

Keller stepped towards him with both hands outstretched.

'I am coming quietly,' he said, in a low voice. 'Thank God!'

Touch and Go

Sapper

THE fair-haired man in the corner had taken no part in the conversation. He made the fifth of the group that had gathered itself together in the corner of the smoking-room, and I don't think any of us even knew his name. He had come on board the day before at Marseilles with his wife, and it was she who had attracted my attention at dinner to such an extent that I had remarked on her to Sturgis of the Gunners, who was sitting next me.

A pretty woman—extremely pretty, and judging by her face somewhere about thirty. Certainly not more, for there was not a wrinkle to be seen, and her arms and neck were those of a young woman. It was her hair that surprised one, and made one wonder if the age estimate was wrong. For though there was a lot of it, it was snow white.

'Some newfangled fashion,' grunted Sturgis in answer to my comment. 'Next year it will be pea-green. I'll bet you that woman is not out of the twenties yet.'

But somehow she didn't look in the least the type who go in for freak fancies of that sort. And her husband seemed to be the last man in the world who would marry one of the type. A more prosaic, matter-of-fact-looking Englishman I have seldom seen, and he was quiet to the point of dullness.

It was his first trip out East, we gathered, whereas we calculated that between the rest of us we had just topped the half-century. Which quite possibly accounted for his silence: we were talking of seas and places that, to him, were merely names out of an atlas. And also, as the evening grew older and tongues grew looser, some pretty tall stories began to fly around. Some were perfectly true; some—— However, I will not labour the point.

I forget who it was who first started the discussion on tight corners, and terrifying experiences generally. Cartwright spun a fairly useful one about three days in the company of some Chinese pirates waiting for a ransom he knew would never come; Sturgis specialized on a singularly unpleasant sect of priests somewhere up in Tibet. In fact, none of us disgraced ourselves, and I think we all had a comfortable feeling that our fair-haired friend was suitably impressed with the perils that lay in wait for the unwary.

'Of course,' said Cartwright, reassuringly, 'it's only when you get off the beaten track that there's any danger. Otherwise you're as safe as you are in England.'

The fair-haired man smiled a little thoughtfully.

'What age would you put my wife at, gentlemen?' was his somewhat astounding remark.

'Well, really,' said Sturgis, after a slightly embarrassed silence, 'I—er——'

'I think you noticed her at dinner,' went on the other, quietly. 'And I have a reason for my apparently strange question.'

'Twenty-five,' I said, determined to err on the right side.

'My wife will be twenty next July,' he answered. 'And seven months ago, when she was just nineteen, her hair was as dark as yours. Not illness, gentlemen: nothing of that sort. But when you made use of the phrase "as safe as you are in England", I couldn't help thinking of that change of colour.'

'You mean she had some terrible shock?' said someone.

'Nothing to compare, of course, with that sect of priests in Tibet,' he answered mildly, and Sturgis became engrossed in the bowl of his pipe. 'Yes, she had a terrible shock.'

'Which turned her hair white?' Cartwright looked at him with interest. 'I've heard of such cases second-hand, but—— Is it a matter which you can pass on, sir?'

The fair-haired man was silent for a moment or two.

'Well, gentlemen,' he said at length, 'you will understand that it's not a thing which I care to talk about as a general rule. But on the condition that it goes no further, and above all on the condition that no allusion should ever be made to it in front of my wife, I have no objection to telling you what happened.

'You will understand, of course, that much of it has been pieced together by me from what she told me after it happened: I was not there at the time. If I had been——'

His fists clenched suddenly, and a strained look came into his eyes.

'We had been married three months when it took place. Our honeymoon was over—I couldn't afford the time for a very long one—and we were settling into the house I had managed to get not far from Sunningdale.

'It was a nice little house—ten bedrooms sort of size, with a well-laid-out garden and about a couple of acres of rough ground in which my predecessor had planted a whole lot of prize rhododendrons. It had a tennis court and a garage, and the marvel to me was that it hadn't been snapped up the instant it came on the market. We found it by mere chance when we were motoring to look at another place, and the instant we saw it we knew that it would do us, and further that we meant to have it. An old caretaker—a strange-looking old woman—showed us over it, and we found that the inside was in just as good condition as the exterior. Which was not to be wondered at, seeing that she told us it had only been unoccupied about nine months.

'"How comes it that it has remained empty all this time?" I asked her, for nine months in that locality is more than nine years elsewhere.

'She shrugged her shoulders, and looked more bovine than before. Yes—the drains were all right, and the house wasn't damp and there weren't any rats—she could assure us of that. And the house agents could give us all other particulars.

'So off we went to the house agent. The rent was eminently satisfactory, and since he seemed a very decent sort of fellow I decided to put the matter to him point-blank.

'"Look here," I said, "as man to man, is there a catch somewhere? I know it's your job to let the house, but this lady and I are shortly going to get married and we don't want to be let down. And from what I know of the housing problem it's a mighty strange thing that a house of that type, in this locality, should have remained empty for nearly a year."

'He didn't answer for a bit, but just sat at his desk fingering the plans.

'"Are you a stranger to these parts?" he said at length.

'"Complete," I answered.

'"Well," he said, "it's unprofessional, I suppose, but in view of the circumstances I'll tell you. Mark you, personally I think it's the most hopeless rot. It's a first-class property in first-class order; of its type and size it's out and away the best value I have on my books. But three years ago a singularly brutal murder was committed there."

'"Three years!" I cried. "But it's only been empty nine months!"

'"The next party that had it after the crime took place moved to a larger house," he answered.

'"And you promise me that that is all there is against it?" I said.

'"Absolutely all," he assured me. "You may have any tests you like carried out." And then he looked at my fiancée and rubbed his chin. "Dash it all," he burst out, "I got married myself once upon a time. The real trouble is—servants. There—I've let the cat out of the bag. You know what they are: difficult at the best of times these days. But that is where the rub comes. The party I told you of certainly did move to a larger house, but I don't think they would have if they had been able to keep a servant. Silly, hysterical girls—swearing that they saw things and heard noises: you know the sort of thing."

'We thanked him warmly for having been so frank with us, and told him we'd think it over.

'"If I can do anything for you," were his parting words, "let me know. I've got a few possibles on my books, though none of them compare with that one. But if you do decide to take it I would not, if I were you, get your servants locally."

'Well, we went away, and we thought it over. It may sound perhaps a small point to some of you fellows—this servant question—but it isn't a small point to us stay-at-homes. And there was no doubt about it—the drawback was a very serious one. So serious that for a week we tried to find something else. But nothing that we saw approached the house at Sunningdale, either for comfort or convenience. And finally, to cut a long story short, we made up our minds to chance it.

'So I wrote and told the house agent of our decision, and in the stress and bustle of getting married the matter more or less passed from my mind. Furniture I had in plenty, and it was not until the house had been completely repapered and fixed-up generally that I went down again.

'I went alone, I remember, as my fiancée was busy that day. It was principally to get some measurements, and I took down a sandwich lunch with me. The old caretaker was there, and I thought she eyed me a bit strangely as she opened the door, though she said nothing. In fact, I don't think I saw her again until just before I was going, when she came into the hall and stood looking at me.

'"What is it, Mrs Gulliver?" I said. "Do you want to ask me anything?"

'"So you've taken the house," she remarked, quietly.

'"I certainly have," I answered. "And a very charming little house it is."

'She nodded her head once or twice and her eyes never left my face.

'"What's the matter?" I cried, irritably. "Have you got something at the back of your mind about it? If so, please tell me."

'"I've nothing at the back of my mind that you would be paying attention to," she said. "But that's not saying that I haven't got something there."

'"Well, what is it?" I said. "I shall certainly pay attention to it if it's anything serious."

'"There's death in this house, Mr Morgan," she answered gravely. "It's hanging over us: I can feel it."

'Well, gentlemen, I can tell you I was furious. Just the sort of damned silly fatuous remark which would scare the average servant stiff and send her flying from the house. At least, that's how it struck me at the time. Now—well, now I'm not so certain.

'Looking back on the little interview I favoured Mrs Gulliver with in that sunny, fresh-painted hall, there is one thing that stands out very clearly in my mind. And that was her impassive demeanour. She never raised her voice, even when I became thoroughly annoyed. She just stood there listening to what I had to say, and her quiet, steady eyes never wavered.

'"It's ridiculous," I cried. "Perfectly ridiculous. It's remarks like that which make it impossible to keep servants."

'"Better that," she said, "than the other. For it will be a terrible death."

'"But what earthly reason have you for making such a statement?" I fumed.

'"Maybe it's not earthly," she answered.

'"Just because a murder was committed here," I grunted. And then her last remark struck me. "What do you mean—not earthly?"

'"There are things, Mr Morgan, beyond our ken," she said, gravely. "It was my mother's gift, and my grandmother's before her, and in turn it has come to me. Second sight, I believe they call it. But sometimes we know what is going to happen. And we are never wrong."

'"And who, might I ask, is going to die?" I said, facetiously.

'"Don't mock me, sir," she said. "No good ever came of that. I cannot tell you who is going to be killed, or when it is going to happen. But it is written."

'"Be killed?" I repeated. "Do you mean another murder?"

'"Aye," she said, gravely. "Another murder. The thoughts come thronging into my mind sometimes, till I have to get up from my chair and go out of doors. Then they leave me. But I tell you there is evil threatening this house and they who live in it. Where it comes from I know not; but always it is the same thing—death. Death by violence."

'There was no good saying anything or trying to argue about it. The woman was firmly convinced that what she said was right, and I had to leave it at that. The only thing I did do was to extract a promise from her that she would not mention the matter to the servants when they came.

'"I'll not mention it," she said, quietly, "but for all that you won't keep them."

'"And why not?" I snapped.

'"The tradesmen," she answered. "When they call of a morning—they'll talk. They'll tell the cook what happened here three years ago. They'll tell her that you may hear strange sounds and see strange things in this house, and she will believe them."

'"Exactly," I said, bitterly. "And then they promptly will begin to hear strange sounds. Whereas if nothing was said to them they wouldn't."

'"Maybe," she answered. "Maybe not."

'She took a step towards me, almost her first movement since the interview had started.

'"There's something, Mr Morgan, that threatens this house. Don't ask me what it is, for that I can't tell you. I don't know myself. But it's there—it's always there. That I do know."

'And the next instant she was gone, and I was alone in the cheerful sunlight. Now, what would any of you have done in my place? Probably just what I did—cursed furiously. While she had been with me her strange personality had impressed me in spite of myself; now that she had gone I merely remembered the stupid vapourings of a silly woman. And a servantless future. She wouldn't be able to hold her tongue, for all her promise to the contrary, when she met the servants. Not she; she wasn't the type. And there and then I determined that whatever else happened there should be no overlap. Mrs Gulliver should be out of the house before the servants came in, even if it did mean some inconvenience to us. In ordinary circumstances, of course, we should have had the house open, with the servants installed, all ready for us on our return from our honeymoon. Now I decided that we would keep on Mrs Gulliver until we came back, and then get rid of her one morning and bring the servants in in the afternoon. I felt that tradesmen's boys were, at any rate, less likely to unsettle the staff than that sombre-eyed woman.'

The fair-haired man took a sip of his drink and knocked out his pipe.

'Well,' he continued, 'we returned. Two months ago, almost to a day, we returned. Mrs Gulliver was at the door to meet us and we spent the afternoon in exploring the house. Everything was perfectly charming, and my wife was delighted. In fact, the only fly in the ointment was Mrs Gulliver's cooking. I hadn't told my wife of the conversation I had had with the woman, and I had taken the first opportunity—when I saw Mrs Gulliver alone—of telling her that if she said one word to my wife of what she had said to me a death by violence would occur in the house and her prophecy would be fulfilled. Because my wife thought that my idea of not having any overlap was merely due to my wish to prevent Mrs Gulliver giving gruesome details of the murder to the servants, which might unsettle them.

'That, then, was the position when we arrived back at the house. The servants were due in in three days, and until then we should have to put up with the cooking.

'Well, as I've said before, it was a charming little place. I spent the next day pottering around with my wife, planning out improvements in the garden, and the more I saw of it the less I thought of Mrs Gulliver's strange words to me a few weeks previously. She had said nothing more, but then, save for one brief interview when I had sworn her to silence, I had not seen her alone. Her face was expressionless, and she performed her work—save the cooking—quietly and efficiently.

'The following day I had to go up to London. There were a lot of arrears of work waiting for me in the office, and I only just got back in time for dinner. And the first thing I noticed was that my wife seemed a little thoughtful and preoccupied.

'"Marjorie Thurston came to see me this afternoon," she said, as we sat down.

'Mrs Thurston was a pal of hers who lived at Ascot.

'"And what had she got to say for herself?" I asked.

'"Jack," she said, "I rather wish we hadn't taken this house."

'I swore under my breath, and consigned Mrs Thurston elsewhere. I could guess what she had been saying.

'"She gave me the details of the murder," went on my wife. "Perfectly horrible. A brute of a man who lived here and killed his wife. He——" and I could see that she was looking a bit white—"he cut off her head."

'"Well, my dear," I said, prosaically, "it seems to me that if you're going to murder someone it doesn't much matter how you do it. The result is much the same."

'"Oh, I know that," she cried. "But it all seems so horrible. And they say that he haunts the place."

'"Confound Marjorie Thurston," I said, angrily. "She'd got no right to fill you up with a cock-and-bull story of that sort. You don't believe it, of course?"

'"No, of course not," she answered, but it wasn't a very convincing "no". "It's the servants I'm thinking of. They're bound to hear of it."

'"Let's leave that trouble till it comes," I said.

'And on the surface, at any rate, we did leave it. We discussed the moving of furniture to different places, and what particular car we were going to buy, and a hundred and one other things, till it was time to go to bed. In fact, I thought she had forgotten about it, until I noticed her glance over her shoulder suddenly as we went upstairs. The hall was in darkness, and she clutched my arm.

'"Jack," she whispered, "Jack—don't you feel it?"

'"Feel what?" I said, impressed in spite of myself.

'"Something evil," she said, and her voice was shaking. "Horrible and black. It's gone now, but——"

'With a little shiver she went on up the stairs, and I followed her. And you can take it from me that for the first time in my life I was annoyed with her. I had felt absolutely nothing, and I put it down to imagination. I didn't say anything. I didn't see that there was any good to be gained by doing so. But the thing annoyed me. If she was going to give way to these hysterical fears, there certainly would be no chance of keeping any servants.

'However, she said nothing more, and when the next morning dawned bright and sunny she seemed to be her normal self again. Which was a relief, seeing that I had to go up to London again.

'But before I went I asked Mrs Gulliver if she had said anything to my wife. She absolutely denied it, and denied it so quietly and convincingly that I believed her. And in view of what happened, gentlemen, that fact is an interesting one. Mark you, I advance no explanation, and yet it seems clear to me that two people—my wife and Mrs Gulliver—both experienced the same sensation in that house. I have since asked my wife if she thought she saw or heard anything in the hall, and her answer is that she did not. In fact, the nearest that I can get to her sensation is that she suddenly felt herself opposed by a dreadful malign influence—one that wished her harm. She is positive that it was not imagination: she says that the sudden sensation was so marked as to be almost physical. Now, if her experience on the stairs had been due to what Mrs Thurston had told her that afternoon, my contention is that she would have been affected differently. If it indeed had been imagination, as I thought at the time, it would have taken a more material form. In fact, I believe that Mrs Thurston represented—if I may put it that way—the errand-boy school of thought, which grew out of idle tittle-tattle. And I believe that my wife's experience that night was a manifestation of what Mrs Gulliver had told me. In short, that the house was, in the accepted sense of the word, not haunted, but that there was a sinister influence present—which, if we knew more of the things that lie on the borderline, should have warned us of the terrible danger we were in.'

The sweat was gleaming in beads on the fair-haired man's forehead, and his neglected pipe lay beside him on the table.

'Gentlemen,' he said, 'I still find it difficult to talk calmly of that next night. I was unavoidably detained in London till the last train, and what happened has been told me disjointedly by that poor child. God! when I think of it, it almost drives me mad!

'I'd telephoned through to her to say that I couldn't get down till late. I asked her how she was, and she assured me she was quite all right. She was going to bed early, and she was going to have a fire lit in her bedroom to make it more cosy. Sandwiches and whisky would be left for me in the dining-room. Mrs Gulliver was there, and she didn't feel in the least uneasy. It must have been just imagination the night before, and anyway I wasn't to dream of coming down early. And with that I left it, and went back to a business dinner with a quiet mind.

'I've got the rest of it out of her a bit here and a bit there, and I'll piece it together for you in the telling. She had her dinner at eight o'clock, and at ten o'clock she went to bed. I had a latchkey, of course, so she locked the front door, but left the light on in the hall. Then she went upstairs, and of one thing she is very positive: there was no repetition of the strange feeling she had experienced the night before.

'The fire was burning brightly in her bedroom, and after she had read for a bit she began to feel sleepy. So she switched off the light, having first glanced at the time to see how much longer I should be. It was eleven o'clock, and twelve-fifteen was the earliest at which I could be back. Then she dozed off.

'She seemed, she told me, hardly to have been asleep at all when she found herself wide awake again. Something had disturbed her, but she doesn't know what. And the time was a quarter to twelve. The fire had died down a bit and was throwing that flickering jumping light about the room which makes it difficult to see clearly.

'She lay there in bed motionless and rigid, conscious only of one thing—that something was going to happen. And then she heard an unmistakable creak on the stairs, followed by a strange muttering noise. Again the stairs creaked and yet again, and she realized that someone was coming up.

'She knew it couldn't be me: she knew Mrs Gulliver had gone to bed hours ago. Who was it—what was it—that was coming up the stairs? Well, it's easy to sit here in a well-lit smoking-room and ask why she didn't get out and lock the door. I asked her the same thing myself. The kid was just too pulverized with terror to move, gentlemen: she lay there in bed listening to those footsteps coming closer and her legs simply refused to act.

'And at last the footsteps ceased outside her door. Clear as anything she could hear the thing—whatever it was—muttering and chuckling to itself, and she just lay there rigid and sick with fear, staring at the door—waiting. After a moment or two the handle was cautiously turned, and the door commenced to open. Inch by inch it was pushed back, but since it didn't open on to the bed she couldn't see who was on the other side. And then quite suddenly there came a hoarse chuckle.

'She almost screamed; may Heaven be praised that it was only almost! For the next instant a man came into the room carrying a bundle in his hands. He walked slowly past the bed and sat down in a chair by the fire with his back to my wife. And she realized he hadn't seen her. He was muttering to himself and laughing, and after a while he deposited the bundle on the hearth-rug at his feet. It was about the size of a football, and it was wrapped up in what looked like a towel. And there he remained for three or four minutes whilst my wife, not daring to move, watched him from the bed. She tried to make out what he was saying to himself, but the few words she caught were just meaningless gibberish.

'At last a thought struck her. By the side of the bed was a push which rang a bell just outside Mrs Gulliver's room. She glanced at the clock; it was still twenty minutes before I could hope to be back. And she felt that she would go mad if she had to endure this any longer. So with infinite care she stretched out her arm and rang the bell. She knew she couldn't hear it—it was too far away; but she also knew that it had been working that evening. So she waited—but nothing happened. She rang again and again—still nothing. And all the time the man sat there muttering and chuckling away to himself, whilst every now and then he lifted the bundle in his hands and held it in front of him.

'Another five minutes passed, and then the strain became too great. She must have given a little cry or made some sound, for the man swung round suddenly and stared at her. He stared at her in absolute silence; then he placed his bundle carefully on the floor and stood up. And I suppose utter despair and terror gave her the strength to move. For even as the man took a step towards her she flung the bed-clothes off and darted through the door, banging it behind her. Then she fled downstairs and into the drawing-room. Behind her pounded the man, and by a second only did she get the door locked. There were French windows leading into the garden, and anything—anything to escape from the house.'

The fair-haired man mopped his forehead, and his hand was shaking uncontrollably.

'You've seen the fantastic shadows cast by moonlight, haven't you? Well, there was a moon that night, shining fitfully through the clouds—and on the windows through which she meant to escape two great shadows were dancing. There were men there—more men, and, clear above the mad pounding on the door behind her, she could hear them trying to force the window. And at that moment she gave up hope. The door was creaking on its hinges; she could hear the man on the other side hurling himself against it. And the crash of broken glass and the splintering of the door came simultaneously. She had a fleeting vision of the man who had been in her bedroom rushing in with something in his hand that gleamed, just as the other two men dashed aside the curtains and sprang into the room also. And the two of them hurled themselves at him savagely. One took him round the legs and brought him crashing to the floor; the other hit him a fearful blow behind the head with a loaded stick. And the man who had been upstairs lay still.

'"Good God, man!" said one of the newcomers, "that was touch and go."

'"Who is he?" said my wife, faintly. "He's been in my bedroom for twenty minutes."

'The two men looked at one another significantly.

'"Are you all alone in the house, mum?" said the other.

'"My husband ought to be back at any moment," she answered.

'"Well, I guess we'll stop with you anyway till he comes. Because we'll have to get a conveyance of some sort to take this bloke away in."

'And it was just about then that I walked in.

'"A marvellous escape, sir," said one of them to me when I'd heard briefly what had happened. "He's a homicidal maniac, and he gave us the slip this evening."

'"You followed him here, I suppose?"

'"Not exactly, sir. We guessed he'd come here. You see, he's the man that did the murder in this house three years ago. And if we hadn't come in time there would have been another done tonight."'

The fair-haired man paused, and for a while no one spoke.

'What a ghastly experience!' said Sturgis. 'I don't wonder your wife's hair turned white.'

The other smiled grimly.

'It wasn't that that did it. I was talking to the two warders below, when I heard scream after scream from my wife's bedroom. You see, the warders hadn't come in time to prevent a murder. For when I got to her, I found her staring at something that lay on the hearth-rug—something from which the coverings had slipped—something about the size of a football. Mrs Thurston had been right as to how the original murder had been committed. He'd cut off his victim's head. And the only thing that had saved my wife was that the maniac had been to Mrs Gulliver's room first. That was why the bell had not been answered.'

'Great Scott!' muttered Cartwright. 'Great Scott!'

'The psychology of the thing, gentlemen, is beyond me. The foolish talk about the house being haunted in the accepted sense of the word may be dismissed. But I do believe firmly that in some way or other beyond our ken the poor demented mind of that madman was able to project itself through space and make itself felt by certain personalities at its destination. How else can you account for the unfortunate housekeeper's feeling of impending evil—for my wife's sudden vivid impression as she went up the stairs? They told me that sometimes he used to lie in a sort of coma for hours at a time. Was it then that his tortured spirit fled from his body, going always to the spot which drew it like a magnet? I know not. But there's one thing I do know. If any of you gentlemen require a nice unfurnished house in the Sunningdale district——'

'Holy smoke!' said Sturgis. 'I'd sooner have my monastery in Tibet.'

Waxworks

W. L. George

Henry Badger rapidly paced the City churchyard; his air of anxiety seemed to overweigh his small, though not unpleasing, features. He was an insignificant little man, dressed in pepper-and-salt tweeds. His hair was cut very close, except where a love-lock, plastered down with jasmine-oil, trailed over his forehead from under his hard black hat. Whenever he completed the circuit of the churchyard he peered towards the gate through which must come disturbance and romance. Henry Badger was in love, and he could not escape the consequences of his share in our common delight and affliction.

Suddenly brightness overspread his sharp features. It was she! She, in a pink crêpe-de-Chine blouse, disconnected rather than connected with her white serge skirt by a patent-leather belt. Above the pink blouse was an equally pink neck, and a rather pretty face, all soft curves. She was bright blue of eye and tumbled in pleasant fairness about the hair, under a large straw hat from which drooped on one side a fragment of ivy that might with advantage have been placed elsewhere. But her name was Ivy, and she liked to live in harmony.

'I'm late,' she said, with pretty briskness, as they shook hands. 'So sorry, Henry. Only the boss got dictating, and he likes to hear himself talk, even if it is only to little me. Still, better late than never,' she added, with a smile indicating wit.

Henry Badger replied 'Yes,' and wondered if it would be good policy to attack her for being late. Since he felt at fault, no doubt it would. Only—an argument with Ivy, one never knew what that would lead to.

'Well, you dummy,' she said, 'is that all you've got to say? Got the tickets?'

'Er——,' said Henry Badger, 'no.'

'What do you mean?' said Ivy, crossly.

'What I say,' replied Henry Badger, with feeble determination. 'Fact is, Ivy, I'm sorry, but I forgot.'

The blue eyes stared at him, incredulous.

'Forgot! What you been and done that for?'

Henry Badger explained profusely. The night before he'd had an awful headache, and it had slipped his memory to go round to the Imperial Music Hall, and this morning the manager——

Ivy trampled upon these confused excuses. 'All I can see,' she said, 'is here we are landed on a Saturday afternoon with nowhere to go except the pictures. And it's so hot in those places. Last time I was fair melted. I do think it's too bad of you.'

It was then that Henry Badger expressed himself. 'Fact is, Ivy, I been thinking.'

'Hope you didn't break anything,' said Ivy, 'but since you done it, what's the ideer?'

'I been thinking that we don't know the town we live in. I was reading a book the other day. *Strange Sights of London*, it was called. And, would you believe it, Ivy? there's lots of things I got to learn.'

'Ah, I do believe it,' said Ivy.

'For instance,' said Henry, 'did you know that the church of St Ethelburga wasn't burnt down in the Fire of London?'

'No,' said Ivy, 'and now I do know it I don't seem to be much better off.'

'Ah!' said Henry, 'that's where you're wrong, Ivy. It improves your mind to know that sort of thing. And that's how I got my ideer. I been thinking we might go round to the docks.'

'What for?'

'Oh, I dunno. Just to mooch round. Ever been to the docks? No? Well, why not try 'em? You know, Ivy, people spend a lot of money going to the Riviera, and they never see the place round the corner. See your own country first,' he added, with originality.

'Well,' said Ivy, after a moment, 'seeing you've mucked up this afternoon, and mother's gone out and there won't be any tea, I suppose we may as well.'

*

The two little people, for neither of them was quite five-foot-six, made their way along the East India Dock Road, where an omnibus had deposited them. For an hour they wandered the tragic land where none live for pleasure, and where slowly the soot falls to obliterate sooty footmarks. They were too tired to be pleased when, behind a long brick wall, they found the docks. They perceived the smell of the East, oil of macassar, piled logs of sandalwood, barrels of copra; at a point against the sky, where now the dark clouds were racing, they saw outlined tall spars, while a funnel striped in yellow and blue threw out a shower of sparks against the sky like a dun veil touched with tinsel. The heat seemed to grow.

They lost their direction, not liking to ask their way of the rough inhabitants, not knowing where they wanted to go. They were astray, unprotected lambs in a land of slender law. Ivy began to drag her feet as loudly as she could, to show that she was displeased. Both were secretly oppressed because that day they had not kissed.

At that moment came rain. Very slowly at first in separate warm drops that made upon the pavement spots as large as a coin. '*My!*' said Henry, 'it's going to come down like billy-oh!'

'I don't care,' said Ivy.

'Come on,' said Henry, 'let's see if we can get under shelter somewhere.' But they were still progressing along another brick wall; opposite, the warehouses were closed. They ran, for now the rain was beginning to fall with greater determination.

'Here,' gasped Henry, as he ran, 'we must get in somewhere; you'll be sopped through. Let's go into a shop.'

They stopped irresolutely at the corner of a side-street. As it was almost entirely occupied by warehouses no living creature could be seen. But just as they prepared to run on through the rain, Henry observed a tottering post, bearing a battered sign. The sign was in the shape of a hand pointing up the lane, and upon it were painted the words: 'To the Waxworks.'

'Here,' he cried, dragging Ivy along, 'that'll do. I didn't know they had waxworks in this part of the world, but it'll save us getting wet.' They ran up the street, expecting a veranda and a commission-aire. At the end of the lane they had found nothing, and paused irresolute, when upon the door of a three-floored house Ivy saw the word 'Waxworks', with the addition: 'Mrs Groby, Proprietress.' Henry seized the door handle, which resisted for a moment. The door jammed, but with a great effort he forced it open. It made a great clatter as he flung it against the wall. Breathless, and wiping their wet faces, the two stood giggling in the hall. Then, feeling alone, suddenly they kissed. The excitement of the run and of the caress sheltered them against an impression which the place imposed upon them only by degrees. They were in the hall of a house, of a house like any other house. There was no noise, except for a slight sound. It felt deserted. The door handle on the right was covered with dust. Nobody had gone into that room for a long time. An unaccountable emotion developed in them. The house was still except that at last they identified the slight sound: far away a tap was leaking. They found themselves listening to the drip which came regularly from the basement.

'Well,' said Henry, with forced cheerfulness, 'here we are.' And as if to reassure himself: 'Anyhow, we sha'n't get wet.'

They stood for a moment looking out at the rain, which now came faster. The effect of this falling water, soft and hot, the dusty silence of the place except for that regular drip far away, combined to cast upon them a sort of uneasiness, an almost physical oppression. Ivy began to look about her with unexplainable anxiety. The darkness of the stairs, the banisters broken in several places, the dusty door handle, stirred in her a vague fear; she looked about her like a cat in a strange place and preparing to flee. As the feeling communicated itself to Henry his manliness revolted. It would be too silly to have the jumps. So he said: 'Ive, since we're here, why not go upstairs and see the show?'

After a moment's hesitation, Ivy dominated her disturbance and said: 'All right.'

They went up the stairs, firmly, but with instinctive slowness, troubled by the sound of their feet upon the boards, followed by the fainter drip of the distant tap. The first floor was like the ground floor. Here, too, the door handles were dusty, and here, too, there came no sound from beyond the doors. They had to make an effort to go up further. The sense that here was emptiness made emptiness frightful. But Henry was leading and still went up. He didn't know why, but knew he must go up. Perhaps because he was a man and couldn't run away from anything, not even from nothing. The second floor comforted them, for here was a pay-box, empty it is

true, but marked: 'Pay here.' Henry released a great sigh. It really
was a show. It had a human air.

'Come on, Ivy,' he said, in a loud voice which rang unpleasantly
down the uncarpeted stairs. 'Since there's nobody down here we
can pay when we get to the top.'

Ivy silently followed him up, and so they reached what seemed
to be a large attic. Once again a reluctant door yielded to their
hands, and Henry stepped into the doorway with a sort of jaunti-
ness, but Ivy paused for a moment at his back. Waxworks, yes, but,
she didn't know why, at once she was terrified. One couldn't see
very well in the attic, for the dust of years lay upon the skylight,
and the avaricious light of the sullen sky hardly penetrated. The
walls had been whitewashed, but now were stained black with
damp, soiled by the touch of hands, the smoke of lamps. About the
door hung rags of dirty red damask. And in the immense silence of
the place, hearing not even the drip of the distant tap, they found
themselves alone with the wax figures.

Some stood upon little thrones of red-painted wood, here a man
in day clothes, staring emptily from a yellow countenance, here a
woman spreading crimson nostrils to an absent scent. The two were
still in the doorway, not knowing why they did not go in. They
were conscious of a secret vileness in these faces. The things stood
so still, but sure of themselves, as if they had always stood in the
dust and twilight. But at last Henry seized Ivy's arm more firmly
and they went in.

Altogether there were fourteen figures. Three of the men were
labelled Charles Peace, Dr Crippen, and Gouffé. The woman with
the intense gaze was Mrs Maybrick, and there were two other
women, one with bright red hair over which a spider had built its
web. But Henry and Ivy, as they stood before them, did not at once
read the legends telling how Crippen had killed his wife and burnt
her body in the furnace, nor did they gaze at Gouffé, the bailiff,
who had been carved into pieces and packed in a trunk. A little later
Ivy read that ticket to the end and shudderingly stepped away from
the invitation to draw apart the figure's clothing and see indicated
the lines along which the body had been cut up. At that moment
she was cowering against Henry, who instinctively had laid an arm
about her shoulders, for the single figures were less terrifying than
two groups represented in action. One of the groups comprised a

man and a woman in a pink flannelette dressing-gown. With an expression of pinched determination the murderer was forcing the female figure down into a bath, where a sheet of mica, tinted green, represented water. In the grasp of a bony hand, the female figure held the edge of the bath, wildly raising the other arm, while into her distorted mouth floated the green edge of the water that was to drown her. It was a work of art of indescribable horror. It was as if the snake-like fingers moved, as if in another moment the head would disappear under that still green surface.

With an exclamation Henry turned aside to the other group, that stood dim within the shadow, away from the faint rays that fell through the skylight. This represented a very old woman, lying on her face, her white hair scattered and stained with blood, while kneeling over her, a sandbag still half-raised, was a short man in the clothes of the day, his face set and coated with a horrible scarlet flush.

Now a new sound made them start. It was the growing rain, pattering upon the skylight, as if goblins raced across it. In a sudden desire for union again they kissed, quickly falling apart, as if espied.

They turned away for a moment, fascinated, they did not know how, in this gallery of crime; the still things about them seemed to have a motion, a vibration of their own. They found themselves looking sharply into corners as if something were there after all, as if these were not creatures of wax, but actually poisoners, men and women experienced in violence and still capable of evil. The great horror, which always drew them back to itself, was that bath, soiled, chipped, and streaked with black rivulets of dirt, into which the murderer was endlessly pressing down the figure that endlessly strove for life.

So great was the tension that Henry tried to rejoin the ordinary world. He whispered: 'We ought to have paid someone,' but while he spoke he looked from side to side, as if begging some material custodian to appear with a familiar ticket and a sounding punch. Ivy did not reply; she was holding his arm in a nervous clutch; once or twice she moved away from him, and then came back, as if her fingers grasped him independently of the processes of her brain. She was opening and closing her mouth, striving to speak and finding her tongue dry. Only at last did she find a whisper: 'I don't like it. Let's go.'

Henry Badger also wanted to go, but he was so unaccountably afraid that he dared not go. His virility spoke: it told him that if he went now he would be everlastingly ashamed. He was afraid to tell himself that he was afraid. So, in a voice the loudness of which half-startled him, he replied: 'Oh, rot! Since we've come up we may as well see the lot of them.' So, Ivy still grasping his arm, they circled the attic, stopping in turn before each figure. Ivy did not want to see, but she could not look away. It was as if she must meet material, human eyes. It was always the eyes she looked at. There was a challenge in them. It was the defiance of the dead which she must meet. She must again view the bath, look down through the green surface of the water upon the agonized limbs which twisted in the dimness that was to be their grave. But now there was a change. Perhaps because habit made that first seem less awful, the second group gained in horror. It was not only the sight of the blood coagulated on the white hair, it was something else, something unnamable. The art of the sculptor had gone too far; here was mere and abominable reality. Real hair, and crouching above, with drooping eyelids, the figure of the murderer, ill-shaven and flushed with health. Something twisted in Ivy's body as she thought that upon the still mask she could discern beads of sweat. They stayed staring, half-conscious that they had been here a long time, though little more than a minute had passed. The beating of their hearts deafened them, and combined with the hissing sound of the rain, as if thin ghosts shod in cloud were racing across the skylight. Her eyes still fixed upon the creature with the sandbag, Ivy whispered again: 'Let's go.'

Then, in the far distance, they heard the front door slam.

At that sound a confused terror seized them both. The contrast between incoming humanity and the unearthly silence here affected them like a blow. Heat and weakness rushed up their limbs, and in Ivy's ears was a sound like the distant unwinding of an endless chain. Henry was the first to recover; a compound emotion formed in him: the proprietress—of course—he wanted to get out—they really ought to pay—he'd better see. This summarized itself in an inarticulate sound. Turning, he ran to the landing and looked down the stairs. He did not know what he expected to see, but something, and after a few seconds, as he heard nothing, such a weakness overcame him that he let himself go against the balustrade, his head hanging down over the well of the stairs, where all was silence and darkness.

But almost at once he recovered, for suddenly behind him there came a long cry, a cry with a strange, torn quality, like that of a beast in pain, that jerked him to his feet as it dragged from his pores a sheet of cold sweat. As he turned, Ivy came tumbling out of the attic, her arms outstretched before her as if she fumbled for her way. She could not see, for her eyes were so retroverted that only the whites showed under the falling lids. He caught her just as she was going to throw herself down the stairs. As he touched her she flung her arms about his neck with maniacal strength and he could not free himself from that grasp. As they stumbled together down the stairs, he thought that it was like being held by bones. They fell together at the foot of the second landing, and somehow struggled to their feet. There was a moment of incredible effort before they could pull open the outer door, which had been closed by the wind. They halted for an instant upon the steps, close-locked under the falling hot rain, and Henry did not understand what drove him then, what strange relief or exaltation, what insane excitement made him press his mouth to the lips drawn tightly into pallid lines. At the kiss Ivy's nerves suddenly relaxed. She became a bundle in his arms, something he dragged along, staggering as he fled, he knew not from what. They shared but one idea: to get away. The pavement streamed before them as they ran with downcast eyes. Then, with a shock, they were stopped by two policemen in oilskins, with whom they nearly collided at the junction of the lane and the main road. The policemen stared at these two, instinctively holding them by the arm, not understanding that they were at the limit of terror, and already suspecting that they had committed some crime. Indeed, Henry and Ivy were struggling in their grasp, still dominated by their one desire: to get away. At last, when they grew quiet and stood breathing hard, their mouths relaxed by nervous exhaustion, the elder policeman, who was a sergeant, said: 'Now then, what's all this?'

'I don't know,' said Henry.

'Come on,' said the sergeant, 'you don't put me off like that. What you been up to, you two?' Henry did not reply. 'Mark you, it'll be all the worse for you if you don't talk. What's happened?' He shook his prisoner, suggesting that he'd make him talk yet, but failing to draw a reply he turned to the girl: 'You, why were you running?'

Ivy seemed to have recovered more quickly than her companion. Though her eyelids did not cease to twitch, she managed to say: 'I saw something.'

'Saw something?' said the sergeant. 'Saw what?'

'Oh, I couldn't,' said Ivy.

'I expect they're drunk,' said the constable.

'No,' said the sergeant, meditatively, 'I can't smell it on 'em.'

'Oh, no,' cried Ivy, 'no, of course not, only it's the waxworks— the waxworks.'

'Waxworks?' said the sergeant. 'What waxworks?'

'I know, sergeant,' said the constable, nodding up the lane. 'Mrs Groby's place.'

'Oh, yes,' said the sergeant, 'I know now. Sort of chamber of 'orrors. Well, you been to the waxworks. What about it?'

'I saw something,' whispered Ivy.

'Saw what?' said the constable. 'Saw Mrs Groby, I suppose. Funny old dame, sergeant. She's been living in that house all by herself for the last forty years, alone with them things. Used to make a lot of money out of them, and they say she's got a lot saved up. Between you and me and the lamp-post I'm surprised no one's knocked her on the head yet and walked off with her money.'

Ivy gave a low cry: 'Yes—that's it—there's a man in there—he's killed her—blood all over her head.'

'What's all this?' asked the sergeant, professionally incredulous. 'What's all this story? And how do you know anything about it?'

'There was a noise,' said Ivy. 'The door slammed—Henry ran out. I couldn't move for a moment—she was on the floor, and the man——' Her voice became shrill: 'as I turned to look after Henry I just—he raised his arm and rubbed it—just with the corner of my eye—I——' She gave a heavy sigh, and her head fell back upon the policeman's chest.

But she had not fainted, and in a moment the policemen were striding up the lane, followed by Henry and Ivy, who clung to the companionship of these tall, loud-speaking men. As they went the sergeant theorized:

'I see the dodge. He did the old woman in; then he heard this pair come up the stairs, and rigged himself up as a wax figure. Got cramp, I suppose, and took the chance to rub his arm when he thought she wasn't looking. Cheer up, missy,' he added to Ivy, who was crying out of weakness. 'We'll soon get him.' As they reached the door of the museum he winked at her and drew his truncheon. 'Better stay downstairs, missy,' he added, as he led the way up. But after a moment Ivy and Henry could not bear their loneliness, and tiptoed up the stairs behind the blue shapes that walked with such assurance, making no attempt to muffle their tread. When they reached the attic, the policeman looked in a puzzled way into the twilight.

'Which one is it?' said the policeman, and instinctively his voice fell to a whisper. Ivy, who was just behind him, pointed at the kneeling shape carrying the sandbag.

'That one,' she said. The sergeant did not understand his own feeling, but he received some dim impression from the grey place. He walked only three feet into the room. Then, in an uneasy voice, he addressed the kneeling figure: 'Now then, my man. The game's up. You better go quietly.'

There was no reply, and the echoes died away, repeating a quivering uncertainty in the policeman's voice.

After a moment's pause the sergeant, irritated by the silence, strode into the room; raising his truncheon, he went up to the kneeling figure and touched it on the shoulder. He drew back his hand, touched the body again. Then, suddenly, he burst into a roar of laughter, as with a derisive gesture he passed his hand up and down over the waxen face.

'Wax!' he cried. 'Bert! have you ever seen such a pair of gabies as these two? Been here and got the 'orrors, the two of them, and ran out like a pair of loonies to tell us this dummy is Jack the Ripper posing for the Russian bally. Oh, my!'

'Wax!' whispered Ivy, 'oh, no. Oh, please don't touch it. It's not wax. No, it's not.'

'Come on,' said the sergeant, kindly, 'touch it yourself.'

'Oh, I couldn't,' said Ivy, quivering, but with a laugh the policeman seized her wrist, and, drawing her towards the figure, forced her to lay her hand upon the waxen coldness of the cheek.

'Wax,' said the policeman, 'you silly kid. That's only wax. And so's this wax,' he added, as he bent down and negligently laid his hand upon the blood-stained white hair. But, in the same movement almost, the policeman jumped up and recoiled, his staring eyes glaring at his hand. For less than a second did he gaze at it; then, with a cry, as if seized by ungovernable hysteria, he brought down his truncheon upon the head of the kneeling man, which, under the blow, scattered into tiny fragments of tinted wax. Then the other policeman drew back as he saw his comrade's hand stained with fresh blood.

'A waxwork,' he gasped. 'What—how? It isn't a waxwork. It's Mrs Groby.' He laid a single finger on the woman's head, stared at his own blood-stained hand. 'Dead—still warm.' His voice rose high: 'Killed—by what?'

In the silence, far below, could be heard the thin drip of the leaky tap.

White Spectre

B. L. Jacot

I T was the waiting.

Our fuel was gone and the engines were dead. It was pitch black all round, but we knew the mountains were there. There was just the screech of the slipstream as we waited. It's the waiting that tears you apart.

When the crash came it was like something exploding in your face. We hit a shelf in the rockface and bounced. The second strike was soft by comparison, but by that time I'd died a thousand deaths.

We had time to get out. All the six of us. At a time like that most of you is missing, but something takes over and you move by instinct. You move like a sleep-walker. Then there was a crack like a whiplash and she went up in a column of white flame. You couldn't get near.

That's the picture I'll always have. That white column tearing up, and the crackle and the roar: seeing the metal settle down and fuse into pools: the searing light that turned blood-red on the rocks and frozen gravel.

It's a strange feeling, coming back from the dead. When you've been out of a place and come back, it's never the same again. You, or the place.

There were the flames, a mile high . . . and then I heard the pilot shouting at us. He put us to work, and, as far as I can remember, all of us, in a daze, spent the night piling rocks round the mouth of a cave the pilot had found. Perhaps he knew where we were. It was very cold.

I remember Leach looking at me, puzzled, from time to time. As if he couldn't make out who I was. *Me*, who'd worked with him for years.

I had seen the fear leap into Leach's eyes when the second pilot came back into the cabin and woke us up. We were over the Atlantic then, and he said we had engine trouble and were making for Reykjavik, in Iceland. He didn't tell us then that the radio was out.

We got to Reykjavik—but that's a queer place and they weren't expecting us. The airport goes right down into the town itself and on the other side is the sea. The British built Reykjavik airport in the war, and the Americans built Keflavik further along the coast.

When the pilot couldn't see which was airport lighting and which was lighting on the boulevards he decided to try for Keflavik. They must have heard an unknown aircraft cruising overhead, for they put up a cone of searchlights to guide us through the mountains—some of them never yet explored.

Before the cloud hid it, we saw the cone—just that once. There were the mountains all round us and the night was just an empty black space, but you knew the mountains were there. Sooner or later we had to hit them. You can feel the strain creaking like a hinge on your brain. It wasn't only Leach who'd taken it badly. There was no need for the pilot to shout. He was the man who'd got us here, wasn't he?

We were still carrying lumps of lava, with the pilot snarling at the flight engineer and the engineer yelling back, when the sun came up. Everything was purple. It was rich. It made you catch your breath. The grey of the rock was streaked with it; the frozen black gravel was washed over with the flood, like paint; the mountains running up into the Arctic Circle were brushed with pastel crimson that seemed to throb on the peaks. You must try to picture the space and the emptiness. It's important. It's hard to think of anything without thinking of an end or a finish to it somewhere. You knew there was no finish to this sort of space. Just space and colour. You've never imagined such colour.

There was a lake that was green jade. It filled an extinct crater and was fed by the streams from the glaciers. There was dove-grey moss on the boulders on the sides away from the wind. And there was a curious heather-like scrub, ankle high where the winds couldn't get at it. The winds blew in gales out of the Arctic and cut like a knife. You've never heard such winds as blew round that cave. If you stopped to look at the mountains you got a feeling like looking down from a high building. You swayed towards them and wanted to hold back on to something.

I don't remember much about that first day. It just seemed to slide by. It went while I was still trying to adjust myself with the background and believe in the situation. But I shall never forget the next morning.

The doctor woke us in that cave where we were sleeping. He had found the pilot with his head battered in. Someone had used a lump of lava on him and he was dead as mutton.

I saw Leach turn instinctively to look at the flight engineer who'd been wrangling with the pilot. I felt sick in my stomach. My brain was numb.

We buried the pilot under the stones and the engineer took charge. Straight away he ordered us to gather scrub to see if we could make it burn. He seemed to be shouting a lot.

I have known Leach all my life. We went to school together. I was glad to have my best friend and business partner with me at a time like this. The scrub wouldn't burn and you would have thought it was someone's fault. 'Take it easy, Mac!' the doctor said.

'I'm responsible now,' the engineer shouted, 'and I'm going to have discipline. Get going!'

It was curious now the way we secretly watched each other. We knew, each one of us, we had a killer amongst us. And we kept alert. No one crossed the engineer. He kept the rations saved from the plane by the ship's officers, and he doled them out. He was a bully. He was unbalanced, too. Suffering from the strain that was eating into all of us. And he kept a tight grip on us.

Not a thing moved in the whole wide sweep of the horizon. I knew they'd never find us. The mountains seemed to have moved in on us. They seemed to stand there watching. Sometimes the wind would drop and there would be a dead calm and you could sit and get nothing except the colour and the emptiness.

The third passenger, the doctor, kept pretty close to Leach and me. He was always wanting to talk. He said: 'If you've anything brooding in your system bring it out. Talk about it. Get it before it gets you. I should know what I'm talking about.'

'Psychologist?' Leach asked him.

'Look at those two,' the doctor pointed out. The engineer and the second pilot were sitting apart staring at nothing. 'Get an idea into your head in a place like this and it's a seed in a hothouse.'

'So what?' Leach demanded. 'Someone killed the pilot. Perhaps you know who?'

'Maybe I do. Maybe I don't,' the doctor told him.

We were sleeping huddled together at one end of the cave. Only the engineer slept apart. Others besides me were watchful that night, but I couldn't sleep. The moon was up when I left the cave, and in the thin light everything looked unreal. I had the feeling of being light, without weight. I felt that if I raised my arms I would float up into space. Loneliness can bring up strange fantasies and the setting was awesome.

Aurora borealis, the Northern Lights, were flickering like whip-lashes on a cosmic scale across the whole spread of the steely sky, and you could hear the cold creaking in the rock-face. And I was thinking all the time that the engineer would get us all, one by one, as the rations shrank and days passed without sight of a plane.

Next morning the engineer was dead.

He lay in his blankets and his head was battered in. No one had heard anything in the night. We dragged the body out from the cave and buried it under the stones. No one spoke, but between Leach and me was an awareness of the doctor. We remembered his mad talk about a hothouse seed in his brain. Fear can be a terrible spectre. And fear of fear is worse.

First the pilot. Now the engineer. Someone, cunning as a fox, was killing us off, one by one. Who would be next? That was the thought Leach and I had between us. Four left, and one of them a killer, cunning as a fox . . . it was enough to affect anyone's reason.

Not a thing moved in the sky next day. We lay in the cave. Each watchful and suspicious of any sudden move. Leach and I kept together. And so did the other two. I woke several times that night and lay in the silence listening for the sound of anyone moving. But in the morning we still mustered four.

The second pilot talked to us next day. The rations would last us eleven more days—three biscuits a day with a piece of chocolate and two spoons of milk. That boy was the surviving officer and he had three passengers to deal with. There was no harm in him. He was doing his duty and he was going to see his orders were obeyed.

The doctor took it badly. He demanded his share, there and then. He wanted to go his own way. But he was out-voted. I was thinking of what he might have let grow in his brain . . . the white spectre of fear.

I warned Leach: 'Watch the doctor. The second pilot'll be the next.' Leach said: 'That's what I think, brother.'

But it wasn't the second pilot. It was the doctor.

Leach found him, dead as a doornail, with his head pulped. He was beside the pool from which we drew our drinking water. He had evidently got up in the night and gone for a drink . . . and one of those left in the cave must have heard him.

There were three of us then, cooped up in that crack in the mountain, eating our breakfast in silence. Hot chocolate warmed on the solid alcohol tablets and the two biscuits. There was that wall of lava stones between us and the grey light outdoors, a protective barrier against the vastness of space and the moaning winds.

I thought my head would burst. There was the heaped moss and heather on which we slept in separate corners. There were the odd things, such as torches, the first-aid box, lying round. You couldn't get away from it, and the second pilot wasn't looking at us. He was keeping away from Leach and me.

When my head cleared, I thought: The rations would stretch further now. How was it Leach and I had survived? *We had stuck together*. We never said this out loud, but it lay between us to give us common strength. But it was a terrible thought that it had been this boy all along, and that he must be planning even now to get us apart, Leach and me.

I went out into the blizzard later, praying for a speck in the sky that would put an end to all this. I was thinking, they've *got* to find us, haven't they? We can't just die like rats.

But the horizon stayed as empty as when God made it, and when I searched the mountains, looking for the speck, they seemed to close up on me then draw back. I was careful to see that no one came up behind me. The second pilot was the only one who knew where the food was cached. He had the power.

Leach was still sitting hunched under his blanket when I got back to the cave. He started at the silent way I came in. 'Where is he?' I asked.

'Out,' Leach answered and he looked at me. 'We've got to keep an eye on him all the time,' Leach said. 'No letting up—or there'll only be one of us left, and that'll be easy game.'

'We'll stick close,' I agreed. 'Day and night. He can't get us both.' My hands were shaking so, I thought Leach must notice. I thought I was going crazy.

Leach showed me the hatchet he had hidden.

He said: 'From now on one of us must always be awake. The only alternative is to kill that crazy kid now.'

I shook my head. 'We can't do that,' I said, and he hid the hatchet away again.

We slept by turns. It did not affect me because I wasn't sleeping much, anyway. I couldn't get my thoughts away from a speck that would—that *must* grow into the shape of a plane.

We spent two more days and nights with the tension growing between us. We were watching each other like cats, and the slightest sound would bring the muscles taut and ready. We ate in silence, and the moan of the wind outside stretched my nerves until I thought something must give.

At night I imagined I could hear a swish made by the Northern Lights playing in the sky. I watched over Leach, then he took his vigil and watched over me. I didn't see how the second pilot could get us, but the fear was always there.

What if I woke up one morning and found Leach dead and that it was now—him and me?

On the eighth day after the doctor's death Leach made a decision. I was living in a haze, weak from being cooped up and waiting. 'The way I see it is this,' Leach said. 'They'd have found us by now if they'd been going to find us. Let's share out what's left and each will know what he's got, and can make his own decision what to do.'

'It suits me,' I agreed, when it had soaked in, but the second pilot pushed himself to his feet. He wasn't too strong either.

'I'm against it,' he croaked. 'One of us will finish his share—and then the others will have to watch him starve. There'll be trouble.'

'It's two to one, my friend,' Leach said. 'Get the stuff from where

you've got it hidden—and get all of it. I'm coming with you to see.'
Leach got up, too, and he had the hatchet in his hand.

'I'll take any trouble that's coming,' the second pilot said. 'You two have been sticking together pretty close, but I'm the only one who knows where the rest of the food is. As long as I keep that pull, I have to survive. So drop that hatchet.'

I could see Leach working it out, then he tossed the hatchet over his blankets and lurched out of the cave. I followed him closely, bent double against the force of the wind. There was murder in Leach's eyes, and I didn't like the cornered look I had seen in the face of the second pilot. The moan of the wind seemed pinned to my eardrums and the mountains heaved and shrank. The steely sky had all the colours of a drop of oil spreading over still waters. *He's killed three*, I was thinking. *He'll strike again soon now!* I stopped trailing Leach and peeled off, hiding among the rocks all day.

That night, they were both in the cave when I got back. I worked my way into the heather so that I had my head and shoulders in a crack of the rock-wall. I was taking no chances, even though Leach was on guard while I slept.

When I climbed out of my blankets in the morning, Leach was standing square in the middle of the cave. He had a ghastly look on his face. I saw a box of rations at his feet and I thought: 'So he's found out where the boy kept the food!'

Leach stooped over and, keeping a wary eye on me, counted the biscuits out into two piles. There were two tins of milk. He kept one and rolled the other over to me. Then he stood up and his head turned.

I followed his eyes and saw that the boy was dead. The same technique. A rock on his head while he slept.

It took time for the significance of it to reach me. All I seemed able to get at first was the moan of the wind and the creak of the cold. The swish of the Northern Lights and the quiet in the cave. It seemed to hold me in another world from which it was getting more and more difficult to work back. My stomach was squeezing up and falling. *Leach!*

I backed away from him without a word and got out of the cave. I don't remember the rest of that day. I chewed my biscuit in the shelter of the burned-out plane that evening, and I wondered if Leach would consider my life was worth the seven biscuits I now had left. He had given them to me, hadn't he? Why kill me to get them back? Perhaps he didn't mean to kill me, too? I couldn't risk it.

I did not return to the cave. I crawled further into the twisted strands of tortured metal and spent the night watching the stars. The cold left me numb and dazed in the morning . . .

That was the day the plane came.

I don't know how I can describe that last morning. They've got me here now safe in this little room with the doctors and the male nurses to look after me. But I can't begin to think yet. It's all too close. It's all too real. And yet I know there's something wrong somewhere, and it can't be true.

For that last morning when I went to the cave, I found Leach lying on the floor with his head battered in.

III

ODD MAN OUT

'"Tickets, Please!"' is the only story by *D. H. Lawrence* (1885–1930) to appear in the *Strand* and it is difficult to understand why the editor, Greenhough Smith, accepted it in the first place. It is not, by any margin, a '*Strand* story'. It was published in 1919 (the April issue), and perhaps an explanation for its appearance is that after five years of war and the loss of many of the magazine's most reliable contributors Smith was desperate for new blood. The period 1917–21 was by no means the *Strand*'s finest hour: there was a dearth of Wodehouse, Conan Doyle was engaged in his interminable history of the war and then became enmeshed in Spiritualism and fairy-photographs; other writers, such as E. Nesbit, had, after long careers, simply written themselves out. During this period names appear on the Contents pages which had never appeared before and were never to appear again; rather more stories were 'bought in' from American publications than at any other time; so hard pressed was Smith that, at one stage, he took the unprecedented step of reprinting an old (and non-*Strand*) story by the romance writer Ethel M. Dell, even blazoning it on the issue's cover. What regular readers made of '"Tickets, Please!"' is anyone's guess. On the face of it a rather jolly tale of female *jacquerie*, it yet features a denouement which is genuinely one of the most unsettling in this entire collection. When the story later appeared in book form, in *England, My England* (1922), it was in a significantly cut-down form.

'Tickets, Please!'

D. H. Lawrence

THERE is in the North a single-line system of tramcars which boldly leaves the county town and plunges off into the black, industrial countryside, up hill and down dale, through the long, ugly villages of workmen's houses, over canals and railways, past churches perched high and nobly over the smoke and shadows, through dark, grimy, cold little market-places, tilting away in a rush past cinemas and shops down to the hollow where the collieries are, then up again, past a little rural church under the ash-trees, on in a bolt to the terminus, the last little ugly place of industry, the cold little town that shivers on the edge of the wild, gloomy country beyond. There the blue and creamy coloured tramcar seems to pause and purr with curious satisfaction. But in a few minutes—the clock on the turret of the Co-operative Wholesale Society's shops gives the time—away it starts once more on the adventure. Again there are the reckless swoops downhill, bouncing the loops; again the chilly wait in the hill-top market-place: again the breathless slithering round the precipitous drop under the church: again the patient halts at the loops, waiting for the outcoming car: so on and on, for two long hours, till at last the city looms beyond, the fat gasworks, the narrow factories draw near, we are in the sordid streets of the great town, once more we sidle to a standstill at our terminus, abashed by the great crimson and cream-coloured city cars, but still jerky, jaunty, somewhat daredevil, pert as a blue-tit out of a black colliery garden.

To ride on these cars is always an adventure. The drivers are often men unfit for active service: cripples and hunchbacks. So they have the spirit of the devil in them. The ride becomes a steeplechase. Hurrah! we have leapt in a clean jump over the canal bridges—now for the four-lane corner! With a shriek and a trail of sparks we are clear again. To be sure a tram often leaps the rails—but what matter! It sits in a ditch till other trams come to haul it out. It is quite common for a car, packed with one solid mass of living people, to come to a dead halt in the midst of unbroken blackness, the heart of nowhere on a dark night, and for the driver and the girl-conductor to call: 'All get off—car's on fire.' Instead of rushing out in a panic, the passengers stolidly reply: 'Get on—get on. We're not coming out. We're stopping where we are. Push on, George.' So till flames actually appear.

The reason for this reluctance to dismount is that the nights are howlingly cold, black and windswept, and a car is a haven of refuge. From village to village the miners travel, for a change of cinema, of girl, of pub. The trams are desperately packed. Who is going to risk himself in the black gulf outside, to wait perhaps an hour for another tram, then to see the forlorn notice 'Depot Only'—because there is something wrong; or to greet a unit of three bright cars all so tight with people that they sail past with a howl of derision? Trams that pass in the night!

This, the most dangerous tram-service in England, as the authorities themselves declare, with pride, is entirely conducted by girls, and driven by rash young men, or else by invalids who creep forward in terror. The girls are fearless young hussies. In their ugly blue uniforms, skirts up to their knees, shapeless old peaked caps on their heads, they have all the sang-froid of an old non-commissioned officer. With a tram packed with howling colliers, roaring hymns downstairs and a sort of antiphony of obscenities upstairs, the lasses are perfectly at their ease. They pounce on the youths who try to evade their ticket-machine. They push off the men at the end of their distance. They are not going to be done in the eye—not they. They fear nobody—and everybody fears them.

'Halloa, Annie!'

'Halloa, Ted!'

'Oh, mind my corn, Miss Stone! It's my belief you've got a heart of stone, for you've trod on it again.'

'You should keep it in your pocket,' replies Miss Stone, and she goes sturdily upstairs in her high boots.

'Tickets, please.'

She is peremptory, suspicious, and ready to hit first. She can hold her own against ten thousand.

Therefore there is a certain wild romance aboard these cars—and in the sturdy bosom of Annie herself. The romantic time is in the morning, between ten o'clock and one, when things are rather slack: that is, except market-day and Saturday. Then Annie has time to look about her. Then she often hops off her car and into a shop where she has spied something, while her driver chats in the main road. There is very good feeling between the girls and the drivers. Are they not companions in peril, shipmates aboard this careering vessel of a tramcar, for ever rocking on the waves of a hilly land?

Then, also, in the easy hours the inspectors are most in evidence. For some reason, everybody employed in this tram-service is young: there are no grey heads. It would not do. Therefore the inspectors are of the right age, and one, the chief, is also good-looking. See him stand on a wet, gloomy morning in his long oilskin, his peaked cap well down over his eyes, waiting to board a car. His face is ruddy, his small brown moustache is weathered, he has a faint, impudent smile. Fairly tall and agile, even in his waterproof, he springs aboard a car and greets Annie.

'Halloa, Annie! Keeping the wet out?'

'Trying to.'

There are only two people in the car. Inspecting is soon over. Then for a long and impudent chat on the footboard—a good, easy, twelve-mile chat.

The inspector's name is John Joseph Raynor: always called John Joseph. His face sets in fury when he is addressed, from a distance, with this abbreviation. There is considerable scandal about John Joseph in half-a-dozen villages. He flirts with the girl-conductors in the morning, and walks out with them in the dark night when they leave their tramcar at the depot. Of course, the girls quit the service frequently. Then he flirts and walks out with a newcomer: always providing she is sufficiently attractive, and that she will consent to walk. It is remarkable, however, that most of the girls are quite comely, they are all young, and this roving life aboard the car gives them a sailor's dash and recklessness. What matter how they behave when the ship is in port? Tomorrow they will be aboard again.

Annie, however, was something of a tartar, and her sharp tongue had kept John Joseph at arm's length for many months. Perhaps, therefore, she liked him all the more; for he always came up smiling, with impudence. She watched him vanquish one girl, then another. She could tell by the movement of his mouth and eyes, when he flirted with her in the morning, that he had been walking out with this lass, or the other the night before. She could sum him up pretty well.

In their subtle antagonism, they knew each other like old friends; they were as shrewd with one another almost as man and wife. But Annie had always kept him fully at arm's length. Besides, she had a boy of her own.

The Statutes fair, however, came in November, at Middleton. It happened that Annie had the Monday night off. It was a drizzling, ugly night, yet she dressed herself up and went to the fairground. She was alone, but she expected soon to find a pal of some sort.

The roundabouts were veering round and grinding out their music, the side-shows were making as much commotion as possible. In the coconut shies there were no coconuts, but artificial substitutes, which the lads declared were fastened into the irons. There was a sad decline in brilliance and luxury. None the less, the ground was muddy as ever, there was the same crush, the press of faces lighted up by the flares and the electric lights, the same smell of naphtha and fried potatoes and electricity.

Who should be the first to greet Miss Annie, on the show-ground, but John Joseph! He had a black overcoat buttoned up to his chin, and a tweed cap pulled down over his brows, his face between was ruddy and smiling and hardy as ever. She knew so well the way his mouth moved.

She was very glad to have a 'boy'. To be at the Statutes without a fellow was no fun. Instantly, like the gallant he was, he took her on the dragons, grim-toothed, round-about switchbacks. It was not nearly so exciting as a tramcar, actually. But then, to be seated in a shaking green dragon, uplifted above the sea of bubble faces, careering in a rickety fashion in the lower heavens, whilst John Joseph leaned over her, his cigarette in his mouth, was, after all, the right style. She was a plump, quick, alive little creature. So she was quite excited and happy.

John Joseph made her stay on for the next round. And therefore she could hardly for shame to repulse him when he put his arm round her and drew her a little nearer to him, in a very warm and cuddly manner. Besides, he was fairly discreet, he kept his movement as hidden as possible. She looked down, and saw that his red, clean hand was out of sight of the crowd. And they knew each other so well. So they warmed up to the fair.

After the dragons they went on the horses. John Joseph paid each time, she could but be complaisant. He, of course, sat astride on the outer horse—named 'Black Bess'—and she sat sideways towards him, on the inner horse—named 'Wildfire'. But, of course, John Joseph was not going to sit discreetly on 'Black Bess', holding the brass bar. Round they spun and heaved, in the light. And round he swung on his wooden steed, flinging one leg across her mount, and perilously tipping up and down, across the space, half-lying back, laughing at her. He was perfectly happy; she was afraid her hat was on one side, but she was excited.

He threw quoits on a table, and won her two large, pale-blue hatpins. And then, hearing the noise of the cinema, announcing another performance, they climbed the boards and went in.

Of course, during these performances, pitch darkness falls from time to time, when the machine goes wrong. Then there is a wild whooping, and a loud smacking of simulated kisses. In these moments John Joseph drew Annie towards him. After all, he had a wonderfully warm, cosy way of holding a girl with his arm, he seemed to make such a nice fit. And, after all, it was pleasant to be so held; so very comforting and cosy and nice. He leaned over her and she felt his breath on her hair. She knew he wanted to kiss her on the lips. And, after all, he was so warm and she fitted in to him so softly. After all, she wanted him to touch her lips.

But the light sprang up, she also started electrically, and put her hat straight. He left his arm lying nonchalant behind her. Well, it was fun, it was exciting to be at the Statutes with John Joseph.

When the cinema was over they went for a walk across the dark, damp fields. He had all the arts of love-making. He was especially good at holding a girl, when he sat with her on a stile in the black, drizzling darkness. He seemed to be holding her in space, against his own warmth and gratification. And his kisses were soft and slow and searching.

So Annie walked out with John Joseph, though she kept her own boy dangling in the distance. Some of the tram-girls chose to be huffy. But there, you must take things as you find them, in this life.

There was no mistake about it, Annie liked John Joseph a good deal. She felt so pleasant and warm in herself, whenever he was near. And John Joseph really liked Annie, more than usual. The soft, melting way in which she could flow into a fellow, as if she melted into his very bones, was something rare and gratifying. He fully appreciated this.

But with a developing acquaintance there began a developing intimacy. Annie wanted to consider him a person, a man; she wanted to take an intelligent interest in him, and to have an intelligent response. She did not want a *mere* nocturnal presence— which was what he was so far. And she prided herself that he could not leave her.

Here she made a mistake. John Joseph intended to remain a nocturnal presence, he had no idea of becoming an all-round individual to her. When she started to take an intelligent interest in him and his life and his character, he sheered off. He hated intelligent interest. And he knew that the only way to stop it was to avoid it. The possessive female was aroused in Annie. So he left her.

It was no use saying she was not surprised. She was at first startled, thrown out of her count. For she had been so *very* sure of holding him. For a while she was staggered, and everything became uncertain to her. Then she wept with fury, indignation, desolation, and misery. Then she had a spasm of despair. And then, when he came, still impudently, on to her car, still familiar, but letting her see by the movement of his eyes that he had gone away to somebody else, for the time being, and was enjoying pastures new, then she determined to have her own back.

She had a very shrewd idea what girls John Joseph had taken out. She went to Nora Purdy. Nora was a tall, rather pale, but well-built girl, with beautiful yellow hair. She was somewhat secretive.

'Hey!' said Annie, accosting her; then, softly: 'Who's John Joseph on with now?'

'I don't know,' said Nora.

'Why tha does,' said Annie, ironically lapsing into dialect. 'Tha knows as well as I do.'

'Well, I do, then,' said Nora. 'It isn't me, so don't bother.'

'It's Cissy Meakin, isn't it?'

'It is for all I know.'

'Hasn't he got a face on him!' said Annie. 'I don't half like his cheek! I could knock him off the footboard when he comes round me!'

'He'll get dropped on one of these days,' said Nora.

'Ay, he will when somebody makes up their mind to drop it on him. I should like to see him taken down a peg or two, shouldn't you?'

'I shouldn't mind,' said Nora.

'You've got quite as much cause to as I have,' said Annie. 'But we'll drop on him one of these days, my girl. What! don't you want to?'

'I don't mind,' said Nora.

But as a matter of fact Nora was much more vindictive than Annie.

One by one Annie went the round of the old flames. It so happened that Cissy Meakin left the tramway service in quite a short time. Her mother made her leave. Then John Joseph was on the qui vive. He cast his eyes over his old flock. And his eyes lighted on Annie. He thought she would be safe now. Besides, he liked her.

She arranged to walk home with him on Sunday night. It so happened that her car would be in the depot at half-past nine: the last car would come in at ten-fifteen. So John Joseph was to wait for her there.

At the depot the girls had a little waiting-room of their own. It was quite rough, but cosy, with a fire and an oven and a mirror and table and wooden chairs. The half-dozen girls who knew John Joseph only too well had arranged to take service this Sunday afternoon. So as the cars began to come in early, the girls dropped into the waiting-room. And instead of hurrying off home they sat round the fire and had a cup of tea.

John Joseph came on the car after Annie, at about a quarter to ten. He poked his head easily into the girls' waiting-room.

'Prayer meeting?' he asked.

'Ay,' said Laura Sharp. 'Ladies' effort.'

'That's me!' said John Joseph. It was one of his favourite exclamations.

'Shut the door, boy,' said Muriel Baggaley.

'On which side of me?' said John Joseph.

'Which tha likes,' said Polly Birken.

He had come in and closed the door behind him. The girls moved in their circle to make a place for him near the fire. He took off his greatcoat and pushed back his hat.

'Who handles the teapot?' he said.

Nora silently poured him out a cup of tea.

'Want a bit o' my bread and dripping?' said Muriel Baggaley to him.

'Ay, all's welcome.'

And he began to eat his piece of bread.

'There's no place like home, girls,' he said.

They all looked at him as he uttered this piece of impudence. He seemed to be sunning himself in the presence of so many damsels.

'Especially if you're not afraid to go home in the dark,' said Laura Sharp.

'Me? By myself I am!'

They sat till they heard the last tram come in. In a few minutes Emma Housely entered.

'Come on, my old duck!' cried Polly Birkin.

'It *is* perishing,' said Emma, holding her fingers to the fire.

'"But I'm afraid to go home in the dark,"' sang Laura Sharp, the tune having got into her mind.

'Who're you going with tonight, Mr Raynor?' asked Muriel Baggaley, coolly.

'Tonight?' said John Joseph. 'Oh, I'm going home by myself tonight—all on my lonely-o.'

'That's me!' said Nora Purdy, using his own ejaculation. The girls laughed shrilly.

'Me as well, Nora,' said John Joseph.

'Don't know what you mean,' said Laura.

'Yes, I'm toddling,' said he, rising and reaching for his coat.

'Nay,' said Polly. 'We're all here waiting for you.'

'We've got to be up in good time in the morning,' he said, in the benevolent official manner. They all laughed.

'Nay,' said Muriel. 'Don't disappoint us all.'

'I'll take the lot, if you like,' he responded, gallantly.

'That you won't, either,' said Muriel. 'Two's company; seven's too much of a good thing.'

'Nay, take one,' said Laura. 'Fair and square, all above board, say which one.'

'Ay!' cried Annie, speaking for the first time. 'Choose, John Joseph—let's hear thee.'

'Nay,' he said. 'I'm going home quiet tonight.' He frowned at the use of his double name.

'Who says?' said Annie. 'Tha's got to ta'e one.'

'Nay, how can I take one?' he said, laughing uneasily. 'I don't want to make enemies.'

'You'd only make *one*,' said Annie, grimly.

'The chosen *one*,' said Laura. A laugh went up.

'Oh, ay! Who said girls!' exclaimed John Joseph, again turning as if to escape. 'Well, good-night!'

'Nay, you've got to take one,' said Muriel. 'Turn your face to the wall, and say which one touches you. Go on—we shall only just touch your back—one of us. Go on—turn your face to the wall, and don't look, and say which one touches you.'

They pushed him to a wall and stood him there with his face to it. Behind his back they all grimaced, tittering. He looked so comical.

'Go on!' he cried.

'You're looking—you're looking!' they shouted.

He turned his head away. And suddenly, with a movement like a swift cat, Annie went forward and fetched him a box on the side of the head that sent his cap flying. He started round.

But at Annie's signal they all flew at him, slapping him, pinching him, pulling his hair, though more in fun than in spite or anger. He, however, saw red. His blue eyes flamed with strange fear as well as fury, and he butted through the girls to the door. It was locked. He wrenched at it. Roused, alert, the girls stood round and looked at him. He faced them, at bay. At that moment they were rather horrifying to him, as they stood in their short uniforms. He became suddenly pale.

'Come on, John Joseph! Come on! Choose!' said Annie.

'What are you after? Open the door,' he said.

'We sha'n't—not till you've chosen,' said Muriel.

'Chosen what?' he said.

'Chosen the one you're to marry,' she replied. The girls stood back in a silent, attentive group.

He hesitated a moment:

'Open the confounded door,' he said, 'and get back to your senses.' He spoke with official authority.

'You've got to choose,' cried the girls.

He hung a moment; then he went suddenly red, and his eyes flashed.

'Come on! Come on!' cried Annie.

He went forward, threatening. She had taken off her belt and, swinging it, she fetched him a sharp blow over the head with the buckle end. He rushed with lifted hand. But immediately the other girls flew at him, pulling him and pushing and beating him. Their blood was now up. He was their sport now. They were going to have their own back, out of him. Strange, wild creatures, they hung on him and rushed at him to bear him down. His tunic was torn right up the back. Nora had hold at the back of his collar, and was actually strangling him. Luckily the button-hole burst. He struggled in a wild frenzy of fury and terror, almost mad terror. His tunic was torn off his back as they dragged him, his shirt-sleeves were torn away, one arm was naked. The girls simply rushed at him, clenched their hands and pulled at him; or they rushed at him and pushed him, butted him with all their might.

At last he was down. They rushed him, kneeling on him. He had neither breath nor strength to move. His face was bleeding with a long scratch.

Annie knelt on him, the other girls knelt and hung on to him. Their faces were flushed, their hair wild, their eyes were all glittering strangely. He lay at last quite still, with face averted, as an animal lies when it is defeated and at the mercy of the captor.

Sometimes his eye glanced back at the wild faces of the girls. His breast rose heavily, his wrists were scratched and bleeding.

'Now then, my fellow!' gasped Annie at length.

'Now then—now——'

At the sound of her terrifying, cold triumph, he suddenly started to struggle as an animal might, but the girls threw themselves upon him with unnatural strength and power, forcing him down.

'Yes—now then!' gasped Annie at length. And there was a dead silence, in which the thud of heartbeating was to be heard. It was a suspense of pure silence in every soul.

'Now you know where you are,' said Annie.

The sight of his white, bare arm maddened the girls. He lay in a kind of trance of fear and antagonism. They felt themselves filled with supernatural strength.

Suddenly Polly started to laugh—to giggle wildly—helplessly—and Emma and Muriel joined in. But Annie and Nora and Laura remained the same, tense, watchful, with gleaming eyes. He winced away from these eyes.

'Yes,' said Annie, recovering her senses a little.

'Yes, you may well lie there! *You* know what you've done, don't you? You know what you've done.'

He made no sound nor sign, but lay with bright, averted eyes and averted, bleeding face.

'You ought to be *killed*, that's what you ought,' said Annie, tensely.

Polly was ceasing to laugh, and giving long-drawn oh-h-h's and sighs as she came to herself.

'He's got to choose,' she said, vaguely.

'Yes, he has,' said Laura, with vindictive decision.

'Do you hear—do you hear?' said Annie. And with a sharp movement, that made him wince, he turned his face to her.

'Do you hear?' she repeated, shaking him. But he was dumb. She fetched him a sharp slap on the face. He started and his eyes widened.

'Do you hear?' she repeated.

'What?' he said, bewildered, almost overcome.

'You've got to *choose*,' she cried, as if it were some terrible menace.

'What?' he said, in fear.

'Choose which of us you'll have, do you hear, and stop your little games. We'll settle you.'

There was a pause. Again he averted his face. He was cunning in his overthrow.

'All right then,' he said. 'I choose Annie.'

'Three cheers for Annie!' cried Laura.

'Me!' cried Annie. Her face was very white, her eyes like coal. 'Me——!'

Then she got up, pushing him away from her with a strange disgust.

'I wouldn't touch him,' she said.

The other girls rose also. He remained lying on the floor.

'Oh, if he's chosen——' said Polly.

'I don't want him—he can choose another,' said Annie, with the same rather bitter disgust.

'Get up,' said Polly, lifting his shoulder. 'Get up.'

He rose slowly, a strange, ragged, dazed creature. The girls eyed him from a distance, curiously, furtively, dangerously.

'Who wants him?' cried Laura, roughly.

'Nobody,' they answered, with derision.

And they began to put themselves tidy, taking down their hair, and arranging it. Annie unlocked the door. John Joseph looked round for his things. He picked up the tatters, and did not quite know what to do with them. Then he found his cap, and put it on, and then his overcoat. He rolled his ragged tunic into a bundle. And he went silently out of the room, into the night.

The girls continued in silence to dress their hair and adjust their clothing, as if he had never existed.

IV

SHEER MELODRAMA

'A Torture by Hope' by the French Symbolist writer *Philippe-Auguste, Comte de Villiers de l'Isle-Adam* (1838–89), is arguably one of the cruellest stories ever written. Unlike Mirabeau or de Sade, whose work featured explicit physical torture or degradation, de l'Isle-Adam pioneered the *conte cruel* in which the protagonist or victim suffers mentally. Like the American writer Ambrose Bierce, he was adept at the twist ending and had a mordant sense of humour; a number of his stories were translated into English as *Sardonic Tales* (1927). A descendant of the last Grand Master of the Knights of Malta, de l'Isle-Adam was hailed during his lifetime by fellow writers (such as his friend J. K. Huysmans) but not by the public. He interested himself in devil worship and black magic and wrote a handful of science fiction stories, including *L'Eve Future* (1886), in which a British nobleman falls in love with an android. He died, in extreme poverty, of cancer.

L. T. Meade (1854–1914) was one of the most indefatigable of Victorian/Edwardian writers. Her canon runs to at least 265 published books, many of which were for the juvenile, particularly the girls', market, written for publishers who issued them as prizes or 'rewards' for Sunday School attendance. She wrote socio-realistic novels such as *A Girl of the People* (1890) and *A Princess of the Gutter* (1895), as well as tracts, domestic dramas, and 'little-girl-lost' stories (at which she was particularly skilful). After nearly twenty years of churning out tales for juveniles Mrs Meade found a new and lucrative career as a crime writer. She was especially resourceful at dreaming up diabolically ingenious murder-methods, often in collaboration with 'Robert Eustace' or 'Clifford Halifax' who supplied the technical know-how. The plot for 'The Man Who Disappeared' (1901, with Eustace), in which the victim is frozen into solidity with liquid air then pounded into dust in a stone-breaker, is by no means her most extravagant. She was equally proficient at exploiting common, everyday fears, as in 'A Horrible Fright', which, when published, must surely have touched a nerve amongst the *Strand*'s female readership.

A superlative editor, *H. Greenhough Smith* (1855–1935) was, at best, a journeyman fiction writer, as his handful of novels attests. He gravitated to journalism in his twenties, later joining the staff of *Temple Bar*, the prosperous though stuffy monthly which was reckoned to be nearest to the *Cornhill* in circulation. Once the *Strand* had been launched, and for many years thereafter, it was George Newnes who was credited with the idea of a brighter monthly; but when Smith died (long after Newnes) his obituarist claimed that Smith himself had been the originator, Newnes merely the catalyst. This makes sense: it is likely that Smith tried out the idea on George Bentley, proprietor of *Temple Bar*, then in his seventies and wary of change, and, thwarted, turned to Newnes, much younger and far more adventurous. Smith was an authority on French poetry and a pugnacious poker-player; he had an interest in true crime, about which he wrote divertingly even when elderly. He retired from active editorship at the somewhat advanced age of 75, though he continued to advise on policy. In the early days of the *Strand* he contributed a number of stories, of which 'The Case of Roger Carboyne', which features an impossible vanishment, has the cleverest central idea.

Ianthe Jerrold (fl. 1918–52) was a descendant of the journalistic Jerrolds, of whom the most famous members were the prodigiously talented Douglas (1803–57), editor, *Punch* wit, and author of the highly entertaining *Mrs Caudle's Curtain Lectures* (1845), and Blanchard (1826–84), novelist, campaigning journalist, and associate of the artist Gustave Doré. She was by no means as prolific, her *œuvre* amounting to less than a dozen novels over a 30-year period. Together with such luminaries as R. Austin Freeman, Dorothy L. Sayers, G. K. Chesterton, John Dickson Carr, and E. C. Bentley, she was a member of the prestigious Detection Club, having been proposed by Anthony Berkeley Cox (who wrote as 'Anthony Berkeley' and 'Francis Iles', and was not known for his aversion to female companionship) on the strength of an ingeniously clued detective story called *The Studio Crime* (1929). She wrote one or two further crime novels as well as a number of psychological romances, of which *The Coming of Age* (1950) is by far the most interesting. 'The Orchestra of Death', published when Jerrold was just 20, is a quite superb slice of melodrama.

A Torture by Hope

Villiers de l'Isle-Adam

BELOW the vaults of the *Oficial* of Saragossa one nightfall long ago, the venerable Pedro Arbuez d'Espila, sixth Prior of the Dominicans of Segovia, third Grand Inquisitor of Spain—followed by a *fra redemptor* (master-torturer), and preceded by two familiars of the Holy Office holding lanterns—descended towards a secret dungeon. The lock of a massive door creaked; they entered a stifling *in pace*, where the little light that came from above revealed an instrument of torture blackened with blood, a chafing-dish, and a pitcher. Fastened to the wall by heavy iron rings, on a mass of filthy straw, secured by fetters, an iron circlet about his neck, sat a man in rags: it was impossible to guess at his age.

This prisoner was no other than Rabbi Aser Abarbanel, a Jew of Aragon, who, on an accusation of usury and pitiless contempt of the poor, had for more than a year undergone daily torture. In spite of all, 'his blind obstinacy being as tough as his skin', he had refused to abjure.

Proud of his descent and his ancestors—for all Jews worthy of the name are jealous of their race—he was descended, according to the Talmud, from Othoniel, and consequently from Ipsiboe, wife of this last Judge of Israel, a circumstance which had sustained his courage under the severest of the incessant tortures.

It was, then, with tears in his eyes at the thought that so steadfast a soul was excluded from salvation, that the venerable Pedro Arbuez d'Espila, approaching the quivering Rabbi, pronounced the following words:

'My son, be of good cheer; your trials here below are about to cease. If, in presence of such obstinacy, I have had to permit, though with sighs, the employment of severe measures, my task of paternal correction has its limits. You are the barren fig-tree, that, found so oft without fruit, incurs the danger of being dried up by the roots . . . but it is for God alone to decree concerning your soul. Perhaps the Infinite Mercy will shine upon you at the last moment! Let us hope so. There *are* instances. May it be so! Sleep, then, this evening in peace. Tomorrow you will take part in the *auto da fé*, that is to say, you will be exposed to the *quemadero*, the brazier premonitory of the eternal flame. It burns, you are aware, at a certain distance, my son; and death takes, in coming, two hours at least, often three, thanks to the moistened and frozen clothes with which we take care to preserve the forehead and the heart of the holocausts. You will be only forty-three. Consider, then, that, placed in the last rank, you will have the time needful to invoke God, to offer unto Him that baptism of fire which is of the Holy Spirit. Hope, then, in the Light, and sleep.'

As he ended this discourse, Dom Arbuez—who had motioned the wretched man's fetters to be removed—embraced him tenderly. Then came the turn of the *fra redemptor*, who, in a low voice, prayed the Jew to pardon what he had made him endure in the effort to redeem him; then the two familiars clasped him in their arms: their kiss, through their cowls, was unheard. The ceremony at an end, the captive was left alone in the darkness.

Rabbi Aser Abarbanel, his lips parched, his face stupefied by suffering, stared, without any particular attention, at the closed door. Closed? The word, half unknown to himself, awoke a strange delusion in his confused thoughts. He fancied he had seen, for one second, the light of the lanterns through the fissure between the sides of this door. A morbid idea of hope, due to the enfeeblement of his brain, took hold on him. He dragged himself towards this strange thing he had seen; and, slowly inserting a finger, with infinite precautions, into the crack, he pulled the door towards him. Wonder of wonders! By some extraordinary chance the familiar who had closed it had turned the great key a little before it had closed upon its jambs of stone. So, the rusty bolt not having entered its socket, the door rolled back into the cell.

The Rabbi ventured to look out.

By means of a sort of livid obscurity he distinguished, first of all, a half-circle of earthy walls, pierced by spiral stairways, and, opposite to him, five or six stone steps, dominated by a sort of black porch, giving access to a vast corridor, of which he could only see, from below, the nearest arches.

Stretching himself along, he crawled to the level of this threshold. Yes, it was indeed a corridor, but of boundless length. A faint light—a sort of dream-light—was cast over it; lamps suspended to the arched roof, turned, by intervals, the wan air blue; the far distance was lost in shadow. Not a door visible along all this length! On one side only, to the left, small holes, covered with a network of bars, let a feeble twilight through the depths of the wall—the light of sunset apparently, for red gleams fell at long intervals on the flagstones. And how fearful a silence! . . . Yet there—there in the depths of the dim distance—the way might lead to liberty! The wavering hope of the Jew was dogged, for it was the last.

Without hesitation he ventured forth, keeping close to the side of the light-holes, hoping to render himself indistinguishable from the darksome colour of the long walls. He advanced slowly, dragging himself along the ground, forcing himself not to cry out when one of his wounds, recently opened, sent a sharp pang through him.

All of a sudden the beat of a sandal, coming in his direction, echoed along the stone passage. A trembling fit seized him, he choked with anguish, his sight grew dim. So this, no doubt, was to be the end! He squeezed himself, doubled up on his hands and knees, into a recess, and, half dead with terror, waited.

It was a familiar hurrying along. He passed rapidly, carrying an instrument for tearing out the muscles, his cowl lowered; he disappeared. The violent shock which the Rabbi had received had half suspended the functions of life; he remained for nearly an hour unable to make a single movement. In the fear of an increase of torments if he were caught, the idea came to him of returning to his cell. But the old hope chirped in his soul—the divine 'Perhaps', the comforter in the worst of distresses. A miracle had taken place! There was no more room for doubt. He began again to crawl towards the possible escape. Worn out with suffering and with hunger, trembling with anguish, he advanced. The sepulchral corridor seemed to lengthen out mysteriously. And he, never ceasing his slow advance, gazed forward through the darkness, on, on, where there *must* be an outlet that should save him.

But, oh! steps sounding again; steps, this time, slower, more sombre. The forms of two Inquisitors, robed in black and white, and wearing their large hats with rounded brims, emerged into the faint light. They talked in low voices, and seemed to be in controversy on some important point, for their hands gesticulated.

At this sight Rabbi Aser Abarbanel closed his eyes, his heart beat as if it would kill him, his rags were drenched with the cold sweat of agony; motionless, gasping, he lay stretched along the wall, under the light of one of the lamps—motionless, imploring the God of David.

As they came opposite to him the two Inquisitors stopped under the light of the lamp, through a mere chance, no doubt, in their discussion. One of them, listening to his interlocutor, looked straight at the Rabbi. Under this gaze—of which he did not at first notice the vacant expression—the wretched man seemed to feel the hot pincers biting into his poor flesh; so he was again to become a living wound, a living woe! Fainting, scarce able to breathe, his eyelids quivering, he shuddered as the robe grazed him. But— strange at once and natural—the eyes of the Inquisitor were evidently the eyes of a man profoundly preoccupied with what he was going to say in reply, absorbed by what he was listening to; they were fixed, and seemed to look at the Jew *without seeing him*.

And, indeed, in a few minutes, the two sinister talkers went on their way, slowly, still speaking in low voices, in the direction from which the prisoner had come. They had not seen him! And it was so, that, in the horrible disarray of his sensations, his brain was traversed by this thought: 'Am I already dead, so that no one sees me?' A hideous impression drew him from his lethargy. On gazing at the wall, exactly opposite to his face, he fancied he saw, over against his, two ferocious eyes observing him! He flung back his head in a blind and sudden terror; the hair started upright upon his head. But no, no. He put out his hand, and felt along the stones. What he saw was the *reflection* of the eyes of the Inquisitor still left upon his pupils, and which he had refracted upon two spots of the wall.

Forward! He must hasten towards that end that he imagined (fondly, no doubt) to mean deliverance; towards those shadows from which he was no more than thirty paces, or so, distant. He started once more—crawling on hands and knees and stomach—

upon his dolorous way, and he was soon within the dark part of the fearful corridor.

All at once the wretched man felt the sensation of cold *upon* his hands that he placed on the flagstones; it was a strong current which came from under a little door at the end of the passage. O God, if this door opened on the outer world! The whole being of the poor prisoner was overcome by a sort of vertigo of hope. He examined the door from top to bottom without being able to distinguish it completely on account of the dimness around him. He felt over it. No lock, not a bolt! A latch! He rose to his feet: the latch yielded beneath his finger; the silent door opened before him.

'Hallelujah!' murmured the Rabbi, in an immense sigh, as he gazed at what stood revealed to him from the threshold.

The door opened upon gardens, under a night of stars—upon spring, liberty, life! The gardens gave access to the neighbouring country that stretched away to the sierras, whose sinuous white lines stood out in profile on the horizon. There lay liberty! Oh, to fly! He would run all night under those woods of citrons, whose perfume intoxicated him. Once among the mountains, he would be saved. He breathed the dear, holy air: the wind reanimated him, his lungs found free play. He heard, in his expanding heart, the 'Lazarus, come forth!' And, to give thanks to God who had granted him this mercy, he stretched forth his arms before him, lifting his eyes to the firmament in an ecstasy.

And then he seemed to see the shadow of his arms returning upon himself; he seemed to feel those shadow-arms surround, enlace him, and himself pressed tenderly against some breast. A tall figure, indeed, was opposite to him. Confidently he lowered his eyes upon this figure, and remained gasping, stupefied, with staring eyes and mouth drivelling with fright.

Horror! He was in the arms of the Grand Inquisitor himself, the venerable Pedro Arbuez d'Espila, who gazed at him with eyes full of tears, like a good shepherd who has found the lost sheep.

The sombre priest clasped the wretched Jew against his heart with so fervent a transport of charity that the points of the monacal hair-cloth rasped against the chest of the Dominican. And, while the Rabbi Aser Abarbanel, his eyes convulsed beneath his eyelids, choked with anguish between the arms of the ascetic Dom Arbuez, realizing confusedly *that all the phases of the fatal evening had been only a calculated torture, that of Hope!* the Grand Inquisitor, with a look of distress, an accent of poignant reproach, murmured in his ear, with the burning breath of much fasting: 'What! my child! on the eve, perhaps, of salvation . . . you would then leave us?'

A Horrible Fright

L. T. Meade

I DON'T think I am at all nervous, and, therefore, when I say that I am about to describe two hours of absolute agony, I hope my readers will believe that the circumstances were at the best exceptional, and will still give me credit for being at least as brave as most girls of my age.

I have always despised so-called nerves. When a child I quite loved to sleep in the dark. At school I was the prime mover of ghost stories, and I remember now that some of my practical jokes verged strangely upon the unkind and even dangerous. I have been educated quite up to modern ideas. It is only a year since I left Girton, and I am now comfortably established at home with my father and mother. I am the only daughter, and am between twenty-three and twenty-four years of age. We live in a large place about an hour's ride by rail from London. I have my own special horse, and a little pony carriage besides for my exclusive use. I also have my study or boudoir, and can order what books I please for my own benefit, not only from Mudie, but from the local booksellers. I am passionately fond of music, and can play two or three instruments. I think I can say, without any false pride, that my performances on the violin are rather better than those of most amateurs. I am also great at all kinds of outdoor sports and games. I am the champion player of the tennis club to which I belong, and I am at the present time successfully getting up a lady's golf club. In short, I think I may truly say of myself that I represent the average, up-to-date, well-educated, rather strong-minded, nineteenth-century girl.

Now, I must tell about my fright. You can imagine that it must have been something special to put me into such a state of terror that I cannot think of it even now without shuddering.

I received an invitation late last autumn to go to see my grandfather, who lives in Dublin. My mother did not particularly wish me to go. I really think mothers must have premonitions, for there was no apparent reason for my not taking such a simple and easily accomplished journey. I had been abroad a good deal, and had had adventures more than one; therefore, when my mother fretted herself about my going from London to Dublin via Holyhead, I could not help laughing at her.

'If you must go alone, Virginia,' she said, 'had you not better travel by day?'

'Oh, nonsense, nonsense,' I said. 'I *hate* travelling by day, particularly by a route which I already know. Besides, it is such a waste of time. At night, one can sleep and travel together. Oh, say no more about it dear, good mother. I'll take the night mail from Euston, this evening, and have breakfast with grandfather in the morning.'

My mother made no further remonstrances, but I heard her sighing in the most aggravating style, and I knew she was murmuring to herself about my headstrongness and how I never would listen to reason.

Nothing makes me so obstinate as those muttered remonstrances of my relatives. Are they afraid of me, that they don't speak out? I am always amenable to reason, but when people mutter over me, then I become simply mulish. I adore my dear mother, but even for her I cannot be expected to give up my own way when I hear her muttering that it is 'Just like Virginia.'

My things were packed, and I started off in good time to catch the night mail at Euston.

'You had better go in one of the ladies' carriages,' said my father.

I quite gasped in horror when he made this audacious proposal.

'Now, *do* you suppose I am likely to do anything quite so old-maidish?' I replied. 'No, I have fixed on the exact corner where I shall snooze away from Euston to Holyhead.' I led my father, as I spoke, to a carriage where two old gentlemen had already comfortably established themselves. They had spread out their rugs, and taken complete possession of the corners which were out of the draught. I was oblivious to draughts, and chose my corner opposite the old gentleman who was nearest to the entrance door. My father supplied me with three or four evening papers. I had an uncut novel in my bag, and a little reading-lamp, which I could fasten to the window ledge. Two or three moments later I had said farewell to my father, and the great express—the Wild Irish Girl—had steamed in grand style out of the station.

I like the feeling of being whirled through space in an express train going at the top of its speed. I looked at the evening papers. Their contents did not specially interest me. I then gazed at my opposite neighbour. He was very stout and very red. He tucked his travelling rug tightly about him, and before we had passed Willesden was fast asleep. He made a distressing noise with his loud snores, and I thought him decidedly irritating. For a moment or two I almost regretted that I had not gone in an empty ladies' carriage. The other old gentleman was scarcely a more agreeable travelling companion. He had a noisy cough, and a bad cold. He blew his nose, and he coughed about every two minutes, and then he looked around him to see if there were any possible draughts. He not only shut his own window but the ventilator above as well, and then he glared at the ventilator which belonged to the snoring old gentleman and me. I made up my mind that *that* ventilator should only be shut over my fallen body.

The express went on its way without let or hindrance. Now and then it swayed from side to side, as if its own great speed were making it giddy; then again it steadied itself, and rushed on and on with a rhythmic sort of motion, which was infinitely soothing, and caused me to forget my two uninteresting companions, and to sink gradually into the land of dreams.

I was awakened presently from quite a sound nap by the slowing of the train. It was coming into a great station, which I found was Chester. We must have passed Crewe while I was asleep. My two companions were now all alive and brisk. They were fastening up their rugs and folding their papers, and I saw that they intended to leave the train.

'If you are going on to Holyhead,' said the snoring one to me, 'you have ten minutes to wait here—quite time to get a cup of tea, if you want one.'

I thanked him, and thought that I would carry his suggestion into effect. A cup of tea would be perfect, and would set me up for the remainder of my journey. I accordingly stepped on to the platform, and went over the bridge to the great waiting-rooms, which presented at this time a gay scene of eager, hungry, fussy men and women sitting at tables, and standing at counters, each and all of them eating and drinking for bare life.

I ordered my tea, drank it standing at the counter, paid for it, and also for a bun, which I carried away with me in a paper bag, and returned to my carriage. I saw a heap of rugs and a large black bag deposited in the corner away from mine, and wondered with a faint passing curiosity who my new travelling companion was likely to be. The guard came up at this moment to see if I were comfortable. He said that we would not stop again until we reached Holyhead, and asked me if I wanted for anything.

I said 'No.'

'Perhaps you'd like me to lock the carriage door, miss?' he said. 'The train is not too full tonight, and I can manage it.'

I laughed and pointed to the rugs and bag in the opposite corner.

'Someone has already taken possession,' I said.

'But if you wish, miss, I'll put those things in another carriage,' said the guard.

'No, no,' I replied, 'I don't mind company in the least.'

Just then my fellow-traveller put in an appearance. He was a big man, wrapped up in a great ulster and with a muffler round his throat and mouth. The guard looked at him, I thought, a little suspiciously. This made me angry. I have no patience with those squeamish girls who think every man who sees them must offer them either admiration or insult. I looked very cheerful, made way for the traveller to take his seat, and smiled and thanked the guard. A moment later the train started on its way.

We had just got well outside the station when the gentleman in the ulster and muffler carefully unwound the latter appendage from his mouth and throat. He folded it up neatly, and put it into his black bag. Afterwards he took off his ulster. I now saw that he was a fairly good-looking man of about eight and twenty. He wore a full moustache of raven hue, and a short beard. He had very black and piercing eyes. When I looked at him, I discovered that he also looked at me.

'Now, are you getting nervous, Virginia, or are you not?' I

murmured to myself. 'Why may not a man look at a girl if he pleases? There is an old proverb that a cat may look at a king. Let me suppose, therefore, that the man opposite is a well-grown and presentable cat, and that I am his Majesty the king. The cat may stare as long as he pleases. The king will not disturb himself.'

Accordingly, I prepared to light my reading-lamp, as I knew that I could not possibly fall asleep under the gaze of those watchful, dark eyes.

I had just settled myself comfortably, and had taken my uncut novel out of my bag, when the stranger spoke to me.

'Do you object to my opening the window?' he asked.

'Certainly not,' I replied. I gave him a distant little bow, which was meant to say that the cat must keep its distance, and lowered my eyes over the fascinating pages of my novel.

The train was now going at a rattling pace, and I found that the draught from the open window was rather more than I cared to be subjected to. I had just raised my head, and was about to ask my travelling companion if he would be kind enough to close it, when I met a sight which gave me the first premonition of that horror which this story is meant to describe. The man in the opposite corner had opened his black bag, and taken from it a pair of large, sharp-looking scissors, and also a razor. When I glanced at him he had opened the razor, and was gently and dextrously sharpening it on a leather strop which he had fastened to one of the buttons of the window. He met my eye as I met his, and smiled grimly.

I felt that a situation of some sort was imminent, and, closing my book, sat perfectly still with my hands tightly locked together and my heart beating loudly. The light from the reading-lamp fell full upon me, and I turned abruptly and put it out.

'I will thank you to light that lamp again,' said the stranger. 'Do so at once—there is no time to lose.'

'I don't understand you,' I said.

I tried to make my voice imperious and haughty, but I was terribly conscious that it came out of my throat in little gasps and jerks.

'Now, look here,' said the man. 'I know you are frightened, and I am not in the least surprised. I should be frightened if I were in your position. You are alone in a railway carriage with a man who could strangle you and throw your dead body on the line if he felt the least inclined to do so. No no—you don't get to the alarm bell. I am keeping guard over that. Now, I may as well tell you frankly that I have come into this railway carriage on purpose to have the pleasure of your society. I saw you get into the carriage at Euston, and I knew that you would be alone when you got to Chester. From Chester to Holyhead is a long run. The train is now comfortably on its way, and will not stop for nearly two hours. You see, therefore, that you are completely at my mercy. Your only chance of safety is in doing *exactly* what I tell you. Now, have the goodness to light that reading-lamp immediately.'

The stranger's voice was imperious—he had now changed his seat to one opposite mine. His restless, brilliant eyes were fixed full on my face.

'Light the lamp,' he said.

I obeyed him without a moment's hesitation.

When I had lit it he took it from my shaking fingers and fastened it to the cushion of the seat in the centre of the carriage.

'That is better,' he said, 'that is more cheerful. Now, see, I am going to kneel down. Look at my face. Can you see it well?'

'Yes,' I answered.

'I have a good deal of hair, haven't I?'

'You have,' I replied.

'Do you see this pair of scissors?'

'Yes.'

'And this razor?'

'Yes.'

'They're deadly weapons, are they not?'

'They could do mischief,' I answered, in a faltering voice.

'Aye, aye, they could—and they will, too, unless a certain young lady does *exactly* what she is told. Now, come—the moment for action has arrived—take your gloves off.'

I hesitated.

'Take them off,' thundered the man.

They were off in a twinkling.

'Come up close, and begin.'

'Begin what?'

'Don't be a fool. You have plenty of intelligence if you choose to exercise it. Cut off my moustache.'

I drew back.

'I don't know how,' I faltered.

'I'll soon teach you.'

'How, pray?' I asked.

'By sharpening that razor a little more. Now, are you going to try? Take the scissors in your hand.'

He knelt so that the light of the lamp should fall full on him, and gave me the scissors. I took it at once and began my task.

'Hold my chin,' he said. 'You can't do your work properly in that shaky way. Cut, I say—cut.'

I did cut—God alone knows how I managed it, but I got the man's thick and sweeping moustache off. As I worked he gave me imperious directions.

'Cut clean,' he said, 'cut close and clean. You will have to shave me presently.'

'That will be very dangerous for you,' I ventured to retort.

'Fudge,' he replied. 'You will be cool enough by that time. Now, is the moustache all gone?'

'Yes,' I said.

'Cut the whiskers off.'

'No,' I answered.

'*Yes*,' he replied.

He fixed his eyes on me, and I obeyed him. The whiskers were followed by the beard—the beard, by the hair on the man's head.

How my fingers ached! how my heart thumped! how those basilisk eyes seemed to pierce through me, and fill me with sick loathing and abject horror!

When I had finished the cutting process, he took from the depths of his bag some shaving apparatus, poured water into a little flask, made the soap lather, and desired me to shave him. I was now completely meek and subdued, and obeyed his least direction without a word. Fortunately for the man's life, I had on one or two occasions performed this operation on my brother, who taught me how to manage the razor, and complimented me on my skill. It came to my aid now. Notwithstanding the shaking train, and the agitated state of my nerves, I performed my task well. I even became, in the queerest way, proud of my successful shaving. The man's cheeks and upper lip looked as innocent of hair as a baby's before I had done with him.

At last my task was done, and a shaven, uncouth object took the place of the handsome stranger who had come into the train an hour ago.

When my work was over he stooped, collected every scrap of hair, and flung it out of the window. Then he shut the window and told me to put out the reading-lamp.

I obeyed, and crouched back in my corner, trembling in every limb.

'You have only one more thing to do for me,' he said.

'Oh, *is* there any more?' I panted. 'I don't think my strength will hold out.'

'Yes, it will,' he replied. 'This part of your task is easy. Turn your head and look out of the window. Don't look back again under any circumstances, until I give you leave. If you do, you are a dead woman.'

I turned my head.

I looked out into the black night. My eyes were swimming—my throat was dry, my heart continued to thump horribly. I felt that I had already lived through a lifetime. I had a kind of sensation that I should never have courage and buoyancy of heart again. The train went on its way, thumping and bounding. I heard the rustle of my companion's movements. Was he a madman? Yes, of course he must be mad. Was he stealing stealthily up now to murder me with that sharp and shining razor? Would the train ever reach its destination? Would the dreadful night ever go?

At last—at last, thank Heaven, I felt the motion of the great express perceptibly slackening. At the same instant my fellow-traveller spoke to me.

'You can look round now,' he said. 'Your task is over. All you have to do is to give me five minutes' grace, and you are safe.'

I looked round eagerly. What I saw forced a loud exclamation from my lips. The metamorphosis in my companion was now fully accomplished. An elderly clergyman, in complete and most correct clerical costume, was seated at the other end of the carriage. The hair which was seen below his hat was silvery white. He had white eyebrows. The rest of his face was clean shaven.

The train drew into the station.

The moment it did so, the clergyman flung open the door of the carriage. He took off his hat to me with a gracious movement.

'Bénédicité,' he said, in a full and reverent voice.

I saw him no more.

A moment later two detectives came up to the door. They asked eagerly if I were travelling alone, or if I had had a companion with a black moustache and beard.

I was positively too much stunned to reply to them. I don't think, to this day, my elderly clergyman was ever discovered.

The Case of Roger Carboyne

H. Greenhough Smith

THE mysterious and extraordinary circumstances surrounding the death of Mr Roger Carboyne have excited so much interest, that it is not surprising that the room in the Three Crows Inn, which had been set apart for the inquest, was crowded at an early hour. The evidence was expected to be sensational—and most sensational, indeed, it proved to be. But for the even more remarkable denouement of the case it is impossible that any person present could have been prepared.

The jury having returned from viewing the body, and the Coroner having taken his seat, the Court immediately proceeded to call witnesses.

Mr Lewis George Staymer, the dead man's friend and companion, whose name had been in everybody's mouth during the last three days, was of course the first to be examined, and his appearance obviously excited the strongest curiosity. He is a young man of twenty-five, tall, dark, and wearing a slight black moustache. His marked air of self-possession, and his quiet and direct mode of giving his evidence, were manifestly those of a man who had no other motive than to relate the facts exactly as they happened. His testimony, which it will be seen confirmed in every respect the extraordinary rumours with which the public are familiar, was as follows:

'My name is Lewis George Staymer. I am a medical student, studying at London University and at St Bartholomew's Hospital. Mr Carboyne was a fellow student with me; he was two years older than myself, and we were fast friends, attending the same lectures,

and generally spending our vacations together. Ten days ago we
arranged to spend our Easter holidays on a riding tour on ponies
through North Wales. We started on March 15th, and carried out
our programme, day by day, until the 21st—last Friday. On the
afternoon of that day we mounted our ponies at the door of the inn
where we had stopped for lunch, the Golden Harp, at Llanmawr,
and rode forward on our way; it was then about half-past two. The
weather was fine, but very cold for the time of year, and the ground
was whitened by a light fall of snow. It must have been nearly five
o'clock when a slight accident to one of my stirrup-leathers forced
me to dismount. I called to my companion to ride on, and that I
would overtake him immediately, and he did so. The road at that
point runs along the mountainside, between a lofty cliff upon the
left and a precipitous descent upon the right—but the path is broad
and smooth, being, I should say, from ten to fifteen yards wide,
and in no way dangerous. About fifty or sixty yards from the spot
where I dismounted the path turned at a sharp angle round a point
of rock and became lost to sight. I happened to look up, while still
engaged upon the stirrup-leather, and I saw my friend disappear
round the angle of the road. As soon as I had finished my work,
which took me somewhat longer than I had expected, I remounted,
and was about to follow him when I was startled to hear his voice
cry out for help. It was a shriek—a single ringing scream—uttered
as if in extremity of agony or terror. I galloped forward, and on
reaching the angle of the road I was surprised to see his pony
standing in the roadway, some sixty yards ahead, with the saddle
empty. The rider was nowhere to be seen.'

'What time had elapsed since he left you?'

'I should say about four or five minutes—possibly six—but not
more than that, I feel sure.'

'What did you do next?'

'I rode forward, calling his name loudly, and casting my eyes in
all directions; but I could see no trace of him, nor of any living
creature. The cliff, which at that point formed a deep bay, round
which the roadway ran to the corresponding angle at the other
extremity of the arc, was as steep and naked as a wall; on the other
hand was the precipice. When I reached the spot at which the pony
stood, I perceived that it was trembling, as if strongly startled; it
made no effort to escape. One of the stirrups was lying across the

saddle; the other was hanging in the usual position. I saw nothing else unusual about the pony, but on casting my eyes upon the snowy roadway I perceived marks as if a struggle had taken place there.'

'What was the position of these marks?'

'They were in front of the pony, on the forward track, and appeared as if some heavy body had been dragged for a distance of eight or ten yards. Then the marks ceased abruptly; the snow all round was absolutely undisturbed.'

'There were no footprints?'

'None whatever, except those of our two ponies on the way by which we had come. The road in front was a white sheet—it was clear that no one could have passed that way since the snow fell.'

'Did the marks extend to the edge of the precipice?'

'Oh, no; they did not stretch in that direction at all. The snow between them and the verge of the precipice was absolutely smooth and unbroken.'

'Did you approach the verge?'

'Yes; I did. I looked over and saw something white fluttering on the branches of a tree which sprouted from a crevice a few yards below. It was Mr Carboyne's handkerchief; I knew it by the peculiar coloured border. I had seen him use it that morning. I could not discern the bottom of the chasm, which was hidden by the branches of the trees growing at the base. The fall was almost sheer and quite impossible to descend. I was greatly agitated, and for some moments was at a loss what to do. I believed my friend lay at the foot of the precipice, but could form no conjecture as to how he could have got there.'

'Describe your course of action.'

'I returned to the ponies, with the purpose of riding with all speed to find the nearest point of descent, and was in the act of mounting when I saw two men on foot approaching from the angle of the road behind me. They were two working men, and are now in court.'

'You rushed to meet them and told them what had occurred?'

'I did. They informed me that I should find a descent about a mile further on, and offered to guide me to the spot. I gladly accepted; we set forward in the direction in which we had been travelling, and had nearly reached the other angle of the bay round which the path again turned, when some heavy object fell from the cliff upon the road, a few yards from us. We darted forward to the spot, and I took it up. It was Mr Carboyne's field-glass.' (Sensation in court.)

'Proceed, Mr Staymer.'

'We all three then looked up and saw, on the top of a young sapling which shot out almost at right angles to the cliff, a cap hanging. It was about half-way up the cliff—some thirty feet or so.'

'You recognized the cap.'

'Yes; it was Mr Carboyne's.'

'You formed no idea as to how it got there?'

'None. I was completely bewildered, and am still.'

'Did you attempt to reach the cap?'

'No—it was impossible to do so. The cliff was sheer wall—a goat could not have found a foothold.'

'What happened next?'

'I endeavoured, with the aid of my own glasses, to discover any other trace or clue, but failed to do so. At the top the cliff overhung a little, and then appeared to form a plateau, of which, of course, I could not see the surface. I resolved to ascend to it, and to look down; I hardly know what I expected to gain by this. My companions informed me that by making a detour of half-a-mile the summit could be reached. I set off with one instantly, while his comrade stayed below to indicate the spot. After nearly half-an-hour's hard climbing we reached the plateau.'

'What did you discover?'

'We discovered the body of Mr Carboyne.' (Renewed sensation.)

'What was its position?'

'It was lying face downwards in the snow, about three feet from the edge of the cliff. It was clear from the marks in the snow that the deceased had originally lain in a position nearly twenty feet further in—that is, further from the edge—and had crawled from thence towards the verge. There was no indication of any other person having been upon the plateau—none whatever.'

'The snow was absolutely undisturbed?'

'Absolutely.'

'Was the deceased quite dead when found?'

'Yes, quite. He must have died about half-an-hour before.'

'You examined him for injuries?'

'I did. I found bruises and abrasions, but no wound sufficient to account for death. The fatal result, as has since been proved, was due, primarily, to shock acting on a weak heart.'

'Did you observe any damage to the clothing?'

'Yes. The coat was ripped half-way up the back—that is to say, there was a wide and roughly torn rent from the middle of the back to just below the collar.'

'Did you form any opinion as to how the rent was made?'

'No; but it was done by a somewhat blunt instrument; the edges of the rent were ripped—not cut.'

'Was anything missing from the body?'

'Yes; the knapsack which the deceased wore by a strap across his shoulder had disappeared.'

'Anything else?'

'I believe nothing else. His money, which he carried in his breast-pocket, was untouched. His watch and chain were also left, as well as a valuable ring which he always wore, and which was, as I have heard him say, a keepsake.'

'You remained with the body while the workman, John Rhys, went to give information to the police?'

'Yes.'

'What space of time elapsed before they came?'

'I do not know—I should guess about two hours.'

'During that time did you observe any circumstance which would help to explain how the deceased could possibly have got there?'

'Absolutely none.'

'You can form no theory or conjecture on the subject?'

'None whatever. I am completely bewildered, and can only speak to what I saw, without being able to offer any shadow of explanation.'

A Juryman: 'Do you suggest that the deceased threw the glasses over the cliff in order to attract attention?'

'That is the only explanation that occurs to me. It is almost certain that he was alive at the time they fell; probably he found himself too weak to reach the edge, and therefore threw down the glasses as the first article that came to hand. He carried them in his side pocket, ready for use.'

'Could you identify the missing knapsack if you saw it?'

'Certainly. It was a brown leather knapsack, having the corners bound with brass—a very unusual thing. The strap had been broken and mended with twine.'

'You have stated that the snow on the road and also on the plateau showed no footprints of a second person; you are absolutely sure of this?'

'I am absolutely sure.'

The witness then stood down.

John Rhys and William Evans, quarrymen, the two men who had come to the assistance of Mr Staymer, were then called, and confirmed his evidence in every particular, but were unable to throw any new light upon the subject.

Sergeant Wallis, who had been summoned to the scene of the tragedy, was the next witness. He deposed as follows:

'On receiving notice of the case, I and an assistant rode with all speed to the plateau, where the body of the deceased had been found and where it was still lying. I made a most careful investigation both of the body and of the plateau, and afterwards descended to the roadway, which I also thoroughly examined. I found the marks of a struggle in the snow, as described by the previous witnesses. This is, in my opinion, clearly a case of foul play—of robbery and murder. I infer this from the absence of the knapsack. I am aware, of course, that the money, the watch, and the ring were left. I cannot entirely account for this at present, but I have no doubt of doing so shortly.'

'Can you account for the absence of footprints?'

'No.'

'Nor for the extraordinary situation in which the body was found?'

'No.'

'In short, the police are entirely at fault?'

'Not at all. On the contrary, we have every prospect of arresting the criminal within a very few days.'

The Coroner expressed a hope that this would be the case, but hardly seemed to share the sergeant's confidence. He then proceeded to address the jury.

'Gentlemen, I have no hesitation in saying that this is the most remarkable case which I have ever been engaged in investigating. There are three or four points in it which seem to be absolutely unaccountable: the absence of footprints in the snow, the sudden transference of the victim by some mysterious means from the roadway to the plateau sixty feet above, the handkerchief found in the ravine, and the absence of the knapsack, coupled with the safety of the money, watch, and rings. These circumstances are beyond the scope of my experience, which has been a tolerably long one— a tolerably long one, gentlemen. There can, however, be no doubt that a foul crime has been committed.'

At this stage the Coroner's remarks were interrupted by a commotion in the crowd, occasioned by the sudden and violent entrance of a person into the room. The newcomer, a short, middle-aged, grizzled man, who carried a brown-paper parcel under his arm, thrust the spectators excitedly aside, and darted into the midst of the apartment.

The Coroner (angrily): 'What do you want, sir? This conduct is most unseemly.'

The man took the parcel from under his arm, stripped off the paper covering, and displayed before the eyes of the spectators a brown leather knapsack, brass bound at the corners, and having the strap mended with a piece of twine. At this unexpected sight there was a movement in the crowd, which was as much of horror as of wonder. Sergeant Wallis and Mr Lewis Staymer took a step forward, while both exclaimed at the same instant—'The missing knapsack!'

'I desire,' said the man, quietly, 'to give evidence in the case of Mr Carboyne.'

The Coroner: 'What do you know of the matter?'

'I know everything.'

'As an eyewitness?'

'As an eyewitness.'

'You were present when Mr Carboyne met his death?'

'I was present; nay, more—I was the cause of it.' (Sensation.)

'You wish to make a statement?'

'Yes.'

'On oath?'

'Yes.'

The witness then took the oath, and at once proceeded to address the Court. His speech was uttered slowly, clearly, and distinctly, and is given here verbatim:

'My name is James Milford; I am by profession an aeronaut—it is just possible that you may have heard of me. Last Friday—the day on which this sad occurrence happened—I made a private ascent from Chester. I intended to make a journey of a mile or two at most, but when I attempted to descend I found that the escape-valve had stuck fast, and all my efforts to open it were without avail. I must have spent an hour or more in the attempt, during which time I had been driving in a rising wind across North Wales. At last I desisted, and determined to extemporize a valve, as I had done once before, by cutting a small opening in the balloon and thrusting through it the neck of a beer-bottle, broken off, and with the cork still in it. By taking the cork in or out I was enabled to emit or check the flow of gas, and it was not long before I was near enough to the ground to throw out my grapnel. It dragged for some distance along the level summit of a cliff without finding anything to catch on, and finally dropped from the summit into a small bay formed by an indentation in the cliff. I could see the road which ran along the cliff, and a man on horseback riding on it. Almost at the same moment I was menaced by a sudden danger; I saw that I must rise at once at least a hundred feet in order to avoid a pinnacle which lay directly in my path. I thrust the cork into the bottle-neck and threw out every ounce of ballast I possessed, which was about two hundredweight. As I finished I heard a sudden and loud cry beneath me, and, looking downward, was horrified to see that my grapnel in its swing had struck the rider in the back, and had caught firmly in his coat. The sudden rise of the balloon had taken place at the same instant, and had lifted the rider from the saddle, and then, his weight bringing the slant of the rope to the perpendicular, had dragged him several yards along the ground. Then, as the balloon rose, it lifted him clear off it, and it was at this moment that he uttered the cry which attracted my attention. I rushed to the cork and withdrew it; but the escape of gas was no compensation for the tremendous loss of ballast. In a few seconds the grapnel with its burden were above the cliff, which they had hardly cleared when the cloth in which the grapnel held suddenly gave way, and Mr Carboyne fell upon the level summit. The hook of the grapnel had, however, passed under the strap of his knapsack, which it lifted from his shoulders as he fell. I afterwards drew it up into the car, and now produce it. The balloon, released from his weight, shot upwards like an arrow, and in a few minutes he was lost to sight.

Before this I could, however, distinctly see his friend searching for him in the roadway, and going towards the verge of the precipice, into which the handkerchief of the deceased had fluttered; it having fallen from him, as did his hat, before the coat gave way. As for me, it was many hours before I could descend, and when I did so I was taken by some peasants swooning from the car. They tended me with every care, but until last night I was too ill to make any attempt to travel. Now, I have come here with all speed, having heard of this inquiry, and knowing that I, and I only, can prevent suspicion from falling on the innocent.'

The Coroner (turning to the jury): 'Gentlemen, I said just now that this case was the most extraordinary that has ever occurred in my experience, and though Mr Milford's statement has explained by perfectly natural causes every detail of the mystery, I am bound to say so still.'

The Orchestra of Death

Ianthe Jerrold

IT was an evening in the end of November and the roadway
gleamed in the lamplight under a soft drizzle of rain. A long
queue waited at the gallery entrance of the Coliseum, for it was ten
minutes before the opening of the doors. By the shining kerb a bent-
backed man moved up and down, playing a monotonous melody on
a tin whistle, his cap pulled down over his eyes and the collar of his
faded coat turned up against the rain. Nobody heeded him.

A small party of young girls wearing munition badges stood in
the queue near to the doorway, and there was much laughing and
lively talk among them. One of them took a postcard from her
handbag and passed it to the friend at her side.

'Mademoiselle José Dessars in "La Rose de la Syrie"' she read
slowly, as two others peered over her shoulder.

'Yes, that's her; not in this dance, but in the one mother seen her
in at the Pavilion. She dances a treat, mother says . . . No, a kind
of dark rose shade and silver shoulder-straps. She was supposed to
be a rose in the dance, see. She comes on tonight after Lucy Glynn.
Got a penny, Maude?' The whistle-player stood by the kerb
diffidently holding out his tattered cap.

A long line of motor-cars stood now before the open doors, and
the bright vestibule was full of moving people. A poster on a
wooden frame which leaned against the doorway drew the eyes of
every passer-by. It was a black sheet of paper lettered in white, and
bore the words:

JOSÉ DESSARS,
Valse Triste.

The doors opened.

'Two by two, please,' said the policeman. Slowly the long queue began to move in at the narrow entrance. . . .

Josephine Dessars lay on the bed in her big, untidy room and stared with blank eyes at the shaded lamp on her open desk. She was half-dressed, and the quilt which had covered her had been tossed aside and lay in a heap on the floor. A variety of soft garments hung over the high foot of the bedstead. She held a folded newspaper in her outflung hand.

Her short coarse hair was black against the white pillow, and accentuated the pallor of her small face; her round, dark eyes were purple-ringed, and the upper lids were swollen and reddened. There was on her face no sign of tears, but the look of one who has spent many restless nights and days in an absorbing anxiety of mind.

There was a sharp click, and then the sound of a door being cautiously opened. A tall girl, with a thick knot of dull fair hair, came quietly into the room and shut the door softly behind her. She tip-toed to the side of the bed. Josephine looked up and smiled.

'Oh, you're awake! How's the headache?'

'All right now,' said Josephine, and yawned, lifting her small arms above her head. 'What's the time, Phyllis, dear?'

'You don't *look* much better,' said Phyllis, gravely. 'And it's a quarter to seven. I was just going to wake you up. And I've turned your bath on.'

'Thank you, Phyllikins.' Josephine yawned again and sat up. In spite of her thirty-six years she looked a child as she swung her legs over the side of the high bedstead. She was an unusually small woman, with slender limbs and a narrow, oval face. Her thick hair showed very few lines of grey.

Phyllis, her pupil and protégée, picked up the *Telegraph* from the floor.

'Why, you haven't even unfolded the paper yet—you don't seem to take any interest in anything now. What's the matter with you, José? And you've been looking simply awfully ill the last few days!'

Josephine, thrusting her feet into brocaded slippers, laughed.

'I'm all right, silly child. It's my cold still hanging on, that's all.'

'I don't believe you sleep a bit at night, either,' said Phyllis, settling herself down on the bed with the air of one determined to argue the matter out. 'And you talk in your sleep. Last night I was awake and I could hear you. And what do you think you said? You kept muttering over and over again: "They're dead; they're all dead." You kept saying that. It sounded dreadful. Who's dead, Josephine, darling?'

Josephine Dessars laughed nervously.

'Did I say that, dear? How funny! The "Valse Triste" must be getting on my nerves. But I must hurry up.' She flung a dressing-gown around her shoulders and went to the door. 'Sort some clothes out for me while I have a bath, there's an angel.'

Phyllis sighed, and got up slowly from the bed. To Josephine Dessars, as she went down the brightly lit passage, the very click of her own heels on the parquet seemed to repeat the words: 'They're dead; they're all dead.'

Josephine Dessars had danced for nearly thirty years. The daughter of a French circus-rider and a wandering Englishman, she had spent her childhood passing from town to town with her mother's troupe. An elfish and precocious little girl of eight, she had taken her childish part in the acrobatic displays which were a feature of such travelling shows. Later, when she had grown to a graceful girl, she joined a different company and gained a certain reputation in provincial French towns as a ballet-dancer. She had inherited the volatile and adventurous temperament of her father, together with something of the shrewdness of the French bourgeoisie.

So she danced her way from town to town. She had many lovers, for men and women alike fell under the spell of her happy kindness and her soft, slow voice. But she was unemotional and ambitious, and she formed no deep attachments.

She was very happy in those early days.

It was in Vienna, when she was twenty-three, that she committed the one great indiscretion of her life. There she met Otto Geracht. He was an Austrian revolutionary, a dreamer, a fanatic, almost a madman; but he had a great eloquence and a queer attractive personality. Through his influence Josephine Dessars became acquainted with a society of revolutionaries known as 'The Seven'. In a moment of impulse and enthusiasm she joined it. It was a small society and consisted of but seven members. They were all possessed of powerful intellects and a really great enthusiasm, but all had the same curious twist—a disregard of logic, a love of theatrical poses, a contempt of individual suffering together with a real concern for the suffering of humanity. It was their optimism and youthful faith that attracted Josephine.

Their aim was an advanced Socialism; they talked a lot of the brotherhood of man. They had indeed a beautiful faith in a future Golden Age, but, like all fanatics, they were absolutely callous of the suffering they caused, with a firm belief in an ultimate end that should justify any means.

Josephine had looked upon the whole affair as an adventure. Although these people attracted her she was not of them. She did not at first realize that what was a passing enthusiasm, a mere thrilling experience, to her, was to them the whole aim of their existence.

So she listened to the passionate eloquence of Otto Geracht and joined 'The Seven'. She never forgot the night of her initiation. The members met at the dwelling-place of Geracht, a big, ugly house in a narrow back street. Ten o'clock was the hour for their meeting, and Josephine had gone to it straight from the theatre; she had hurried through the gaily lit streets with an enjoyable sense of romantic adventure.

It was not until she had entered the bare gas-lit meeting-room that the first apprehension came upon her. She realized for the first time the immense earnestness of Geracht and his associates. She saw herself as she was, practical, happy, ambitious, and knew most certainly that she had nothing in common with these absorbed unworldly dreamers. She had felt suddenly hysterical and had become conscious of a desire to leave the house before she committed herself too far. But Otto Geracht had come to her and talked to her while they waited for the arrival of two late members, and the old feeling of adventure had in part returned to her. So she had remained, and when all the members had come they had seated themselves around a small square table, and she had been given a chair at the right hand of Otto Geracht.

As Josephine Dessars drove through the rainy streets of London to the Coliseum she lived again through that night of thirteen years ago. She seemed to see again the massive figure of old Geracht as he stood with square finger-ends upon the table addressing those few

people in that great half-furnished room. She felt again, as she had
felt so many times during the last five days, the old sensation of
growing anxiety and repentance. She heard again Geracht's deep,
rather harsh, voice as he formally introduced her. She remembered
how the others had drunk to her health in some pale, sickly wine,
and how Anna Petro, a Czech singer and the only other woman
present, had looked at her across the table with a sort of contempt
and pity in her melancholy eyes.

She had stood up as if in a dream and had repeated after Otto
Geracht a pledge of lifelong loyalty to the brotherhood. Then
Geracht had opened an old brown-covered book and had read aloud
the rules of the society, which were few. He had paused and had
looked around the table slowly from one tense face to another;
finally his large light eyes had rested upon those of Josephine.

'And it is required of each member when elected to take a pledge
of loyalty to this society. It is forbidden for any member to divulge
to the outside world the names of any of his fellow-members, and it
is forbidden for any member to divulge any of the secret affairs of
this society. The punishment for any infringement of this rule is
death.'

Here he had paused, and Josephine remembered how she had
watched, as if hypnotized, his big black-nailed fingers playing with
the leaves of the book.

'Any member,' he had repeated slowly, 'who proves guilty of
disloyalty will be discovered and put to death, no matter where he
may be. He may hide himself in the remotest parts of earth, but
sooner or later he will be found. He will receive a sign of his
approaching death in the form of a black cross. In less than twenty-
four hours from that time he will die.'

'*He will receive a sign of his approaching death in the form of a black
cross: in less than twenty-four hours from that time he will die.*' The words
echoed through the mind of Josephine Dessars as clearly as if they
had but just been spoken. Then she found herself repeating, like
one who strives to comfort with a parrot-phrase of consolation: 'But
they're dead; they're all dead.'

Sitting there in the darkness she began silently to tell over the
names of those who had belonged to the Secret Society of Seven.

'——Otto Geracht, died three years ago in Leipzig; Diedrich
Kummer, killed in the Prague riots; Anna Petro, killed herself in

Vienna the year after I came to England. They're dead, all of them. I have nothing to fear, nothing. They're all dead.'

But her restless mind reverted once again to that far-off night in Vienna, and she seemed to see again the large eyes of Otto Geracht looking into her own with their vague peculiar gaze. For nearly a week she had seen those eyes, all through the days and in her dreams at night.

'You have been false,' they seemed to say to her. 'False! you have been false.'

Josephine Dessars had been false. It was now three days since the sensational arrest of Sir Marcus Pinder, MP; he was yet awaiting his trial on a charge of high treason. And it was Josephine Dessars who had given the information which had led to his arrest. She had known of him in Vienna as a friend of Otto Geracht; she had indeed once met him at Geracht's house. She knew that he was pledged to the wild idealistic Socialism of the Society of Seven; he had not been a member, but she had heard him often discussed as one of the chief secret tools of the society. She knew that Geracht had had a very great influence over him and had indeed granted him sums of money with which to carry forward the cause. It was he who had arranged, under the directions of Geracht, the assassination of Mousset in 1906.

All this she had known of Marcus Pinder, but during the peaceful, happy years which had elapsed after she came to England, she had heard little of him. She had still felt a certain sympathy for his ideals, although her old enthusiasm had long since died.

But when war broke out the old shadowy dreams of a brotherhood that admitted no nationality faded away. Josephine Dessars knew herself a Frenchwoman, an Englishwoman.

Then one day she had seen in the newspaper the announcement of Sir Marcus Pinder's appointment to a seat on the Treasury Bench. The name had leapt at her eyes from the white page as she had unfolded the paper. Sir Marcus Pinder! A host of recollections had come crowding into her mind. She had stood as one in a trance for a time while her thoughts had gone wandering back to the days when that name had been so familiar to her. Sir Marcus Pinder! Had not his mother been some relation of Diedrich Kummer? Her mind went back to an evening in the house of Otto Geracht. Pinder had been there. He had monopolized the talk at the supper-table.

She remembered him as a short, thickset man with greying hair and a birdlike vivaciousness of manner. Some of his words came back to her:

'The seed we sow will not bear for many years in England or in France, Miss Dessars. In Germany, and in Germany alone of all the great nations, may we hope for quick and good results. The German mind has a broadness, an idealism——'

This man was helping to control the destinies of France and England. Josephine had consulted no one. She was accustomed to bringing her mind to quick decisions. She had written that morning to the Home Office, stating clearly all that she knew of Marcus Pinder; she had explained the way in which she had acquired her knowledge, and had given a detailed account of the Society of Seven. As she wrote she felt like one confessing old childish follies. It was as she had written her signature to the letter that she had felt a curious sudden sensation of being watched. She had looked up. There had been no one in the room. But at that moment there had flashed back to her memory for the first time for many years the picture of a big, bare room and a tall man who held a book in his large white hands.

'And it is required of each member to take a pledge of loyalty to this society. It is forbidden to divulge any of the secret affairs of this society. The punishment for an infringement of this rule is death. . . . He will receive a sign of his approaching death in the form of a black cross. In less than twenty-four hours from that time he will die.'

Josephine Dessars had addressed and posted her letter of information; but from that moment she had existed in a very inferno of restlessness and excitement. All through that night she had not slept, but had lain on her back with wide eyes looking into the darkness, unable to free herself of a terror that she knew was without foundation. So it had been for every night since that one. Memories of her past life possessed her mind utterly; not by any effort of will could she rid herself of them. Neither work nor amusement could divert her thoughts for one moment. She was like one under an obsession; she felt herself dwelling upon the borderland between reason and insanity.

Looking out at the wet dim-lit streets, she found herself wondering how long this obsession would last. She had a sudden impulse to speak, to put into words her vague alarms. She turned and slid her arm around the thin body of the girl at her side.

'Phyllis—Phyllis——'

Phyllis turned to her. But under those clear, thoughtful eyes Josephine fell silent. How could she tell this girl of her shadowy fears? What had Phyllis in common with those old days of intrigue and adventure? Josephine would not alarm and mystify the child with the tale of her own neurotic foolishness.

So she said:

'It's nothing dear. What are you thinking about that you are so quiet?'

'I was thinking about tonight. Oh, Josephine, I do hope the people will like it—I love first nights.'

The car slowed down and came to a standstill. They stepped out into the fine misty rain. The street was almost deserted.

'Oh, I'm excited!' cried Phyllis, as they went up the long passage to Josephine's dressing-room. The bright-lit room was dazzling after the darkness of the street. Josephine took off her cloak and hung it over a chair. She went across the room to switch up the light over the mirrors.

'A—ah!' she cried, with a quick intake of breath. She stood rigid by the table, one hand outstretched towards the electric buttons. Phyllis saw her face go grey as paper. Her eyes dilated, and stared with an intensity of horror at something upon the laden dressing-table.

'What is it? What is it?' cried Phyllis, putting her arms around her. She was rigid to the touch as a dead thing.

Then suddenly her body relaxed; she groped for a chair and sank down upon it. She still looked with a kind of horrified bewilderment towards the dressing-table. The frightened girl followed the direction of her eyes. Two black sticks of grease-paint were upon the corner of the table; by some chance they lay one upon the other, in the form of a cross.

'Oh, what is it?' cried Phyllis again.

Josephine said:

'Nothing.' She began to laugh, and tears came very quickly to her eyes. Her mind seemed filled with a terrible chaos of speculations; she could not force herself to think clearly. Like one who hears voices in his half-sleep, she listened to the terrified questions and endearments of the girl who knelt at her side. Somewhere at the back of her brain a hammer kept time to the throbbing of her heart. 'I shall go mad,' said its every dull thud. 'I shall go mad, I shall go mad.'

Phyllis cried again, her face as white as Josephine's own:

'Oh, José, what is it, what is it?'

'I saw—I thought I saw—— Oh, it's nothing, Phyllis, nothing. I must dress.' Josephine rose to her feet. She put her hand under Phyllis's chin with an attempt to smile; but her eyes had not lost their look of dazed horror.

'It's nothing, really. I'm awfully silly and nervy, I know, Phyl. I shall take a long rest when the season's over. We'll go away somewhere.'

'But——'

'It was nothing, really. Don't think about it any more, Phylly. Help me with my dressing, dear; I think we're a bit late. This will be the first time I've made myself up as an invalid.'

She went on talking vivaciously as she took off her clothes; it was less to reassure Phyllis than to stem the current of her own wild thoughts. But all the while she chattered there floated at the back of her brain a dark image, an ominous black cross.

Phyllis responded soon to her talkativeness and laughed as she stroked the folds of the garment that Josephine was to wear. It lay upon the sofa, a soft white robe of thick silk. The dance had been arranged by Josephine herself, and was set to the eerie music of the 'Valse Triste' of Sibelius. It was to be a strange performance, and Josephine held secret doubts as to its good reception. The dance was an adaptation of the story to which the 'Valse Triste' was written—of a dying woman, who rises from her bed and joins in the wild dance of the spirits that throng her room.

Josephine sang softly the slow opening bars of the music as she slipped her dress over her head. Phyllis watched her from the sofa, admiring the faint flush that excitement brought to her white cheeks.

'You'd better run along now,' said Josephine. 'I'm ready.'

Phyllis turned her from the mirror and surveyed her. Her plain white dress hung in heavy folds to her ankles. It was suggestive of a bedgown. The long hanging sleeves almost reached its hem. She wore no wig, and her thick dark hair stood out around her face; it was without band or ornament.

'Kiss me for luck, Phyl,' she said, 'and run along to the Stracheys.' She turned to her mirror again as Phyllis closed the door behind her.

The safety curtain was being lowered for the interval as Phyllis entered the box where her friends were. The orchestra was playing a selection of popular airs; a buzz of talk had arisen among the audience. Phyllis looked around the auditorium before she sat down. The place was crowded.

As the curtain began slowly to go up there was a sudden hush; the first slow notes dropped on the heavy air like pearls. Phyllis leaned forward and settled her elbows on the edge of the box.

The curtain rose upon a dimly lit stage. The walls were hung with deep purple curtains; the floor was covered in dark felt. In the centre of the stage, at the back, was a high couch draped with purple cloth. A woman clothed in white lay upon it. A small lamp burnt dimly by the bedside. There was not light enough upon the stage to distinguish any details; the purple background seemed full of deep shadows. The soft, slow music from the orchestra was as quiet as sleep.

For a minute or more there was no movement, neither on the stage nor among the audience. Then Josephine stirred upon her couch and moaned softly. The valse rhythm of the sleepy music became more insistent. Josephine turned and let one arm fall listlessly over the side of the bed.

Suddenly a white flickering light appeared upon the purple background and went out. Another appeared, and another, until the dark walls seemed alive with pale dancing flames. It was as if the dim stage were full of will-o'-the-wisps. The music grew louder and lost its dreamy quality. Josephine sighed deeply like one who wakes from an unquiet sleep, and raised herself slowly upon one elbow. The stage became dim again and all the little moving lights went out. Then suddenly one appeared, a patch of wavering flame, upon the hangings of the bed. Josephine put out her hand as if to touch it; it flickered away across the floor and up the wall. Josephine gave a soft hollow laugh and rose slowly from where she lay. She stood unsteadily for one moment; she was like a spirit in her long white robe. Her face was pale, and her bare feet were white as chalk against the purple carpet. Her eyes followed the movements of the dancing flame. She made one or two uncertain steps as if to reach

it; then with a low laugh she sprang after it and the strange dance
began.

Soon other faint wavering flames appeared upon the walls and
floor, until the whole stage was once again flickering with pale
lights. They flashed across the white, smiling face of Josephine as
she swayed in her fantastic dance. They seemed to dance with her
like living things. The dance grew always faster as it proceeded,
until the stage was dazzling to the audience. The dancer's shining
draperies seemed made of the same stuff as the white flames that
leapt around them. It was an eerie performance; but it was beautiful.

Josephine felt nothing now but a great exultation. For her the
facts of life had ceased to exist. She was a dancer, and nothing else;
she was one with the lights that danced about her head and hands,
and with the bright quick sounds that danced and died like invisible
butterflies. For the first time for many tortured days she found
forgetfulness. The smile that was on her lips was not acted, but was
the unconscious expression of sheer happiness and triumph.

Wilder and louder grew the music, and the ghostly dance swifter
and swifter: until the dancer suddenly stood still and put her hand
to her eyes. Then as if exhausted she sank upon the couch. The
moving flames went out; the stage was dim and shadowy again. The
slow theme returned and the music from the orchestra was like soft
calling voices.

All was still for a few moments. Then, as before, the music
quickened and grew loud. The flickering lights appeared again
singly. The dancer lifted her arms, and sprang to her feet like one
who makes an effort. The wild dance began again. But now the
small flames, as they appeared one after another, seemed to merge
together until a pale light flooded the stage. It was a queer soft
radiance, neither brilliant nor harsh; it was as if the stage were full
of moonshine. In this still light Josephine danced, and her white
dress gleamed like a lily under the moon. She felt etherealized, a
spirit dancing on an immaterial plane. Her body moved in such
perfect time with her mind that she seemed to have no body.
Looking straight before her she saw, but without any recognition,
the black and white blur that was her audience. A movement
somewhere between herself and the blur caught her eyes, and all
unconsciously she lowered her gaze to it. It was the baton of the
conductor moving in agitated rhythm with the music. It brought

her mind back to a certain extent from its uplifted state. She felt vaguely irritated by the sight of it; the cold commonplaces of life seemed to start knocking again at the doors of her mind.

The movements of her wild dance took her to the back of the stage, but when she came to the front again her eyes were caught once more by that small object; it seemed to move with a kind of crazy desperation. Her eyes travelled up the black sleeve of the man who held it.

Then the walls of the universe seemed to fall crashing about her ears. For a moment her mind was absolutely empty; then all that she had ever known of fear and evil rushed into it like a tidal river. For she had looked into the light eyes of Otto Geracht.

There he stood, massive and tall as she had always remembered him, his great shoulders rather hunched about his ears, his grey hair hanging in wisps over his forehead. Josephine went on dancing; her limbs moved mechanically. But her mind was filled with a terror more appalling than anything she had ever known.

Round the stage she went in her swift dance, but those clear eyes, she knew, never left her for one moment. She looked into them. There was no hostility in them: large and pale, they met her own with that faint vague questioning look she remembered so well. She could see every detail of his head and shoulders; there was no light shining upon him, but he stood out with clear distinctness. Swifter and swifter moved his arms, and his great body moved with them; but his head was never turned to one side, and neither were his unblinking eyes.

Josephine forced herself to look away from him. She looked around the orchestra in the wild hope of meeting a friendly recognizing glance that might dispel the terrible illusion. She could not see all the members of the orchestra, but a few of them seemed to stand out with a curious distinctness, as if she were looking at them in the light of day. There was something familiar about the downbent head of the first violin, who stood next to the conductor. He raised his eyes from the printed sheet before him, and a cold hand seemed to close around Josephine's heart. It was Diedrich Kummer. He looked at her unseeingly.

In wild horror her eyes went from one figure to another. There were the others: Hugo Spizke and Charles Palacky stood at the right hand of Otto Geracht. They had fiddles; little Palacky was playing with that air of desperate concentrated alacrity which had distinguished all his movements. There to his right sat old Van der Heyder; he held the oboe in his hand and looked at Josephine with gentle dreaminess. Even as her terrified eyes swept his face he raised his plump hand and settled his pince-nez more firmly on his nose; it was an old mannerism of his.

There was the thin, sad Ledstein with the flute, and there Anna Petro sat by the harp. Her dark eyes held those of Josephine for a moment; there was no enmity in them, but the old enigmatical look of mockery and pity. Josephine in her wild fear had an impulse to cry out to her and implore her sympathy and support. In the old days she had been attracted by the woman's mournful beauty, and had been baffled by the atmosphere of mystery that had always surrounded her. Surely Anna Petro was capable of understanding and sympathy! But the dark eyes never changed in their regard, and the long fingers went on touching the strings with lazy indifference.

Josephine's eyes fell again upon Otto Geracht. She felt trapped and helpless. She wanted to stop the dance, to cry out, to leave the stage, but her body seemed hypnotized. Her lips were stiffened in a frozen smile. Her limbs moved without her volition; she had as little command over her movements as if she had been a wooden marionette, and the large hands of Otto Geracht had held the strings instead of the conductor's baton. Faster and faster moved that small gleaming stick, and wilder and louder grew the ghostly music.

In a very agony of terror Josephine looked up to the right in the hope of meeting Phyllis's sane and loving eyes, but she could see nothing. A black mist seemed to hang between her eyes and the auditorium. Only those grotesquely moving figures in the orchestra were distinct. She tried to scream, but no sound left her lips.

The wild music reached its climax. This was the end, then, at last. The light upon the stage went out as Josephine threw herself once again upon the dark couch. The music ended with a few slow bars. The curtain fell.

There was absolute stillness in the theatre for a few seconds. Then the applause burst out. As one man the audience rose to their feet. Volley of clapping followed volley. Someone at the back began to cry 'Encore! Encore!' and the whole audience took up the cry.

*

Behind the curtain on the now brilliantly lit stage four or five people stood with a sort of frightened hesitancy upon their faces. A man in evening-dress was bending over the white figure of Josephine Dessars where she still lay upon the purple couch. He raised his head towards the others with a shocked look upon his face; his lips seemed trembling into the form of a word.

A tall fair-haired girl suddenly came on from the wings. Her cheeks were flushed and her eyes shone. She seemed about to speak, but stopped and stood looking towards the figure on the bed with nothing but surprise in her big eyes. One of the women left the whispering group and laid her hand upon her arm.

'My dear,' she began. But Phyllis pushed her aside. She hurried towards the bed and leant over the small figure lying there. Then, very slowly, she drew back.

'Josephine—Josephine——,' she said in a whisper that had a ringing quality which echoed for a long time in the brains of all who heard it.

But Josephine Dessars was dead.

V

SUPERBEASTS

C. J. Cutcliffe-Hyne (1865–1944) was a hugely popular writer who attained the upper tax bracket and, unlike so many of his peers, did not fall out of it again through stupidity, carelessness, or reckless prodigality. The cause of his wealth were the novels and short-story collections about his character Captain Kettle, a fiery little seaman and adventurer who, like his creator, restlessly roamed the world. Cutcliffe-Hyne himself did not discover lost civilizations amidst the Arctic ice and was only very rarely in peril of his life, but he was assiduous in his wanderings: in one of his entertaining, and not overly boastful, volumes of memoirs he claimed that at one period in his life he travelled 10,000 miles of new territory every year. There seems no reason to dispute this. He was a close friend of Alfred Harmsworth, later Lord Northcliffe, often yachting with him and the writer Cecil Hayter, another prolific wordsmith as well as seasoned traveller. Cutcliffe-Hyne was a natural story-teller and a master of the narrative hook. It was said that during the first two decades of this century Captain Kettle was second only to Sherlock Holmes in the affections of the reading public. Tall, rangy, ebullient, and immensely xenophobic, Cutcliffe-Hyne was not above dropping private jokes into his narratives. The narrator of 'The Lizard' is one Chesney—one of Cutcliffe-Hyne's pseudonyms; the address mentioned in the story's opening paragraph was Cutcliffe-Hyne's own address, when he was not gallivanting around the globe. An unreconstructed romantic, he had a bias towards the weird and the wonderful: *The Lost Continent* (1900) was his contribution to the 'Atlantis' genre. An early fantasy, *Beneath Your Very Boots* (1889, about a race of troglodytes located beneath the Yorkshire dales), is a scandalously rare book in its first edition, while his last, *Wishing Smith* (1940, a larky novel about a man whose wishes come true and which incorporates many of Cutcliffe-Hyne's own obsessions about world-government), is almost as elusive.

An enormously industrious writer of 'library' novels, *L. G. Moberly* (*fl.* 1885–1930) was at one stage publishing two or three books a year, mainly for the eminently respectable firm of Ward, Lock, prodigious suppliers of popular fiction to the subscription libraries. Like Ethel M. Dell (at least, in the judgement of the critic Edward Shanks), Moberly 'could not write but her stories were good'. Readers devoured her pacey narratives and agreed with her essentially simplistic view of the world (which to all intents and purposes meant the British Empire). Her heroines were by no means downtrodden, and often exhibited signs of hoydenish rebelliousness; but invariably, in the final chapter, they bowed to the conventions. Moberly was not a regular *Strand* contributor. 'Inexplicable' was published in 1917 when most of the regulars were engaged elsewhere and Greenhough Smith, the editor, was scratching around to fill his pages. Nevertheless, the story has distinct merits and carries, as with much post-Suffragette popular fiction, a subversive subtext.

The Lizard

C. J. Cutcliffe-Hyne

IT is not in the least expected that the general public will believe
the statements which will be made in this paper. They are written
to catch the eye of Mr Wilfred Cecil Cording (or Cordy) if he still
lives, or in the event of his death to carry some news of his last
movements to any of his still existing friends and relations. Further
details may be had from me (by any of these interested people) at
Poste Restante, Kettlewell, Wharfedale, Yorkshire. My name is
Chesney, and I am sufficiently well known there for letters to be
forwarded to wherever I may be at the moment.

The matters in question happened two years ago on the last day of
August. I had a small, high-ground shoot near Kettlewell, but that
morning all the upper parts of the hill were thick with dense mist, and
shooting was out of the question. However, I had been going it pretty
hard since the Twelfth, and was not sorry for an off-day, the more so
as there was a newly found cave in the neighbourhood which I was
anxious to explore thoroughly. Incidentally I may mention that cave-
hunting and shooting were my only two amusements.

It was my keeper who brought me news to the inn about the
impossibility of shooting, and I suggested to him that he should
come with me to inspect the cave. He made some sort of excuse—I
forget what—and I did not press the matter further. He was a
Kettlewell native, and the dalesmen up there look upon the local
caves with more awe than respect. They will not own up to
believing in bogles, but I fancy their creed runs that way. I used to
have a contempt for their qualms, but latterly I have somehow or
other learned to respect them.

I had taken unwilling helpers cave-hunting with me before, and found them such a nuisance that I had made up my mind not to be bothered with them again; so, as I say, I did not press for the keeper's society, but took candles, matches in a bottle, some magnesium wire, a small coil of rope, and a large flask of whisky, and set off alone.

The clouds above were wet, and a fine rain fell persistently. I tramped off along one of the three main roads that lead from the village, but which road it was had better remain hidden for the present. And in time I got off this road and cut over the moor.

What I was looking for was a fresh scar on the hillside, caused by a roof-fall in one of the countless caves which honeycomb this limestone district; and, although I had got my bearings pretty accurately, the fog was so thick up there that I had to take a good dozen casts before I hit upon the place.

I had not seen it since the 10th of August, when I first stumbled across it by accident whilst I was going over the hill to see how the birds promised for the following Twelfth; and I was a good deal annoyed to find by the boot-marks that quite a lot of people had visited it in the interval. However, I hoped that the larger part of these were made by shepherds, and perhaps by my own keepers, and, remembering their qualms, trusted that I might find the interior still untampered with.

The cave was easy enough to enter. There was a funnel-shaped slide of peat-earth and mud and clay to start with, well pitted with boot-marks; and then there was a tumbled wall of boulders, slanting inwards, down which I crawled face uppermost till the light behind me dwindled. The way was getting pretty murky, so I lit up a candle to avoid accidents, stepped knee-deep into a lively stream of water, and went briskly ahead. It was an ordinary enough limestone cave so far, with inferior stalactites, and a good deal of wet everywhere. It did not appear to have been disturbed, and I stepped along cheerfully.

Presently I got a bit of a shock. The roof above began to droop downwards, slowly but relentlessly. It seemed as though my way was soon going to be blocked. However, the water beneath deepened, and so I waded along to inspect as far on as possible. It was a cold job, for the water was icy, but then I am a bit of an enthusiast about cave-hunting, and it takes more than a trifle of discomfort to stop me.

The roof came down and down till I was forced into the water up to my chin, and the air, too, was none of the best. I was beginning to get disappointed; it looked as if I had got wet through to the bone with freezing cold cave-water for no adequate result.

However, there is no accounting for the freaks of caves. Just when I fancied I was at the end of my tether, up went the roof again; I was able to stand erect once more; and a dozen yards further on I came out on to dry rock, and was able to have a rest and a drop of whisky. The roof had quite disappeared to candle-light overhead, so I burned a foot of magnesium wire for a better inspection. It was really a magnificent cave.

But I did not stop to make any accurate measurements or drawings then, and, for reasons which will appear, I have not been near to do so since. I was too cold to care for prolonged admiration, and I wanted to (so to speak) annex the whole of the cave's main contours before I took my departure. I was first man in, and wished to be able to describe the whole of my find. There is a certain keen emulation about these matters amongst cave-hunters.

So I walked on over the flat floor of rock, stepping over and through pools, and round boulders, and dodging round stalactites, which hung from the unseen roof above, and slipping between slimy palings of stalagmite which sprouted from the floor. And then I came to a regular big subterranean tarn, which stretched right across the cavern.

Spaces were big here, and the candle did little to show them. It burned brightly enough, and that pleased me: one has to be very careful in cave-hunting about foul air, because once overcome by that, it means certain death. The air in this cave, however, did not altogether pass muster; there was something new about it, and anything new in cave smells is always suspicious. It wasn't the smell of peat, or iron, or sandstone, or limestone, or fungus, though all these are common enough in caves; it was a sort of faint musky smell; and I had got an idea that it was in flavour rather sickly. It is hard to define these things, but that smell, although it might very possibly lead to a new discovery, somehow did not cheer me. In fact, at times, when I inhaled a deeper breath of it than usual, it came very near to making my flesh creep.

However, hesitations of this kind are not business. I nipped off another foot of magnesium wire, lit it at the candle, and held the flaming end high above my head. Before me the water of the tarn lay motionless as a mirror of black glass; the sides vignetted away into alleys and bays; the roof was a groined and fretted dome, far overhead; and at the further side was a beach of white tumbled limestone.

I pitched a stone into the black water, and the mirror broke (I was pleased to think) for the first time during a million years into ripples. Yes, it's worth even a year of hard cave-hunting to do a thing like that.

The stone sank with a luscious *plop*. The water was very deep. But I was wet to the neck already, and didn't mind a swim. So with a lump of clay I stuck one candle in my cap, set up a couple more on the dry rock as a lighthouse to guide my return, lowered myself into the black water, and struck out. The smell of musk oppressed me, and I fancied it was growing more pronounced. So I didn't dawdle. Roughly, I guessed the pool to be some five-and-thirty yards across.

I landed amongst the white broken limestone on the further side, with a shiver and a scramble, and there was no doubt about the smell of musk now; it was strong enough to make me cough. But when I had stood up, got the candle in my hand again, and peered about through the dark, a thrill came through me as I thought I guessed at the cause. A dozen yards further on amongst the tumbled stone was a broken 'cast', where some monstrous uncouth animal had been entombed in the forgotten ages of the past, and mouldered away and left only the outer shell of its form and shape. For ages this, too, had endured; indeed, it had only been violated by the eroding touch of the water and some earth tremor within the last few days; perhaps at the same time that the 'slip' was made in the moor far above, which gave an entrance to the caves.

The 'cast' was half full of splintered rubbish, but even as it was I could see the contour of its sides in many places, and with care the debris could be scooped out, and a workman could with plaster of Paris make an exact model of this beast, which had been lost to the world's knowledge for so many weary millions of years. It had been some sort of a lizard or a crocodile, and, in fancy, I was beginning to picture its restored shape posed in the National Museum, with my name underneath as discoverer, when my eye fell on something amongst the rubble which brought me to earth with a jar. I stooped

and picked it up. It was a common white-handled penknife, of the
variety sold by stationers for a shilling. On one side of it was the
name of Wilfred Cecil Cording (or Cordy), scratched apparently
with a nail. The work was neat enough to start with, but the
engraver had wearied with his job; and the 'Cecil' was slipshod, and
the surname too scratchy to be certain about.

On the hot impulse of the moment, I threw the knife far from me
into the black water, and swore. It is more than a bit unpleasant for
an explorer who has made a big discovery to find that he has been
forestalled. But since then I have more than once regretted the hard
things I said against Cording (if that is his name) in the heat of my
first passion. If the man is alive I apologize to him. If, as I strongly
suspect, he came to a horrible end there in the cave, I tender my
regrets to his relatives.

I looked upon the cast of the saurian now with the warmth of
discovery quite gone. I was conscious of cold, and, moreover, the
musky smell of the place was vastly unpleasant. And I think I
should straightway have gone back to daylight and a change of
clothes down in Kettlewell, but for one thing. I seemed somehow
or other to trace on the rock beneath me the outline of another cast.
It was hazy, as a thing of the kind would be if seen through the
medium of sparsely transparent limestone, and by the light of a
solitary paraffin wax candle. I kicked at it petulantly.

Some flakes of stone shelled off, and I distinctly heard a more
extensive crack.

I kicked again, harder—with all my might, in fact. More flakes
shelled away, and there was a little volley of cracks this time. It did
not feel like kicking against stone. It was like kicking against
something that gave. And I could have sworn that the musky smell
increased. I felt a curious glow coming over me that was part fright,
part excitement, part, I fancy, nausea; but plucked up my courage
and held my breath, and kicked again, and again, and again. The
laminae of limestone flew up in tinkling showers. There was no
doubt about there being something springy underneath now, and
that it was the dead carcass of another lizard I hadn't a doubt. Here
was luck, here was a find. Here was I the discoverer of the body of
a prehistoric beast, preserved in the limestone down through all the
ages, just as mammoths have been preserved in Siberian ice.

The quarrying of my boot heel was too slow for me. I stuck my

candle by its clay socket to a rock, and picked up a handy boulder
and beat away the sheets of the stone with that; and all the time I
toiled, the springiness of the carcass beneath distinctly helped me.
The smell of musk nearly made me sick, but I stuck to the work.
There was no doubt about it now. More than once I barked my
knuckles against the harsh, scaly skin of the beast itself—against the
skin of this anachronism, which ought to have perished body and
bones ten million years ago. I remember wondering whether they
would make me a baronet for the discovery. They do make scientific
baronets nowadays for the bigger finds.

Then of a sudden I got a start: I could have sworn the dead flesh
moved beneath me.

But I shouted aloud at myself in contempt. 'Pah!' I said, 'ten
million years: the ghost is rather stale by this!' And I set to work
afresh, beating away the stone which covered the beast from my
sight.

But again I got a start, and this time it was a more solid one.
After I had delivered my blow, and whilst I was raising my weapon
for another, a splinter of stone broke away as if pressed up from
below, flipped up in the air, and tinkled back to a standstill. My
blood chilled, and for a moment the loneliness of that unknown
cave oppressed me. But I told myself that I was an old hand; that
this was childishness; and, in fact, pulled myself together. I refused
to accept the hint. I deliberately put the candle so as to throw a
better light, swallowed back my tremors, and battered afresh at the
laminated rock.

Twice more I was given warnings, and disregarded them in the
name of what I was pleased to call cold common reason; but the
third time I dropped the battering stone as though it burnt me, and
darted back with the most horrible shock of terror which (I make
bold to say) any man could endure and still retain his senses.

There was no doubt about it—the beast was actually moving.

Yes, moving and alive. It was writhing, and straining, and
struggling to leave its rocky bed where it had lain quiet through all
those countless cycles of time, and I watched it in a very petrification
of terror. Its efforts threw up whole basketfuls of splintered stone
at a time. I could see the muscles of its back ripple at each effort. I
could see the exposed part of its body grow in size every time it
wrenched at the walls of that semi-eternal prison.

Then, as I looked, it doubled up its back like a bucking horse, and drew out its stumpy head and long feelers, giving out the while a thin, small scream like a hurt child; and then with another effort it pulled out its long tail and stood upon the debris of the limestone, panting with a new-found life.

I gazed upon it with a sickly fascination. Its body was about the bigness of two horses. Its head was curiously short, but the mouth opened back almost to the forearm; and sprouting from the nose were two enormous feelers, or antennae, each at least 6 ft. long, and tipped with fleshy tendrils like fingers, which opened and shut tremulously. Its four legs were jointless, and ended in mere club-feet, or callosities; its tail was long, supple, and fringed on the top with a saw-like row of scales. In colour, it was a bright grass-green, all except the feelers, which were of a livid blue. But mere words go poorly for a description, and the beast was outside the vocabulary of today. It conveyed, somehow or other, a horrible sense of deformity, which made one physically ill to look upon it.

But worst of all was the musky smell. That increased till it became well-nigh unendurable, and though I half-strangled myself to suppress a sound, I had to yield at last and give my feelings vent.

The beast heard me. I could not see that it had any ears, but anyway it distinctly heard me. Worse, it hobbled round clumsily with its jointless legs, and waved its feelers in my direction. I could not make out that it had any eyes—anyway, they did not show distinct from the rough skin of its head; its sensitiveness seemed to lie in those fathom-long feelers and in the fleshy fingers which twitched and grappled at the end of them.

Then it opened its great jaws—which hinged, as I said, down by the forearm—and yawned cavernously, and came towards me. It seemed to have no trace of fear or hesitation. It hobbled clumsily on, exhibiting its monstrous deformity in every movement, and preceded always by those hateful feelers which seemed to be endued with an impish activity.

For a while I stayed in my place, too paralysed by horror at this awful thing I had dragged up from the forgotten dead, to move or breathe. But then one of its livid blue feelers—a hard, armoured thing like a lobster's—touched me, and the fleshy fingers at the end of it pawed my face and burned me like nettles. I leaped into movement again. The beast was hungry after its fast of ten million years; it was trying to make me its prey: those fearful jaws——

I turned and ran.

It followed me. In the feeble light of the one solitary candle I could see it following accurately in my track, with the waving feelers and their twitching fingers preceding it. It had pace, too. Its gait, with those clumsy, jointless legs, reminded one of a barrel-bellied sofa suddenly endowed with life, and careering over rough ground. But it distinctly had pace, and what was worse, the pace increased. At first it had the rust of those eternal ages to work out of its cankered joints; but this stiffness passed away, and presently it was following me with a speed equal to my own.

If this huge green beast had shown anger, or eagerness, or any of those things, it would have been less horrible; but it was absolutely unemotional in its hunt, and this helped to paralyse me; and in the end, when it drove me into a cul-de-sac amongst the rocks, I was very near surrendering myself through sheer terror to what seemed the inevitable. I wondered dully whether there had been another beast entombed beside it, and whether that had eaten the man who owned the penknife.

But the idea warmed me up. I had a stout knife in my own pocket, and after some fumbling got it out and opened the blade. The feelers with their fringe of fumbling fingers were close to me. I slashed at them viciously, and felt my knife grate against their armour. I might as well have hacked at an iron rail.

Still, the attempt did me good. There is an animal love for fighting stowed away in the bottom of all of us somewhere, and mine woke then. I don't know that I expected to win; but I did intend to do the largest possible amount of damage before I was caught. I made a rush, stepped with one foot on the beast's creeping back, and leaped astern of him; and the beast gave its thin, small whistling scream, and turned quickly in chase after me.

The pace was getting terrific. We doubled, and turned, and sprawled, and leapt amongst the slimy boulders, and every time we came to close quarters I stabbed at the beast with my knife, but without ever finding a joint in its armour. The tough skin gave to the weight of the blows, it is true, but it was like stabbing with a stick upon leather.

It was clear, though, that this could not go on. The beast grew in strength and activity, and probably in dumb anger, though actually it was unemotional as ever; but I was every moment growing more blown and more bruised and more exhausted.

At last I tripped and fell. The beast with its clumsy waddle shot past me before it could pull up, and in desperation I threw one arm and my knees around its grass-green tail, and with my spare hand drove the knife with the full of my force into the underneath part of its body.

That woke it at last. It writhed, and it plunged, and it bucked with a frenzy that I had never seen before, and its scream grew in piercingness till it was strong as the whistle of a steam-engine. But still I hung doggedly on to my place, and planted my vicious blows. The great beast doubled and tried to reach me; it flung its livid blue feelers backwards in vain efforts: I was beyond its clutch. And then, with my weight still on its back, it gave over dancing about the floor of the cavern, and set off at its hobbling gait directly for the water.

Not till it reached the brink did I slip off; but I saw it plunge in; I saw it swim strongly with its tail; and then I saw it dive and disappear for good.

And what next? I took to the water too, and swam as I had never swum before—swam for dear life to the opposite side. I knew that if I waited to cool my thoughts I should never pluck up courage for the attempt. It was then or not at all. It was risk the horrors of that passage, or stay where I was and starve—and be eaten.

How I got across I do not know. How I landed I cannot tell. How I got down the windings of the cave and through that water-alley is more than I can say. And whether the beast followed me I do not know either. I got to daylight again somehow, staggering like a drunken man. I struggled down off the moor, and on to the village, and noted how the people ran from me. At the inn the landlord cried out as though I had been the plague. It seemed that the musky smell that I brought with me was unendurable, though, by this time, the mere detail of a smell was far beneath my notice. But I was stripped from my stinking clothes, and washed, and put to bed, and a doctor came and gave me an opiate; and when twelve hours later wakefulness came to me again, I had the sense to hold my tongue. All the village wanted to know from whence came that hateful odour of musk, but I said, stupidly, I did not know. I said I must have fallen into something.

And there the matter ends for the present. I go no more cave-hunting, and I offer no help to those who do. But if the man who owned that white-handled penknife is alive, I should like to compare experiences with him; and if, as I strongly suspect, he is dead, these pages may be of interest to his relatives. He was not known in Kettlewell or any of the other villages where I enquired, but he could very well have come over the hills from Pateley Bridge way. 'Cording' was the name scratched on the knife, or 'Cordy', I could not be sure which; and, as I have said, mine is Chesney, and I can be heard of at the Kettlewell post office, though I have given up the shooting on the moor near there. Somehow, the air of the district sickens me. There seems to be a taint in it.

Inexplicable

L. G. Moberly

THE hinges were rusty, the gate swinging to behind me creaked dismally, and as the latch clicked into its socket with a sharp clang I started. That clanging sound drew from the depths of my subconscious self some old stories of prison doors and turnkeys. And I actually glanced nervously over my shoulder at the suburban road which trailed to right and left of the gate I had just entered, although anything less calculated to inspire nervous tremors than that stretch of ordinary road lined by ordinary houses could not be imagined!

I had an order to view 119 Glazebrook Terrace, in the very unromantic suburb of Prillsbury, and I was seeking a house in that unromantic suburb merely because it was a healthy place within convenient distance of the London station to which my husband had to travel every morning. The rent of the house was decidedly low, if the house itself came up to the flowery description of it given by the house-agent; but I had made up my mind that this possibility was almost too good to be true. Nevertheless, I confess I was surprised by the outside appearance of the houses in the terrace. They were solidly built, commodious-looking dwellings, and although the scrap of front garden belonging to No. 119 was in the last stages of neglect and weeds, and there was a generally unkempt air about the whole place, still, I reflected, as I walked up the grass-grown path, these faults could soon be remedied. And it was simply absurd to be obsessed by a feeling of traps or prison-bars just because the gate had creaked on its hinges and then clanged-to with a sharpness which gave me such a feeling of finality.

The house-agent's clerk, who waited for me on the steps with the key of the house, was as ordinary as the rest of the surroundings, and my unaccountable attack of nerves passed off under the influence of his self-assured and cockney accents. Like the generality of his profession, he was profuse in praises of the house I had come to see, and I was fain to confess that in this case the praise was not undeserved. No. 119 was a very delightful house, well arranged, well built, with a nice piece of garden at the back, and plenty of accommodation.

But I only discovered its merits after literally wading through seas of dust, for never in the whole course of my existence have I seen any house so dusty as that house. Our feet sank into a thick powder; the windows were grimy, the walls coated, there must have been inches of dust upon every ledge capable of holding a grain of anything.

'I wonder the house has been allowed to get into this condition,' I remarked to my guide when, having visited all the lower rooms, we stood in the big front bedroom; 'it would surely have paid to put a caretaker into the place to keep it cleaned and aired.'

'We found it——' he began, in his self-confident accents, and then he stopped short, and his very fair face flushed. 'Messrs Dyron did not consider it necessary,' he said, rather hurriedly, and was then proceeding to explain to me how expeditiously the establishment could be put into liveable order, when my eye was attracted to a small table standing against the wall by the fireplace. It was octagonal in shape, set on three twisted legs—just a small occasional table such as one may see in any drawing-room. But the way in which it was carved was entirely out of the common, and I crossed the room to look at it more closely, exclaiming as I did so, 'What a perfectly lovely piece of carving! Of course, this has been left here by mistake.' And I turned the table more to the window to let the light fall upon it. The whole top was a crust of carved leaves and flowers, and in each curve of the octagon there was fashioned a small alligator, his head pointing outwards, his tail meeting the tails of the other crocodiles in the centre; and as the light fell full on the scaly bodies they had an extraordinary look of life, and the little sinister heads with the small evil eyes almost seemed to move. I shuddered and drew away from the table, and the voice of Messrs Dyron's clerk seemed to come to me from quite a long way off.

'The table goes with the house,' I heard him say; 'it is really like a fixture, it goes with the house.' I don't suppose he really said the words very often, but in the dimness that had temporarily descended upon my brain I thought he went on repeating, like a parrot-cry, 'It goes with the house. It goes with the house.' Then the dimness cleared away, and I heard him say quietly, whilst it struck me that his face was oddly white:

'I am afraid you are tired, madam.'

I passed my hand over my face. 'I don't know,' I said. 'I think the house must be stuffy. Just for a moment I felt quite faint, and there is such a queer smell in here,' I added, becoming all at once conscious of a strange and penetrating odour I had not before noticed. 'The drains——'

'The drains were set in order before the last tenant vacated the house,' my companion put in quickly. 'I have the sanitary people's certificate about them. I fancy the smell you notice is due to the place having been shut up some time, and to the rankness of the creeper outside.'

Well, what he said sounded reasonable, and when he flung the window open the smell disappeared, and I recovered from my momentary faintness. But I made up my mind that, much as I liked the house, I would have every drain carefully inspected again before I urged Hugh to take it. As I was leaving the front bedroom my mind went back to the carved table.

'Do you really mean to say the former tenants wish to leave that beautiful thing?' I asked. 'I suppose they are not going to leave it for nothing?'

'Oh, yes,' the young man answered, airily, as if exquisitely carved tables were usually bestowed by outgoing upon incoming tenants; 'they have simply left it as—as—well, as a fixture, or as lumber— whichever way one likes to look at it.'

'I should prefer to look on it as a fixture,' I said. 'I can only conclude that its owners are most unusual people. Fancy parting with such an artistic piece of work! If we take the house—and I am very much inclined to think we shall—that table will not be left in a bedroom.' The young man bowed acquiescently and looked from me to the table with an oddly sidelong glance.

Although my temporary faintness had passed off, and after the window was opened the queer smell in the room had also vanished,

I was not sorry to be outside in the fresh air again, for that faintness had left me oddly shaken. However, I forgot all about it long before I reached home, and I was only anxious to impress upon my husband the many charms and conveniences of 119 Glazebrook Terrace. The more I thought about the house the more sure I was that it would suit us in every particular, and by the end of the evening I had planned out all the rooms and fitted our furniture into them. Hugh paid a hurried visit to the house with me next day, and shared my enthusiasm. The windows were all open, there was no longer any strange smell, the sun was shining on our eager plans for the future; we ignored the present air of neglect and forlornness. And as for the table! My husband fell in love with it as much as I had done, and marvelled, as I had marvelled, how anyone in his senses could leave such a fine piece of work behind.

'So much the better for us,' Hugh exclaimed gaily, his fingers running over the delicately carved crust of flowers and leaves, and resting on the head of one of the alligators, a head fashioned with such skill that its loathsome naturalness made one shudder.

'Good heavens, May, the things look so lifelike I could almost have sworn one of them squirmed.' And Hugh stood back from the table, stared at it with round eyes, and then laughed. 'I shall be seeing rats and snakes next,' he said, and laughed again as we left the room together. Before we left the house that day we had definitely decided to take it, supposing the drains were all they should be and the lease a satisfactory one; and in a very few weeks we were actually able to move into our new abode. An expert had declared the drains to be entirely above reproach; no terms could have been easier than those of the lease; in every direction our way seemed to be smoothed for us, and Hugh and I agreed that we were most lucky to have got so wholly delightful a house with so little difficulty or expense. We turned in an army of workpeople, and by the middle of May the house was clean and fresh from attic to basement, the garden had lost its neglected appearance; and when at last we took up our abode there on a sunshiny afternoon, when the lilacs were in bloom and the thrushes singing their loudest, we felt that we had come there to stay, probably for the rest of our natural lives.

'That beautiful table is too good for a bedroom,' Hugh exclaimed, as we were arranging the disposition of our furniture. 'I'll cart it down to the drawing-room.'

'Yes—do, dear,' I answered absently, my thoughts busy over vital questions of curtains and carpets, 'and open the windows wide as you pass—there is still a stuffy smell here. I believe it is those shrubs outside—I shall have them cut back more.' But Hugh had already picked up the small table and vanished with it through the door, and I returned to my calculations, when a great crash interrupted the current of my thoughts—a crash and a sharp cry.

I rushed to the stairs, to see Hugh lying in the hall, the table standing beside him apparently uninjured. I was at my husband's side in a second; he pulled himself up with difficulty, but he could not get upon his feet, and his face was drawn with pain.

'Twisted my ankle or something,' he said, trying to smile reassuringly; 'there must have been a piece of carpet loose. Something seemed to slither between my feet, and I lost my balance. Good job I didn't break my neck,' he added, philosophically, 'and, anyhow, the table's all right.'

Yes—the table was all right. The delicate carving was unbroken, the alligators lay there intact, grinning their sinister, malicious grin.

'Beastly things,' Hugh said, looking at them with a queer little shiver, as I helped him to hobble into the drawing-room. 'The chap who carved them was an artist, if you like.'

Poor old Hugh! He was laid up for days with that bad ankle, and it fretted him to see me setting our house in order whilst he was tied by the leg.

'We certainly must have those shrubs cut back,' he said to me the day after his fall, and he sniffed audibly; 'there's a sort of smell in here of decaying vegetation. I dare say the shrubs have got a bit rank. Good Lord, what's that?' and he pulled himself upright on the couch, as from the small alligator table in the window there came a most prodigious crack. I confess I started too, for, accustomed as one is to the cracking of furniture, the sound did really seem gigantic to come from such a small object as the table.

'Very funny,' Hugh said, eyeing the delicate carving and the grinning heads with a certain hostility. 'I hate things that give one the jumps, and it was such a funny sort of crack, too,' he added, thoughtfully; 'more like—more like—what on earth was it like, May? Not exactly like the sound one associates with cracking furniture.'

'Not quite like anything I ever heard before,' I answered. 'Perhaps the wood is some peculiar kind to which we are not accustomed. Now I know the table has tricks and manners of that kind, it won't startle me so much next time.'

I keep no diary, but I think it must have been on a morning two days later that I found my usually neat cook in a strange state of dishevelment when I went downstairs to order dinner. My heart sank within me. The untidy gown, tousled hair, the general air of having tumbled straight out of bed into the kitchen seemed to tell only one tale, and the horrible conviction that my hitherto sober Maria had been drinking became something like a certainty when she suddenly flung her apron over her head and began to sob.

'I'm sure I never had a better missus,' she said, incoherently, 'but there's things nobody can bear—nor ain't meant to.' I had no clue to her disjointed remarks, excepting the very obvious one that she had been, if she was not at that moment, royally drunk, and I said, sternly:

'Take your apron off your face, Maria, and explain yourself. I don't know what you are talking about.'

'No—nor anyone else either,' she responded, wildly. 'It isn't right, not in any decent house, nor such as flesh and blood can stand. I'm sure I never had a complaint to make before not since I was in your service, but this——'

'Oh, Maria, do stop talking nonsense and tell me what you mean!' I broke in, impatiently. 'What on earth is the matter?'

'Matter enough!' she said, with a quiver in her voice; and she looked nervously over her shoulder, as though she expected to see someone enter the door. 'If I'd been asleep I should say it was a nightmare after the toasted cheese, but I was as wide awake as I am now.'

'But what happened?' I exclaimed. 'Do tell me what you are talking about.'

'I don't know,' came the extraordinary reply. 'If I knew what it was I could tell you, but I don't know no more than the babe unborn,' and she shuddered—a shudder that was certainly one of genuine fear.

'Maria,' I said, gravely, 'I don't like to think——'

'Oh, I haven't been drinking, ma'am—if that's what you were going to say,' she answered, quite civilly, and with that odd glance over her shoulder again; 'but I never slept a wink after two, and I daren't stir to call anybody. I thought it might get me.'

'*What* might get you?' A little chill crept down my own spine on seeing the look in her eyes.

'I don't know,' she repeated. 'I don't know what it was. Only—I lay there awake, and I heard the clock in the hall strike two, and then'—she shrank closer to me and shuddered once more—'then my door opened—I always sleep with it ajar, but it opened wide, and there came—there came——'

'What?' I cried, when she paused.

'I don't know what it was—only I could hear it kind of sliding across the floor—sliding or pattering—there! I can't describe it, but I heard it. And I didn't dare light a candle—I just lay and shivered and shook whilst it went across the floor.'

'Maria, how absurd!' I said, though something in her manner and in her realistic description gave me once more a creeping sensation in my spine. 'Probably the cat got into your room.'

'The cat?' Maria flung back her head and laughed hysterically. 'No cat slides about like that. And there was a great flop, flop. Oh, I couldn't stop here another night, not if you was to pay me twenty thousand pounds!'

It took me an unreasonably long time to argue Maria into common sense, and then she only agreed to stay temporarily and on condition that she might leave her present room and share one with Jane, the housemaid.

'And I wouldn't even do that if you and the master hadn't been so good to me,' was her final remark.

'The woman's dotty,' Hugh said, irritably, when I told him the story, 'but she's a jolly good cook, so freeze on to her, dotty or not. But for Heaven's sake tell all the maids that if we hear any more rubbish about sliding, pattering animals they'll all get such a rowing from me as they won't forget in a hurry.'

The incident gave me a feeling of perturbation—I do not know why—and it was a relief when, that evening, Jack Wilding, an old friend of Hugh's, turned up to dinner. He was a delightful person who had travelled all over the world, and his fund of knowledge, not to mention his stock of good stories, was inexhaustible. At dinner he was in his best vein, and I relegated cook and her terrors into the background of my mind; and in the drawing-room later I prepared to enjoy myself. I sat down to work whilst the two men smoked and chatted.

The windows were wide open. It was a delicious May night, and the air that drifted in brought with it the fragrance of hawthorn and wistaria and fresh-growing things, and I sat enjoying it and giving half an ear to the talk of the two men, when all at once the drifting sweetness from without was tainted by that same strange odour which we had once or twice noticed before. Was I right in thinking it the smell of decaying vegetation, or was it not rather some indescribable smell to which I could give no name? As it drifted across the room our guest suddenly sat bolt upright in his chair, and a curious greyness overspread his naturally bronzed complexion.

'My God!' he said, 'what is that? And why does it smell the same—the same——' His sentence trailed off into silence, and in the intense stillness following his strange words I heard a sound which, for some reason I could not pretend to explain, gave me a feeling of cold fear. I can only describe the sound as like a far-away bellowing—not precisely the bellowing of cattle, but a more sinister, more horrible sound, pregnant with evil.

'You hear it too?' Jack Wilding questioned, under his breath, and as he rose from his chair I saw that his face was ashen and beads of sweat stood upon his forehead. 'You hear it? And the stench is here too! Good God! if I thought I should ever have to cross that swamp again I should go mad!' His words, his tone, his whole appearance were so unlike our usually sane and cheery friend that both Hugh and I stared at him dumbfounded. And there was no doubt that his emotion, to whatever cause it was due, was entirely, even terribly, genuine.

'What's up, old man?' Hugh said, gently. 'There is a most awfully queer smell in here, but it isn't drains, and——'

'*Drains!*' Jack laughed a harsh laugh with a catch in it, then he passed his hand over his forehead and looked from Hugh to me with an oddly bewildered glance. 'I must have had a nightmare—a waking nightmare,' he said, looking round him. 'I could have sworn that I smelt the alligator swamp in New Guinea, the place where——' He broke off short. 'I heard the loathsome brutes bellowing,' he began again; 'but, of course—of course, it was merely some association of ideas.' His voice was still shaken, the whiteness had not left his face, and Hugh put a sympathetic hand upon his shoulder, whilst I remembered that strange, faint bellowing which I too had heard.

'Simply association of ideas, old man.' My husband's voice penetrated to my understanding. 'As likely as not you had been looking at that beautiful little table bequeathed to us by the former tenants. That put alligators into your head.' Jack turned and glanced at the table, and he recoiled when he saw the grinning heads lying amongst the crusted delicacy of leaves and flowers.

'Loathsome beasts!' he said, and again his voice shook. 'You will both think me an absolute fool,' he went on, recovering his self-control with an effort and sinking back into his chair; 'but I crossed an alligator swamp once with a friend.' He spoke in abrupt jerks and turned his head with a curious uneasy movement. 'It was dark, the place swarmed with those unspeakable devils, their stench was everywhere. It was dark—and poor old Danson'—he paused, as if speech were almost impossible—'they dragged him off the path of logs in the darkness.' His voice ended on a sharp high note, and neither Hugh nor I could speak for a minute or two. Somehow his words brought before me the hideous swamp, the darkness, the loathly monsters waiting for their prey, and the remembrance of just such an incident in a book I had once read flashed into my mind.

'I couldn't stand that table in any house I lived in,' Jack resumed presently, in more ordinary tones, and with a forced laugh. 'I never want to see an alligator again, alive or dead, or even carved.' He pushed back his chair abruptly and rose. 'I think I'll go up to bed now, if you don't mind,' he said; 'I'm not very good company.' And having said 'Good-night' he was moving across the room, when all at once he stumbled, flung out his hands to save himself, and, failing to do so, fell heavily to the ground. Something slid from between his feet—I saw a dark shape, a flash of white, and then it had vanished; and I stood staring vacantly at the place where it had been, whilst Hugh helped our guest to his feet.

'Something tripped me up,' he said, in dazed accents.

'I suppose it's that confounded cat of ours,' Hugh answered, and his voice sounded so cheery and normal through the cloud of uncanny, shuddering sensations that were creeping over me. 'Trust a cat to be just where you wish it wasn't! I'm awfully sorry, old man. It gave you a nasty jar.'

'A nasty jar,' Jack repeated, and his eyes were as dazed as his voice.

'Come on upstairs,' Hugh said, gently. 'I'll help you into bed. You've had a bit of a shaking.'

'Yes—a bit of a shaking.' the words were echoed, and the two men left the room together, whilst I, with one fearful glance behind me towards where I had seen that dark shape glide and vanish, left the room too with more haste than dignity, shutting the door firmly behind me and scurrying upstairs to my own bedroom.

When Jane brought my tea next morning the first thing she did was to drop the tray with a crash just inside my door, and then burst into a flood of tears. Hugh had gone out early to see Jack off at the station. I was alone.

'I can't stop here—I can't stop here!' Jane moaned. 'Cook and me—oh, my gracious goodness, I couldn't stop another minute!'

'Cook has been frightening you,' I said, trying to speak sternly, but not wholly succeeding, because of the memory of that something that had slid away from between Jack's feet last night. 'I should have thought you were too sensible to make a fuss about a trifle.'

'A trifle—oh, my lawks!' And Jane, the irreproachable and excellent servant, dropped into a chair and sobbed afresh.

'What has frightened you?' I said, trying to speak calmly, even though my morning tea was trickling over the carpet, and broken china and bread and butter were mingled in inextricable confusion. 'What is it?'

'We all slept together last night.' Jane lifted a scared face. 'After what cook heard, me and her and Dale all slept together.' I nearly groaned aloud. If Dale, my middle-aged parlourmaid, who had been with me for years, was also infected with panic-fear, what should I do? 'We all slept together,' Jane continued, 'and we locked the door'—here she gave a breathless gulp—'so as nothing couldn't get in. But it got in!' Her voice suddenly rose to a little scream. 'I couldn't stop here another night!'

'What got in, Jane?' I said, quietly, though my heart beat fast.

'It smelt something awful,' Jane went on, heedless of my question, and I expected every moment that she would break into a paroxysm of hysterics. 'It got in!' she ended, in a terrified whisper.

'What got in?' I asked. 'I suppose the cat was shut into the room before you went to bed, and gave you a fright.'

'It wasn't no cat,' she answered, under her breath; and try as I would to argue myself into common sense, the hair rose on my head. 'It was bigger than twenty cats, it slipped over the floor—over the floor—and oh!' And Jane finished with just the hysterical scream I had expected.

'Did you see this ridiculous thing?' I asked, sternly, when she was quieter; but, sternly as I spoke, my flesh crept.

'We dursn't light a candle,' she moaned, 'but the curtains was half drawn, and we saw its shape, and there was a white streak in it, and it slid over the floor—over——'

'That will do, Jane,' I said. 'Your master and I will talk the thing over. Meanwhile——'

'There's not one of us will sleep in the house again,' Jane said, shakily. And to this pleasing resolution our three servants adhered, in spite of anything that Hugh and I could say.

'Give them a night or two away to recover their nerves,' Hugh said to me afterwards, with a man's cheerful disregard of the difficulties of running a house without servants. 'Get in a char. We shall be all right.'

I acted on his advice, sent the servants off for two days' holiday, and sought the nearest charwoman. But at four o'clock the good woman came into my sanctum and refused to stay a moment longer. Her face was the colour of ashes, her speech was rambling.

'Which I can't stand it no longer,' she said, 'never bein' accustomed to a place where such animals is kep'.'

'But no animals are kept except a cat,' I answered, my heart sinking into my boots.

'Cats is cats, and dogs is dogs, and troubles though they both may be, and I'm not denyin' they are, still they're what you might call human,' Mrs Jenkins said grandly, but I noticed that for all her grandiloquence she was shaking from head to foot. 'The animals what come slithering in and out o' the scullery and kitchen—they ain't human. Runnin' on their underneaths, with paws as don't seem a bit o' use to 'em. Them as likes such pets must keep such pets, but I couldn't stop, not if it was ever so.' She had not been drinking. She was as sober as I was myself. I could only pay her her money and let her depart, and I telephoned to Hugh that I would meet him in town and dine there. He listened to my story, laughed at me, said that obviously the maids had put notions into Mrs Jenkins's head, and that I mustn't be silly. But when, at ten o'clock, he

opened our own front door, and the stench which had startled Jack
the day before rushed out at us, I shrank back white and trembling.

'Oh, Hugh,' I said, 'oh, Hugh, it frightens me!'

'Nonsense, my dear, stuff and nonsense!' Hugh began, drawing
me in and shutting the door with a sharp clang. 'You mustn't
let——' And then his sentence ended in a sharp exclamation, and
he clutched my arm with a grip that nearly upset my balance.

'Something slid between my feet,' he said, using the very words
Jack had used; 'I was almost down. That cat shall——' He said no
more. A frozen horror must have paralysed his speech, as it
prevented me from uttering a syllable, and we stood there clutching
each other and looking at the stairs, down which in the dusk we
could see a huge shape gliding at lightning speed. Another was
coming more slowly out of the drawing-room door, and from
amongst the dark shadows of the hall came sounds of sliding and
pattering—sounds which made my very blood run cold.

'Hugh!' I found my voice at last, and shrieked my husband's
name. 'Come away, Hugh, come away!' And opening the door
behind me I fled out into the night, dragging my husband with me.
Nothing would induce him to go to any of our neighbours. He said
we should look a pretty pair of fools if we told such a cock-and-bull
story as ours to any rational beings. And we made ourselves as
comfortable as we could for the night in the cottage at the end of
the garden, a cottage we had just furnished for the lady gardener
who was coming to us.

When in the bright sunshine of the next day we re-entered our
house, we were beginning to tell each other that we must have been
suffering the night before from optical delusions, when I saw in the
corner of the hall a flat head in which two malicious eyes gleamed,
whilst a devilish grin exposed two rows of hideous teeth. Hugh saw
it too, and turned white, but before he could reach the corner it had
gone. Then he strode on into the drawing-room, and still without
uttering a word he picked up the little table with its delicate carving
and the gruesome alligators' heads.

'What are you going to do?' I said, fearfully.

'Burn this infernal thing,' was his grim reply.

'But how can a table—just a table——' I began, but Hugh only
laughed sternly.

'I don't know,' he said, 'but I am taking no more chances.' He carried the table out to the back garden, surrounded it with straw, and set fire to it. And never another word did he speak until the beautiful work of art was nothing but a heap of ashes.

'So perish all devilry,' he said, when the last spark had died away; 'and now we will go to the house-agent's.'

But from the house-agent's clerk we got as much satisfaction as one is in the habit of getting from gentlemen of that profession. He looked at us with mild surprise, and answered our remarks urbanely and courteously.

'Any unpleasant stories about the house during the last tenancy? Oh, well—there had been a few silly servants' tales, but nothing of importance. The gentleman had left because he wished to reside in another county.'

'And what about the carved table he left behind him?' Hugh asked, sternly. The clerk shrugged his shoulders.

'The gentleman had not cared to take it. It was merely left as part of the house, that was all.'

'Oh, well, it is not a part of the house any more,' was Hugh's grim retort. 'It's not a part of anything, excepting in so far as matter never dies, and the smoke is doing some useful turn elsewhere.' The clerk stared. 'I have burnt that infernal table,' Hugh went on, forgetting his manners for once; 'nobody will ever see it again. You can tell your late client so, with my compliments. To leave it in the house was an abominable and mean thing to do.' With that he marched out of the office, and we went back to our house, a house which, from that day to this, has shown no sign of abnormality.

But it was many a long day before I could live down those weird experiences, and even now they are to me quite inexplicable.

Does any explanation of it all occur to you?

VI

THE LIGHT FANTASTIC

The 'L' in *L. de Giberne Sieveking* (1896–1972) stood for Lancelot, and as Lance Sieveking he was one of the pioneers of radio and a formidable influence on the medium. Something of a Jack-of-all-Trades—actor, poet, author, composer, producer, assistant inspector of taxes (this last for only a very short while, at the start of his career)—he was yet a master of one: sound-broadcasting, writing quantities of plays and serials during the inter-war years, as well as numerous radio adaptations of stage classics and novels. For many of these he composed his own background music. This wide range of interests was evident at an early age: when he was 13 he wrote a novel called *Stampede* (subsequently published, in 1924, with illustrations by G. K. Chesterton, his godfather), and in his mid-teens, just prior to the First World War, was active in the Women's Suffrage movement (his mother, a cousin of Gerard Manley Hopkins, was an ardent Suffragette). A pilot in the RFC, he was shot down over the Rhine in 1917 and spent a grim year in a prison camp. This does not appear to have affected his sense of humour—whimsical in 'The Prophetic Camera', rather more robust in real life: his friends, including the playwright and song-writer Eric Maschwitz, all recalled his loud laugh and mild addiction to practical jokes (in which his collection of mechanical singing birds sometimes played a part).

Henry A. Hering (*fl.* 1890–1930) wrote prolifically for the monthly and weekly magazines of his day yet seems to have had little interest in seeing the fruits of his prodigious labours translated into a more permanent form. His published books included *The Burglars' Club* (1906, revised with additional stories 1910), an amusing miscellany of round-the-fire yarns spun by various cracksmen, and *Adventures and Fantasy* (1930), a mixed collection of tales of mystery and the imagination. Though he could on occasion sound a gruesome note in his stories he was addicted to farce and was clearly an enthusiast of the 'new humour' of the 1890s, his style and general approach having more than a touch of its chief proponent, Jerome K. Jerome.

'The Queer Story of Brownlow's Newspaper' by *H. G. Wells* (1866–1946) is one of the last fantasy short stories its author composed, if not the very last. Written too late to be included in Wells' mammoth *Collected Short Stories* (1927), its first appearance in book form was tucked away at the back of the Odhams Press issue of *The Soul of a Bishop* in the 'Collected Edition' of 1933, which was then given away in a promotional drive by the *Daily Herald*. By 1932, when the story was published in the *Strand*, Wells, though 'official optimist for the human race', had a darker vision of the future than he cared to admit. His final book, *Mind at the End of its Tether* (1945), is a savage assault on humanity in which all of his pent-up pessimism is unleashed. It is not a comfortable work. Wells was not an infallible prophet despite an enviable track-record (his famous story predicting tank-warfare, 'The Land Ironclads', had originally appeared in the *Strand* in 1903), and he was perhaps happier with the short story than the long. At any rate he rarely wrote an unreadable one.

The Prophetic Camera

L. de Giberne Sieveking

THERE were moments in the life of Mr Muffle when he was glad his wife was not present. She constantly upbraided him for being a 'soft-hearted fool'.

'We may as well put the shutters up at once,' said she, 'if every time I leave you alone in the shop you empty the till into the lap of the first person who brings in a piece of good-for-nothing rubbish.' But then she was made of harder stuff than he was. On this particular evening he was particularly glad that she had gone off to a sale at Islington and would not be back for some time.

He was too distressed at the appearance of the miserable individual who furtively crept up to the counter to appraise with a businesslike eye the thing which the other set down before him. The miserable-looking man fumbled with one hand on the counter, and said:

'What will you allow me on this?'

Mr Muffle picked up the large old box-camera and turned it over once or twice.

'What do you want for it?' he asked.

'What'll you 'llow me?' persisted the other, almost inaudibly.

'Three-and-six,' with a shrug of his shoulders, though he felt sure the camera was worth practically nothing.

'Make it five bob.'

Mr Muffle looked from the camera to its owner. He shook his head. The other's face fell.

"Tisn't really worth half a crown, by rights,' murmured Mr Muffle, thinking of his wife's return that evening.

'It's worth a good deal more than that, indeed it is,' said the other. 'Why, the lens alone——'

Mr Muffle moved about uneasily and glanced at the clock.

'All right,' he said, suddenly, and went to his desk to make out the pawnticket. In another moment the man had gone, and with him went five shillings which would be very hard to account for.

Luckily Mrs Muffle was in a good humour when she returned, having bought some old china and glass very cheaply, and merely snorted with a contemptuous little laugh when she saw the camera, and pushed it out of the way among a lot of unsaleable uniforms that had come from men home from South Africa.

That had been in November. Now it was spring again. The Euston Road was drying up under the hard bright rays of the early May sunlight. Mr Muffle was standing in the doorway of his shop reading a leading article on Campbell-Bannerman in the *Daily News*. He turned when a voice from behind him called his name. His little nephew, who was staying with them, caught hold of his arm.

'Oh, uncle!' he said, 'I shall be going tomorrow, and I forgot to tell you that father made me promise to be sure and not forget to bring back a photo of you and Aunt Mabel.'

'Why, Charlie,' said his uncle, 'me and your aunt ain't had our picture took for nigh on eight years. Your father has seen all those old things.'

'Ain't you got a camera?' asked the boy. 'Then I could just take a snap in no time.'

'Never 'ad a camera in me life,' replied his uncle, peering under his hand at the clock on St Pancras tower.

'What's that?' said his wife's voice from the gloom behind the counter. 'Have you forgotten that thing you lent five good shillings of my money for last year? Might as well say "gave", for all the chance there is of him ever coming back for it!'

'There you are, Uncle Robin!' cried the boy. 'Let's have a look at it.'

Mrs Muffle, muttering to herself, got upon a chair and reached into a dusty corner. Then she returned to the counter and banged the old camera down on it.

'Look out, aunt! You'll smash the works.' Charlie picked it up and carried it out into the light. After blowing the dust off it he had soon pressed the knob which opened the back.

'It'll take quarter-plate,' he announced, cheerfully. And then, pressing the bulb, he looked through the lens at the sky.

'Looks all right,' he said. 'Come on, Uncle Robin, give me a bob and I'll go and buy a packet of plates at the chemist's opposite.'

'Making six good shillings in all thrown away,' observed his aunt, sourly.

Five minutes later Charlie was in the cupboard under the counter, carefully sliding the plates into their sockets as well as he could in the dark. Soon he emerged, radiant but rumpled, and ordered his aunt and uncle out into the street. He made them stand together just beneath the three golden balls.

'Put your arm round my neck, Mabel,' said Mr Muffle, with an effort at jocularity, 'and pretend we're on our 'oneymoon.'

'You button up your coat,' said his wife, severely, 'and smooth your 'air a bit. Then you might look more like a man and less like a cab 'orse.'

Poor Mr Muffle wore a very chastened expression as his nephew pressed the bulb of the old camera.

'Now,' said Charlie, as he pulled the knob and dropped the first plate, 'now you take one of me. Me and Aunt Mabel together.' So saying, he handed his uncle the camera and stood beside his aunt with a perky, self-conscious air.

Mr Muffle pressed the bulb.

'Now I'll take one of the Euston Road,' said he, as a happy thought struck him. 'I've often thought I'd like one took just from this very door. But 'ow do you shift the plates?'

His nephew showed him, and they shook the second plate down. He looked through the viewfinder and saw a little man talking to a policeman in the near foreground, a hansom cab bowling along towards him, and two horse buses drawn up on the further side of the street. The advertisement on the side of the nearer bus caught his eye:

HENRY IRVING IN 'OTHELLO'

He pressed the bulb once again, and, turning to the others: 'But who's a-going to develop them?' he asked.

'The chemist over the way,' replied his nephew. 'I asked him.'

'What'll *that* cost?' demanded his aunt, sharply.

'Ooo, not much.'

Next morning, after breakfast, Charlie went across to the chemist, and returned in a few moments running.

'Look here!' he said, bursting into the parlour. 'This *is* a go! It is a funny camera and no mistake. They've come out all wrong. It's took something altogether different!'

'What do you mean?' said his uncle, stretching out a buttery thumb and forefinger. He looked closely at the print for a few moments, and then he jumped up with an exclamation, and, pushing the boy aside, he gazed incredulously at the other two photographs on the table.

'Aunt Mabel!' cried Charlie up the stair. 'Aunt Mabel, come quickly. The photos have come out mighty queer. You haven't come out at all! And uncle——'

Soon all three of them were staring in blank amazement. In the first photograph Mr Muffle was standing against the shop by himself. On his face a placid, comfortable expression which looked completely unfamiliar to him. He had filled out, apparently, and though he looked perfectly well and happy, and very much better dressed, he seemed to have aged considerably. The cut of his coat and the style of his collar and tie struck them as particularly odd. The name over the shop, above his head, was no longer R. Muffle, but E. Watson. Also the three golden balls were no longer to be seen. The second photograph was that of a young man of about twenty-eight, in overalls, with a large spanner in one hand.

'Why! It's you, Charlie!'

'Can't be me. And yet it *do* seem to be like me some'ow.' And then: 'I say!' in an awestruck tone, 'he's lost two fingers off his left hand.'

Of the third photograph they could make neither head nor tail at first. It appeared to be of a wide, straight thoroughfare completely unknown to them. There were a large number of odd-looking, small, square vehicles, unlike anything they had ever seen before. In the near foreground was a police inspector talking to a man in a bath-chair. On the opposite side of the street there were two omnibuses without horses, on whose sides was an advertisement which stood out in clear letters:

BEERBOHM TREE IN '*JULIUS CÆSAR*'

'Them things,' said Mr Muffle, in a bewildered voice, 'looks like motor-cars, but I'm sure I never seed one that shape before! And what a lot of them! Buses, too.'

'There's the corner of St Pancras!' cried his wife, pointing her finger at it. 'But whatever's that huge building opposite to it? I never saw *that* before.'

'It's the Euston Road,' said Charlie.

'Where's that camera?'

Charlie produced it.

Mr Muffle took it gingerly over to the window of the parlour. Suddenly he gave a little gasp. On the side of the camera was a circle of metal like a clock-face, about two inches in diameter. So discoloured was it that it was hardly distinguishable from the faded leather round it. He rubbed it briskly with his sleeve. The other two crowded round him.

'Whatever are all those figures?' said Charlie. 'And look, there's a little arrow pointing. You can move it round with your finger.'

Mr Muffle did so.

'I wonder what it's for?' he said.

Charlie's face glowed suddenly with inspiration.

'Where was the arrow? What figure was the arrow against when we took the photos?' he asked, in a hushed voice.

'Fourteen, I think,' said his uncle. And then: 'Yes, fourteen.'

'Fourteen *years*!' said Charlie.

'What do you mean—years?' said his aunt, quickly. 'And why didn't I come out in the photos, anyway?'

Something dawned on Mr Muffle.

'Because you're——' said he, and stopped.

There was a long pause. And then she said, looking at the photograph of her husband:

'But you look so well—and happy—Robin.'

There was a step at the door. Charlie turned and saw the chemist from across the road. He was a cheerful-looking man about thirty-five, with a pale moustache.

'Mind if I have another look at those photos I developed?' he asked.

The others said nothing. For a long time he scrutinized the photograph of the Euston Road. Then he picked up the camera and, opening it, he put his hand inside and felt about.

'This arrow in the disc of figures doesn't seem to be connected with anything. Nothing comes through from outside,' he said, at last.

'It's *impossible*,' said Mr Muffle, with an air of finality.

'Nothing is impossible,' said the chemist.

'Well, you developed them,' said Mrs Muffle, accusingly.

'But I didn't take them,' said the chemist. 'And what I want you to let me do is to make a few experiments myself. Now I'll go across to my place and load the camera up full of new plates, and then we'll take six photographs, turning the arrow on five figures each time. Ten—fifteen—twenty——'

'Thirty years,' murmured Mrs Muffle to herself. 'I don't believe it. I *won't* believe it! To think you paid five shillings for this—this——'

The chemist returned almost at once with the camera in his hand.

'Come out in the street,' he said, in an excited voice.

Charlie eyed him open-mouthed. Handing the camera to Mr Muffle, the chemist said:

'Now you take six photos of me, and turn the arrow to five the first time, ten the next time, and so on.'

'Aren't you afraid?' said Mrs Muffle.

'Not me!' said the chemist, stuffing his hands into his trouser pockets. But for all that his face was pale.

With a trembling hand Mr Muffle prepared to do as he was asked. But his nephew took the camera from him, saying:

'You can't do it like that, uncle, you're shaking so.'

After peering once quickly through the viewfinder, Charlie pressed the bulb six times, dropping a plate and turning the arrow on five points between each.

'Right,' said the chemist, taking the camera from him. 'I sha'n't be long.'

'Isn't there room for us in your darkroom?' asked Mr Muffle, eagerly.

'I say! Yes, *is* there?' chimed in Charlie.

'Come along,' said the chemist, and they crossed the road.

'I am sure it can't be right, and I don't believe it, anyway,' muttered Mrs Muffle, turning back into the shop.

However, she was unable to think of anything else. In about a quarter of an hour she locked the front door and followed them across the road to the chemist's shop.

'Where are you?' She raised her voice slightly.

Following the sound of talking which she heard, she went through into the back of the shop. She came to a door which was shut. From the other side of this came the chemist's voice.

'And now the last one,' he said, and his voice was full of emotion.

She waited in silence.

Then she heard Charlie say, 'It's coming out. You're not there!'

For a long time there was only the sound of the plate clicking against the side of the dish as the chemist tilted it.

'Yes, you *are* there; you're sitting down.'

'Hooray!' shouted the chemist. 'I'm sixty-five! And don't I look prosperous just?'

The door opened.

'They're fixing,' he said, on seeing Mrs Muffle. 'I'll show you them in a moment.'

'Then it *is* true,' she said, quietly.

Soon they were all looking at the wet plates as the chemist held them up for a minute to the light before dropping them into clean water. Each one showed him slightly older, and in the third the name over the Muffles' shop had changed to Watson, and the three golden balls had gone. The window was full of books.

'I'm fifty there,' said the chemist.

'What I want to know,' said Mr Muffle, 'is what I'm doing then, if a chap called Watson has got the shop. Oh, by the way, though, I'm fifty-four then. But however did I come to look so rich?'

'It won't be your own doing, you may be sure,' said his wife.

The chemist held up the last three one by one.

'And see,' he said at the last one, 'I'm sixty-five there. I've a good mind to take another six.'

'Which would be tempting Providence,' said Mrs Muffle.

'Tempting your grandmother!' he responded cheerfully. 'That would only bring me to ninety-four.'

'Take a dozen,' suggested Charlie, facetiously.

'You're a Noptimist!' laughed the chemist.

*

That day in the parlour behind the Muffles' shop the four of them could think and talk of nothing else. The chemist was full of tremendous suggestions. At first he was all for advertising the camera's capabilities, and charging so much a head to show people in black-and-white exactly what their fate would be. And then, on second thoughts, he came to the conclusion that it would be better to continue the experiments for a while. For, as Mr Muffle pointed out, the camera did not really belong to them. The chemist replied that, if ever the owner returned to redeem it, they might buy it from him. No sum appeared to him too large for this purpose.

'Of course, telling people the future——Well, we can't do it,' reflected the chemist.

'That's exactly what we *can* do,' said Mr Muffle.

'No; I mean it's illegal.'

And then he went off on the most fantastic flights of imagination.

'We could take photographs of places centuries and centuries ahead, and see exactly what's going to happen. What kind of buildings—architecture—feats of engineering—means of transport—people's clothes. Why,' he cried, 'we could take a photo of the end of the world!'

'Don't be blasphemous,' said Mrs Muffle. 'It would go off bang as a judgement, if you did. Besides, what's all this "we"? It isn't your camera, as I know of.'

'Well, it isn't ours either,' interpolated Mr Muffle.

The chemist judiciously passed this point over.

'It's queer,' he went on. 'The camera shows us what we're going to become——'

'Of course, the camera cannot lie,' snorted Mrs Muffle, in parenthesis.

'And perhaps,' continued the chemist, 'the camera is going to be the means by which we achieve fortune. When we've formed the company—Prophecies, Limited; or Forewarned Fore-armed Trust.'

'Second Sight Syndicate!' cried Mr Muffle, fired by the other's enthusiasm.

The chemist got up and strode about the room.

'By a series of photographs taken according to a calculated time and place we shall be able to foretell social changes, evolutions, revolutions, falls of Governments, wars and their results. Can't you see a series of photographs taken in the House of Commons,

showing who'll be sitting on what benches ten, twenty, forty years
hence? How prices alter from the effect of war! By photographing
shop windows with ticketed objects. If the prices on the tickets
come out double—treble what they are at present, we shall know
that once again England has won a war! We shall be able to go to
Prime Ministers and charge them fabulous sums for photographs of
the House of Commons Register three years hence.'

Mr Muffle objected.

'What would be the good,' he reasoned, 'of showing anybody
anything? We might show one man how he would die by the
hangman's rope, but that wouldn't enable him to avoid it. If it did,
the photo wouldn't be true. It would be merely a suggestion as to
what might happen. We might demonstrate to any number of
people the actual, precise, and detailed result of a revolution that
was inevitably going to take place. Famine—waste—disease—
rioting. But in so much as it was inevitable, it would 'ave to 'appen,
and I'm sure nobody would be any better for the knowing of it.
The politicians could change their way of going on as much as they
pleased, but if what the camera said was going to 'appen *was* going
to 'appen, what they did would be what they would have done in
any case.'

The chemist waved him to silence with an exasperated sweep of
the arm.

'As if those were the only possibilities,' he said. 'Think how we
might get the whole history of the world, backwards and forwards
from beginning to end!'

'The arrow won't go backwards,' said Mr Muffle. 'You can only
push it round one way. From nought right round to nought again.
Besides which, I'm positive it ain't no good knowing the future
unless it's pleasant.'

'Well,' responded the chemist, 'we could take people's photos—
at a price—and we could decide when we developed them whether
their future was a happy one or not. And if it wasn't, why, we
needn't show 'em.'

'That would be worse than showing them!' ejaculated Mrs Muffle.
'Then they'd be quite sure it was bad, only they wouldn't know *how*
bad it was!'

'Anyway,' said the chemist, 'whether it benefits me or not, I'm
going to know all about the future. I am going to take thousands

and thousands of photos. There must be lots of people with money
who would be quite willing to pay and never consider whether it
would do them any good or not. Think of a photograph of New
York or Paris in the year 3000! Perhaps the Channel with bridges
across it—flying machines as big as liners—a new kind of animal—
or even of the Euston Road in five hundred years' time! Why, man!
Only think——'

The shop bell rang.

'Run and see what they want, Charlie,' said his aunt.

Charlie returned with a pawnticket and handed it to his uncle.

Muttering that he would not be a moment, Mr Muffle went into
the shop. In answer to an excited shout, the three of them followed
him a moment later.

'It's HIM! It's HIM!' said Mr Muffle, clutching the chemist's
arm.

The chemist pulled himself together.

'I've took rather a fancy to your camera,' he said to the miserable-
looking individual. 'How'd you like to sell it me for a reasonable
price?'

'I don't want to sell it,' replied the other, in a sad voice.

'Well,' said the chemist, a little breathlessly, 'what would you say
to five pounds? Come, now!'

'I don't want to sell it,' repeated the other.

'Wouldn't you sell it—reelly—not at all?' urged Mr Muffle,
leaning over the counter with his hands clasped and his eyes shining.

'You've got my ticket,' said the sad-looking man, 'and here's the
money. Give me the camera.'

'He's perfectly right,' said Mrs Muffle, in a firm voice, and she
handed him the camera.

'You shut your mouth!' said the chemist. And then to Mr Muffle:
'We can't—we *mustn't* let it go! We must make him a partner or
something. We must hire it. Look here,' he continued, turning to
the stranger, 'do you know what that camera of yours will do?'

The sad-looking man turned towards them with his hand on the
door.

'If you've been using it,' he said, quietly, 'well, you've been using
it, that's all. Good afternoon.'

He stepped out into the street.

The offer of some vast sum framed itself on Mr Muffle's silent lips. For a moment they gazed at each other motionless. Then Mrs Muffle picked up the money and put it in the till. Suddenly the chemist was galvanized into action.

'I must follow him!' he shouted, and rushed to the door.

He looked wildly up and down the Euston Road, where the heavy afternoon traffic was rumbling by.

But the sad-faced man had disappeared.

Cavalanci's Curse

Henry A. Hering

1675

CAVALANCI DA SALÒ was one day in his workshop opposite the old Palace of the Podestà in Brescia. On the shelves around were numerous examples of his work, their rich gold varnish, for which he was afterwards so famous, glistening in the sunlight. But Cavalanci sat on a bench disconsolate.

'Diavolo,' he at length exclaimed, letting a half-purfled scroll fall unheeded from his hand, 'is this to be the end of Brescian dreams? Here is music lying dead, enough to charm the ears of half Italy, and yet, forsooth, he who wants viol or violin must needs hasten to Cremona for the imitations of the Amati, Guarneri, or of Antonio Stradivari. Times are indeed changed that I, Gasparo's grandson, must offer my work and find no purchasers, unless it be the mountebanks of the village fairs. Truly, I pay dearly for a father's folly. Instead of roaming Western seas, why stayed he not at home to earn the mantle which fell on Maggini's shoulders, from whom I had to learn all a father should have taught? And his son Carlo, in like manner, is content to merce flimsy silk rather than pursue immortal work. We are ingrates here, while in Cremona loyalty, at any rate, thrives, and son succeeds father to Brescian hurt.'

Then he rose and paced the room savagely, kicking what tools or wood fell in his way.

'But what mends it,' he muttered, 'mouthing of fallen hopes? Present claims are more urgent. Sixteen lire were due to Carlo for rent more than a month ago. His grace expires tomorrow, and well

I know no memories of the past will stay his hand. My stock and tools alone are worth a hundred lire; therefore old Tubal would give me ten. Perchance I might haggle the whole sixteen, and then—Corpo di Bacco, that it should come to this!—Gasparo's grandson an outcast, while Guarneri and Stradivari, base copiers, flourish! By all that is unholy, I swear I'd sell my soul to the Evil One himself could I but outdo them in fame.'

There was a blinding flash of lightning, followed by a fearful thunder-peal, and then, sulphurous darkness filled the shop. When light came Cavalanci was conscious of the presence of another. He half-hoped, half-dreaded, to see the Devil on whom he had so impiously called—but it was seemingly only a chance customer. Yet it was afterwards said that he was something more, for Cavalanci paid his rent next day, the fame of his instruments increased forthwith, and he died a rich, though not a happy, man.

1875

'DEAR SIR,'—the letter ran—'We are instructed by Messrs Ware and Foster, executors under the will of the late Mr Josephus Wilson, to intimate to you that the testator bequeathed to you his violin. We are sending it you by special messenger herewith, and will thank you to sign inclosed acknowledgement of receipt.

'Yours respectfully,
'DANES AND DANES'

I handed the letter to Dawson.

'Well, I've heard of heaping coals of fire on your enemy's head,' he remarked, when he had read it, 'but I never came across such a remarkable instance of the operation as this. Are you going to take it?'

'Why not? I will accept it as the peace-offering for which it was obviously intended. As a matter of fact, a post-mortem reconciliation was the only one I would have agreed to. Yes, certainly I will take it.'

So I signed the receipt and accepted the bequest.

I undid the parcel and took the violin from its battered case.

'Why, it's as yellow as a guinea,' I exclaimed, in surprise; I had never seen such a light one.

'Wilson was uncommonly proud of the colour,' said Dawson, 'and he was simply infatuated with the instrument. Latterly they couldn't tear him away from it. He never would play it before anyone, though. That was another of his cranks. He used to shut himself up with it all day long, and play both it and the piano simultaneously.'

I expressed my doubts as to this possibility.

'At any rate, Wilson did it: I've heard him myself, though I never actually saw the operation.' Saying which, Dawson sat down on the stool and resumed the interrupted nocturne.

Then a remarkable thing happened. He had not played half-a-dozen chords before a long-drawn-out note came from the violin I was still fingering. I nearly dropped it in my amazement.

'Here, stop that,' said Dawson, wheeling round.

'I did not touch a string. It made that noise of itself.'

'Humbug! Don't do it again, that's all,' he replied, snappishly, resuming his interrupted piece.

Again, as he struck the keyboard, the violin sounded. Without stopping Dawson turned his head, and when he saw me a couple of yards away from the violin, his expression of annoyance changed to one of open-eyed amazement, for he was still playing the piano, and the notes that continued to proceed from the violin were in harmony with his piece.

He stopped suddenly, and with him the violin.

'Did you hear that?' he asked, in a scared voice.

I was too much astonished to reply, and we both stared at the instrument for some minutes in absolute silence.

'It's a sympathetic fiddle,' I said, at length, for the mere sake of saying something.

'It seems a bit that way,' replied Dawson, drily; 'but I never heard one so sympathetic as all that.'

He turned round to the piano and commenced afresh, and again the violin joined in. This time Dawson did not stop, and the duet continued in absolute harmony.

I bent over the instrument. The varnish seemed brighter than before. The sun glinted topaz lights upon it, with changing gleams of purple and brown; the strings quivered as though touched by an unseen bow. I felt a cold shiver run down my spine as I watched; it was altogether too uncanny.

The piano stopped: simultaneously the violin. Dawson wheeled round and gazed at it.

'Well, of all the extraordinary things!' he ejaculated. 'What on earth does it mean?'

'Let's see if it will follow me,' I said, irrelevantly, taking his seat.

Once I learnt to play on the piano, and I still remember the treble of two tunes—'Haydn's Surprise' and 'God bless the Prince of Wales'. I played the first, but the violin remained impassive. Maybe the bass I improvised puzzled it: at any rate, it did not join in. Then I tried the second air, and with no better success. Then Dawson played with his right hand only, and it struck in at once.

'It isn't particularly respectful to its owner,' I remarked. 'It seems to me, Dawson, this fiddle has taken an altogether unnecessary liking for you. Wilson should have left it to you instead.'

'If you want to part with it I shall be glad to offer it a home,' said Dawson with what appeared to me indelicate haste.

'You can take it away now, Dawson,' I rejoined. 'I want no unwilling visitor here.'

He seemed singularly pleased with the present, and he left me that evening with the fiddle-case in his hand.

Immediately after this I made a long foreign tour, and it was nearly twelve months before I saw him again. I wrote advising him of my return, and asked him to look me up, but as he neither did so nor wrote, I called upon him.

He lived in rooms in Bloomsbury. The servant told me he was in, but added that she did not think he would see me.

'Is he ill?' I asked.

'No, sir, but he's playing; and he won't ever see anyone then.'

This was a new development in his character. Telling the servant it would be all right, I made my way upstairs.

Yes, Dawson was undoubtedly playing, and someone was helping him, for there were piano and violin.

I tapped and then turned the handle, but the door was locked. I knocked loudly and called to Dawson to open it.

There was a moment's pause—or rather the piano stopped, but the violin went on.

'Who's there?' shouted Dawson, in a peevish voice.

'Saunders!'

'Wait a minute,' was the curt reply; and on the piano galloped as if to overtake its companion. I don't think it accomplished this, for the violin shrieked as if in anger at the delay, and the piano rushed on blindly and apologetically. Then in a fierce crescendo of disgust the fiddle ceased. The piano put on the brake, slowed down, and stopped.

The door opened and Dawson bade me enter. He was alone.

'Where's your friend?' I asked; and then, catching sight of a yellow violin on the table, I suddenly remembered: I had just been listening to another duet between Dawson and my self-acting legacy.

Dawson made no reply, but sank into a chair and wiped the perspiration from his face with trembling hands. He seemed altogether out of condition.

'What's the matter, old man?' I asked. 'You don't seem well.'

Dawson gloomily pointed to the fiddle.

'That's what's the matter,' he replied, with a ghastly smile.

'What, my sympathetic fiddle? You don't mean to say you've had too much of it already? I'll take it back if you don't like it.'

'You can't take it back. It's a Cavalanci.'

'Well, it won't bite, will it?'

'When a man once gets a Cavalanci and plays to it, it sticks to him like the Old Man of the Sea, and no power on earth can take it away from him,' said Dawson, sententiously.

'Humbug!'

'Look at the wreck I am,' he replied. 'There's no humbug about that, is there? And I've only the Cavalanci to thank for it.'

'You do look bad,' I admitted. 'But tell me all about it. What do you mean by a Cavalanci?'

Dawson leaned back in his chair and gazed at the ceiling.

'Cavalanci,' said he, slowly, 'was a competitor of Stradivarius, and he determined to outshine his rival. According to the legend, which I for one now implicitly believe, he sold his soul to the Devil to gain his ends. His instruments became all the rage, till it was found that their owners invariably went mad, as I am going. Then the demand ceased and bonfires were made of them whenever possible. I have learnt that there are only four extant now, and this cursed thing is one of them.'

'Why not burn that as well, if it annoys you?'

'I dare not. Its owner can only destroy his Cavalanci on his death-bed. Wilson could have done it, but as he owed you a grudge he passed it on to you instead. Would to Heaven you'd been the first to play in its diabolic presence.'

'I'll destroy it, if you won't,' I said. I grabbed at it, and was about to break it across my knee when Dawson sprang forward with a terrible cry.

'No, no, Saunders. You'd kill me if you did it.' He caught the instrument in his hands and huddled it to him as if it were a child.

It was a painful spectacle. I watched him pityingly.

'Saunders,' he said, at length, 'you don't know what a time of it I've had since I got hold of this infernal thing.'

'You seemed pleased enough to get it at the time.'

'And so I was. It seemed scarcely credible, but as I played with the thing in your room, an overwhelming desire for possession came over me. I pretty well asked for it, and if you had refused to give it me, I think I should have taken it by main force. I simply craved for that fiddle.'

'Then if you wanted it so badly, why does its possession worry you?'

'Because, Saunders, it makes my life a perfect misery. Man, I'm its slave. It takes the lead now. When it wishes to play—and it is always wishing it—I have to accompany it wherever I am. Distance makes no difference, and I have to play till it is satisfied. I found that out about a week after I got it. I was at the Venables'. In the middle of dinner I felt a terrible longing stealing over me. I wanted to play. I tried to control myself, but play I must or go mad. Scarcely apologizing, I left the table, ran into the drawing-room, and sat down at the piano. I don't know what I played, but the moment my fingers touched the keys I was filled with a feeling of content and delight. I was still playing when the ladies entered. Mrs Venables must have thought me mad, for I did not stop. She sent for her husband, who came and asked me to return to the table. I nodded to him and went on. Suddenly my feelings changed, and I was only aware that I was making a terrible fool of myself. The full force of my social enormity fell upon me, and, livid with confusion, I made some incoherent apology and fled from the house.

'From that night my reputation for eccentricity was firmly established, and I have added to it from time to time, for I am never safe, and can go nowhere without the danger of a similar occurrence. The following Sunday I went to the Wilmers'. There were plenty of delightful people there, and for a time I forgot my wretched position. Suddenly the same mad impulse came over me. There was a long-haired German at the piano, but it didn't matter. I flicked him off the stool, and, surrounded by a gaping crowd, went through Heaven knows what composition. But I did not care: I was happy. Then when my master was satisfied again the terrible awakening came, and I flung myself out of the room like a madman—they all thought I was. It's just fiendish, Saunders. I rarely can go anywhere without making a fool of myself. It's just maddening to think of the ignominy of it all.'

'But, my dear chap, why don't you lose it? Put it in an express train, with a fictitious address, and wash your hands of it.'

'I've tried it,' said Dawson, wearily. 'Before I knew all I have since learnt from bitter experience, I packed it off by P&O boat, addressed to the Grand Llama of Tibet. I thought he might be able to deal with it if he ever got it. I suffered agonies from the separation, and it must have been very lively on the journey. For I had to play to it just the same. And then, after all, it came back to me marked "Gone—Left no address", and I don't know what I hadn't to pay for carriage. How they found out the sender, goodness only knows. I have left it in trains, but it *never fails* to come back, and I have always suffered during its absence. I took it to a pawnshop and destroyed the ticket, but the yearning for it was so fearful I had to get it out by making a false declaration about the ticket before a magistrate. I can't bear to be away from it. When I play its accompaniments a feeling of intense happiness and satisfaction steals over me, but afterwards the sense of the ignominy of it all is terrible. I can do nothing in life but minister to the caprices of a Cavalanci violin—and finally go crazy.'

Just as he ended there was a tap at the door, and the servant appeared with a parcel. It was a disreputable-looking object. The paper was ragged and dirty, the string knotted and loosely tied.

Dawson looked at it doubtfully.

'Are you sure it's for me?' he asked. 'Who brought it?'

'He looked like a circus man, sir,' replied the maid, 'and he was most particular in saying it was for you.'

'A circus man,' muttered Dawson, as he tore off the wrapper. A violin-case was exposed to view. He opened it, and then gave vent to a yell of dismay. I looked at the contents. It was a yellow violin.

'What, another Cavalanci!' I exclaimed.

'It looks like it,' said Dawson, bitterly. 'One's quite enough for any family. I don't know to whom I'm indebted for this particular attention, but I should like to wring his precious neck.' Then he banged the lid to.

'Here, Saunders,' said he, 'you can do me this good turn at any rate. Take this outside—leave it in a 'bus or pitch it into a dustbin; do anything you like with it, only take it away, and it will work its passage to its owner. But do it at once. I may have to play any minute to satisfy my own fiddle, and I don't know what complication would result. Take it, man, this minute.'

To satisfy him I took hold of the thing, put on my hat and opened the door. I nearly fell over the servant, who was about to knock; behind her was a tall, fur-coated man whom I did not remember to have seen before. And, good heavens! in his hand was a violin-case! The place seemed infested with fiddles.

I was brushing past him, but he laid a heavy hand on my shoulder and forced me back into the room. He himself followed, closed the door, and placed himself before it.

'Excuse my roughness, sir,' said he, with a strong nasal twang, 'but air you James Dawson?'

'No,' I replied: 'that's the gentleman,' pointing to Dawson, who was standing with eyes staring out of his head, fixed on the stranger's violin-case.

'Don't stay, Saunders,' he almost shrieked, 'take it away. There's not a moment to be lost.'

But the newcomer effectually barred the way.

Dawson was almost beside himself. He grabbed hold of the poker, but the stranger coolly threw his case on the table and from his breast produced a tiny revolver.

'Two can play at that pertic'ler game, sir,' said he, 'and I reckon the betting's on my side today.'

And there we stood.

'Perhaps you'll kindly explain what you mean by this intrusion?' I said, hotly.

'No objection at all,' said the American, for so I judged him to be. 'I'd have done so at once if James Dawson hadn't been so demonstrative. You see, Colonel, it's thish-yer way. That infernal cuss, Cavalanci——'

Again the door opened, and this time a heavily muffled foreigner with spectacles and long hair appeared, and, ye gods! he also had a violin-case.

'Goot,' said the latest arrival, 'I see dat I am joost in de nick off time. Goot evenings, shentlemens all,' and with this he placed his case and hat on the table and proceeded to divest himself of his wraps.

'Bravo,' said the Yankee, 'I'm glad to see you, Bloomstein. We are now complete—the four extant Cavalanci and the four owners.'

'I'm not an owner,' I said, in alarm, for I did not at all like the turn things were taking.

'You're the Baboo from Benares, ain't you?' asked the American.

'No, sir, I'm not. I'm a friend of Mr Dawson. I was simply calling upon him, and I think I'll go now. I don't wish to intrude on your proceedings.'

'No, you don't, sir,' said he, turning the key in the door and pocketing it. 'Not till I'm clear on the subject. Whose fiddle's that?' pointing to the one I held.

'It's just come in a parcel,' said I.

'Allow me to look at it, please,' said the Yankee, still toying with his revolver.

He placed the case on the table, opened it, and drew forth the violin. Underneath it was a letter.

'Ah, thishyer's thingumy's fist,' said he, 'and no doubt it will explain. Here, Colonel, you look like an Oriental scholar, so, perhaps, you'll decipher it.' And he handed me the letter.

The handwriting was like a copy-book heading, but the composition was peculiar. This is what I read:

'Honoured Sir—It mortifies me deeply not to intrude at happy conversazione. I have made blue in the Wiski of Scotchland the rupees obligingly forwarded so there is no ability in me to pay for a transit. Today the Gangees receives a solid addition but my fiddle of spanking yellow will reach you timely by a holy gentleman of Shoreditch.—Faithful and truly,

DONNERGEE JUGGERNAUT.'

'The cur!' exclaimed the Yankee, when I had finished reading this singular epistle. 'Why didn't he destroy his Cavalanci before he committed suicide instead of passing it on here? Someone will have to own it or the whole scheme will fall through. Here, Colonel,' addressing me, 'you're the odd man out. You've got to take possession of that Cavalanci.'

'I beg to decline the honour,' I replied, firmly.

The Yankee lifted his revolver threateningly.

'Nein, nein,' broke in the German, 'do not shet his blood. Egsblain de matter to de shentlemans und he vill understand.'

'Right,' said the Yankee, seating himself astride of a chair, with his back to the door, revolver still in hand. 'It's thishyer way, and maybe if I had told you at first I should have had a warmer reception from James Dawson. My name is Masters—Simpson K. Masters, of Tontine, Dak. I am the unfortunate owner of this instrument, and I need hardly tell you what its possession entails.'

A groan broke from the German. 'Ja, ja; dat is so,' he said.

'It was left me about five years ago by a lady who had lost her breach of promise action against me, and when I fully realized that I should probably grow woolly if I could not get rid of it, I determined to devote what leisure the infernal instrument left me to making inquiries about Cavalanci and his curse—for, as most poisons have their antidote, I reckoned the same arrangement held good for curses. I spent all last year at Brescia, where these things were manufactured. I bought up every vestige of a relic of Cavalanci, took his shop for a spell of 999 years, and was prepared to stay my lease out unless I got what I wanted. I searched every corner and cranny of that-air shop after the manner prescribed by the late E. A. Poe. I spent days in the chimneys, and wasted a power of time in the roof; I took his old tester-bed to bits, and probed every inch of its wood; and worked at the anatomy of the building till the authorities sent word it was likely to fall, but all to no purpose.

'I had about given up hope when I chanced upon a lineal descendant of Cavalanci—a decayed Italian nobleman in the retail macaroni business. From him I learnt of the existence of a tradition that Cavalanci on his death-bed was annoyed to think of the trouble he had started, and got the Devil to promise that, when a combined band of all his fiddles played a certain air, the Curse should be removed. Why the Old Gentleman agreed to this arrangement my informant couldn't guess, unless he did it to soothe his friend's last moments, no doubt feeling pretty certain that the combined band would never play till he'd got a lot of fun out of the Curse.

220 *Henry A. Hering*

'It sounded like a cock-and-bull tale, but the Italian nobleman seemed so certain about it, and was so much hurt when I doubted him, that I sort of began to believe in it myself. As luck had it, I had discovered a roll of manuscript music up the shop chimney, of which I had taken no pertic'ler account, but which now assumed considerable importance. As I had no piano handy in those days, I had been playing to my fiddle on a concertina, and it rather seemed to take to the instrument; so the very next time it wanted me to accompany it, I started to work through that bunch of tunes on the same article. Now, whether it was the concertina it suddenly took a dislike to, or whether the tunes didn't agree with it, I don't pretend to say, but it turned sulky and wouldn't take a hand in noway, that is until I came to one pertic'ler air. It was a weird affair—a sort of mixture of the "Dead March in Saul" and "Hail, Columbia!" It struck in from the first note in a nasty nagging way, and if ever a fiddle played unwillingly that one did. It lagged behind and put in commas and full-stops where they were not wanted, and in every other bar it screeched out a note of exclamation that wasn't down in my part. But I took it out of that Cavalanci, gentlemen, and made it sit up, for when I'd run through the ditty I started it all over again, and that instrument followed me like a whipped cur. And then another remarkable thing happened. It changed colour—from yellow to orange and then to a dirty brown. I guess I'd touched it up at last; and when I saw this I closed the concert and gave that Italian nobleman an order for macaroni that surprised him.

'Although it regained its old colour, I was firmly convinced from the behaviour of my violin that the nobleman was right, and that if I could get the whole extant Cavalanci together the Curse could be broken; and the last few months I have spent in tracing Bloomstein, the Baboo, and our friend James Dawson, and in making arrangements for this happy meeting. I thought it better to keep the notion from you, James, until now, for fear of incredulity on your part. And now, Colonel,' turning to me, 'you must assume possession of that Baboo's fiddle. It won't take ten minutes to break that-air Curse.'

'But if it doesn't break?' I urged.

'It will break,' said Simpson K. Masters.

'Saunders,' said Dawson, who had worked himself up into a state of great excitement, 'I implore you to help us destroy this Curse.

You owe it to me to do so, for it's all through you I got into the trouble at all.'

'I'm awfully sorry, Dawson,' I replied, 'but I cannot. I was very strictly brought up, and my family would not like me to mix myself up in anything of this nature. You must respect my scruples.'

'And you must respect this, sir,' said the Yankee, holding his revolver at an extremely unpleasant angle.

There was no help for it. 'All right,' I said, 'I'll do it for my old friend Dawson's sake. Nothing else would have induced me. But I can't play any instrument,' I added, triumphantly.

'Mein Gott!' exclaimed the German.

'Why, I have heard you play "Haydn's Surprise",' said Dawson.

'Only on one finger,' I modestly urged.

'Try it, sir, with your toes if you like,' said the Yankee. 'And I shall be surprised if that fiddle don't respond. A Cavalanci ain't pertic'ler when it wants an owner.'

I sat down at the piano and played what I knew of the air. A shadow of despair came over Dawson's face, and the German put his fingers in his ears, but Simpson K. Masters encouraged me to persevere.

'Keep it up, Colonel,' said he. 'Put the pedal on, it'll help you round the corners.'

Before I had played a dozen notes a sound came from the table.

'Hurrah!' cried Dawson.

'The Baboo's fiddle has bit,' said Simpson K. Masters.

Sure enough the violin had joined in, and I turned cold at the thought that I was now the owner of a Cavalanci violin.

I played all I knew of the air and then stopped. The violin ceased as well.

'It would not let you off so easily in a week or two, Colonel,' said the Yankee, grimly. 'Now, gentlemen, here we are—the four extant Cavalanci and the four owners. All we have to do is to run through Cavalanci's Antidote and our troubles are over.'

With eager impatience Dawson sat down at the piano, the German produced a flageolet, and Masters a flute.

'What am I to play?' said I, in dismay. 'You mustn't leave me out.'

'Haven't you got anything, James?' said the Yankee. 'A drum would do.'

'I've nothing that I know of,' replied Dawson.

'Then we must send out for something.'

'I have it,' said Dawson. 'I bought a triangle some years ago, and ought to have it still.'

'A driangle—goot!' said Mr Bloomstein, and Masters nodded his satisfaction.

After some little delay the triangle was found, and when I had received a few instructions on the manipulation of this simple instrument Dawson sat down, and the quartet—or rather octet—commenced.

I don't think it was a success from a musical point of view, for we were all excited. Even the flute was off-colour. Still, we hung together pretty well, and stuck to the notes as well as we could. I tapped my triangle with considerable effect.

The four Cavalanci joined in from the first note. It was a weird and mournful composition, and the violins kept up the pathos of the thing with remarkable effect. It was like the prolonged wail of a soul in torment, with sudden outbursts of Satanic joviality. Our feelings were strung to the highest pitch, for we were playing for our lives. The sweat rolled off Bloomstein's face, and Dawson's hands trembled like aspen leaves. Simpson K. Masters tried to appear unconcerned—and failed.

The others were intent on the notes, but as I played from ear I was able to observe the fiddles. I could feel my heart thumping as I watched them. Would the 'Antidote' act, or was it all a delusion of the Yankee's? Was I not saddled for life with a fearful monstrosity which would finally undermine my reason?

Ha! it was touching them. Masters was right. They were changing colour! They were a rich yellow when we started, but with every bar their hue deepened through varying shades of orange, brown, walnut, darker, darker still, till at last four coal-black violins lay upon the table. As the final bars came their notes shrieked out as if in terrible protest, and as the last chord was struck sixteen strings snapped with one crack.

'Gentlemen,' said the Yankee, 'I guess Signor Cavalanci's Curse is off.'

The Queer Story of Brownlow's Newspaper

H. G. Wells

I CALL this a Queer Story because it is a story without an explanation. When I first heard it, in scraps, from Brownlow I found it queer and incredible. But—it refuses to remain incredible. After resisting and then questioning and scrutinizing and falling back before the evidence, after rejecting all his evidence as an elaborate mystification and refusing to hear any more about it, and then being drawn to reconsider it by an irresistible curiosity and so going through it all again, I have been forced to the conclusion that Brownlow, so far as he can tell the truth, has been telling the truth. But it remains queer truth, queer and exciting to the imagination. The more credible his story becomes the queerer it is. It troubles my mind. I am fevered by it, infected not with germs but with notes of interrogation and unsatisfied curiosity.

Brownlow is, I admit, a cheerful spirit. I have known him tell lies. But I have never known him do anything so elaborate and sustained as this affair, if it is a mystification, would have to be. He is incapable of anything so elaborate and sustained. He is too lazy and easy-going for anything of the sort. And he would have laughed. At some stage he would have laughed and given the whole thing away. He has nothing to gain by keeping it up. His honour is not in the case either way. And after all there is his bit of newspaper in evidence—and the scrap of an addressed wrapper. . . .

I realize it will damage this story for many readers that it opens with Brownlow in a state very definitely on the gayer side of sobriety. He was not in a mood for cool and calculated observation, much less for accurate record. He was seeing things in an exhilarated manner. He was disposed to see them and greet them cheerfully and let them slip by out of attention. The limitations of time and space lay lightly upon him. It was after midnight. He had been dining with friends.

I have enquired what friends—and satisfied myself upon one or two obvious possibilities of that dinner party. They were, he said to me, 'just friends. They hadn't anything to do with it.' I don't usually push past an assurance of this sort, but I made an exception in this case. I watched my man and took a chance of repeating the question. There was nothing out of the ordinary about that dinner party, unless it was the fact that it was an unusually good dinner party. The host was Redpath Baynes, the solicitor, and the dinner was in his house in St John's Wood. Gifford, of the *Evening Telegraph*, whom I know slightly, was, I found, present, and from him I got all I wanted to know. There was much bright and discursive talk and Brownlow had been inspired to give an imitation of his aunt, Lady Clitherholme, reproving an inconsiderate plumber during some rebuilding operations at Clitherholme. This early memory had been received with considerable merriment—he was always very good about his aunt, Lady Clitherholme—and Brownlow had departed obviously elated by this little social success and the general geniality of the occasion. Had they talked, I asked, about the Future, or Einstein, or J. W. Dunne, or any such high and serious topic at that party? They had not. Had they discussed the modern newspaper? No. There had been nobody whom one could call a practical joker at this party, and Brownlow had gone off alone in a taxi. That is what I was most desirous of knowing. He had been duly delivered by his taxi at the main entrance to Sussex Court.

Nothing untoward is to be recorded of his journey in the lift to the fifth floor of Sussex Court. The liftman on duty noted nothing exceptional. I asked if Brownlow said, 'Good-night'. The liftman does not remember. 'Usually he says Night O,' reflected the liftman—manifestly doing his best and with nothing particular to recall. And there the fruits of my enquiries about the condition of Brownlow on this particular evening conclude. The rest of the story comes directly from him. My investigations arrive only at this: he was certainly not drunk. But he was lifted a little out of our normal harsh and grinding contact with the immediate realities of existence. Life was glowing softly and warmly in him, and the unexpected could happen brightly, easily, and acceptably.

He went down the long passage with its red carpet, its clear light, and its occasional oaken doors, each with its artistic brass number. I have been down that passage with him on several occasions. It was his custom to enliven that corridor by raising his hat gravely as he passed each entrance, saluting his unknown and invisible neighbours, addressing them softly but distinctly by playful if sometimes slightly indecorous names of his own devising, expressing good wishes or paying them little compliments.

He came at last to his own door, number 49, and let himself in without serious difficulty. He switched on his hall light. Scattered on the polished oak floor and invading his Chinese carpet were a number of letters and circulars, the evening's mail. His parlourmaid-housekeeper, who slept in a room in another part of the building, had been taking her evening out, or these letters would have been gathered up and put on the desk in his bureau. As it was, they lay on the floor. He closed his door behind him or it closed of its own accord; he took off his coat and wrap, placed his hat on the head of the Greek charioteer whose bust adorns his hall, and set himself to pick up his letters.

This also he succeeded in doing without misadventure. He was a little annoyed to miss the *Evening Standard*. It is his custom, he says, to subscribe for the afternoon edition of the *Star* to read at tea-time and also for the final edition of the *Evening Standard* to turn over the last thing at night, if only on account of Low's cartoon. He gathered up all these envelopes and packets and took them with him into his little sitting-room. There he turned on the electric heater, mixed himself a weak whisky-and-soda, went to his bedroom to put on soft slippers and replace his smoking jacket by a frogged jacket of llama wool, returned to his sitting-room, lit a cigarette, and sat down in his armchair by the reading lamp to examine his correspondence. He recalls all these details very exactly. They were routines he had repeated scores of times.

Brownlow's is not a preoccupied mind; it goes out to things. He is one of those buoyant extroverts who open and read all their letters and circulars whenever they can get hold of them. In the daytime his secretary intercepts and deals with most of them, but at night he escapes from her control and does what he pleases, that is to say, he opens everything.

He ripped up various envelopes. There was a formal acknowledgement of a business letter he had dictated the day before, there was a letter from his solicitor asking for some details about a settlement he was making, there was an offer from some unknown gentleman with an aristocratic name to lend him money on his note of hand alone, and there was a notice about a proposed new wing to his club. 'Same old stuff,' he sighed. 'Same old stuff. What bores they all are!' He was always hoping, like every man who is proceeding across the plains of middle-age, that his correspondence would contain agreeable surprises—and it never did. Then, as he put it to me, *inter alia*, he picked up the remarkable newspaper.

It was different in appearance from an ordinary newspaper, but not so different as not to be recognizable as a newspaper, and he was surprised, he says, not to have observed it before. It was enclosed in a wrapper of pale green, but it was unstamped; apparently it had been delivered not by the postman, but by some other hand. (This wrapper still exists; I have seen it.) He had already torn it off before he noted that he was not the addressee.

For a moment or so he remained looking at this address, which struck him as just a little odd. It was printed in rather unusual type: 'Evan O'Hara Mr, Sussex Court 49.'

'Wrong name,' said Mr Brownlow; 'Right address. Rummy. Sussex Court 49. . . . 'Spose he's got *my Evening Standard* . . . 'Change no robbery.'

He put the torn wrapper with his unanswered letters and opened out the newspaper.

The title of the paper was printed in large slightly ornamental black-green letters that might have come from a kindred fount to that responsible for the address. But, as he read it, it was the *Evening Standard*! Or, at least, it was the 'Even Standrd'. 'Silly,' said Brownlow. 'It's some damn Irish paper. Can't spell—anything—these Irish. . . .'

He had, I think, a passing idea, suggested perhaps by the green wrapper and the green ink, that it was a lottery stunt from Dublin.

Still, if there was anything to read he meant to read it. He surveyed the front page. Across this ran a streamer headline: 'WILTON BORING REACHES SEVEN MILES: SUCCES ASSURED.'

'No,' said Brownlow. 'It must be oil. . . . Illiterate lot these oil chaps—leave out the "s" in "success".'

He held the paper down on his knee for a moment, reinforced himself by a drink, took and lit a second cigarette, and then leant back in his chair to take a dispassionate view of any oil-share pushing that might be afoot.

But it wasn't an affair of oil. It was, it began to dawn upon him, something stranger than oil. He found himself surveying a real evening newspaper, which was dealing, so far as he could see at the first onset, with the affairs of another world.

He had for a moment a feeling as though he and his armchair and his little sitting-room were afloat in a vast space and then it all seemed to become firm and solid again.

This thing in his hands was plainly and indisputably a printed newspaper. It was a little odd in its letterpress, and it didn't feel or rustle like ordinary paper, but newspaper it was. It was printed in either three or four columns—for the life of him he cannot remember which—and there were column headlines under the page streamer. It had a sort of art-nouveau affair at the bottom of one column that might be an advertisement (it showed a woman in an impossibly big hat), and in the upper left-hand corner was an unmistakable weather chart of Western Europe, with *coloured* iso-bars, or isotherms, or whatever they are, and the inscription: 'Tomorrow's Weather.'

And then he remarked the date. The date was November 10th, 1971!

'Steady on,' said Brownlow. 'Damitall! Steady on.'

He held the paper sideways, and then straight again. The date remained November 10th, 1971.

He got up in a state of immense perplexity and put the paper down. For a moment he felt a little afraid of it. He rubbed his forehead. 'Haven't been doing a Rip Van Winkle, by any chance, Brownlow, my boy?' he said. He picked up the paper again, walked out into his hall and looked at himself in the hall mirror. He was reassured to see no signs of advancing age, but the expression of mingled consternation and amazement upon his flushed face struck him suddenly as being undignified and unwarrantable. He laughed at himself, but not uncontrollably. Then he stared blankly at that familiar countenance. 'I must be half-way *tordu*,' he said, that being his habitual facetious translation of 'screwed'. On the console table was a little respectable-looking adjustable calendar bearing witness that the date was November 10th, 1931.

'D'you see?' he said, shaking the queer newspaper at it reproach-fully. 'I ought to have spotted you for a hoax ten minutes ago. 'Moosing trick, to say the least of it. I suppose they've made Low editor for a night, and he's had this idea. Eh?'

He felt he had been taken in, but that the joke was a good one. And, with quite unusual anticipations of entertainment, he returned to his armchair. A good idea it was, a paper forty years ahead. Good fun if it was well done. For a time nothing but the sounds of a newspaper being turned over and Brownlow's breathing can have broken the silence of the flat.

Regarded as an imaginative creation, he found the thing almost too well done. Every time he turned a page he expected the sheet to break out into laughter and give the whole thing away. But it did nothing of the kind. From being a mere quip, it became an immense and amusing, if perhaps a little over-elaborate, lark. And then, as a lark, it passed from stage to stage of incredibility until, as anything but the thing it professed to be, it was incredible altogether. It must have cost far more than an ordinary number. All sorts of colours were used, and suddenly he came upon illustrations that went beyond amazement; they were in the colours of reality. Never in all his life had he seen such colour printing—and the buildings and scenery and costumes in the pictures were strange. Strange and yet credible. They were colour photographs of actuality forty years from now. He could not believe anything else of them. Doubt could not exist in their presence.

His mind had swung back, away from the stunt-number idea altogether. This paper in his hand would not simply be costly beyond dreaming to produce. At any price it could not be produced. All this present world could not produce such an object as this paper he held in his hand. He was quite capable of realizing that.

He sat turning the sheet over and—quite mechanically—drinking whisky. His sceptical faculties were largely in suspense; the barriers of criticism were down. His mind could now accept the idea that he was reading a newspaper of forty years ahead without any further protest.

It had been addressed to Mr Evan O'Hara, and it had come to him. Well and good. This Evan O'Hara evidently knew how to get ahead of things. . . .

I doubt if at that time Brownlow found anything very wonderful in the situation.

Yet it was, it continues to be, a very wonderful situation. The wonder of it mounts to my head as I write. Only gradually have I been able to build up this picture of Brownlow turning over that miraculous sheet, so that I can believe it myself. And you will understand how, as the thing flickered between credibility and incredibility in my mind, I asked him, partly to justify or confute what he told me, and partly to satisfy a vast expanding and, at last, devouring curiosity: 'What was there in it? What did it have to say?' At the same time, I found myself trying to catch him out in his story, and also asking him for every particular he could give me.

What was there in it? In other words, What will the world be doing forty years from now? That was the stupendous scale of the vision, of which Brownlow was afforded a glimpse. The world forty years from now! I lie awake at nights thinking of all that paper might have revealed to us. Much it did reveal, but there is hardly a thing it reveals that does not change at once into a constellation of riddles. When first he told me about the thing I was—it is, I admit, an enormous pity—intensely sceptical. I asked him questions in what people call a 'nasty' manner. I was ready—as my manner made plain to him—to jump down his throat with 'But that's preposterous!' at the very first slip. And I had an engagement that carried me off at the end of half an hour.

But the thing had already got hold of my imagination, and I rang up Brownlow before tea-time, and was biting at this 'queer story' of his again. That afternoon he was sulking because of my morning's disbelief, and he told me very little. 'I was drunk and dreaming, I suppose,' he said. 'I'm beginning to doubt it all myself.' In the night it occurred to me for the first time that, if he was not allowed to tell and put on record what he had seen, he might become both confused and sceptical about it himself. Fancies might mix up with it. He might hedge and alter to get it more credible. Next day, therefore, I lunched and spent the afternoon with him, and arranged to go

down into Surrey for the weekend. I managed to dispel his huffiness
with me. My growing keenness restored his. There we set ourselves
in earnest, first of all to recover everything he could remember
about his newspaper and then to form some coherent idea of the
world about which it was telling.

It is perhaps a little banal to say we were not trained men for the
job. For who could be considered trained for such a job as we were
attempting? What facts was he to pick out as important and how
were they to be arranged? We wanted to know everything we could
about 1971; and the little facts and the big facts crowded on one
another and offended against each other.

The streamer headline across the page about that seven-mile
Wilton boring, is, to my mind, one of the most significant items
in the story. About that we are fairly clear. It referred, says
Brownlow, to a series of attempts to tap the supply of heat beneath
the surface of the earth. I asked various questions. 'It was *explained*,
y'know,' said Brownlow, and smiled and held out a hand with
twiddling fingers. 'It was explained all right. Old system, they
said, was to go down from a few hundred feet to a mile or so and
bring up coal and burn it. Go down a bit deeper, and there's no
need to bring up and burn anything. Just get heat itself straight-
away. Comes up of its own accord—under its own steam. See?
Simple.

'They were making a big fuss about it,' he added. 'It wasn't only
the streamer headline; there was a leading article in big type. What
was it headed? Ah! The Age of Combustion has Ended!'

Now that is plainly a very big event for mankind, caught in mid-
happening, November 10th, 1971. And the way in which Brownlow
describes it as being handled, shows clearly a world much more
preoccupied by economic essentials than the world of today, and
dealing with them on a larger scale and in a bolder spirit.

That excitement about tapping the central reservoirs of heat,
Brownlow was very definite, was not the only symptom of an
increase in practical economic interest and intelligence. There was
much more space given to scientific work and to inventions than is
given in any contemporary paper. There were diagrams and math-
ematical symbols, he says, but he did not look into them very
closely because he could not get the hang of them. '*Frightfully*
highbrow, some of it,' he said.

A more intelligent world for our grandchildren evidently, and also, as the pictures testified, a healthier and happier world.

'The fashions kept you looking,' said Brownlow, going off at a tangent, 'all coloured up as they were.'

'Were they elaborate?' I asked.

'Anything *but*,' he said.

His description of these costumes is vague. The people depicted in the social illustrations and in the advertisements seemed to have reduced body clothing—I mean things like vests, pants, socks and so forth—to a minimum. Breast and chest went bare. There seem to have been tremendously exaggerated wristlets, mostly on the left arm and going as far up as the elbow, provided with gadgets which served the purpose of pockets. Most of these armlets seem to have been very decorative, almost like little shields. And then, usually, there was an immense hat, often rolled up and carried in the hand, and long cloaks of the loveliest colours and evidently also of the most beautiful soft material, which either trailed from a sort of gorget or were gathered up and wrapped about the naked body, or were belted up or thrown over the shoulders.

There were a number of pictures of crowds from various parts of the world. 'The people looked fine,' said Brownlow. 'Prosperous you know, and upstanding. Some of the women—just lovely.'

My mind went off to India. What was happening in India?

Brownlow could not remember anything very much about India. 'Ankor,' said Brownlow. 'That's not India, is it?' There had been some sort of Carnival going on amidst 'perfectly lovely' buildings in the sunshine of Ankor.

The people there were brownish people but they were dressed very much like the people in other parts of the world.

I found the politician stirring in me. Was there really nothing about India? Was he sure of that? There was certainly nothing that had left any impression in Brownlow's mind. And Soviet Russia? 'Not as Soviet Russia,' said Brownlow. All that trouble had ceased to be a matter of daily interest. 'And how was France getting on with Germany?' Brownlow could not recall a mention of either of these two great powers. Nor of the British Empire as such, nor of the USA. There was no mention of any interchanges, communications, ambassadors, conferences, competitions, comparisons, stresses in which these governments figured, so far as he could remember. He racked his brains. I thought perhaps all that had been going on so entirely like it goes on today—and has been going on for the last hundred years—that he had run his eyes over the passages in question and that they had left no distinctive impression on his mind. But he is positive that it was not like that. 'All that stuff was washed out,' he said. He is unshaken in his assertion that there were no elections in progress, no notice of Parliament or politicians, no mention of Geneva or anything about armaments or war. All those main interests of a contemporary journal seem to have been among the 'washed out' stuff. It isn't that Brownlow didn't notice them very much; he is positive they were not there.

Now to me this is a very wonderful thing indeed. It means, I take it, that in only forty years from now the great game of sovereign states will be over. It looks also as if the parliamentary game will be over, and as if some quite new method of handling human affairs will have been adopted. Not a word of patriotism or nationalism; not a word of party, not an allusion. But in only forty years! While half the human beings already alive in the world will still be living! You cannot believe it for a moment. Nor could I, if it wasn't for two little torn scraps of paper. These, as I will make clear, leave me in a state of—how can I put it?—incredulous belief.

After all, in 1831 very few people thought of railway or steamship travel, and in 1871 you could already go round the world in eighty days by steam, and send a telegram in a few minutes to nearly every part of the earth. Who would have thought of that in 1831? Revolutions in human life, when they begin to come, can come very fast. Our ideas and methods change faster than we know.

But just forty years!

It was not only that there was this absence of national politics from that evening paper, but there was something else still more fundamental. Business, we both think, finance that is, was not in evidence, at least upon anything like contemporary lines. We are not quite sure of that, but that is our impression. There was no list of Stock Exchange prices, for example, no City page, and nothing in its place. I have suggested already that Brownlow just turned that page over, and that it was sufficiently like what it is today that he passed and forgot it. I have put that suggestion to him. But he is quite sure that that was not the case. Like most of us nowadays, he is watching a number of his investments rather nervously, and he is convinced he looked for the City article.

November 10th, 1971, may have been Monday—there seems to have been some readjustment of the months and the days of the week; that is a detail into which I will not enter now—but that will not account for the absence of any City news at all. That also, it seems, will be washed out forty years from now.

Is there some tremendous revolutionary smash-up ahead, then? Which will put an end to investment and speculation? Is the world going Bolshevik? In the paper, anyhow, there was no sign of, or reference to, anything of that kind. Yet against this idea of some stupendous economic revolution we have the fact that here forty years ahead is a familiar London evening paper still tumbling into a private individual's letter-box in the most uninterrupted manner. Not much suggestion of a social smash-up there. Much stronger is the effect of immense changes which have come about bit by bit, day by day, and hour by hour, without any sort of revolutionary jolt, as morning or springtime comes to the world.

These futile speculations are irresistible. The reader must forgive me them. Let me return to our story.

There had been a picture of a landslide near Ventimiglia and one of some new chemical works at Salzburg, and there had been a picture of fighting going on near Irkutsk. (Of that picture, as I will tell presently, a fading scrap survives.) 'Now that was called——' Brownlow made an effort, and snapped his fingers triumphantly. '——"Round-up of Brigands by Federal Police."'

'*What* Federal Police?' I asked.

'There you have me,' said Brownlow. 'The fellows on both sides looked mostly Chinese, but there were one or two taller fellows, who might have been Americans or British or Scandinavians.

'What filled a lot of the paper,' said Brownlow, suddenly, 'was gorillas. There was no end of a fuss about gorillas. Not so much as about that boring, but still a lot of fuss. Photographs. A map. A special article and some paragraphs.'

The paper had, in fact, announced the death of the last gorilla. Considerable resentment was displayed at the tragedy that had happened in the African gorilla reserve. The gorilla population of the world had been dwindling for many years. In 1931 it had been

estimated at nine hundred. When the Federal Board took over it
had shrunken to three hundred.

'*What* Federal Board?' I asked.

Brownlow knew no more than I did. When he read the phrase, it
had seemed all right somehow. Apparently this Board had had too
much to do all at once, and insufficient resources. I had the
impression at first that it must be some sort of conservation board,
improvised under panic conditions, to save the rare creatures of the
world threatened with extinction. The gorillas had not been sufficiently observed and guarded, and they had been swept out of
existence suddenly by a new and malignant form of influenza. The
thing had happened practically before it was remarked. The paper
was clamouring for inquiry and drastic changes of reorganization.

This Federal Board, whatever it might be, seemed to be something of very considerable importance in the year 1971. Its name
turned up again in an article of afforestation. This interested
Brownlow considerably because he has large holdings in lumber
companies. This Federal Board was apparently not only responsible
for the maladies of wild gorillas but also for the plantation of trees
in—just note these names!—Canada, New York State, Siberia,
Algiers, and the East Coast of England, and it was arraigned for
various negligences in combating insect pests and various fungoid
plant diseases. It jumped all our contemporary boundaries in the
most astounding way. Its range was world-wide. 'In spite of the
recent additional restrictions put upon the use of big timber in
building and furnishing, there is a plain possibility of a shortage of
shelter timber and of rainfall in nearly all the threatened regions for
1985 onward. Admittedly the Federal Board has come late to its
task, from the beginning its work has been urgency work; but in
view of the lucid report prepared by the James Commission, there
is little or no excuse for the inaggressiveness and over-confidence it
has displayed.'

I am able to quote this particular article because as a matter of
fact it lies before me as I write. It is indeed, as I will explain, all
that remains of this remarkable newspaper. The rest has been
destroyed and all we can ever know of it now is through Brownlow's
sound but not absolutely trustworthy memory.

*

My mind, as the days pass, hangs on to that Federal Board. Does that phrase mean, as just possibly it may mean, a world federation, a scientific control of all human life only forty years from now? I find that idea—staggering. I have always believed that the world was destined to unify—'Parliament of Mankind and Confederation of the World', as Tennyson put it—but I have always supposed that the process would take centuries. But then my time sense is poor. My disposition has always been to underestimate the pace of change. I wrote in 1900 that there would be aeroplanes 'in fifty years' time'. And the confounded things were buzzing about everywhere and carrying passengers before 1920.

Let me tell very briefly of the rest of that evening paper. There seemed to be a lot of sport and fashion; much about something called 'Spectacle'—with pictures—a lot of illustrated criticism of decorative art and particularly of architecture. The architecture in the pictures he saw was 'towering—kind of magnificent. Great blocks of building. New York, but more so and all run tógether' . . . Unfortunately he cannot sketch. There were sections devoted to something he couldn't understand, but which he thinks was some sort of 'radio programme stuff'.

All that suggests a sort of advanced human life very much like the life we lead today, possibly rather brighter and better.

But here is something—different.

'The birth-rate,' said Brownlow, searching his mind, 'was seven in the thousand.'

I exclaimed. The lowest birth-rates in Europe now are sixteen or more per thousand. The Russian birth-rate is forty per thousand, and falling slowly.

'It was seven,' said Brownlow. 'Exactly seven. I noticed it. In a paragraph.'

But what birth-rate, I asked. The British? The European?

'It said the birth-rate,' said Brownlow. 'Just that.'

That I think is the most tantalizing item in all this strange glimpse of the world of our grandchildren. A birth-rate of seven in the thousand does not mean a fixed world population; it means a population that is being reduced at a very rapid rate—unless the death-rate has gone still lower. Quite possibly people will not be dying so much then, but living very much longer. On that Brownlow could throw no light. The people in the pictures did not look to him an 'old lot.' There were plenty of children and young or young-looking people about.

'But Brownlow,' I said, 'wasn't there any crime?'

'Rather,' said Brownlow. 'They had a big poisoning case on, but it was jolly hard to follow. You know how it is with these crimes. Unless you've read about it from the beginning, it's hard to get the hang of the situation. No newspaper has found out that for every crime it ought to give a summary up-to-date every day—and forty years ahead they hadn't. Or they aren't going to. Whichever way you like to put it.

'There were several crimes and what newspaper men call stories,' he resumed; 'personal stories. What struck me about it was that they seemed to be more sympathetic than our reporters, more concerned with the motives and less with just finding someone out. What you might call psychological—so to speak.'

'Was there anything much about books?' I asked him.

'I don't remember anything about books,' he said . . .

And that is all. Except for a few trifling details such as a possible thirteenth month inserted in the year, that is all. It is intolerably tantalizing. That is the substance of Brownlow's account of his newspaper. He read it—as one might read any newspaper. He was just in that state of alcoholic comfort when nothing is incredible and so nothing is really wonderful. He knew he was reading an evening newspaper of forty years ahead and he sat in front of his fire, and smoked and sipped his drink and was no more perturbed than he would have been if he had been reading an imaginative book about the future.

Suddenly his little brass clock pinged Two.

He got up and yawned. He put that astounding, that miraculous newspaper down as he was wont to put any old newspaper down; he carried off his correspondence to the desk in his bureau, and with the swift laziness of a very tired man he dropped his clothes about his room anyhow and went to bed.

But somewhen in the night he woke up feeling thirsty and grey-minded. He lay awake and it came to him that something very strange had occurred to him. His mind went back to the idea that he had been taken in by a very ingenious fabrication. He got up for a drink of Vichy water and a liver tabloid, he put his head in cold water and found himself sitting on his bed towelling his hair and doubting whether he had really seen those photographs in the very colours of reality itself, or whether he had imagined them. Also running through his mind was the thought that the approach of a world timber famine for 1985 was something likely to affect his investments and particularly a trust he was setting up on behalf of an infant in whom he was interested. It might be wise, he thought, to put more into timber.

He went back down the corridor to his sitting-room. He sat there in his dressing-gown, turning over the marvellous sheets. There it was in his hands complete in every page, not a corner torn. Some sort of autohypnosis, he thought, might be at work, but certainly the pictures seemed as real as looking out of a window. After he had stared at them some time he went back to the timber paragraph. He felt he must keep that. I don't know if you will understand how his mind worked—for my own part I can see at once how perfectly irrational and entirely natural it was—but he took this marvellous paper, creased the page in question, tore off this particular article and left the rest. He returned very drowsily to his bedroom, put the scrap of paper on his dressing-table, got into bed and dropped off to sleep at once.

When he awoke again it was nine o'clock; his morning tea was untasted by his bedside and the room was full of sunshine. His parlourmaid-housekeeper had just re-entered the room.

'You were sleeping so peacefully,' she said; 'I couldn't bear to wake you. Shall I get you a fresh cup of tea?'

Brownlow did not answer. He was trying to think of something strange that had happened.

She repeated her question.

'No. I'll come and have breakfast in my dressing-gown before my bath,' he said, and she went out of the room.

Then he saw the scrap of paper.

In a moment he was running down the corridor to the sitting-room. 'I left a newspaper,' he said. 'I left a newspaper.'

She came in response to the commotion he made.

'A newspaper?' she said. 'It's been gone this two hours, down the chute, with the dust and things.'

Brownlow had a moment of extreme consternation.

He invoked his God. 'I wanted it *kept*!' he shouted. 'I wanted it *kept*.'

'But how was *I* to know you wanted it kept?'

'But didn't you notice it was a very extraordinary-looking newspaper?'

'I've got none too much time to dust out this flat to be looking at newspapers,' she said. 'I thought I saw some coloured photographs of bathing ladies and chorus girls in it, but that's no concern of mine. It didn't seem a proper newspaper to me. How was I to know you'd be wanting to look at them again this morning?'

'I must get that newspaper back,' said Brownlow. 'It's—it's vitally important . . . If all Sussex Court has to be held up I want that newspaper back.'

'I've never known a thing come up that chute again,' said his housekeeper, 'that's once gone down it. But I'll telephone down, sir, and see what can be done. Most of that stuff goes right into the hot-water furnace, they say . . .'

It does. The newspaper had gone.

Brownlow came near raving. By a vast effort of self-control he sat down and consumed his cooling breakfast. He kept on saying 'Oh, my God!' as he did so. In the midst of it he got up to recover the scrap of paper from his bedroom, and then found the wrapper addressed to Evan O'Hara among the overnight letters on his bureau. That seemed an almost maddening confirmation. The thing *had* happened.

Presently after he had breakfasted, he rang me up to aid his baffled mind.

I found him at his bureau with the two bits of paper before him. He did not speak. He made a solemn gesture.

'What is it?' I asked, standing before him.

'Tell me,' he said. 'Tell me. What are these objects? It's serious. Either——' He left the sentence unfinished.

I picked up the torn wrapper first and felt its texture. 'Evan O'Hara, Mr,' I read.

'Yes. Sussex Court, 49. Eh?'

'Right,' I agreed and stared at him.

'*That's* not hallucination, eh?'

I shook my head.

'And now this?' His hand trembled as he held out the cutting. I took it.

'Odd,' I said. I stared at the black-green ink, the unfamiliar type, the little novelties in spelling. Then I turned the thing over. On the back was a piece of one of the illustrations; it was, I suppose, about a quarter of the photograph of that 'Round-up of Brigands by Federal Police' I have already mentioned.

When I saw it that morning it had not even begun to fade. It represented a mass of broken masonry in a sandy waste with bare-looking mountains in the distance. The cold, clear atmosphere, the glare of a cloudless afternoon were rendered perfectly. In the foreground were four masked men in a brown service uniform intent on working some little machine on wheels with a tube and a nozzle projecting a jet that went out to the left, where the fragment was torn off. I cannot imagine what the jet was doing. Brownlow says he thinks they were gassing some men in a hut. Never have I seen such realistic colour printing.

'What on earth is this?' I asked.

'It's *that*,' said Brownlow. 'I'm not mad, am I? It's really *that*.'

'But what the devil is it?'

'It's a piece of a newspaper for November 10th, 1971.'

'You had better explain,' I said, and sat down, with the scrap of paper in my hand, to hear his story. And, with as much elimination of questions and digressions and repetitions as possible, that is the story I have written here.

I said at the beginning that it was a queer story and queer to my mind it remains, fantastically queer. I return to it at intervals, and it refuses to settle down in my mind as anything but an incongruity with all my experience and beliefs. If it were not for the two little bits of paper, one might dispose of it quite easily. One might say that Brownlow had had a vision, a dream of unparalleled vividness and consistency. Or that he had been hoaxed and his head turned by some elaborate mystification. Or, again, one might suppose he had really seen into the future with a sort of exaggeration of those previsions cited by Mr J. W. Dunne in his remarkable 'Experiment with Time.' But nothing Mr Dunne has to advance can account for an actual evening paper being slapped through a letter-slit forty years in advance of its date.

The wrapper has not altered in the least since I first saw it. But the scrap of paper with the article about afforestation is dissolving into a fine powder and the fragment of picture at the back of it is fading out; most of the colour has gone and the outlines have lost

their sharpness. Some of the powder I have taken to my friend
Ryder at the Royal College, whose work in micro-chemistry is so
well known. He says the stuff is not paper at all, properly speaking.
It is mostly aluminium fortified by admixture with some artificial
resinous substance.

Though I offer no explanation whatever of this affair I think I will
venture on one little prophesy. I have an obstinate persuasion that
on November 10th, 1971, the name of the tenant of 49, Sussex
Court, will be Mr Evan O'Hara. (There is no tenant of that name
now in Sussex Court and I find no evidence in the Telephone
Directory, or the London Directory, that such a person exists
anywhere in London.) And on that particular evening forty years
ahead, he will not get his usual copy of the *Even Standrd*: instead he
will get a copy of the *Evening Standard* of 1931. I have an incurable
fancy that this will be so.

There I may be right or wrong, but that Brownlow really got and
for two remarkable hours, read, a real newspaper forty years ahead
of time I am as convinced as I am convinced that my own name is
Hubert G. Wells. Can I say anything stronger than that?

VII

UNNATURAL DISASTERS

Edgar Wallace (1875–1932) was the most successful and popular crime fiction writer of his generation: during the latter half of the 1920s one in every four books sold in the UK was by him. His forte was the thriller, a genre he virtually created. Although outwardly a determined materialist, Wallace was attracted to fantasy and made use of many of the genre's central themes in his work (there are some notable weird tales in the 'Sanders of the River' canon, and his 1922 novel *Captains of Souls* concerned posthumous soul-transference). The 'catastrophe' plot in particular appealed to him as a vehicle for drama on the grand scale: in *The Green Rust* (1919) world supplies of wheat are menaced by a man-made blight; *The Day of Uniting* (1926) postulates what might happen if the Earth were to be threatened with collision by a huge extra-terrestrial body; the short story 'The Sodium Lines' (1923) deals with the sudden and calamitous cessation of all electrical power. An ex-reporter, nurtured on Lord Northcliffe's lively *Daily Mail*, Wallace knew well how to dab atmosphere and colour into his stories and present nationwide turmoil in a few telling phrases. In 'The Black Grippe' he effectively exploits an age-old and universal terror.

Morley Roberts (1857–1942), too, could paint scenes of dire catastrophe, perhaps even more vividly than Wallace. Before he turned to writing Roberts had had an adventurous life in Australia and America, and made good use of his gruelling experiences in Canada and the Texas Panhandle region in his first book, *The Western Avernus* (1887), a critical though not a financial success. He numbered amongst his friends George Gissing and the naturalist W. H. Hudson. After juvenile aspirations to be a poet ('to rival Rossetti, or get on a level with Browning'), Roberts served before the mast, coolied as a stevedore in South African ports, worked on Australian sheep stations, and was a sawmill hand in Canada (erstwhile friends in British Columbia, after reading the largely uncomplimentary *The Western Avernus*, threatened to hang him if he ever set foot in the region again). He wrote over fifty novels of varying quality and numerous short stories, a good many of which dealt with nautical subjects. There were also some impressive weird tales, of which 'The Fog' is one of his most atmospheric and (especially in his vivid descriptions of a London gone mad) harrowing.

Grant Allen (1848–99) is a perfect epitome of the late-Victorian polymath, a man who wrote philosophical and evolutionist treatises (he was a disciple of Herbert Spencer), as well as popular biographies, nature studies, travel guides, and an enormous quantity of fiction, much of it sensational. Cursed with ill health for most of his life he still managed a final tally of over eighty titles in only twenty years. In his day Allen outraged the conventionally-minded with 'new woman' novels such as the notorious *The Woman Who Did* (1895) and *The British Barbarians* (1895), in both of which contemporary morality is flouted; he was not above cloaking his identity to get his proto-feminist views across, publishing *The Type-Writer Girl* (1897) under the impenetrable pseudonym 'Olive Pratt Rayner'. His friends, such as Darwin, T. H. Huxley, Spencer, and the natural philosopher Alfred Russel Wallace, viewed his fiction writing with consternation and were especially mortified that the man whose works included *Physiological Aesthetics* (1877) and *The Colour-Sense: An Essay In Comparative Psychology* (1879) should write a trumpery serial for *Tit-Bits*, although, as Allen pointed out, the £1,000 he received for it went some way to compensate for the drudgery of writing on scientific subjects. Allen appeared in the very first issue of the *Strand* and regularly thereafter, either wearing his fiction hat or as a science-popularizer. 'The Thames Valley Catastrophe' cleverly combines sensation and suspense with careful scientific observation (despite the story's somewhat absurd premise).

As a novelist *Martin Swayne* flourished in the period 1909 to 1918, publishing a handful of light comedies of no special merit, and one science fiction novel, *The Blue Germ* (1918), which dealt humorously with immortality and still has a certain reputation. His *Strand* short stories, however, exhibit variety of plots, a fertile and lively imagination, and a refreshing irony rarely to be found in popular fiction of the day: 'An Awkward Situation' (1924) is the witty but gripping tale of a man who fakes his own death and then can get no one to believe him, while 'Life-Like' (1913) is a brilliant little chiller about an ex-officer who finds himself the reluctant star in what can only be described as a snuff movie. 'A Sense of the Future' is an unusually prophetic tale which, over sixty years ago, dealt with a worry—the finite nature of fossil fuel—that is all too relevant today. Swayne's solution to the problem is one that ecologists and Green Party activists the world over would doubtless applaud.

The Black Grippe

Edgar Wallace

D R HEREFORD BEVAN was looking thoughtfully at a small Cape rabbit; the rabbit took not the slightest notice of Dr Hereford Bevan. It crouched on a narrow bench, nibbling at a mess of crushed mealies and seemed perfectly content with its lot, in spite of the fact that the bench was situated in the experimental laboratory of the Jackson Institute of Tropical Medicines.

In the young principal's hand was a long porcelain rod with which from time to time he menaced the unconscious feeder, without, however, producing so much as a single shiver of apprehension. With his long ears pricked, his sensitive nostrils quivering—he was used to the man-smell of Hereford Bevan by now—and his big black eyes staring unwinkingly ahead, there was little in the appearance of the rabbit to suggest abnormal condition.

For the third time in a quarter of an hour Bevan raised the rod as though to strike the animal across the nose, and for the third time lowered the rod again. Then with a sigh he lifted the little beast by the ears and carried him, struggling and squirming, to a small hutch, put him in very gently, and closed the wire-netted door.

He stood staring at the tiny inmate and fetched a long sigh. Then he left the laboratory and walked down to the staff study.

Stuart Gold, his assistant, sat at a big desk, pipe in mouth, checking some calculations. He looked up as Bevan came in.

'Well,' he said, 'what has Bunny done?'

'Bunny is feeding like a pig,' said Bevan, irritably.

'No change?'

Bevan shook his head and looked at his watch.

'What time——' he began.

'The boat train was in ten minutes ago,' said Stuart Gold. 'I have been on the 'phone to Waterloo. He may be here at any minute now.'

Bevan walked up and down the apartment, his hands thrust into his trousers pockets, his chin on his breast.

Presently he walked to the window and looked out at the busy street. Motor-buses were rumbling past in an endless procession. The sidewalks were crowded with pedestrians, for this was the busiest thoroughfare in the West End of London and it was the hour of the day when the offices were absorbing their slaves.

As he looked, a taxi drew up opposite the door and a man sprang out with all the agility of youth, though the iron-grey whiskers about his chin and the seamed red face placed him amongst the sixties.

'It is he!' cried Hereford Bevan, and dashed from the room to welcome the visitor, taking the portmanteau from his hand.

'It is awfully good of you to come, professor,' he said, shaking the traveller warmly by the hand. 'Ever since I telegraphed I have been scared sick for fear I brought you on a fool's errand.'

'Nonsense,' said the elder man, sharply; 'I was coming to Europe anyway, and I merely advanced my date of sailing. I'd sooner come by the *Mauretania* than the slow packet by which I had booked. How are you? You are looking bright.'

Hereford Bevan led the newcomer to the study and introduced him to Gold.

Professor Van der Bergh was one of those elderly men who never grow old. His blue eye was as clear as it had been on his twentieth birthday, his sensitive mouth was as ready to smile as ever it had been in the flower of his youth. A professor of pathology, a great anatomist, and one of the foremost bacteriologists in the United States, Bevan's doubts and apprehensions were perhaps justified, though he was relieved in mind to discover that he had merely accelerated the great man's departure from New York and was not wholly responsible for a trip which might end in disappointment.

'Now,' said Van der Bergh, spreading his coat-tails and drawing his chair to the little fire, 'just give me a second to light my pipe and tell me all your troubles.'

He puffed away for a few seconds, blew out the match carefully and threw it into the grate, then before Bevan could speak he said:

'I presume that the epidemic of January has scared you?'

Hereford Bevan nodded.

'Well,' said the professor, reflectively, 'I don't wonder. The 1918 epidemic was bad enough. I am not calling it influenza, because I think very few of us are satisfied to affix that wild label to a devastating disease which appeared in the most mysterious fashion, took its toll, and disappeared as rapidly and mysteriously.'

He scratched his beard, staring out of the window.

'I haven't heard any theory about that epidemic which has wholly satisfied me,' he said. 'People talk glibly of "carriers" of "infection", but who infected the wild tribes in the centre of Africa on the very day that whole communities of Eskimos were laid low in parts of the Arctic regions which were absolutely isolated from the rest of the world?'

Bevan shook his head.

'That is the mystery that I have never solved,' he said, 'and never hope to.'

'I wouldn't say that,' said the professor, shaking his head. 'I am always hoping to get on the track of first causes, however baffling they may be. Anyway, I am not satisfied to describe that outbreak as influenza, and it really does not matter what label we give to it for the moment. You might as truly call it the Plague or the Scourge. Now let's get down to the epidemic of this year. I should like to compare notes with you because I have always found that the reports of this Institute are above suspicion. I suppose it has been suggested to you,' he went on, 'that the investigation of this particular disease is outside the province of tropical medicines?'

Stuart Gold laughed.

'We are reminded of that every day,' he said, dryly.

'Now just tell me what happened in January of this year,' said the professor.

Dr Bevan seated himself at the table, pulled open a drawer, and took out a black-covered exercise book.

'I'll tell you briefly,' he said, 'and without attempting to produce statistics. On the 18th January, as near three o'clock in the afternoon as makes no difference, the second manifestation of this disease attacked this country, and, so far as can be ascertained, the whole of the Continent.'

The professor nodded.

'What were the symptoms?' he asked.

'People began to cry—that is to say, their eyes filled with water and they felt extremely uncomfortable for about a quarter of an hour. So far as I can discover the crying period did not last much more than a quarter of an hour, in some cases a much shorter time.'

Again the professor nodded.

'That is what happened in New York,' he said, 'and this symptom was followed about six hours later by a slight rise of temperature, shivering, and a desire for sleep.'

'Just the same sort of thing happened here,' said Bevan, 'and in the morning everybody was as well as they had been the previous morning, and the fact that it had occurred might have been overlooked but for the observation made in various hospitals. Gold and I were both stricken at the same time. We both took blood and succeeded in isolating the germs.'

The professor jumped up.

'Then you are the only people who have it,' he said, 'nobody else in the world seems to have taken that precaution.'

Stuart Gold lifted a big bell-shaped glass cover from a microscope, took from a locked case a thin microscopic slide, and inserted it in the holder. He adjusted the lens, switched on a shaded light behind the instrument, and beckoned the professor forward.

'Here it is, sir,' he said.

Professor Van der Bergh glued his eye to the instrument and looked for a long time.

'Perfect,' he said. 'I have never seen this fellow before. It looks rather like a trypnasome.'

'That's what I told Bevan,' said Stuart Gold.

The professor was still looking.

'It is like and it is unlike,' he said. 'Of course, it is absurd to suggest that you've all had an attack of sleeping sickness, which you undoubtedly would have had if this had been a trypnasome, but surely this bug is a new one to me!'

He walked back to his chair, puffing thoughtfully at his pipe.

'What did you do?'

'I made a culture,' said Bevan, 'and infected six South African rabbits. In an hour they developed the first symptoms. Their eyes watered for the prescribed time, their temperature rose six hours later, and in the morning they were all well.'

'Why South African rabbits?' asked Van der Bergh, curiously.

'Because they develop secondary symptoms of any disease at twice the rate of a human being—at least that has been my experience,' explained Bevan. 'I found it by accident whilst I was in Grahamstown, in South Africa, and it has been a very useful piece of knowledge to me. When I wired to you I had no idea there were going to be any further developments. I merely wanted to make you acquainted with the bug——'

The professor looked up sharply.

'Have there been further developments?' he asked, and Bevan nodded.

'Five days ago,' he said, speaking slowly, 'the second symptom appeared. I will show you.'

He led the way back to the laboratory, went to the little hutch, and lifted the twisting, struggling rabbit to the bench under a blaze of electric light. The professor felt the animal gingerly.

'He has no temperature,' he said, 'and looks perfectly normal. What is the matter with him?'

Bevan lifted the little beast and held his head toward the light.

'Do you notice anything?' he asked.

'Good heavens!' said Van der Bergh; 'he's blind!'

Bevan nodded.

'He's been blind for five days,' he said.

'But——' Van der Bergh stared at him. 'Do you mean——'

Bevan nodded.

'I mean, that when the secondary symptom comes, and it should come in a fortnight from today——'

He stopped.

He had replaced the animal upon the bench and had put out his hand to stroke his ears when suddenly the rabbit groped back from him. Again he reached out his hand and again the animal made a frantic attempt to escape.

'He sees now,' said the professor.

'Wait,' said Bevan.

He took down a board to which a paper was pinned, looked at his watch, and jotted a note.

'Thank God for that,' he said; 'the blindness lasts for exactly one hundred and twenty hours.'

'But do you mean,' asked Van der Bergh, with an anxious little frown, 'that the whole world is going blind for five days?'

'That is my theory,' replied the other.

'Phew!' said the professor, and mopped his face with a large and gaudy handkerchief.

They went back without another word to the study and Van der Bergh began his technical test. For his information sheet after sheet of data were placed before him. Records of temperature, of diet and the like were scanned and compared, whilst Bevan made his way to another laboratory to examine the remaining rabbits.

He returned as the professor finished.

'They can all see,' he said; 'I inspected them this morning and they were as blind as bats.'

Presently the professor finished.

'I am going down to our Embassy,' he said, 'and the best thing you boys can do is to see some representative of your Government. Let me see, Sir Douglas Sexton is your big man, isn't he?'

Bevan made a wry face.

'He is the medical gentleman who has the ear of the Government,' he said, 'but he is rather an impossible person. He's one of the old school——'

'I know that school,' said the professor, grimly, 'it's a school where you learn nothing and forget nothing. Still, it's your duty to warn him.'

Bevan nodded and turned to Stuart Gold.

'Will you cancel my lecture, Gold?' he said; 'let Cartwright take the men through that demonstration I gave yesterday. I'll go down and see Sexton though he wither me!'

Sir Douglas Sexton had a large house in a very large square. He was so well-off that he could afford a shabby butler. That shrunken man shook his head when Dr Bevan made his enquiry.

'I don't think Sir Douglas will see you, sir,' he said. 'He has a consultation in half an hour's time and he is in his library, with orders that he is not to be disturbed in any circumstances.'

'This is a very vital matter and I simply must see Sir Douglas,' said Bevan, firmly.

The butler was gone for some time and presently returned to

usher the caller into a large and gloomy room, where Sir Douglas
sat surrounded by open books.

He greeted Bevan with a scowl, for the younger school were not
popular with the Sextonians.

'Really, it is most inconvenient, doctor, for you to see me at this
moment,' he complained, 'I suppose you want to ask about the
Government grant to the Jackson Institute. I was speaking to the
Prime Minister yesterday and he did not seem at all inclined to
agree to spend the country's money——'

'I haven't come about the grant, Sir Douglas,' replied Bevan, 'but
a matter of much greater importance.'

In as few words as possible he gave the result of his experiment,
and on the face of Sir Douglas Sexton was undisguised incredulity.

'Come, come,' he said, when Dr Bevan had finished, and permitted his heavy features to relax into a smile. 'Now, that sort of stuff
is all very well for the Press if you want to make a sensation and
advertise your name, but surely you are not coming to me, a medical
man, and a medical man, moreover, in the confidence of the
Government and the Ministry of Health, with a story of that kind!
Of course, there was some sort of epidemic, I admit, on the 18th. I
myself suffered a little inconvenience, but I think that phenomena
could be explained by the sudden change of wind from the south-
west to the north-east and the corresponding drop in temperature.
You may have noticed that the temperature dropped six degrees
that morning.'

'I am not bothering about the cause of the epidemic,' said Bevan,
patiently. 'I am merely giving you, Sir Douglas, a rough account of
what form the second epidemic will take.'

Sir Douglas smiled.

'And do you expect me,' he asked with acerbity, 'to go to the
Prime Minister of England and tell him that in fourteen days the
whole of the world is going blind? My dear good man, if you
published that sort of story you would scare the people to death and
set back the practice of medicine a hundred years! Why, we should
all be discredited!'

'Do you think that if I saw the Prime Minister——' began Bevan,
and Sir Douglas stiffened.

'If you know the Prime Minister or have any friends who could
introduce you,' he said, shortly, 'I have not the slightest objection

to your seeing him. I can only warn you that the Prime Minister is certain to send for me and that I should give an opinion which would be directly contrary to yours. I think you have made a very grave error, Dr Bevan, and if you were to take the trouble to kill one of your precious rabbits and dissect it you would discover another cause for this blindness.'

'The opinion of Dr Van der Bergh,' began Bevan, and Sir Douglas snorted.

'I really cannot allow an American person to teach me my business,' he said. 'I have nothing to say against American medicines or American surgery, and there are some very charming people in America—I am sure this must be the case. And now, doctor, if you will excuse——'

He turned pointedly to his books and Bevan went out.

For seven days three men worked most earnestly to enlist the attention of the authorities. They might have given the story to the Press and created a sensation, but neither Bevan nor Van der Bergh favoured this method. Eminent doctors who were consulted took views which were extraordinarily different. Some came to the laboratories to examine the records. Others 'pooh-poohed' the whole idea.

'Have you any doubt on the matter yourself?' asked the professor, and Bevan hesitated.

'The only doubt I have, sir,' he said, 'is whether my calculations as to the time are accurate. I have noticed in previous experiments with these rabbits the disease develops about twice as fast as in the human body, but I am far from satisfied that this rule is invariable.'

Van der Bergh nodded.

'My Embassy has wired the particulars to Washington,' he said, 'and Washington takes a very serious view of your discovery. They are making whatever preparations they can.'

He went back to his hotel, promising to call on the morrow. Bevan worked all that day testing the blood of his little subjects, working out tables of reaction, and it was nearly four o'clock when he went to bed.

He slept that night in his room at the Institute. He was a good sleeper, and after winding the clock and drawing down the blind he jumped into bed and in less than five minutes was sound asleep. He awoke with the subconscious feeling that he had slept his usual allowance and was curiously alive and awake. The room was in pitch darkness and he remembered with a frown that he had not gone to bed until four o'clock in the morning. He could not have slept two hours.

He put out his hand and switched on the light to discover the time. Apparently the light was not working.

On his bedside table was a box of matches, his cigarette holder, and his cigarettes. He took the box, struck a light, but nothing happened. He threw away the match and struck another—still nothing happened.

He held the faithless match in his hand and suddenly felt a strange warmth at his fingertips. Then with a cry he dropped the match—it had burnt his fingers!

Slowly he put his legs over the edge of the bed and stood up, groping his way to the window and releasing the spring-blind. The darkness was still complete. He strained his eyes but could not even see the silhouette of the window-frame against the night. Then a church-bell struck the hour . . . nine, ten, eleven, twelve!

Twelve o'clock! It was impossible that it could be twelve o'clock at night. He gasped. Twelve midday and dark!

He searched for his clothes and began to dress. His window was open, yet from outside came no sound of traffic. London was silent—as silent as the grave.

His window looked out upon the busy thoroughfare in which the Jackson Institute was situated, but there was not so much as the clink of a wheel or the sound of a pedestrian's foot.

He dressed awkwardly, slipping on his boots and lacing them quickly, then groped his way to the door and opened it. A voice outside greeted him. It was the voice of Gold.

'Is that you, Bevan?'

'Yes, it is I, what the dickens——' and then the realization of the catastrophe which had fallen upon the world came to him.

'Blind!' he whispered. 'We're all blind!'

Gold had been shell-shocked in the war and was subject to nerve-storms. Presently Bevan heard his voice whimpering hysterically.

'Blind!' he repeated. 'What a horrible thing!'

'Steady yourself!' said Bevan, sternly. 'It has come! But it's only for five days, Gold. Now don't lose your nerve!'

'Oh, I sha'n't lose my nerve!' said Gold, in a shaky voice. 'Only it is rather awful, isn't it? Awful, awful! My God! It's awful!'

'Come down to the study!' said Bevan. 'Don't forget the two steps leading down to the landing. There are twenty-four stairs, Gold. Count 'em!'

He was half-way down the stairs when he heard somebody sobbing at the foot and recognized the voice of the old housekeeper who attended to the resident staff. She was whimpering and wailing.

'Shut up!' he said, savagely. 'What are you making that infernal row about?'

'Oh, sir,' she moaned. 'I can't see! I can't see!'

'Nobody can see or will see for five days!' said Bevan. 'Keep your nerve, Mrs Moreland.'

He found his way to the study. He had scarcely reached the room before he heard a thumping on the door which led from the street to the staff quarters. Carefully he manœuvred his way into the hall again, came to the door, and unlocked it.

'Halloa,' said a cheery voice outside, 'is this the Jackson Institute?'

'Thank God you're safe, professor. You took a risk in coming round.'

The professor came in with slow, halting footsteps, and Bevan shut the door behind him.

'You know your way, I'll put my hand on your shoulder if you don't mind,' said Van der Bergh. 'Luckily I took the trouble to remember the route. I've been two hours getting here. Ouch!'

'Are you hurt?' asked Bevan.

'I ran against an infernal motor-bus in the middle of the street. It had been left stranded,' said the professor. 'I think the blindness is general.'

Stuart had stumbled into the room soon after them, had found a chair and sat down upon it.

'Now,' said Van der Bergh, briskly, 'you've got to find your way to your Government offices and interview somebody in authority. There's going to be hell in the world for the next five days. I hope your calculations are not wrong in that respect, Bevan!'

Hereford Bevan said nothing.

'It is very awkward!' it was Gold's quivering voice that spoke, 'but, of course, it'll be all right in a day or two.'

'I hope so,' said the professor's grim voice. 'If it's for five days little harm will be done, but—but if it's for ten days!'

Bevan's heart sank at the doubt in the old man's voice.

'If it's for ten days?' he repeated.

'The whole world will be dead,' said the professor, solemnly, and there was a deep silence.

'Dead?' whispered Gold and Van der Bergh swung round toward the voice.

'What's the matter with you?'

'Shell-shock,' muttered Bevan under his breath, and the old man's voice took on a softer note.

'Not all of us, perhaps,' he said, 'but the least intelligent. Don't you realize what has happened and what will happen? The world is going to starve. We are a blind world, and how shall we find food?'

A thrill of horror crept up Bevan's spine as he realized for the first time just what world-blindness meant.

'All the trains have stopped,' the professor went on; 'I've been figuring it out in my room this morning just what it means. There are blind men in the signal-boxes and blind men on the engines. All transport has come to a standstill. How are you going to get the food to the people? In a day's time the shops, if the people can reach them, will be sold out and it will be impossible to replenish the local stores. You can neither milk nor reap. All the great power-stations are at a standstill. There is no coal being got out of the mines. Wait, where is your telephone?'

Bevan fumbled for the instrument and passed it in the direction of the professor's voice. A pause, then:

'Take it back,' said the professor, 'of course, that will not be working. The exchange cannot see!'

Bevan heard a methodical puff-puff and the scent of tobacco came to him, and somehow this brought him comfort. The professor was smoking.

He rose unsteadily to his feet.

'Put your hand on my shoulder, professor, and, Gold, take hold of the professor's coat or something.'

'Where are you going?' asked Van der Bergh.

'To the kitchen,' said Bevan; 'there's some food there and I'm starving.'

The meal consisted in the main of dry bread, biscuits, and cheese, washed down by water. Then Hereford Bevan began his remarkable pilgrimage.

He left the house, and keeping touch with the railings on his right, reached first Cockspur Street and then Whitehall. Half-way along the latter thoroughfare he thumped into a man and, putting out his hand, felt embossed buttons.

'Halloa,' he said, 'a policeman?'

'That's right, sir,' said a voice; 'I've been here since the morning. You're in Whitehall. What has happened, sir? Do you know?'

'It is a temporary blindness which has come upon everybody,' said Bevan, speaking quickly. 'I am a doctor. Now, constable, you are to tell your friends if you meet them and everybody you do meet that it is only temporary.'

'I'm not likely to meet anybody,' said the constable. 'I've been standing here hardly daring to move since it came.'

'What time did it happen?'

'About ten o'clock, as near as I can remember,' said the policeman.

'How far from here is Downing Street?'

The constable hesitated.

'I don't know where we are,' he said, 'but it can't be very far.'

Two hours' diligent search, two hours of groping and of stumbling, two hours of discussing with frantic men and women whom he met on the way, brought him to Downing Street.

That journey along Whitehall would remain in his mind a horrible memory for all his days. He heard oaths and sobbings. He heard the wild jabberings of somebody—whether it was man or woman he could not say—who had gone mad under the stress of the calamity, and he came to Downing Street as the clock struck three.

He might have passed the Prime Minister's house but he heard voices and recognized one as that of Sexton.

The great man was moaning his trouble to somebody who spoke in a quiet unemotional voice.

'Halloa, Sexton!'

Bevan stumbled toward, and collided with the great physician.

'Who is it?' said Sexton.

'It is Hereford Bevan.'

'It's the man, Prime Minister, the doctor I spoke to you about.'

A cool hand took Bevan's.

'Come this way,' said the voice; 'you had better stay, Sexton, you'll never find your way back.'

Bevan found himself led through what he judged to be a large hall and then suddenly his feet struck a heavy carpet.

'I think there's a chair behind you,' said the new voice, 'sit down and tell me all about it.'

Dr Bevan spoke for ten minutes, his host merely interjecting a question here and there.

'It can only last for five days,' said the voice, with a quiver of emotion, 'and we can only last out that five days. You know, of course, that the food supply has stopped. There is no way of averting this terrible tragedy. Can you make a suggestion?'

'Yes, sir,' said Bevan. 'There are a number of blind institutes throughout the country. Get in touch with them and let their trained men organize the business of industry. I think it could be done.'

There was a pause.

'It might be done,' said the voice. 'Happily the telegraphs are working satisfactorily, as messages can be taken by sound. The wireless is also working and your suggestion shall be carried out.'

The days that followed were days of nightmare, days when men groped and stumbled in an unknown world, shrieking for food. On the evening of the second day the water supply failed. The pumping stations had ceased to work. Happily it rained and people were able to collect water in their mackintosh coats.

Dr Bevan made several excursions a day and in one of these he met another bold adventurer who told him that part of the Strand was on fire. Somebody had upset a lamp without noticing the fact. The doctor made his way toward the Strand but was forced to turn back by the clouds of pungent smoke which met him.

He and his informant (he was a butcher from Smithfield) locked arms and made their way back to the Institute. By some mischance they took a wrong turning and might have been irretrievably lost but they found a guardian angel in the shape of a woman against whom they blundered.

'The Jackson Institute?' she said. 'Oh yes, I can lead you there.'

She walked with unfaltering footsteps and with such decision that the doctor thought she had been spared the supreme affliction. He asked her this and she laughed.

'Oh, no,' she said, cheerfully. 'You see, I've been blind all my life. The Government has put us on point duty at various places to help people who have lost their way.'

She told them that, according to her information, big fires were raging in half-a-dozen parts of London. She had heard of no railway collisions and the Prime Minister told her——

'Told you?' said Bevan in surprise, and again she laughed.

'I've met him before, you see,' she said. 'I am Lord Selbury's daughter, Lillian Selbury.'

Bevan remembered the name. It is curious that he had pictured her, for all the beauty of her voice, as a sad, middle-aged woman. She took his hand in hers and they walked slowly toward his house.

'You'll think I'm horrid if I say I am enjoying this,' she said, 'and yet I am. It's so lovely to be able to pity others! Of course, it is very dreadful and it is beginning to frighten me a little, and then there's nobody to tell me how pretty I am, because nobody can see. That is rather a drawback, isn't it?' and she laughed again.

'What does the Government think about this?'

'They are terribly upset,' she said, in a graver tone; 'you see, they cannot get at the people—they are so used to depending on the newspapers, but there are no newspapers now, and if there were nobody could read them. They have just stopped—— You step down from the kerb here and walk twenty-five paces and step up again. We are crossing Whitehall Gardens. They have wonderful faith in this Dr Bevan.'

Hereford Bevan felt himself going red.

'I hope their faith is justified,' he said, grimly; 'I happen to be the wonderful doctor.'

He felt her fingers grip him in an uncontrollable spasm of surprise.

'Are you really?' she said, with a new note of interest. 'Listen!'

They stopped, and he heard the tinkle of a bell.

'That is one of our people from St Mildreds,' she said; 'the Government is initiating a system of town-criers. It is the only way we can get news to the people.'

Bevan listened and heard the sing-song voice of the crier but could not distinguish what he said. The girl led him to his house and there left him. He felt her hand running down his right arm and wondered why until she took his hand and shook it.

Old Professor Van der Bergh roared a greeting as he came into the room.

'Is that you, Bevan?' he asked. 'I've got a knuckle of cold ham here, but be careful how you cut it, otherwise you're going to slice your fingers.'

He and Stuart Gold had spent the day feeding the various specimens in the laboratory. The fourth day dawned and in the afternoon came a knock at the door. It was the girl.

'I've been ordered to place myself at your disposal, Dr Bevan,' she said; 'the Government may need you.'

He spent that day wandering through the deserted streets with the girl at his side and as the hundred and twentieth hour approached he found himself looking forward not so much to the end of the tragic experience which he shared with the world, but to seeing with his own eyes the face of this guide of his. He had slept the clock round and just before ten struck he made his way to the street. He heard Big Ben boom the hour and waited for light, but no light came. Another hour passed and yet another, and his soul was seized with blind panic. Suppose sight never returned, suppose his experiments were altogether wrong and that what happened in the case of the rabbits did not happen to Man! Suppose the blindness was permanent! He groaned at the thought.

The girl was with him, her arm in his, throughout that day. His nerves were breaking, and somehow she sensed this fact and comforted him as a mother might comfort a child. She led him into the park with sure footsteps and walked him up and down, trying to distract his mind from the horror with which it was oppressed.

In the afternoon he was sent for to the Cabinet Council and again told the story of his experiments.

'The hundred and twenty hours are passed, are they not, doctor?' said the Premier's voice.

'Yes, sir,' replied Bevan in a low voice, 'but it is humanly impossible to be sure that that is the exact time.'

No other question was asked him but the terror of his audience came back to him like an aura and shrivelled his very heart.

He did not lie down as was his wont that night, but wandered out alone into the streets of London. It must have been two o'clock in the morning when he came back to find the girl standing on the step talking with Van der Bergh.

She came toward him at the sound of his voice.

'There is another Cabinet meeting, doctor,' she said, 'will you come with me?'

'I hope I haven't kept you long,' he said, brokenly. His voice was husky and so unlike his own that she was startled.

'You're not to take this to heart, Dr Bevan,' she said, severely, as they began their pilgrimage to Whitehall. 'There's a terrible task waiting for the world which has to be faced.'

'Wait, wait!' he said, hoarsely, and gripped the rail with one hand and her arm with the other.

Was it imagination? It was still dark, a fine drizzle of rain was falling, but the blackness was dappled with tones of less blackness. There was a dark, straight thing before him, something that seemed to hang in the centre of his eye, and a purple shape beyond, and he knew that he was looking at a London street, at a London lamp-post, with eyes that saw. Black London, London devoid of light, London whose streets were packed with motionless vehicles that stood just where they had stopped on the day the darkness fell, London with groping figures half mad with joy, shrieking and sobbing their relief—he drew a long breath.

'What is it? What is it?' said the girl in a frightened voice.

'I can see! I can see!' said Bevan in a whisper.

'Can you?' she said, wistfully. 'I—I am so glad. And now——'

He was near to tears and his arms went about her. He fumbled in his pocket for a match and struck a light. That blessed light he saw, and saw, too, the pale spiritual face turned up to his.

'I can see you,' he whispered again. 'My God! You're the most beautiful thing I have ever seen!'

London slept from sheer force of habit and woke with the grey dawn to see—to look out upon a world that had been lost for five and a half days, but in the night all the forces of the law and the Crown had been working at feverish pace, railways had dragged their drivers from their beds, carriers and stokers had been collected by the police, and slowly the wheels of life were turning again, and a humble world, grateful for the restoration of its greatest gift, hungered in patience and was happy.

The Fog

Morley Roberts

THE fog had been thickening for many weeks, but now, moving like a black wall, it fell on the town. The lights that guided the world were put out—the nearest were almost as invisible as the stars; a powerful arc-lamp overhead was but a blur. Traffic ceased, for drivers could not see; screams were heard in the streets, and cries for help, where none could help themselves.

'I'm blind,' said Tom Crabb, as he leant against the pillar outside the Café Français in Regent Street. He said it with a chuckle, for he, alone of a street full of the lost, did not feel lost. 'I'm blind, but know my way home!'

Day by day and night by night he patrolled the street with a placard upon his breast marked in big letters, 'Blind'. People with eyes saw him. Out of a thousand one gave him a penny; out of ten thousand one gave him sixpence. The millionth, or some charitable madman, made it half a crown. The red-letter day of his blind life was when he found a sovereign in his palm, put there by a soft little hand that touched his. He heard a gentle girl's voice say, 'Poor blind man.' He had a hard life, and was a hard and lonely man, but he remembered that voice, as he did all voices.

As he stayed by the pillar a man stumbled against him and apologized.

'That's Mr Bentley,' said Tom Crabb.

'Who are you?'

'I'm blind Crabb, sir, bless your heart. You've given me many a copper, haven't you?'

Bentley was a chauffeur and engineer. He drove for Lord Gervase

North, the balloonist and motor-racer, and was for ever about the
West End and Regent Street, as Lord Gervase often dined at the
Français.

'To be sure. I know your voice,' said Bentley. 'It's an awful night,
Crabb.'

'Must be,' said Crabb. 'But fog or none is the same for an eyeless
man. To hear the folks, it might be the end of the world, sir.'

'There never was such a fog,' replied Bentley; 'it's just awful. I
can't see you; no, nor my hand before my face.'

'You can't get home, then. What are you doing?'

'I've come for my boss and the lady he's to marry. They're dining
here with her mother. But we'll never get home.'

'Bentley!' called a voice.

'Yes, my lord,' said the chauffeur.

'What are we to do?'

'Don't know, my lord.'

'Can we get to an hotel?'

'They're crammed already, I hear, my lord.'

Crabb put out his hand and touched Bentley.

'Where does he want to go? Perhaps I could lead you.'

It was a strange notion, but then the blind know their way.

'Aye, perhaps you could. The ladies live in Eccleston Square and
my lord in Pont Street.'

'I don't know either of them, but I could take them and you to
your place.'

'My place?' said Bentley. Then his master spoke.

'Who's that with you, Bentley?'

'A blind man, my lord. He thought he might take you all
home, but he doesn't know Eccleston Square. All he knows is my
place.'

'Better be there than in the street,' said Crabb. He had a sense of
power in him. All the rest of the world were blind. He alone had
some sight.

'If the hotels are full we must go somewhere,' said Lord Gervase.
'There's no room here, nor a bed. They want to shut up now. I'll
speak to the ladies.'

'Good bloke that,' said Crabb. 'He gave me a shilling once and
said a kind word.'

The darkness was thicker than ever. It was incredibly thick and choking—it made the useless eyes ache. It was a threat, a terror. So might the end of the world come.

'Bentley!' said Lord Gervase once more.

'Yes, my lord.'

'Come here.'

Bentley found him, and his employer put his hand upon his shoulder. 'Can you trust this man? If so, the ladies will come to your place till it clears, if you will take us in.'

'My wife will do her best, my lord. I know this Crabb to speak to. He says you once gave him a shilling. I'm sure he'll lead us right. But what about the car?'

'You must leave it, or get him to bring you back. I want you with us. Come, Lady Semple; come, Julia.'

The mother and daughter, who had been close behind him, moved timidly.

'Let me lead her ladyship,' said Bentley.

'Thank you, Bentley,' said Lady Semple. There was a painful note in her voice. She was never strong, and the fog alarmed her. Julia clung to her lover and did not speak.

'Crabb, take us to my place, then, if you can,' said Bentley.

'I'll give you a fiver if we get there all right,' said Lord Gervase.

'You gave me a shilling once, my lord, and after that I'd take you for nothing,' said Crabb. ''Tisn't often I get so much.'

He led the way and Bentley took hold of his coat.

'Keep close, all of you,' said Crabb. 'The Circus is packed terrible, but if I can get across Piccadilly, 'twill be easy.'

They were on the west side of Regent Street and went down Air Street into Piccadilly. Out of the darkness wandering folks came and met them. Some wailed, some asked for help, some seemed dazed or half mad, as all folks get in deep fog. And every now and again there was a crash of glass.

They came to Piccadilly and heard the trampling of horses. People in carriages spoke. The darkness was a visible, awful darkness, and in it a mad world was buried.

'Here's the way across to Eagle Place,' said Crabb. 'But can we get across?'

It was a passage of such peril as might be found in war, or upon an unknown mountain in heavy snow, or in a wreck upon a reef of sharp rocks. They heard the dreadful cry of a hurt man. Crabb's foot came upon one who lay on the pavement. He was dead, or so Crabb averred when he stooped and felt him.

'I've seen many dead when I was soldiering in India,' said Crabb. Julia trembled to hear him say so.

There were many people in the street; some were drunk, and many wild, but most were fearful. Yet the darkness released some from fear and let loose their devilry. It seemed that two men in front of them smashed every window as they passed, and laughed wildly. Once Julia called out, and her lover said, 'What is it?'

'Did you kiss me, Gervase?'

There was horror in her voice. He had not kissed her.

'My God!' said Gervase. 'My God!'

There was a strange laugh in the darkness. He leapt at the laugh, caught it by the throat, and dashed the laugher on the pavement. And Julia's cry brought him back to her. But they crossed at Duke Street, and wondered how they did it.

'Now it's easy,' said Crabb. 'We're as good as there, my lord.'

In St James's Square there were few people, and they rested. Julia spoke again.

'Did you—did you hurt him?'

But Crabb heard her speak.

'Who spoke?' he said, suddenly.

''Twas Miss Semple spoke,' answered Bentley.

'Young lady, did you ever give a poor blind man a sovereign?' asked Crabb, in a strange, far-off voice.

'Yes, once, many years ago,' said Julia, wondering.

'And you said, "Poor blind man." God bless you, miss. I knew your voice just now,' said Crabb. ''Twas the fifth of July, five years ago; I never forget a voice.'

He went on in silence and led them by way of Pall Mall and the Square down Whitehall and Parliament Street, going through many perils, till the Houses of Parliament were on their left and the Abbey on their right.

'We're close now,' said Crabb. ''Tis strange it should be the same to me as any other night. Is it better now?'

'It's worse,' said Bentley, gloomily.

But they came to the stairway of the flat that Bentley lived in.

'Is this it?' asked Bentley, in surprise. He could see nothing.

'You live here, or I'm a fool,' said Crabb. 'I've led you straight. Go up and see.'

On the first floor his flat was, and Bentley's young wife opened the door and cried out as she took hold of him.

'A blind man led me, dear,' said Bentley, 'and we've brought Lord Gervase North and Lady Semple and Miss Semple. They cannot get home. We must keep them till tomorrow, when the fog goes.'

So shadow spoke to shadow, and she whom they could not see spoke to them and bade them welcome in a trembling voice, and found chairs for them. But Bentley and Lord Gervase went out again to Crabb, who took his five pounds gratefully.

'Will this fog last?' asked Lord Gervase. But none could answer him. Ere Crabb went off to his solitary house close by, Bentley said to him:

'If the fog's like this tomorrow, come in and see us, Crabb.'

They shook hands, for the danger brought them close, and Crabb went off murmuring to himself. Bentley went back upstairs again, and it seemed to him that the fog was thicker still. In the room was lighted darkness, and the lamps showed the night feebly.

'There never was such a fog,' he said, cheerfully. But Lady Semple moaned and shed tears, and nothing they could say consoled her. To be in her own home in such a fog would be bad enough, but to be here! Poor Mrs Bentley, only lately married, was terrified to think she had three such folks to deal with, but she had sense and some energy in her. She took her husband aside.

'The Thompsons are away,' she began. These people lived in the opposite flat on their landing. 'Why shouldn't we break in there and take their beds for these ladies?'

'Break in!' cried Bentley. 'Suppose they came back?'

'They've gone for a week, and how can they come back in this fog? Besides, what can we do?'

'It's a notion after all,' said her husband. 'I'll propose it to his lordship.'

As a result of the proposal he and Lord Gervase put their heads and shoulders together and turned housebreakers inside five minutes. They lighted fires and lamps and mitigated the horrid darkness as much as they could, and sent Lady Semple and Julia to bed. Mrs Bentley soon followed, and left her husband and his employer together.

'This is a queer situation, Bentley. I wonder if it will last?' said Lord Gervase.

'It's a rum start, my lord,' replied Bentley; 'and, to look at it, it might last for ever.'

'Then what will become of London and of us?'

'We'll have to leave in your balloon, my lord,' said Bentley, with a grim laugh. 'But let's hope it will be better in the morning.'

Lord Gervase slept in the Bentleys' spare room, and slept soundly. When he woke it was pitch-dark. He looked at his watch by the light of a match and could not discern the figures. It seemed as if he was blind. But on opening the watch and feeling the hands he found it was eight o'clock in the morning. The fog was worse than ever. The gloom that was outside settled on their hearts. They had breakfast together and hardly spoke. Lady Semple cried continually, and Julia could hardly restrain her own tears.

'It's like the end of the world,' sobbed Lady Semple. 'We—we shall die of it.'

In truth Mrs Bentley wondered where food was to come from if it continued. She had nothing left after breakfast but a loaf of bread. And they could not see each other. When they opened the window the outside fog was as thick as a black blanket. It inspired a helpless, hopeless horror. They sat about till nearly noon and said nothing. At ten Crabb came to the outer door and knocked. When they let his dark shadow in he put something on the table.

'It's grub,' he said. 'I thought you might want it.'

He came to them from the outer world; they asked him for news.

'Things are awful, my lord,' he said, quietly. But there was a strange ring in his voice. 'They're awful; I can't tell you all that's going on. 'Tis madness. There are awful things being done; fires, murders, and horrible screams about. I was in Trafalgar Square and folks cried out suddenly, "Light! Light!" Something broke in the fog overhead and a great light shone. People cried out, and then— then the fog came down again. Terror is in us all, but many have broken into liquor shops and are drunk; the whole town's mad.'

'Oh, will it last?' asked Julia. 'What do the papers say?'

There were no papers; there was nothing, said Crabb. The very electric lights were out; it seemed no one worked, no one could work. There was a blind mob in the streets, and all were lost. They sought to escape, and knew not which way to run. When he had

finished Lady Semple fainted, falling into her daughter's arms. Julia
and Mrs Bentley took hold of her, and Crabb and Bentley and Lord
Gervase went apart.

'What's to be done?' asked Lord Gervase, in a kind of despair.

'Nothing but wait, my lord,' said Bentley.

'Could you lead us out of London, Crabb?' asked Lord Gervase.

'I don't know more than my beat and a bit over,' said Crabb.
'What I know I know like the inside of my hat, but beyond it there's
a sort of blackness for me. But I'll get you food.'

'How did you get what you brought?' asked Bentley.

'Out of an open shop,' said Crabb. 'There was a dead man in it.'

They said nothing for a time.

'Folks are going mad and jumping into the river,' said Crabb.
'And I heard women shrieking awfully. Wicked people are about.
There's fires already here and there.'

'What can we do?' asked Lord Gervase.

'It can't last,' said Bentley.

'Why can't it?' asked Crabb, after a pause.

'It might last a week, eh?' said Bentley; 'or—or more?'

'Where's London's food to come from? Where are folks to find it?'
asked Crabb. 'In three days they'll be eating each other. I heard
horrid things said in the dark by blind voices, my lord. They gave
me the shivers and shakes.'

'Where's that balloon, Bentley?' asked Lord Gervase, in a shaken
voice. 'Could we—could we use it? We *must* get Lady Semple out
of this; we must, or she will die!'

It was in a store close by the gasworks, but Bentley couldn't find
it. Crabb said he knew the gasworks if Bentley could find the place
in which the balloon was.

'But what will you do with it, my lord?'

'Go up in it and out of this, and drift away,' said Lord Gervase.
'It could be done.'

'Will there be any gas left?' asked Bentley, and then he clapped
his thigh as if he thought of something.

'What is it, Bentley?'

'There'll be none working at the gasworks, my lord!'

'No?'

'Crabb and I will go down and turn off the supply if we can,' said
Bentley; 'turn it off before it's gone.'

'Do it,' said Lord Gervase; 'this is horrible—my eyes ache. It's driving me mad. Poor Julia!'

'Will you help me, Crabb?' asked Bentley.

So they went out together, and passed murder in the streets, and saw the glare of fires, and heard awful things. And Bentley was blind. But Crabb had eyes in his mind. So at last they came to the works, and smote on the door to see if by happy chance there were any there. The watchman came running; he had lost his nerve, and cried as he held to them, telling how the men had left him all alone. But he lived there, and they had their homes elsewhere.

'What gas have you left?' they asked him, and when he could answer he said that one gasometer was half full, but that it went quickly.

'Come and turn it off, so that it won't waste any more,' cried Bentley. And they turned it off, knowing they brought bitter darkness to many. But Crabb said he would bring food to the watchman, and he was easier in his mind.

'London's being destroyed,' said the watchman. 'I hear dreadful things.'

'Dreadful things are being done,' said Crabb. 'But dreadful things are always being done, my lad. I'm not so blind I can't see that.'

'This *is* blindness,' said the watchman. 'I can't smoke even. 'Tis dreadful. Shall we all die?'

'Some day,' said Crabb. 'I can see that.'

And he and Bentley tried to find the store where the balloon was, and, in trying, Crabb once got lost and said so. Bentley's blood ran cold, for Crabb was his sight, his life, and the life of those he loved. For he loved not only his wife, but Gervase North and Julia Semple, since they were made to be loved, both of them, and Bentley was kind-hearted.

Yet Crabb found himself again, and they went back to the Square without discovering the balloon shed.

'We'll try tomorrow,' said Crabb.

They tried next day and failed.

They tried the next day—and still failed. But Crabb brought them food, very fine food, wonderful things in pots and jars.

'I went up to Piccadilly and smashed a window for 'em,' said Crabb. 'God's truth I did. I hope they're good. Is it too dark to see?'

They, too, had no gas.

'We can taste,' they answered. But they tasted fog—fog thick, inspissated, yellow, a pasty fog. And they tasted horror, for there were lamentable voices in the streets, voicing death and murder.

'What's this in the bottom of the sack?' asked Bentley, when he had taken out the jars and the fine glasses of preserved foods.

'Jewels, I think,' said Crabb, in a strange voice. 'I thought the ladies might like 'em. I found 'em on the pavement in an open bag, and by the feel of 'em thought they might be di'monds. And I passed another shop and smashed the window and grabbed a handful. Why not? Who wants 'em? London's dying. But you've your balloon.'

Again a heavy silence fell on them. Crabb went away—he wanted news, he said. So he went lightly through the gloom, the paste of darkness and night. London was like the Pit: it was silent, but in the silence were cries. Horses lay dead; others wandered loose. There were fires in the streets, made of smashed vehicles; gloomy shadows burnt themselves and cooked horseflesh by the leaping hidden flames; some danced drunkenly and fell in the fires. Many offered golden loot for food, jewels for a mouthful, and went about hunting. They said—voices said—that the river was thick with floating corpses already, and fires increased. Out of the night came the mad shrieks of women and the wildest laughter. Dying men played with death and fell on fire and crime and the awfullest disasters. Some went madly crying for their wives and daughters, their little children and their old people who were lost. In churches they prayed; a blind organist made mad music to Heaven in a church that Crabb passed. For him a madman blew.

''Tis an awful strange world,' said Crabb. 'Darkness fell on me years ago. But this city's blind.'

Some he spoke to were quiet and some wild. They told him rumours—the strangest. It was wonderful how rumours went in the dark. Wild crowds were marching east and west and south and north, or trying to march. But few had any guidance. 'Twas said one man had a compass and led a thousand to the river and there fell in. The parks were full of wanderers. Rich people offered thousands from windows, and were slain for money that the slayers could not find. One man lighted a fire with banknotes. A voice said that men were in the Bank, in all the banks, stealing the sacks of gold. The pavements were slippery with a thick fluid, and the dead lay everywhere. Folks drank at the river and fell in. They threw themselves from windows and fell on blind wanderers.

The railways were quiet; nothing moved there. Ships were deserted in the lower river. The telegraphs were quiet; men fled from them. The telephone exchanges were empty. The outside world had deserted London and cut it off. It was sunk in a pit; it lay at the bottom of a well. And these things Crabb gathered up and, going back to his friends, told them. But he brought them food and they ate in the darkness. He took them wine and they drank in the night. And they lost count of the days and the nights. But every day (or night) Bentley and Crabb sought for the place where the balloon was stored.

On the tenth day they found it. That day Lady Semple seemed near to death.

With infinite labour, though they had the help of the watchman, they took the balloon to the gasworks, and then Lord Gervase came with them, leaving Julia with her sick mother.

'It's our only chance, my darling,' he said, as he left her.

He kissed her in the darkness, and kissed the dying woman—for, indeed, unless they got her out of darkness she was dead—and went away with Crabb and Bentley.

With blind eyes they worked; their eyes ached and saw nothing; their hearts laboured, for the air was thick and foul, and ever fouler and thicker, since the fires of the town grew by the folly and madness of lost men. And once again for an hour it grew lighter overhead. They saw each other. Then the darkness fell again. With the help of the watchman, now their slave and the slave of Crabb—who did the work of many and was the calmest of all—they started the inflating of the great balloon. In the blackness of things they had to use infinite care lest they should wound the gigantic ship which was to save them. Yet at last the monster commenced to grow wonderfully, like a huge toadstool in the night. As it grew it straightened out the gear, and they felt its proportions and recognized this and that and felt easier.

'We shall get out,' said Lord Gervase. He yearned to live. He was young and loved a woman, and the world was big for him and fine. But he found Bentley a bigger man than himself; and Crabb was bigger than either, though he had been no more than a soldier, wounded in a foolish fight in far-off India. He gave them courage to drink—he held up their hearts. For he loved the voice of Julia Semple, and remembered her gift, and was glad to help her and her lover.

'You shall want nothing after this, Crabb,' said Gervase.

'I shall want much, or little always,' returned Crabb, in a strange exaltation. For he had never loved a woman till now, though he had kissed many. And her whom he loved he could never kiss.

The world outside was not their world. They were lost in London in the darkness, and were cut off. But the balloon grew and grew. And then it ceased to grow. There was no more gas.

That night it was a little lighter (for it was night, though they knew it not), and the four men laboured in the works, and set the retorts going and made more gas. Crabb was a man of strength, and now he grew more strong. He held them up and laboured, and made the watchman, who was a poor creature, do all that he should do. He made him feel brave. This is the gift of the strong; the gift by which men know them. And at last the balloon stood up and tugged upon its ropes, made fast to an old boiler in the open space.

'It will carry—how many?' asked Crabb. This was a thing none had asked. It was a great balloon, built for a special race and for purposes of science, but it could not carry them all, and they knew it.

Lord Gervase whispered to him.

'Five at the most, Crabb.'

Including the watchman they were seven.

'I'll stay, my lord,' said Crabb. 'I can get on by myself, as you see.'

'You're a brave man,' said Lord Gervase.

He was more than a brave man, this poor blind fellow. But for him what would they have done? By now they would have been dead. Through him they had one chance.

But if Crabb stayed, who was the other to be? They fought it out that night in the flat among the three—Lord Gervase, Crabb, and Bentley. The women stayed apart in another room, where some feared Lady Semple was dying.

'I'll stay with those who can't go,' said Crabb. They understood him. He could live. For him it was not dark. He had, as he said, eyes, and his strong and quiet mind could endure the horrors of which he told them. They knew he never told half, but their minds told them the rest.

'Let it be so, Crabb. You've saved us,' said Lord Gervase. 'When this is over, ask what you like and you shall have it.'

'I'll stay with Crabb, sir,' said Bentley. He too was brave, but his heart sank as he spoke.

'Your wife must go, then!'

'She must,' said Bentley.

'What about the watchman?' asked Crabb.

'If I stay he can go,' said Bentley. 'He has helped; but for him we couldn't have filled the balloon. Let him go.'

Bentley called to his wife. She came from the other flat and went to his voice, and leant upon him while he told her what they meant to do. She was a young girl still, no more than nineteen, and her soul was her husband's in this hour.

'I'll stay with you, Will.'

They could not move her. For when they spoke urgently she laughed at them in scorn. Every reason they urged for her safety was one for her man's.

'I'd rather die with him. Don't say any more. Let the watchman go,' said she. Bentley kissed her in the darkness, which was lighted for him by her faith and love, and she wept upon his heart.

'Take poor Lady Semple out of this place quickly,' she said, 'or she will die.'

They knew it was the truth. Lord Gervase spoke.

'Then it's Lady Semple and Miss Semple, myself and the watchman. Yet the balloon might carry five. It's a pity.'

'So much the better chance for you, my lord,' said Bentley.

The higher they could rise the greater chance there was of getting an air-current to carry them away from London. But they knew there might be none.

'Lose no time,' said Crabb. He was the strongest there.

They needed a strong man, for if the fog could be worse it was now worse indeed. The heavy smoke of many fires ran along the ground; nothing but the calm that destroyed them kept them from being destroyed.

'Let's go now,' said Crabb. He carried Lady Semple to the works in his arms, and as they went she spoke to him.

'Save my daughter, Crabb. I shall never get out alive.'

'We'll save you both, and all of you, my lady,' said Crabb, cheerfully.

'Oh, it's dreadful,' she moaned. 'Am I blind, Crabb? I see nothing—nothing! I choke!'

'You'll be in sunlight, God's sunlight, in half an hour, my lady,' said Crabb. 'Up above this there's light—there must be; think of it—fine sunlight shining such as I've not seen these ten years, since I saw it out in India. 'Tis a sun there, my lady. I remember shining temples, gold and marble. Oh, yes, there's sunlight up above.'

They came to the works and entered. The watchman greeted them nervously.

'You must take me, gentlemen; you must take me,' he cried, fearfully.

'Shut up,' said Crabb. 'You're going to be taken. Don't act the cur.'

But the watchman was half mad. There were thousands mad that hour in London, and tens of thousands would be. Yes, there was sunlight up above, said Crabb. Oh, the brave man he was! Could there be sunlight, or had the sun been put out?

They laid the sick woman in the car, and she rested her head upon Julia's knees. The watchman held to the basket-work and leapt in hurriedly. But Gervase North spoke with Crabb and Bentley.

'Stay here if you can, Crabb. You, Bentley, go back to your wife. She'll be lonely. You're both brave men—the bravest. I feel a cur to leave you. But you stay, Crabb. If there's no wind up aloft we shall come down *here*—here! You understand?'

They understood and shook hands.

'I'd like to shake hands with Miss Julia, my lord,' said Crabb, in a queer, strained voice.

'Yes, yes,' said Lord Gervase.

So Crabb spoke to the girl.

'Will you shake hands, miss?'

Julia cried softly.

'Oh, yes; you're a brave man.'

'You said years ago, "Poor blind man,"' said Crabb. He kissed her hand gently.

'Goodbye, miss.'

Gervase was in the car.

'You can let go, Crabb,' he said. 'Goodbye, Bentley; goodbye, Crabb.'

'Good luck and God's sunlight to you all,' said the blind man.

He and Bentley let the rope run slowly, easing it off round a heavy pipe of iron that lay by the big boiler.

'I'm at the end of the rope,' said Crabb. 'Stand clear, Bentley. Goodbye, sir. Goodbye, miss.'

The balloon was invisible, the car unseen; the world was blank and awful.

'Let go,' said Gervase.

He heard a far dim voice below him cry 'Goodbye,' and knew the earth had dropped away. He grasped Julia's hand. Lady Semple fainted and was quiet. The watchman laughed. But Gervase looked up—up!

Above him he saw something—a dimness, a blur, a space. It was almost black, but visible; it was brown, it was yellow, and then grey. There was a dash of wonderful blue in it, and then they shot out into a magic and intolerable day of noon! The sun shone upon them, and far below lay a wonderful cloud with sunlight on it.

And the watchman giggled strangely. Julia shrank from him and held out her hand to her lover. They saw each other once more—their sight was their own again. But Gervase was grimed with the labour he had done; she hardly knew him. Even his voice was strange.

'Thank God! It's wonderful!' she said. He bent and kissed her.

'My dearest!' he answered. And Lady Semple moaned and woke.

'Where am I?' she asked.

'In the daylight,' said Gervase.

'The poor men who were left!' cried Julia. She had never seen this Crabb with her eyes; she only knew him as a big shadow, a voice that was strong and yet trembled when he spoke to her. She knew he was a hero, and knew, as women must know, that he loved her. He was in the darkness beneath them.

But how wonderful the world was! The sun was glorious, the heaven above a perfect blue. The far cloud below was white, and yet in places a strange dun colour. It heaved and moved and rose and sank. Out of it came strange pillars of yellow clouds.

'What are they?' asked Julia, pointing into the void.

'Fires,' said her lover. He wondered if the balloon moved, and could not see that it did. There was no speck of cloud above them to say if the air moved.

Far away from the city, to the east and west, they saw a shining gleam of the river. The great cloud rested only on the town. They saw far off blue hills, and the far, far country adorned with happy little towns. Wrath lay only on the city; far away was peace. The lower river was full of ships. The outer world wondered at the end of things.

They rose no further. And they did not move. Gervase grasped Julia's hand.

'You're brave, my dear?'

It was a question, and she knew it.

'What is it, Gervase?'

'We don't move, Julia. Neither up nor away from here.'

'What does that mean?'

She saw how grave he looked.

'What does it mean?'

'You're brave and will be,' he said.

So she understood. He knew the balloon was slowly sinking. Perhaps there was a little leak in it.

They came slowly, very slowly, from the heights. But still the watchman chuckled, for he watched no longer. The golden cloud heaved close beneath them.

'We're going down, down,' said the lovers. It was as though a ship sank in a turbid sea. A little grey cloud gathered about them. The sun lost its golden clear sharpness. And the watchman saw it and watched, and ceased to laugh.

'Do we go down again, sir?' he asked.

'Aye,' said Gervase. Lady Semple heard him, but saw nothing. The light of day grew dim. It was as though night fell about them. The sun went out and darkness gathered where they sank. They breathed uneasily and sank into utter blackness.

Down below Crabb waited, quietly wondering. He had taken Bentley home and had come back to the works by himself. He sat quiet as a stone—hoping, happy and unhappy. She was, at any rate, in sunshine. He thanked what gods there were for that. The time went. Perhaps a wind blew high up in the sunlight!

As he waited he heard a little sharp cry like that of a bat, and then a sudden rushing sound, and the flat sound of something striking earth not many yards from him. It was very horrible, for what fell was soft—humanly soft—and he knew it. He groped his way to where the thing fell, and his hands were wet when he touched it, and his heart failed him. But he felt again, and knew it was a man, or had been one, and not a woman. He felt a beard. It was the watchman. He sat by the body—by the wreck of the body—and wondered. Had Lord Gervase thrown him out? That was possible. Anything was possible. Or perhaps the man had gone mad. He knew he was unbalanced. There were few wholly sane in the great city. But if the balloon had been coming down, it must have ascended again.

'I'll wait,' said Crabb. How long he waited he did not know. No clocks chimed. He had no sense of the hours; there was no light for him or for any. But at last—at last—he heard a far dim voice. It was not in the street, for now none came there, or if they came they cried lamentably. It was far above him. The next moment he heard the faint light impact of the car; heard it rebound lightly and come down again, not twenty yards from where it had ascended.

'Is that you, my lord?' he asked.

A voice within two yards of him answered, 'Yes, Crabb.'

'I'm sorry, sorry, my lord.'

'It can't be helped,' said Gervase. 'Did you hear anything fall, Crabb?'

'Aye, my lord.'

'The watchman went mad and jumped out. We rose again, but sank once more. There's no wind up there, Crabb. And Lady Semple's dead, Crabb.'

Crabb heard Julia Semple weeping quietly, but he found a sheet of iron and dragged it over the hollow in which the watchman's body lay before he went to the car.

'Make the ropes fast, Crabb,' said Lord Gervase.

Then they lifted Julia and her dead mother from the car. They laid the body apart.

'God help us,' said Gervase. 'Where's Bentley?'

'With his wife,' said Crabb.

'We must keep the balloon full and try again,' said Gervase. Crabb brought Bentley, and his wife came with him. The men fired the retorts and made more gas with infinite labour. Once more the balloon, which had become limp and flaccid, stood up boldly. There were five of them left. The car could carry five, but even with four they had done nothing. Before they did anything else they buried

Lady Semple, and heaped earth upon the battered watchman. They thought then that it was day.

'We must go,' said Gervase.

Crabb stood apart once more, but Julia Semple spoke.

'Let Crabb come.'

'Oh, no, miss.'

'You must come, or I will not go.'

She took the blind man by the arm.

'Yes; come, Crabb. We owe everything to you,' said Gervase.

'I'll come, then,' said Crabb. His voice was strained. They remembered it afterwards. Some folks have gifts in their voices: they mark the power of their nature, the strength of them.

Before they went up they lightened the car of every superfluous thing and cut away the guide-rope. They took little food with them, and even cast away their boots.

'It's our last chance, Bentley,' said Lord Gervase. 'We can't make more gas, Crabb says.'

They got into the car again.

'I'll cut the rope, my lord,' said Crabb.

'Aye,' said Gervase.

'Are we ready?'

'Yes.'

Crabb cut the rope, and they rose. But overhead the darkness was intense.

'We came through black and dun and yellow and grey before,' said Gervase. 'And then the light—the light!'

Now they breathed again and saw a faint greyness, and then stars sparkling suddenly in deep dark blue, and far away to the west a thin, thin moon. It was night, the dark hour before the dawn. Towns shone with lights far below them, sparkling on the horizon.

'It's night still,' they said.

Even as they spoke they saw in the east a little grey flame of dawn, a faint whiteness, a growth as of a lily opened.

'There's the day!'

'I wish I could see it,' said Crabb.

'Poor blind man,' said Julia, and she pressed his big hand.

'That's better than gold, missy. Oh, if I could see your face!' said Crabb.

'I've never seen yours,' she said, softly.

But the dawn rose like a magic palm in a desert. There was gold in the flame of it, and a heart of gold, and the upper limb of the sun grew out of the east, and she saw Crabb at last. Grimed though he was by labour she saw a strangely carved face, which was very calm and strong. The lids upon his sightless eyes were full and hid them. His mouth was like that of some strange Egyptian. It had power in it, and resolution.

'I see you now, Crabb,' she said to him.

The others looked at the dawn. Mrs Bentley wept softly.

'If I could only see you! May I touch your face, missy?'

She raised his hand to it and he felt its sweet, soft contours.

'You must be very beautiful,' he murmured. Then he said to Lord Gervase:

'Do we still rise, my lord?'

'I think so, Crabb,' Gervase answered.

'Look up, my lord. Is there a cloud above us?'

High in the zenith there was a faint wisp of vapour in a cool current.

'That cloud above moves, my lord,' said Bentley.

'We don't move,' said Gervase, dully. ''Tis a thousand feet above us.'

'Can we cast out anything?' said Crabb, in an eager voice.

They cast out some clothes—aye, and some food and water.

'It's not enough,' said Gervase. 'But there's a strong current high above us.'

'Oh, there's enough,' said Crabb.

But they only stared at him.

'You're blind, Crabb.'

'I can see things,' said Crabb. 'I see if we go down we shall not rise again. I see that—and more.'

He bent his head to Julia.

'You see me, missy? Will you remember me?'

'Oh, yes, Crabb.'

He stood up and held the edge of the car.

'Sit down, man!' cried Bentley.

But he stared at the warmth of the sun, which he felt upon his pallid cheek.

'Oh, the sun's good, though I cannot see it! And I've a sense of light in me! Goodbye, missy.'

He said that to Julia, and ere they knew what he did he threw himself from the car.

They saw his body fall, and Julia shrieked vainly. He fell into the cloud, but the balloon rose and entered the great wind of the upper air. And the heavy cloud below them slipped to the east.

The Thames Valley Catastrophe

Grant Allen

IT can scarcely be necessary for me to mention, I suppose, at this time of day, that I was one of the earliest and fullest observers of the sad series of events which finally brought about the transference of the seat of Government of these islands from London to Manchester. Nor need I allude here to the conspicuous position which my narrative naturally occupies in the Blue-book on the Thames Valley Catastrophe (vol. ii, part vii), ordered by Parliament in its preliminary Session under the new regime at Birmingham. But I think it also incumbent upon me, for the benefit of posterity, to supplement that necessarily dry and formal statement by a more circumstantial account of my personal adventures during the terrible period.

I am aware, of course, that my poor little story can possess little interest for our contemporaries, wearied out as they are with details of the disaster, and surfeited with tedious scientific discussions as to its origin and nature. But in after years, I venture to believe, when the crowning calamity of the nineteenth century has grown picturesque and, so to speak, ivy-clad, by reason of its remoteness (like the Great Plague or the Great Fire of London with ourselves), the world may possibly desire to hear how this unparalleled convulsion affected the feelings and fortunes of a single family in the middle rank of life, and in a part of London neither squalid nor fashionable.

It is such personal touches of human nature that give reality to history, which without them must become, as a great writer has finely said, nothing more than an old almanac. I shall not apologize, therefore, for being frankly egoistic and domestic in my reminiscences of that appalling day: for I know that those who desire to seek scientific information on the subject will look for it, not in vain, in the eight bulky volumes of the recent Blue-book. I shall concern myself here with the great event merely as it appeared to myself, a Government servant of the second grade, and in its relations to my own wife, my home, and my children.

On the morning of the 21st August, in the memorable year of the calamity, I happened to be at Cookham, a pleasant and pretty village which then occupied the western bank of the Thames just below the spot where the Look-out Tower of the Earthquake and Eruption Department now dominates the whole wide plain of the Glassy Rock Desert. In place of the black lake of basalt which young people see nowadays winding its solid bays in and out among the grassy downs, most men still living can well remember a gracious and smiling valley, threaded in the midst by a beautiful river.

I had cycled down from London the evening before (thus forestalling my holiday), and had spent the night at a tolerable inn in the village. By a curious coincidence, the only other visitor at the little hotel that night was a fellow-cyclist, an American, George W. Ward by name, who had come over with his 'wheel', as he called it, for six weeks in England, in order to investigate the geology of our southern counties for himself, and to compare it with that of the far western cretaceous system. I venture to describe this as a curious coincidence, because, as it happened, the mere accident of my meeting him gave me my first inkling of the very existence of that singular phenomenon of which we were all so soon to receive a startling example. I had never so much as heard before of fissure-eruptions; and if I had not heard of them from Ward that evening, I might not have recognized at sight the actuality when it first appeared, and therefore I might have been involved in the general disaster. In which case, of course, this unpretentious narrative would never have been written.

As we sat in the little parlour of the White Hart, however, over our evening pipe, it chanced that the American, who was a pleasant, conversable fellow, began talking to me of his reasons for visiting England. I was at that time a clerk in the General Post Office (of which I am now secretary), and was then no student of science; but his enthusiastic talk about his own country and its vastness amused and interested me. He had been employed for some years on the Geological Survey in the Western States, and he was deeply impressed by the solemnity and the colossal scale of everything American. 'Mountains!' he said, when I spoke of Scotland; 'why, for mountains, your Alps aren't in it, and as for volcanoes, your Vesuviuses and Etnas just spit fire a bit at infrequent intervals; while ours do things on a scale worthy of a great country, I can tell you. Europe is a circumstance: America is a continent.'

'But surely,' I objected, 'that was a pretty fair eruption that destroyed Pompeii!'

The American rose and surveyed me slowly. I can see him to this day, with his close-shaven face and his contemptuous smile at my European ignorance. 'Well,' he said, after a long and impressive pause, 'the lava-flood that destroyed a few acres about the Bay of Naples was what we call a trickle: it came from a crater; and the crater it came from was nothing more than a small round vent-hole; the lava flowed down from it in a moderate stream over a limited area. But what do you say to the earth opening in a huge crack, forty or fifty miles long—say, as far as from here right away to London, or further—and lava pouring out from the orifice, not in a little rivulet, as at Etna or Vesuvius, but in a sea or inundation, which spread at once over a tract as big as England? That's something like volcanic action, isn't it? And *that's* the sort of thing we have out in Colorado.'

'You are joking,' I replied, 'or bragging. You are trying to astonish me with the familiar spread eagle.'

He smiled a quiet smile. 'Not a bit of it,' he answered. 'What I tell you is at least as true as Gospel. The earth yawns in Montana. There are fissure-eruptions, as we call them, in the Western States, out of which the lava has welled like wine out of a broken skin— welled up in vast roaring floods, molten torrents of basalt, many miles across, and spread like water over whole plains and valleys.'

'Not within historical times!' I exclaimed.

'I'm not so sure about that,' he answered, musing. 'I grant you, not within times which are historical right there—for Colorado is a very new country: but I incline to think some of the most recent fissure-eruptions took place not later than when the Tudors reigned in England. The lava oozed out, red-hot—gushed out—was squeezed out—and spread instantly everywhere; it's so compara-

tively recent that the surface of the rock is still bare in many parts,
unweathered sufficiently to support vegetation. I fancy the stream
must have been ejected at a single burst, in a huge white-hot dome,
and then flowed down on every side, filling up the valleys to a
certain level, in and out among the hills, exactly as water might do.
And some of these eruptions, I tell you, by measured survey, would
have covered more ground than from Dover to Liverpool, and from
York to Cornwall.'

'Let us be thankful,' I said, carelessly, 'that such things don't
happen in our own times.'

He eyed me curiously. *'Haven't* happened, you mean,' he
answered. 'We have no security that they mayn't happen again
tomorrow. These fissure-eruptions, though not historically
described for us, are common events in geological history—com-
moner and on a larger scale in America than elsewhere. Still, they
have occurred in all lands and at various epochs; there is no reason
at all why one shouldn't occur in England at present.'

I laughed, and shook my head. I had the Englishman's firm
conviction—so rudely shattered by the subsequent events, but then
so universal—that nothing very unusual ever happened in England.

Next morning I rose early, bathed in Odney Weir (a picturesque
pool close by), breakfasted with the American, and then wrote a
hasty line to my wife, informing her that I should probably sleep
that night at Oxford; for I was off on a few days' holiday, and I
liked Ethel to know where a letter or telegram would reach me each
day, as we were both a little anxious about the baby's teething.
Even while I pen these words now, the grim humour of the situation
comes back to me vividly. Thousands of fathers and mothers were
anxious that morning about similar trifles, whose pettiness was
brought home to them with an appalling shock in the all-embracing
horror of that day's calamity.

About ten o'clock I inflated my tyres and got under way. I meant
to ride towards Oxford by a leisurely and circuitous route, along
the windings of the river, past Marlow and Henley; so I began by
crossing Cookham Bridge, a wooden or iron structure, I scarcely
remember which. It spanned the Thames close by the village: the
curious will find its exact position marked in the maps of the period.

In the middle of the bridge, I paused and surveyed that charming
prospect, which I was the last of living men perhaps to see as it then

existed. Close by stood a weir; beside it, the stream divided into three separate branches, exquisitely backed up by the gentle green slopes of Hedsor and Cliveden. I could never pass that typical English view without a glance of admiration; this morning, I pulled up my bicycle for a moment, and cast my eye downstream with more than my usual enjoyment of the smooth blue water and the tall white poplars whose leaves showed their gleaming silver in the breeze beside it. I might have gazed at it too long—and one minute more would have sufficed for my destruction—had not a cry from the tow-path a little further up attracted my attention.

It was a wild, despairing cry, like that of a man being over-powered and murdered.

I am confident this was my first intimation of danger. Two minutes before, it is true, I had heard a faint sound like distant rumbling of thunder; but nothing else. I am one of those who strenuously maintain that the catastrophe was *not* heralded by shocks of earthquake.*

I turned my eye upstream. For half a second I was utterly bewildered. Strange to say, I did not perceive at first the great flood of fire that was advancing towards me. I saw only the man who had shouted—a miserable, cowering, terror-stricken wretch, one of the abject creatures who used to earn a dubious livelihood in those days (when the river was a boulevard of pleasure) by towing boats up-stream. But now, he was rushing wildly forward, with panic in his face; I could see he looked as if close pursued by some wild beast behind him. 'A mad dog!' I said to myself at the outset; 'or else a bull in the meadow!'

I glanced back to see what his pursuer might be; and then, in one second, the whole horror and terror of the catastrophe burst upon me. Its whole horror and terror, I say, but not yet its magnitude. I was aware at first just of a moving red wall, like dull, red-hot molten metal. Trying to recall at so safe a distance in time and space the feelings of the moment and the way in which they surged and succeeded one another, I think I can recollect that my earliest idea was no more than this: 'He must run, or the moving wall will overtake him!' Next instant, a hot wave seemed to strike my face. It

---

* For an opposite opinion, see Dr Haigh Withers's evidence in Vol. iii of the Blue-book.

was just like the blast of heat that strikes one in a glasshouse when you stand in front of the boiling and seething glass in the furnace. At about the same point in time, I was aware, I believe, that the dull red wall was really a wall of fire. But it was cooled by contact with the air and the water. Even as I looked, however, a second wave from behind seemed to rush on and break: it overlaid and outran the first one. This second wave was white, not red—at white heat, I realized. Then, with a burst of recognition, I knew what it all meant. What Ward had spoken of last night—a fissure-eruption!

I looked back. Ward was coming towards me on the bridge, mounted on his Columbia. Too speechless to utter one word, I pointed upstream with my hand. He nodded and shouted back, in a singularly calm voice: 'Yes; just what I told you. A fissure-eruption!'

They were the last words I heard him speak. Not that he appreciated the danger less than I did, though his manner was cool; but he was wearing no clips to his trousers, and at that critical moment he caught his leg in his pedals. The accident disconcerted him; he dismounted hurriedly, and then, panic-stricken as I judged, abandoned his machine. He tried to run. The error was fatal. He tripped and fell. What became of him afterward I will mention later.

But for the moment I saw only the poor wretch on the tow-path. He was not a hundred yards off, just beyond the little bridge which led over the opening to a private boat-house. But as he rushed forwards and shrieked, the wall of fire overtook him. I do not think it quite caught him. It is hard at such moments to judge what really happens; but I believe I saw him shrivel like a moth in a flame a few seconds before the advancing wall of fire swept over the boat-house. I have seen an insect shrivel just so when flung into the midst of white-hot coals. He seemed to go off in gas, leaving a shower of powdery ash to represent his bones behind him. But of this I do not pretend to be positive; I will allow that my own agitation was far too profound to permit of my observing anything with accuracy.

How high was the wall at that time? This has been much debated. I should guess, thirty feet (though it rose afterwards to more than two hundred), and it advanced rather faster than a man could run down the centre of the valley. (Later on, its pace accelerated greatly with subsequent outbursts.) In frantic haste, I saw or felt that only one chance of safety lay before me: I must strike uphill by the field path to Hedsor.

I rode for very life, with grim death behind me. Once well across the bridge, and turning up the hill, I saw Ward on the parapet, with his arms flung up, trying wildly to save himself by leaping into the river. Next instant he shrivelled, I think, as the beggar had shrivelled; and it is to this complete combustion before the lava-flood reached them that I attribute the circumstance (so much commented upon in the scientific excavations among the ruins) that no casts of dead bodies, like those at Pompeii, have anywhere been found in the Thames Valley Desert. My own belief is that every human body was reduced to a gaseous condition by the terrific heat several seconds before the molten basalt reached it.

Even at the distance which I had now attained from the central mass, indeed, the heat was intolerable. Yet, strange to say, I saw few or no people flying as yet from the inundation. The fact is, the eruption came upon us so suddenly, so utterly without warning or premonitory symptoms (for I deny the earthquake shocks), that whole towns must have been destroyed before the inhabitants were aware that anything out of the common was happening. It is a sort of alleviation to the general horror to remember that a large proportion of the victims must have died without even knowing it; one second, they were laughing, talking, bargaining; the next, they were asphyxiated or reduced to ashes as you have seen a small fly disappear in an incandescent gas flame.

This, however, is what I learned afterward. At that moment, I was only aware of a frantic pace uphill, over a rough, stony road, and with my pedals working as I had never before worked them; while behind me, I saw purgatory let loose, striving hard to overtake me. I just knew that a sea of fire was filling the valley from end to end, and that its heat scorched my face as I urged on my bicycle in abject terror.

All this time, I will admit, my panic was purely personal. I was too much engaged in the engrossing sense of my own pressing danger to be vividly alive to the public catastrophe. I did not even think of Ethel and the children. But when I reached the hill by Hedsor Church—a neat, small building, whose shell still stands, though scorched and charred, by the edge of the desert—I was able to pause for half a minute to recover breath, and to look back upon the scene of the first disaster.

It was a terrible and yet I felt even then a beautiful sight—

beautiful with the awful and unearthly beauty of a great forest fire, or a mighty conflagration in some crowded city. The whole river valley, up which I looked, was one sea of fire. Barriers of red-hot lava formed themselves for a moment now and again where the outer edge or vanguard of the inundation had cooled a little on the surface by exposure: and over these temporary dams, fresh cataracts of white-hot material poured themselves afresh into the valley beyond it. After a while, as the deeper portion of basalt was pushed out, all was white alike. So glorious it looked in the morning sunshine that one could hardly realize the appalling reality of that sea of molten gold; one might almost have imagined a splendid triumph of the scene-painter's art, did one not know that it was actually a river of fire, overwhelming, consuming, and destroying every object before it in its devastating progress.

I tried vaguely to discover the source of the disaster. Looking straight upstream, past Bourne End and Marlow, I descried with bleared and dazzled eyes a whiter mass than any, glowing fiercely in the daylight like an electric light, and filling up the narrow gorge of the river towards Hurley and Henley. I recollected at once that this portion of the valley was not usually visible from Hedsor Hill, and almost without thinking of it I instinctively guessed the reason why it had become so now: it was the centre of disturbance—the earth's crust just there had bulged upward slightly, till it cracked and gaped to emit the basalt.

Looking harder, I could make out (though it was like looking at the sun) that the glowing white dome-shaped mass, as of an electric light, was the molten lava as it gurgled from the mouth of the vast fissure. I say vast, because so it seemed to me, though, as everybody now knows, the actual gap where the earth opened measures no more than eight miles across, from a point near what was once Shiplake Ferry to the site of the old lime-kilns at Marlow. Yet when one saw the eruption actually taking place, the colossal scale of it was what most appalled one. A sea of fire, eight to twelve miles broad, in the familiar Thames Valley, impressed and terrified one a thousand times more than a sea of fire ten times as vast in the nameless wilds of Western America.

I could see dimly, too, that the flood spread in every direction from its central point, both up and down the river. To right and left, indeed, it was soon checked and hemmed in by the hills about

Wargrave and Medmenham; but downward, it had filled the entire valley as far as Cookham and beyond; while upward, it spread in one vast glowing sheet towards Reading and the flats by the confluence of the Kennet. I did not then know, of course, that this gigantic natural dam or barrier was later on to fill up the whole low-lying level, and so block the course of the two rivers as to form those twin expanses of inland water, Lake Newbury and Lake Oxford. Tourists who now look down on still summer evenings where the ruins of Magdalen and of Merton may be dimly descried through the pale green depths, their broken masonry picturesquely overgrown with tangled water-weeds, can form but little idea of the terrible scene which that peaceful bank presented while the incandescent lava was pouring forth in a scorching white flood towards the doomed district. Merchants who crowd the busy quays of those mushroom cities which have sprung up with greater rapidity than Chicago or Johannesburg on the indented shore where the new lakes abut upon the Berkshire Chalk Downs have half forgotten the horror of the intermediate time when the waters of the two rivers rose slowly, slowly, day after day, to choke their valleys and overwhelm some of the most glorious architecture in Britain. But though I did not know and could not then foresee the remoter effects of the great fire-flood in that direction, I saw enough to make my heart stand still within me. It was with difficulty that I grasped my bicycle, my hands trembled so fiercely. I realized that I was a spectator of the greatest calamity which had befallen a civilized land within the ken of history.

I looked southward along the valley in the direction of Maidenhead. As yet it did not occur to me that the catastrophe was anything more than a local flood, though even as such it would have been one of unexampled vastness. My imagination could hardly conceive that London itself was threatened. In those days one could not grasp the idea of the destruction of London. I only thought just at first, 'It will go on towards Maidenhead!' Even as I thought it, I saw a fresh and fiercer gush of fire well out from the central gash, and flow still faster than ever down the centre of the valley, over the hardening layer already cooling on its edge by contact with the air and soil. This new outburst fell in a mad cataract over the end or van of the last, and instantly spread like water across the level expanse between the Cliveden hills and the opposite range at Pinkneys. I realized with a throb that it was advancing towards

Windsor. Then a wild fear thrilled through me. If Windsor, why not Staines and Chertsey and Hounslow? If Hounslow, why not London?

In a second I remembered Ethel and the children. Hitherto, the immediate danger of my own position alone had struck me. The fire was so near; the heat of it rose up in my face and daunted me. But now I felt I must make a wild dash to warn—not London—no, frankly, I forgot those millions; but Ethel and my little ones. In that thought, for the first moment, the real vastness of the catastrophe came home to me. The Thames Valley was doomed! I must ride for dear life if I wished to save my wife and children!

I mounted again, but found my shaking feet could hardly work the pedals. My legs were one jelly. With a frantic effort, I struck off inland in the direction of Burnham. I did not think my way out definitely; I hardly knew the topography of the district well enough to form any clear conception of what route I must take in order to keep to the hills and avoid the flood of fire that was deluging the lowlands. But by pure instinct, I believe, I set my face London-wards along the ridge of the chalk downs. In three minutes I had lost sight of the burning flood, and was deep among green lanes and under shadowy beeches. The very contrast frightened me. I wondered if I was going mad. It was all so quiet. One could not believe that scarce five miles off from that devastating sheet of fire, birds were singing in the sky and men toiling in the fields as if nothing had happened.

Near Lambourne Wood I met a brother cyclist, just about to descend the hill. A curve in the road hid the valley from him. I shouted aloud:

'For Heaven's sake, don't go down! There is danger, danger!'

He smiled and looked back at me. 'I can take any hill in England,' he answered.

'It's not the hill,' I burst out. 'There has been an eruption—a fissure-eruption at Marlow—great floods of fire—and all the valley is filled with burning lava!'

He stared at me derisively. Then his expression changed of a sudden. I suppose he saw I was white-faced and horror-stricken. He drew away as if alarmed. 'Go back to Colney Hatch!' he cried, pedalling faster, and rode hastily down the hill, as if afraid of me. I have no doubt he must have ridden into the very midst of the flood, and been scorched by its advance, before he could check his machine on so sudden a slope.

Between Lambourne Wood and Burnham I did not see the fire-flood. I rode on at full speed among green fields and meadows. Here and there I passed a labouring man on the road. More than one looked up at me and commented on the oppressive heat, but none of them seemed to be aware of the fate that was overtaking their own homes close by, in the valley. I told one or two, but they laughed and gazed after me as if I were a madman. I grew sick of warning them. They took no heed of my words, but went on upon their way as if nothing out of the common were happening to England.

On the edge of the down, near Burnham, I caught sight of the valley again. Here, people were just awaking to what was taking place near them. Half the population was gathered on the slope, looking down with wonder on the flood of fire, which had now just turned the corner of the hills by Taplow. Silent terror was the prevailing type of expression. But when I told them I had seen the lava bursting forth from the earth in a white dome above Marlow, they laughed me to scorn; and when I assured them I was pushing forward in hot haste to London, they answered, 'London! It won't never get as far as London!' That was the only place on the hills, as is now well known, where the flood was observed long enough beforehand to telegraph and warn the inhabitants of the great city; but nobody thought of doing it; and I must say, even if they had done so, there is not the slightest probability that the warning would have attracted the least attention in our ancient Metropolis. Men on the Stock Exchange would have made jests about the slump, and proceeded to buy and sell as usual.

I measured with my eye the level plain between Burnham and Slough, calculating roughly with myself whether I should have time to descend upon the well-known road from Maidenhead to London by Colnbrook and Hounslow. (I advise those who are unacquainted with the topography of this district before the eruption to follow out my route on a good map of the period.) But I recognized in a moment that this course would be impossible. At the rate that the flood had taken to progress from Cookham Bridge to Taplow, I felt sure it would be upon me before I reached Upton, or Ditton Park at the outside. It is true the speed of the advance might slacken somewhat as the lava cooled; and strange to say, so rapidly do realities come to be accepted in one's mind, that I caught myself thinking this thought in the most natural manner, as if I had all my life long been accustomed to the ways of fissure-eruptions. But on the other hand, the lava might well out faster and hotter than before, as I had already seen it do more than once; and I had no certainty even that it would not rise to the level of the hills on which I was standing. You who read this narrative nowadays take it for granted, of course, that the extent and height of the inundation was bound to be exactly what you know it to have been; we at the time could not guess how high it might rise and how large an area of the country it might overwhelm and devastate. Was it to stop at the Chilterns, or to go north to Birmingham, York, and Scotland?

Still, in my trembling anxiety to warn my wife and children, I debated with myself whether I should venture down into the valley, and hurry along the main road with a wild burst for London. I thought of Ethel, alone in our little home at Bayswater, and almost made up my mind to risk it. At that moment, I became aware that the road to London was already crowded with carriages, carts, and cycles, all dashing at a mad pace unanimously towards London. Suddenly a fresh wave turned the corner by Taplow and Maidenhead Bridge, and began to gain upon them visibly. It was an awful sight. I cannot pretend to describe it. The poor creatures on the road, men and animals alike, rushed wildly, despairingly on; the fire took them from behind, and, one by one, before the actual sea reached them, I saw them shrivel and melt away in the fierce white heat of the advancing inundation. I could not look at it any longer. I certainly could not descend and court instant death. I felt that my one chance was to strike across the downs, by Stoke Poges and Uxbridge, and then try the line of northern heights to London.

Oh, how fiercely I pedalled! At Farnham Royal (where again nobody seemed to be aware what had happened) a rural policeman tried to stop me for frantic riding. I tripped him up, and rode on. Experience had taught me it was no use telling those who had not seen it of the disaster. A little beyond, at the entrance to a fine park, a gatekeeper attempted to shut a gate in my face, exclaiming that the road was private. I saw it was the only practicable way without descending to the valley, and I made up my mind this was no time for trifling. I am a man of peace, but I lifted my fist and planted it

between his eyes. Then, before he could recover from his astonish-
ment, I had mounted again and ridden on across the park, while he
ran after me in vain, screaming to the men in the pleasure-grounds
to stop me. But I would not be stopped; and I emerged on the road
once more at Stoke Poges.

Near Galley Hill, after a long and furious ride, I reached the
descent to Uxbridge. Was it possible to descend? I glanced across,
once more by pure instinct, for I had never visited the spot before,
towards where I felt the Thames must run. A great white cloud
hung over it. I saw what that cloud must mean: it was the steam of
the river, where the lava sucked it up and made it seethe and boil
suddenly. I had not noticed this white fleece of steam at Cookham,
though I did not guess why till afterwards. In the narrow valley
where the Thames ran between hills, the lava flowed over it all at
once, bottling the steam beneath; and it is this imprisoned steam
that gave rise in time to the subsequent series of appalling earth-
quakes, to supply forecasts of which is now the chief duty of the
Seismologer Royal; whereas, in the open plain, the basalt advanced
more gradually and in a thinner stream, and therefore turned the
whole mass of water into white cloud as soon as it reached each
bend of the river.

At the time, however, I had no leisure to think out all this. I only
knew by such indirect signs that the flood was still advancing, and,
therefore, that it would be impossible for me to proceed towards
London by the direct route via Uxbridge and Hanwell. If I meant
to reach town (as we called it familiarly), I must descend to the
valley at once, pass through Uxbridge streets as fast as I could,
make a dash across the plain, by what I afterwards knew to be
Hillingdon (I saw it then as a nameless village), and aim at a house-
crowned hill, which I only learned later was Harrow, but which I
felt sure would enable me to descend upon London by Hampstead
or Highgate.

I am no strategist; but in a second, in that extremity, I picked out
these points, feeling dimly sure they would lead me home to Ethel
and the children.

The town of Uxbridge (whose place you can still find marked on
many maps) lay in the valley of a small river, a confluent of the
Thames. Up this valley it was certain that the lava-stream must
flow; and, indeed, at the present day, the basin around is completely

filled by one of the solidest and most forbidding masses of black basalt in the country. Still, I made up my mind to descend and cut across the low-lying ground towards Harrow. If I failed, I felt, after all, I was but one unit more in what I now began to realize as a prodigious national calamity.

I was just coasting down the hill, with Uxbridge lying snug and unconscious in the glen below me, when a slight and unimportant accident occurred which almost rendered impossible my further progress. It was past the middle of August; the hedges were being cut; and this particular lane, bordered by a high thorn fence, was strewn with the mangled branches of the may-bushes. At any other time, I should have remembered the danger and avoided them; that day, hurrying downhill for dear life and for Ethel, I forgot to notice them. The consequence was, I was pulled up suddenly by finding my front wheel deflated;* this untimely misfortune almost unmanned me. I dismounted and examined the tyre; it had received a bad puncture. I tried inflating again, in hopes the hole might be small enough to make that precaution sufficient. But it was quite useless. I found I must submit to stop and doctor up the puncture. Fortunately, I had the necessary apparatus in my wallet.

I think it was the weirdest episode of all that weird ride—this sense of stopping impatiently, while the fiery flood still surged on towards London, in order to go through all the fiddling and troublesome little details of mending a pneumatic tyre. The moment and the operation seemed so sadly out of harmony. A countryman passed by on a cart, obviously suspecting nothing; that was another point which added horror to the occasion—that so near the catastrophe, so very few people were even aware what was taking place beside them. Indeed, as is well known, I was one of the very few who saw the eruption during its course, and yet managed to escape from it. Elsewhere, those who tried to run before it, either to escape themselves or to warn others of the danger, were overtaken by the lava before they could reach a place of safety. I attribute this mainly to the fact that most of them continued along the high roads in the valley, or fled instinctively for shelter towards their homes, instead of making at once for the heights and the uplands.

---

* The bicycles of that period were fitted with pneumatic tubes of india-rubber as tyres—a clumsy device, now long superseded.

The countryman stopped and looked at me.

'The more haste the less speed!' he said, with proverbial wisdom.

I glanced up at him, and hesitated. Should I warn him of his doom, or was it useless? 'Keep up on the hills,' I said, at last. 'An unspeakable calamity is happening in the valley. Flames of fire are flowing down it, as from a great burning mountain. You will be cut off by the eruption.'

He stared at me blankly, and burst into a meaningless laugh. 'Why, you're one of them Salvation Army fellows,' he exclaimed, after a short pause. 'You're trying to preach to me. I'm going to Uxbridge.' And he continued down the hill towards certain destruction.

It was hours, I feel sure, before I had patched up that puncture, though I did it by the watch in four and a half minutes. As soon as I had blown out my tyre again I mounted once more, and rode at a breakneck pace to Uxbridge. I passed down the straggling main street of the suburban town, crying aloud as I went, 'Run, run, to the downs! A flood of lava is rushing up the valley! To the hills, for your lives! All the Thames bank is blazing!' Nobody took the slightest heed; they stood still in the street for a minute with open mouths: then they returned to their customary occupations. A quarter of an hour later, there was no such place in the world as Uxbridge.

I followed the main road through the village which I have since identified as Hillingdon; then I diverged to the left, partly by roads and partly by field paths of whose exact course I am still uncertain, towards the hill at Harrow. When I reached the town, I did not strive to rouse the people, partly because my past experience had taught me the futility of the attempt, and partly because I rightly judged that they were safe from the inundation; for as it never quite covered the dome of St Paul's, part of which still protrudes from the sea of basalt, it did not reach the level of the northern heights of London. I rode on through Harrow without one word to anybody. I did not desire to be stopped or harassed as an escaped lunatic.

From Harrow I made my way tortuously along the rising ground, by the light of nature, through Wembley Park, to Willesden. At Willesden, for the first time, I found to a certainty that London was threatened. Great crowds of people in the profoundest excitement stood watching a dense cloud of smoke and steam that spread rapidly over the direction of Shepherd's Bush and Hammersmith. They were speculating as to its meaning, but laughed incredulously when I told them what it portended. A few minutes later, the smoke spread ominously towards Kensington and Paddington. That settled my fate. It was clearly impossible to descend into London; and indeed, the heat now began to be unendurable. It drove us all back, almost physically. I thought I must abandon all hope. I should never even know what had become of Ethel and the children.

My first impulse was to lie down and await the fire-flood. Yet the sense of the greatness of the catastrophe seemed somehow to blunt one's own private grief. I was beside myself with fear for my darlings; but I realized that I was but one among hundreds of thousands of fathers in the same position. What was happening at that moment in the great city of five million souls we did not know, we shall never know; but we may conjecture that the end was mercifully too swift to entail much needless suffering. All at once, a gleam of hope struck me. It was my father's birthday. Was it not just possible that Ethel might have taken the children up to Hampstead to wish their grandpapa many happy returns of the day? With a wild determination not to give up all for lost, I turned my front wheel in the direction of Hampstead Hill, still skirting the high ground as far as possible. My heart was on fire within me. A restless anxiety urged me to ride my hardest. As all along the route, I was still just a minute or two in front of the catastrophe. People were beginning to be aware that something was taking place; more than once as I passed they asked me eagerly where the fire was. It was impossible for me to believe by this time that they knew nothing of an event in whose midst I seemed to have been living for months; how could I realize that all the things which had happened since I started from Cookham Bridge so long ago were really compressed into the space of a single morning?—nay, more, of an hour and a half only?

As I approached Windmill Hill, a terrible sinking seized me. I seemed to totter on the brink of a precipice. Could Ethel be safe? Should I ever again see little Bertie and the baby? I pedalled on as if automatically; for all life had gone out of me. I felt my hip-joint moving dry in its socket. I held my breath; my heart stood still. It was a ghastly moment.

At my father's door I drew up, and opened the garden gate. I hardly dared to go in. Though each second was precious, I paused and hesitated.

At last I turned the handle. I heard somebody within. My heart came up in my mouth. It was little Bertie's voice: 'Do it again, Granpa; do it again; it amooses Bertie!'

I rushed into the room. 'Bertie, Bertie!' I cried. 'Is Mammy here?'

He flung himself upon me. 'Mammy, Mammy, Daddy has comed home.' I burst into tears. 'And Baby?' I asked, trembling.

'Baby and Ethel are here, George,' my father answered, staring at me. 'Why, my boy, what's the matter?'

I flung myself into a chair and broke down. In that moment of relief, I felt that London was lost, but I had saved my wife and children.

I did not wait for explanations. A crawling four-wheeler was loitering by. I hailed it, and hurried them in. My father wished to discuss the matter, but I cut him short. I gave the driver three pounds—all the gold I had with me. 'Drive on!' I shouted, 'drive on! Towards Hatfield—anywhere!'

He drove as he was bid. We spent that night, while Hampstead flared like a beacon, at an isolated farmhouse on the high ground in Hertfordshire. For, of course, though the flood did not reach so high, it set fire to everything inflammable in its neighbourhood.

Next day, all the world knew the magnitude of the disaster. It can only be summed up in five emphatic words: There was no more London.

I have one other observation alone to make. I noticed at the time how, in my personal relief, I forgot for the moment that London was perishing. I even forgot that my house and property had perished. Exactly the opposite, it seemed to me, happened with most of those survivors who lost wives and children in the eruption. They moved about as in a dream, without a tear, without a complaint, helping others to provide for the needs of the homeless and houseless. The universality of the catastrophe made each man feel as though it were selfishness to attach too great an importance at such a crisis to his own personal losses. Nay, more; the burst of feverish activity and nervous excitement, I might even say enjoyment, which followed the horror, was traceable, I think, to this self-same cause. Even grave citizens felt they must do their best to dispel the universal gloom; and they plunged accordingly into a round of dissipations which other nations thought both unseemly and un-English. It was one way of expressing the common emotion. We had all lost heart—and we flocked to the theatres to pluck up our courage. That, I believe, must be our national answer to M. Zola's strictures on our untimely levity. 'This people,' says the great French author, 'which took its pleasures sadly while it was rich and prosperous, begins to dance and sing above the ashes of its capital— it makes merry by the open graves of its wives and children. What an enigma! What a puzzle! What chance of an Œdipus!'

A Sense of the Future

Martin Swayne

G EORGE BALLANCE was a financier with a sense of the future. He was also purely English.

He was a tall, lean man, clean-shaven, with a half-humorous and half-sardonic expression, and a roguish, boyish blue eye. He looked on life not from the point of view of one who is immediately interested in what goes on, but as one who wishes only to discover what things are leading to. This attitude gives an effect of detachment which is enigmatical, especially if, as in Ballance's case, it is accompanied by a very shrewd knowledge of affairs.

I encountered him in the lounge of the Blitz Hotel one evening. We were both waiting for friends with whom we were to dine. I discovered him sitting behind a palm tree, eyeing the crowd of well-dressed folk who were passing into the dining-room. It was some time since I had seen him.

'What are you up to nowadays?' I asked, taking a seat beside him. 'I've heard nothing of your exploits recently.'

'I'm buying horses,' he said, with a peculiar light in his eye.

'Horses!' I exclaimed. 'Do you expect another war, or what?'

'No, I don't expect another war. The war-chests are too empty still. We sha'n't have another war for some time.'

'Then why are you buying horses?'

'I'm buying horses because I like them.' He crooked his fingers round the fine gold chain that suspended his eyeglasses, and smiled at me in his peering, short-sighted way. 'They're nice animals. I feel I can't possess enough of 'em. I'm buying them everywhere. I've got agents working for me in Asia Minor, in America, in

Australia, and in Africa. Think what a useful animal the horse is.
It's got four legs.'

'That's true,' I replied.

'And nice strong muscles.'

'Yes.'

'It's a patient animal, too.'

'Quite. Still, they eat a lot.'

'There's plenty of grass and oats and bran. There is always plenty
of that. I don't worry about what comes from the surface of the
earth, Millington.'

'What do you worry about?'

'I worry about what comes from below the surface. Now, horses
aren't interested in what comes from below the surface of the earth.
No animal is. That shows their good sense. They're only interested
in what's on the surface. So am I.'

I was still quite in the dark, and told him so.

'If I were to tell you why I'm buying horses, you wouldn't believe
me. Nobody would.' He tinkled his glasses against the gold ring
that he wore on the little finger of his left hand, and his eyes looked
sardonically upon the crowd of diners who passed up the steps
towards the glass doors of the huge dining-room. 'Nobody ever
believes in what happens. That's why it happens. Why don't you
buy some horses?'

'I really don't need any. I've just got another car.'

'What make?'

'A thirty-horse-power Crusader. It's about the only car turned
out nowadays with engines and parts that will last more than a
couple of years. She's a fine engineering proposition, Ballance. It's
a treat to drive her.'

'I'd rather have thirty horses,' he said.

'What on earth would be the good of having thirty horses?' I
exclaimed, vexed that he did not share the enthusiasm I felt for my
new Crusader. 'If you used the whole thirty together you wouldn't
be able to go faster than one of them could go. My car can average
thirty-five in a long trip comfortably. A horse—no!'

'The horse has definite limitations.'

'It certainly has.'

He nodded.

'The more I think about limitations, the more sense I see in them.

If you had thirty horses under the bonnet of your car, you could feed 'em on grass and oats. But you've got a lot of machinery instead. What do you have to feed it on?'

'Petrol, of course.'

'Yes. Petrol, of course. You never saw petrol growing in a field, did you? There isn't a petrol shrub or a petrol flower. You can't sow petrol. If you could, I wouldn't buy horses, even if they had six legs apiece and muscles as big as bolsters. Petrol comes from beneath the surface of the earth. Everything that is a damned nuisance comes from there. Diamonds, for instance.'

I was silent.

'How much does your car do on a gallon of petrol?'

'About twenty miles.'

'Twenty miles with a gallon of petrol. Where's the petrol gone when you've gone twenty miles? There's no manure in petrol vapour. It doesn't go back to the earth. No, it's gone for ever, and you have to get another gallon out of the earth. Now with the horse it's different.'

'Are you going to try and re-introduce the horse into Western civilization?'

'I'm not going to try. I'm going to be the man who owns the horses when Western civilization goes to the earth for another gallon of petrol and finds there ain't any left.'

At that moment he rose and left me with a nod. A party of men and women had just come in and he went to greet them. My own friends arrived a little later. During dinner I mentioned that Ballance was buying horses all over the world.

'What for?' they asked.

'I don't know. As far as I can make out he believes that petrol will give out.'

There was a chorus of laughter at the absurdity of the idea.

'Why, petrol came down twopence only last week, because they struck new oil four months ago in Mexico,' said one.

Ballance is a strangely impressive man. He has the power of being impressive without intending to be. I could not shake off the memory of his words. We went to a music-hall after dinner, and everything was merry enough. There was plenty of laughter, of colour and noise, of jokes and bright eyes and pretty dresses. I possessed my new Crusader. My bank balance was satisfactory. I felt in good health. There had been no cloud on my horizon until my conversation with Ballance that evening. And the cloud that now hung there had no proper reason to exist. I did not believe Ballance, and in any case what concern was it of mine if petrol did fail in the far future? Yet in the midst of laughter I constantly found myself staring at the cloud, which I could not get rid of.

If I had known Ballance merely as a dismal prophet, I would have paid no attention to him, and his words would have had no effect on me. But he was not in any sense a dismal prophet. He was a remarkably shrewd man, whose calculations, though simple enough, were usually right. He was very wealthy. He had made his money, as far as I could make out from what I had heard, by foreseeing a few very simple and plain events—plain enough, that is, after they had taken place. But the spectacle of his agents throughout the world silently getting a controlling interest in horses, while he sat, with his half-humorous, half-sardonic expression, in London, amidst all the evidences of the increasing popularity of motoring, with petrol coming steadily down in price and machinery getting cheaper, and mass production on the increase and facilities for easy purchase alluring the most impecunious inhabitant of flatland and villadom to possess a car—this spectacle seemed so paradoxical and absurd that I could not understand why it gained such a hold on my imagination. It was, perhaps, the absurdity of it that made my imagination play round it that night while I lay in bed unable to sleep.

Next morning I took out my new Crusader and went for a fine spin into the country. Its glittering aluminium body was beautiful to behold. I felt that she was a living goddess obedient to my desire. What a marvellous thing a car is! Is there any piece of mechanism so beautifully organized and so easy to handle? I stopped in a village a hundred miles from London to fill up with petrol. A red-painted pump was fixed in the road outside a cycle shop, and I drew up beside it. As the man filled my tank I reflected that nearly every village in Great Britain had these pumps. Everywhere, in all directions, in town or country, petrol was systematically supplied. Everywhere, going in every direction, north, east, south, and west, were motor-cars of every description. Millions of explosions in millions of cylinders, millions of pistons dashing up and down, millions of gallons of petrol gurgling into tanks, millions of tyred wheels turning—all the world over. What a tremendous activity! What a tremendous giant organism it all was! How impossible to conceive that it should ever die and fall away into nothing because there was no more petrol to course through its arteries! How could that be possible when all the machinery of its vast body was standing, all the enamelled cars with their ingenious engines, and the factories behind them continually turning out new ones? Motors had come to stay. They would never disappear. What, as one of my guests had said the evening before, did people do in the days when there were no motors?

I turned my Crusader towards London, pushed down the accelerator and ate up the miles, and five gallons of petrol as well.

It occurred to me that evening that I would ring up Ballance and ask him to dine with me. I did not expect that he would accept my invitation. He was a great man, simple enough in his habits, but nevertheless a great man. I was agreeably surprised to hear his manservant reply on the telephone that Sir George would be pleased if I would come and dine with him instead at eight. After I had dressed I found I had half an hour to spare, so I decided to walk to Ballance's house, which was across St James's Park. As I strolled along Piccadilly, the great roar of London traffic filled the air. The streets seemed to contain an endless band of moving cars and buses. I tried to cast back my mind to the days before motors were common, but my recollection was dim and I could not construct the picture clearly. This great mass of traffic, these thundering and swaying buses, the continual pulsation of engines, that began in the early morning and continued until far into the night—for it only ceased, or almost ceased, for a brief space every twenty-four hours—had become a part of daily existence, and to think myself out of it, back into the days of horse traffic, was not possible. As well might I try to think myself into a London before gas was introduced and before water-pipes had been laid, or when the grass grew in the fields round Mayfair.

Ballance had a genial, hospitable vein in him. We dined in a small room in his big house, and were waited upon by a single servant. After dinner I asked if the subject of conversation of the previous evening was permissible, as I wanted to ask some questions.

'You ask any questions you like,' he said. 'I always tell people anything I know.'

'Isn't that rather risky for a financier?'

'Not in my case. It may be for some. When you make money out of the general tendency of things, as I do, and not out of artificial situations, as most others do, there is no risk.'

'Why do you think petrol is going to fail?'

He screwed up his eyes and looked towards the ceiling as if he were listening for an answer. Then he lowered his head and carefully moved his wineglass further away from his plate.

'I don't exactly think,' he said. 'Have you ever noticed that it is quite true that troubles never come singly?'

'I have noticed that,' I replied, eagerly. 'It took me years to notice it, but it is quite true. They come in waves.'

'You knew the saying long before you realized it?'

'Yes.'

'When you realized it, in fact, you probably thought you had made a remarkable discovery, until you happened to remember the proverb that you had used yourself a hundred times without realizing what it meant?'

I nodded. He nodded also and moved his wineglass back.

'That is how things go,' he said. 'You live to discover only a small fraction of what you say every day in familiar phrases. Now I began to realize for myself that Nature increases to excess what she is just going to take away. I thought I had made a discovery. I struggled with the dim idea and tried to pin it down, when I suddenly found it lying pat before me in a book that I happened to pick up. It is an ancient Chinese proverb. There it was, in those words. Nature increases to excess what she is just going to take away. I understood it at once. You may have read it yourself. But I bet you haven't discovered it. You can read all the wisdom of the world in a week or a day, or perhaps an hour. But you can't understand a millionth part of it unless you have lived it into realization.'

'Then you thought that petrol would give out because there is so much motoring?'

'I knew that something must give way, and I wondered what. So I began to make enquiries—very careful ones, too, I assure you. I went into oil and the distribution of oil and the life of oil-bearing regions. After I had finished these enquiries I began to buy horses.'

'So you believe that motoring is doomed?'

'Doomed? Why use such a word? It will die out. And not only motoring, but machinery in general. It is finished.'

'But not for hundreds of years.'

'Oh, some men live a kind of existence for fifty years after they are finished. But if I thought the age of motoring would last for hundreds of years yet, I wouldn't buy horses.' He pointed a finger at me. 'See here,' he continued, 'the end of motoring will be very quick. If you knew as much as I do about oil and had my sense of what's coming you would understand why. I'll put it in this way. This earth we live on isn't any darned old thing. It isn't blind, senseless, helpless, without any affairs of its own. It's alive and cute, but because it's built on another scale it seems a bit slow in the uptake.'

'That's only a fanciful idea.'

'Is it?' He snorted. 'Two fleas on your skin might say the same to one another about your body. But let them nip far enough and long enough and they'll be surprised at what happens to them.' He grinned. 'How is the new Crusader?'

'She's not short of petrol yet.'

He circled his hand round in the air and pursed up his lips, giving me a sly look.

'She won't be just yet.'

'How long will it be until she is?'

'It might be a year.'

'Well, that's some relief to hear. We've got another year!'

'A year's a long time, isn't it? About the time it takes for the earth to turn round and scratch. Have some more wine. There'll always be enough wine, Millington. There's no harm in wine. It's from the surface of the earth.'

It is remarkable how soon we forget things. We forget even our grandest moments of insight and our most inspiring ideas. A couple of months after dining with Ballance—he had gone abroad in the meanwhile—I had almost forgotten what we had spoken about, forgotten the train of imagination I had had, forgotten almost that petrol came out of the earth. The Crusader was still, of course, the delight of my soul, but I had seen another make of car that was certainly very good. In fact, I had had a run in this other car and she seemed to go quite divinely. But, as I had said to the agent of the firm, I was perfectly satisfied with my Crusader—which was built, it will be remembered, to last for years—and could not think of changing her, although, of course, there was no doubt that she was inclined to—but this is not the place to describe her defects.

In the meanwhile petrol, after touching the lowest price on record, had begun to climb again. There was a good deal of outcry at this, and I was one amongst the many who penned indignant letters to the papers with my head filled with visions of fleshy oil kings, with long cigars stuck between yellow teeth, manipulating the market after twenty-course dinners, with chorus-girls dancing down the centre of the table. Anything that touches the pocket certainly does rouse violent fancies. Petrol, however, continued to rise in spite of my letter. I had dined with Ballance in the early autumn. By the spring petrol was three shillings, and almost at once it jumped to three-and-sixpence a gallon.

In my own case I could afford to buy it at this price, but it was vexatious and damped the pleasure of motoring considerably. To fill up my eight-gallon tank and have to pay almost thirty shillings for it was irritating. How that yellow-toothed oil king hovered in my mind! Petrol rose relentlessly to four shillings. There was now a universal clamour, and questions were asked in the House of Commons. Everyone suspected that somebody was juggling. It was pointed out that an enormous number of people were buying cars on the hire-purchase system, and that they could not afford to use them if petrol was likely to remain at that level. As it was, they did not know whether to forfeit the cars or continue to pay for them, or what to do, and as most of these people could not really afford to have cars at all, whatever the price of petrol, they easily became overwrought.

As is always the case in such situations, the announcement that there was an actual shortage of petrol was made so obscurely that nobody grasped it. I, for one, certainly did not grasp it, but remained convinced that somebody was playing the fool with the public. Endless articles appeared on the subject, but none of them referred to the central fact that oil was running dry in all countries.

It was Sir George Ballance who pointed it out. In the course of a published interview, Sir George stated in the simplest words that petrol was obtained from beneath the surface of the earth, and came up in the form of crude oil which had to be refined. The supply of crude oil coming up from the depths of the earth was diminishing rapidly both west and east, hence it had been necessary to raise the price of petrol because it was becoming more and more precious and there *was not enough to go round*. This last phrase astonished everyone. It seemed incredible.

The newspapers quoted Ballance's words all the world over. They hailed him as a great authority, a man with extraordinary insight and marvellous penetration. His golden phrase that there was not enough oil to go round enlightened the whole of humanity. The oil kings ceased to be the object of vindictive declamation. People no longer shook their fists at them far into the night in clubland, flatland, and villadom. They were not to blame. Sir George—who was an extraordinary man, of course—had explained the situation in a way that no newspaper and none of the well-known journalists of the day—who are so copious in striking articles which never mean anything—had been able to explain it. There wasn't enough oil to go round. Oil was failing. In a report of a further interview with Sir George, it was stated that he had said that the output of oil was not only rapidly diminishing, but that it would probably entirely cease. This was a most startling assertion. It caused a tremendous sensation. No one had expected it. People had understood, from the report of the first interview with Sir George, that the rise in the price of petrol was not due to the nefarious machinations of the oil kings, but to the fact that there was not enough oil to go round. But the public had not got as far as the realization that oil might cease to exist. The genius of Sir George Ballance was necessary to point that out, and when it did so an extraordinary nervousness swept over the entire Western civilization.

The confidence in Western civilization seemed to be menaced.

The morning upon which the second interview was published in the newspapers I received a letter from Sir George. It was laconic.

'Would you like to buy thirty horses?—G. B.'

I threw it aside and opened my newspaper. I looked first at the price of petrol. It had risen to eight shillings and sixpence a gallon. My eye then caught the heavy type in which the headings of the interview with Ballance were printed.

'NO MORE OIL. EARTH RUNNING DRY. STARTLING THEORY. INTERVIEW WITH SIR GEORGE BALLANCE.'

I read every word of that article and laid down the newspaper. It was impossible. I could not believe it. I recalled the conversation in the lounge of the Blitz Hotel in the autumn of the previous year, but it still seemed fanciful and unlikely, even though petrol was so high. I was ready to accept the view that petrol was high because there was a temporary shortage. I had ceased to blame the oil kings and wish them in the fires of hell. I had decided to use my car—by the way, I had sold my Crusader and bought a Juno, a most wonderful car, as pliant as a willow—only for the weekends until the price of petrol became easier.

But I could not agree with Ballance in thinking that petrol would cease to exist. The earth might be running dry of oil, but petrol— well, of course, if the earth really was running dry of oil, petrol would cease to exist, and as that was quite unthinkable, it was impossible that the earth was running dry of oil. The earth was an enormous size. Imagine a can of petrol in comparison to the size of the earth! I heartily wished somebody would publish one of those illustrated articles on the subject with the dome of St Paul's and Mount Everest on it. How many cans of petrol, piled on top of one another, would reach the height of Cleopatra's Needle? What was the daily consumption of petrol in the world? Would the tins reach the top of St Paul's or the top of Mount Everest? I really scarcely knew if the world used a million or a hundred thousand or ten million gallons of petrol a day.

After breakfast I strolled round to the garage where I kept my new Juno. The manager of the garage, an ex-officer, looked glum.

'What's the matter?' I asked.

'Matter? Did you see what Sir George Ballance says? No more oil! Earth running dry! That's a nice outlook for me.' His eye roved over the rows of shining cars that were congregated under the glass roof of the garage.

'It's all nonsense,' I said, warmly. 'Ballance doesn't know what the earth contains. Why, since the internal-combustion engine was invented we can't have used more than what amounts to a cupful of the total quantity of oil lying in the earth. This shortage is temporary. They'll strike new oil before a week is out.'

'But the oil's failing in Baku, in Peru, in Mexico, and all over the place. I've heard of one oil-well failing or one district running dry, but never of the whole lot failing together.'

'Bah!' I said; 'it's nonsense. Why, if petrol gave out, the whole of civilization would have to change its habits. It's inconceivable.'

'Then it seems to me the whole of civilization *will* have to change its habits,' he muttered. 'I don't like it. It's never happened before in this way. They say petrol will jump to double the price before tonight. We can't get it. There have been five hundred gallons on order for the garage for a week past, and I can't get a drop. They've taken off half the London buses, and are jerking the fares up every hour. Look at all these cars here. A month ago most of them would have been out by this time. Now the owners leave them all the week and take them out on Sunday.'

'It doesn't matter to you. They pay rent for them just the same.'

'Do you suppose I depend only on the rent paid for garaging them?' he said, angrily. 'Petrol, oil, repairs, tyres, cleaning, over-hauling—all that brings me in cash. The more a man uses his car, the better pleased I am.'

'I shouldn't worry. Nothing will happen.'

He looked at me with sombre fiery eyes.

'Were you in the war, Mr Millington?'

'Yes.'

'Didn't that teach you that things you can't imagine *can* happen?' He laughed shortly and turned away. It was only natural that he should be nervy. I went to my new Juno. Her lines were splendid, and on the road she was all she looked.

I left the garage and walked up a side street into Piccadilly. As the manager of the garage had said, they had taken half the London buses off the road. This made a considerable difference to the volume of traffic. There was also a much smaller number of private cars and tradesmen's vans. It was possible to cross the street with ease.

Looking down Piccadilly and seeing the wide gaps in the stream of vehicles gave a faint sense of disaster. The volume of traffic and the great din of its passage had hitherto sung a brazen triumphant song that reassured the Londoner. It was the harsh song of progress in an age which, hurrying with increasing complexities, required a strident loud music to drown its anxieties. It was a visible and audible proof that all was well, that things worked properly, that business was prosperous, that people were going the right way, that money was plentiful, that God was in His heaven, that there was nothing to fear. The streets are all roaring with traffic—all's well with the world! This was the unconscious influence of the traffic, which I only became aware of through its absence. A chill feeling crept over me as I watched the broken and narrowed stream flowing intermittently past me. A newspaper poster caught my eye: '*Earth running dry of oil. Petrol nine shillings.*'

Petrol was fourteen shillings a gallon next day, and that was an entirely prohibitive price. All the London buses were withdrawn from the streets. All lorries and commercial vehicles ceased running. Only a very few private cars appeared. *The streets of London were almost empty.* People could walk across from pavement to pavement without looking round. They could stand in groups in the middle of Ludgate Circus and discuss the weather, if they wanted to, without danger. The dislocation of trade was incalculable.

Of course, it was rather enjoyable because it was novel, and people got some new sensations, but everyone felt a growing apprehension of disaster in the air. This sudden withdrawal of mechanical power was mysterious. What would happen next? Would coal cease? If coal ceased, machinery could not be kept going, and without machinery where would modern civilization find itself? Factories would close, railways would be unused, tubes would be silent, there would be no electricity, no gas, no oil. Animal or vegetable fat would become the sole illuminant. It would take an hour to get from Hampstead to the City. It would take days to get to Manchester and weeks to reach America. Newspapers would be handprinted by candle-light. Civilization would be thrown back one hundred, two hundred, a thousand years.

We should still have telephones and telegraphs, but no means of swift locomotion. We should know what occurred in Australia or Japan in a few seconds, but what a singular discrepancy there would be between the swiftness of the transmission of news and the slowness of the transmission of our bodies! England would become large again. York would be far distant by coach, and Edinburgh an adventurous expedition. The entire spirit of life would change. A new race would emerge in every Western land, a race of craftsmen who rooted themselves in their native ground. Character and dialect would arise again. The towns would contract. The great combines in business would break up and the movements of centralization, the modern substitution for roots, cease.

But there was no evidence of coal ceasing. That layer of modern civilization and all that belonged to it was not threatened. But the superimposed layer of motor traffic was removed at one stroke.

I had a tank full of petrol in my Juno, so I took her out into the deserted streets. People stared at me. Their looks were almost hostile. It was as if the first days of motoring had returned, when a car was regarded as an invention of the devil, and the drivers of horse-buses vented their wit on it. I felt it was awkward having to sound my horn. People resented it. I went out into the country north of London. I did not see a single car of any kind. The trains were running as usual. I met a string of horses moving towards London, led by a man chewing a straw. He stared at my car. A few miles further on I met more horses.

I drew up on a lonely heath, where the gorse was flaming. I felt sad. The sense of disaster had gripped me. At last I realized that petrol had perhaps ceased for ever. I walked slowly over the heathland. What did it mean to me? It meant a great deal. A motor-car had become the chief factor of my life. I was always motoring, motoring here and motoring there, always arranging trips and going to places for the sake of motoring to them. I liked taking people out. I liked lunching in the country, driving out to distant golf courses, driving down to the sea, driving up to Scotland, driving to and fro. I liked my car to be admired. I liked to talk motoring shop. It gave me most of the meaning I found in life. A strange admission, perhaps, but true enough. What would I do without a motor—without speed—without independence?

There stood my Juno in the sunlight amid the golden gorse, perfectly shaped, faultlessly neat and complete, almost living—and was she already a thing of the past, finished, *dead*? Down the road the strings of horses were moving slowly towards London.

Well, there was one man who knew what to do at this strange moment, when fate had turned the wheel of progress back with sudden violence. That man was Sir George Ballance. Horses were moving all the world over, and Ballance was the controller of them. He would be busy enough. People would gradually find out that he was the Horse King. Some would recollect that he had said he was buying horses for months past, and they would understand, as I now understood, why he had been doing it. I smiled at myself. At the Blitz Hotel and at his house I could not comprehend him, although he had told me enough. Now it was all quite plain.

I climbed into my Juno and turned her south for our last ride together.

On coming into London, I happened to turn up the Euston Road, where second-hand motor shops abound. I descended upon one of them and enquired—merely out of curiosity—what they would give me for the car. I was told that they were not buying any more cars. They were quite polite until I said I would take two hundred for her. One of them, a little dark man with a cigarette between his lips, spoke:

'Take the darned thing away! What the devil do you think us want with cars?'

He spoke so violently that I thought it wise to retire. All down the Euston Road and Great Portland Street little groups of men with anxious faces stood at the doors of the motor-showrooms. I drove my Juno into her garage and left here there with half an inch of petrol in her tank. That was the last time I drove her. Petrol was now over a pound a gallon, and rapidly mounting.

No one knew what to do. The feeling of disaster had increased. Civilization seemed menaced. Of course, religious-minded folk saw a warning from Heaven in the situation. I must confess that I did not entirely escape from this notion myself. The sudden cessation of oil was curious. It looked almost as if a supernatural agency was at work. I think most people felt this even if they did not say so. Vast bodies of men were thrown out of employment, but there were no riots. People were touched with a kind of awe. No one, perhaps, had realized before how vulnerable our modern civilization was, and how easily it could be thrown into disorder, and even paralysed. I may be wrong, but it often seemed to me that with the awe people felt there was a trace of relief. Could it be possible that people were relieved that motor-cars had vanished? Was it possible that people didn't really believe in modern civilization? I have often wondered.

The Government tried to deal with the situation. Doles were distributed. It was still hoped that oil would be struck again, and that the former wells would begin to yield. Some scientist tried to account for the cessation of oil by a theory connected with the attractive forces of the moon and planets, and talked of an oil-tide; others advanced the idea that there had been some deep subterranean displacement which had caused the oil levels to sink beyond reach; others said it was due to an actual exhaustion. Nobody knew how the situation should be taken. Motor-car makers did not know if they should continue making cars. People who had cars did not know whether they should keep on paying garage fees. The omnibus companies, with their thousands of motor-buses, did not know whether to buy horses or not. A week passed by in this great uncertainty. Tradesmen began to buy horses and order vans. The carriage-builders began to get busy. Garages began to be turned into stables. Very gradually horse traffic began to increase in the streets. A few ancient horse-buses appeared, the drivers wearing top-hats and flicking their whips as of old. Hansom cabs and four-wheelers crept out of odd corners and were snapped up eagerly. A new traffic appeared, slow-moving—incredibly slow-moving it seemed at first—singing another song, and exhaling another odour. The harsh music of the age of progress was softened. New expressions appeared on people's faces. They looked calmer. They were less hurried.

By the end of a month motor-cars were things of the past. They were nowhere to be seen. The volume of horse traffic steadily increased. Horses began to pour into Europe. They poured into England. The former roar in the streets was replaced by a rumble and the clip-clop of hoofs. Processions of horse-drawn lorries bore motor-cars away from garages—where, I know not. You could buy a thousand of the finest cars ever produced for the price of taking them away. They were utterly useless. Enormous fortunes were lost. Companies smashed right and left. All the money in oil, in rubber, vanished into thin air. All sorts and conditions of people were hit. It was extraordinary to realize how many concerns and how many people depended directly and indirectly on the existence of motor-cars. And all the great industries connected with oil in every form crumbled into nothing. It seemed at first impossible for Western civilization to stand the racket. But, somehow, things very slowly adjusted themselves. It was found possible for people to exist without oil.

By the end of three months the horses were everywhere. As Ballance had said, the horse has its limitations. Just before the disappearance of petrol, the buses had been increased in size.

But when the horses came back the little horse-bus came back too. And aeroplanes disappeared for good, to everyone's relief. What use were they ever? How diminutive the horse-buses looked! All the vehicles looked diminutive, like toys. They gave up erecting the huge, ugly shops along Regent Street. Somehow they did not seem necessary. That kind of architecture began to look dead and staring. They began, within a year, to build in a different style. Style in everything, in fashion, art, and architecture, in dancing, in drama, in cinema films, in novels, in manners, began to change. Domestic life began to reappear. People stayed at home. Newspapers changed. The nervous, meaningless, sensational style of journalism faded away. The short snappy paragraph vanished. Phrases changed. Familiar words passed away. People's voices altered. And, strangely enough, there seemed to be more room in the world. There seemed to be fewer people.

I met Sir George Ballance driving in the Park in his carriage and pair. He was said to be the wealthiest man in Europe. He was kind enough to tell his coachman to stop. 'Have you got a horse?' he enquired.

'Yes,' I said. 'I have got two horses. I live outside London now.'

'Nice animals, aren't they?'

I nodded.

'They steady us human beings, you know,' he continued. 'Got a nice atmosphere about them. We're made of flesh and blood like them. We're not made of steel and petrol. I hear the doctors say that nervous complaints are on the decline.'

'Is that so?'

'You look better yourself. You used to be a jumpy sort of fellow. Wonderful things, horses.'

VIII

TWO STORYTELLERS

Arthur Conan Doyle (1859–1930) is, and will always be, inextricably linked to Sherlock Holmes, and yet the Holmes canon, novels and short stories, takes up less than a third of its creator's output. Doyle's first love was the historical genre—it depressed him that novels such as *The White Company* (1891) and *Sir Nigel* (1906) were not the roaring bestsellers he thought they ought to have been. But in truth they are over-worthy. His Brigadier Gerard tales, on the other hand, are still eminently readable today since Gerard is a scamp and a posturer, a character of flesh and blood. All of Doyle's story-telling skills came to the fore when he hit on a hero who was just that much larger than life. Pre-eminent in this respect is Professor Challenger, two of whose novel-length adventures, *The Lost World* (1912) and *The Poison Belt* (1913), are triumphs of the tale-teller's art. *The Land of Mist* (1926), however, the third Challenger novel, fails dismally because Doyle's interest is transferred to Malone, the journalist, leaving Challenger, for all his barkings and bluster, a curiously muted figure; it did not help, either, that the book was written as propaganda for Doyle's Spiritualist convictions. Contrary to popular belief, Doyle had been attracted to Spiritualism long before the First World War (in which his son died); he joined the Society for Psychical Research as early as 1883, though it was only one of a wide range of interests he pursued. It is arguable that when he vigorously espoused the cause, almost to the exclusion of all else, he lost a good deal of his story-telling craft. After 1919 Greenhough Smith was forever cracking the editorial whip in an endeavour, mostly vain, to drag his star-author away from life-after-death and back to fictional fancies. Doyle's fervent championship of the 'Cottingley Fairies' (photographs of dancing elves, in fact faked up by two young girls) must have proved a trying experience to the older, and surely wiser, man. It is difficult to believe that Smith, something of a cynic, published these pictures and Doyle's subsequent articles with any great enthusiasm, and it seems more than likely that Doyle himself pulled rank to get them into the magazine. In general, those who believe in the paranormal tend not to make a very good fist of writing supernatural fiction. This is not entirely the case with Doyle, yet it must be said that his pre-war weird tales carry rather more fictional conviction than the stories he wrote after the year 1915. Even a mildly propagandist tale like 'How It Happened' has a not entirely expected twist to it. In 'The Silver Mirror' one can tell the author is enjoying himself immensely: there is humour, horror, and (his favourite genre) history. 'The Horror of the Heights' is surely one of his most riveting tales: even though we know his basic premise (that something terrible lurks high above the clouds) is wildly absurd, it yet remains a little masterpiece of imaginative writing.

E. Nesbit (1858–1924) led a life quite at variance with the image summoned up by her most famous writings. A celebrated children's author whose reputation has increased rather than otherwise over the past sixty years, she successfully combined magic and fantasy in her books (most of which were first serialized in the *Strand*) with a down-to-earth realism (her child heroes and heroines are in the main pugnacious pragmatists, whatever extraordinary and fantastical events are occurring around them). The American novelist Gore Vidal judged her to be 'rigorously honest . . . about how children and adults lived . . . [and] one of the few writers who realized that children, like Jews and Negroes, are a persecuted minority'. In this she followed Kenneth Grahame, in whose *The Golden Age* (1895) and *Dream Days* (1898) adults are generally excoriated as 'Olympians', whose sole purpose in life, as seen through the children's eyes, seems to be to quarrel amongst themselves and be a nuisance. Nesbit was an early and ardent socialist and founder-member of the Fabian Society. Her marriage to the journalist Hubert Bland did not lack stress, partly due to Bland's incessant and flagrant infidelities (the only females he seems not to have tried to seduce were his own daughters), partly due to her own rather quieter efforts in the same line, with various much younger artists and writers. Nevertheless, the Bland ménage seems to have rubbed along, albeit in a decidedly Bohemian manner (Nesbit's best friend, Alice Hoatson, lived with them for a while, giving birth to more of Bland's children, whom Nesbit brought up as her own). Although fiercely feminist, in some respects she had a conservative streak, rejecting the notion of female suffrage. Nesbit wrote some notable supernatural stories, many with a distinct bias towards the gruesome. Her novel *Salome and the Head* (1909) features a striking sequence in which the heroine, Alexandra, discovers she has been dancing the Dance of the Seven Veils with the still bloody head of a dead man (a year later, one of Nesbit's protégés, the young novelist Edgar Jepson, utilized the severed head idea in the first chapter of his Tsarist Secret Service thriller *The Girl's Head*). Although 'The Haunted House' and 'The Power of Darkness' contain no element of the supernatural, both are convincingly horrid.

The Silver Mirror

Arthur Conan Doyle

JAN. 3.—This affair of White and Wotherspoon's accounts proves to be a gigantic task. There are twenty thick ledgers to be examined and checked. Who would be a junior partner? However, it is the first big bit of business which has been left entirely in my hands. I must justify it. But it has to be finished so that the lawyers may have the result in time for the trial. Johnson said this morning that I should have to get the last figure out before the 20th of the month. Good Lord! Well, have at it, and if human brain and nerve can stand the strain I'll win out at the other side. It means office-work from ten to five, and then a second sitting from about eight to one in the morning. There's drama in an accountant's life. When I find myself in the still early hours while all the world sleeps, hunting through column after column for those missing figures which will turn a respected Alderman into a felon, I understand that it is not such a prosaic profession after all.

On Monday I came on the first trace of defalcation. No heavy game hunter ever got a finer thrill when first he caught sight of the trail of his quarry. But I look at the twenty ledgers and think of the jungle through which I have to follow him before I get my kill. Hard work—but rare sport, too, in a way! I saw the fat fellow once at a City dinner, his red face glowing above a white napkin. He looked at the little pale man at the end of the table. He would have been pale too if he could have seen the task that would be mine.

Jan. 6.—What perfect nonsense it is for doctors to prescribe rest when rest is out of the question! Asses! They might as well shout to a man who has a pack of wolves at his heels that what he wants is absolute quiet. My figures must be out by a certain date; unless they are so I shall lose the chance of my lifetime, so how on earth am I to rest? I'll take a week or so after the trial.

Perhaps I was myself a fool to go to the doctor at all. But I get nervous and highly-strung when I sit alone at my work at night. It's not a pain—only a sort of fullness of the head with an occasional mist over the eyes. I thought perhaps some bromide, or chloral, or something of the kind might do me good. But stop work! It's absurd to ask such a thing. It's like a long-distance race. You feel queer at first and your heart thumps and your lungs pant, but if you have only the pluck to keep on you get your second wind. I'll stick to my work and wait for my second wind. If it never comes—all the same I'll stick to my work. Two ledgers are done, and I am well on in the third. The rascal has covered his tracks well; but I pick them up for all that.

Jan. 9.—I had not meant to go to the doctor again. And yet I have had to. 'Straining my nerves, risking a complete breakdown, even endangering my sanity.' That's a nice sentence to have fired off at one. Well, I'll stand the strain and I'll take the risk; but so long as I can sit in my chair and move a pen I'll follow the old sinner's slot.

By the way, I may as well set down here the queer experience which drove me this second time to the doctor. I'll keep an exact record of my symptoms and sensations, because they are interesting in themselves—'a curious psycho-physiological study', says the doctor—and also because I am perfectly certain that when I am through with them they will all seem blurred and unreal, like some queer dream betwixt sleeping and waking. So now, while they are fresh, I will just make a note of them, if only as a change of thought after the endless figures.

There's an old silver-framed mirror in my room—it was given me by a friend who had a taste for antiquities, and he, as I happen to know, picked it up at a sale and had no notion where it came from. It's a large thing, three feet across and two feet high, and it leans at the back of a side-table on my left as I write. The frame is flat, about three inches across, and very old; far too old for hallmarks or other methods of determining its age. The glass part projects, with a bevelled edge, and has the magnificent reflecting power which is only, as it seems to me, to be found in very old mirrors.

Arthur Conan Doyle

There's a feeling of perspective when you look into it such as no modern glass can ever give.

The mirror is so situated that as I sit at the table I can usually see nothing in it but the reflection of the red window curtains. But a queer thing happened last night. I had been working for some hours, very much against the grain, with continual bouts of that mistiness of which I have complained. Again and again I had to stop and clear my eyes. Well, on one of these occasions I chanced to look at the mirror. It had the oddest appearance. The red curtains which should have been reflected in it were no longer there, but the glass seemed to be clouded and steamy, not on the surface, which glittered like steel, but deep down in the very grain of it. This opacity, when I stared hard at it, appeared to slowly rotate this way and that, until it was a thick white cloud swirling in heavy wreaths. So real and solid was it, and so reasonable was I, that I remember turning, with the idea that the curtains were on fire. But everything was deadly still in the room—no sound save the ticking of the clock, no movement save the slow gyration of that strange woolly cloud deep in the heart of the old mirror.

Then, as I looked, the mist, or smoke, or cloud, or whatever one may call it, seemed to coalesce and solidify at two points quite close together, and I was aware, with a thrill of interest rather than of fear, that these were two eyes looking out into the room. A vague outline of a head I could see—a woman's, by the hair, but this was very shadowy. Only the eyes were quite distinct; such eyes—dark, luminous, filled with some passionate emotion, fury or horror, I could not say which. Never have I seen eyes which were so full of intense, vivid life. They were not fixed upon me, but stared out into the room. Then as I sat erect, passed my hand over my brow, and made a strong conscious effort to pull myself together, the dim head faded into the general opacity, the mirror slowly cleared, and there were the red curtains once again.

A sceptic would say, no doubt, that I had dropped asleep over my figures and that my experience was a dream. As a matter of fact, I was never more vividly awake in my life. I was able to argue about it even as I looked at it, and to tell myself that it was a subjective impression—a chimera of the nerves—begotten by worry and insomnia. But why this particular shape? And who is the woman, and what is the dreadful emotion which I read in those wonderful brown eyes? They come between me and my work. For the first time I have done less than the daily tally which I had marked out. Perhaps that is why I have had no abnormal sensations tonight. Tomorrow I must wake up, come what may.

Jan. 11.—All well, and good progress with my work. I wind the net, coil after coil, round that bulky body. But the last smile may remain with him if my own nerves break over it. The mirror would seem to be a sort of barometer which marks my brain pressure. Each night I have observed that it had clouded before I reached the end of my task.

Dr Sinclair (who is, it seems, a bit of a psychologist) was so interested in my account that he came round this evening to have a look at the mirror. I had observed that something was scribbled in crabbed old characters upon the metalwork at the back. He examined this with a lens, but could make nothing of it. 'Sanc. X. Pal.' was his final reading of it, but that did not bring us any further. He advised me to put it away into another room; but, after all, whatever I may see in it is, by his own account, only a symptom. It is in the cause that the danger lies. The twenty ledgers—not the silver mirror—should be packed away if I could only do it. I'm at the eighth now, so I progress.

Jan. 13.—Perhaps it would have been wiser after all if I *had* packed away the mirror. I had an extraordinary experience with it last night. And yet I find it so interesting, so fascinating, that even now I will keep it in its place. What on earth is the meaning of it all?

I suppose it was about one in the morning, and I was closing my books preparatory to staggering off to bed, when I saw her there in front of me. The stage of mistiness and development must have passed unobserved, and there she was in all her beauty and passion and distress, as clear-cut as if she were really in the flesh before me. The figure was small, but very distinct—so much so that every feature, and even every detail of dress, is stamped in my memory. She is seated on the extreme left of the mirror. A sort of shadowy figure crouches down beside her—I can dimly discern that it is a man—and then behind them is cloud, in which I see figures—figures which move. It is not a mere picture upon which I look. It is a scene in life, an actual episode. She crouches and quivers. The man beside her cowers down. The vague figures make abrupt

movements and gestures. All my fears were swallowed up in my
interest. It was maddening to see so much and not to see more.

But I can at least describe the woman to the smallest point. She
is very beautiful and quite young, not more than five-and-twenty, I
should judge. Her hair is of a very rich brown, with a warm
chestnut shade fining into gold at the edges. A little flat-pointed cap
comes to an angle in front, and is made of lace edged with pearls.
The forehead is high, too high perhaps for perfect beauty, but one
would not have it otherwise, as it gives a touch of power and
strength to what would otherwise be a softly feminine face. The
brows are most delicately curved, over heavy eyelids, and then
come those wonderful eyes—so large, so dark, so full of overmastering emotion, of rage, of horror, contending with a pride of self-
control which holds her from sheer frenzy. The cheeks are pale, the
lips white with agony, the chin and throat most exquisitely rounded.
The figure sits and leans forward in the chair, straining and rigid,
cataleptic with horror. The dress is black velvet, a jewel gleams like
a flame in the breast, and a golden crucifix smoulders in the shadow
of a fold. This is the lady whose image still lives in the old silver
mirror. What dire deed could it be which has left its impress there
so that now in another age, if the spirit of a man be but attuned to
it, he may be conscious of its presence?

One other detail: down on the left side of the skirt of the black
dress was what I thought at first was a shapeless bunch of white
ribbon. Then, as I looked more intently or as the vision defined
itself more clearly, I perceived what it was. It was the hand of a
man, clenched and knotted in agony, which held on with a
convulsive grasp to the fold of the dress. The rest of the crouching
figure was a mere vague outline, but that strenuous hand shone
clear on the dark background, with a sinister suggestion of tragedy
in its frantic clutch. The man is frightened—horribly frightened.
That I can clearly discern. What has terrified him so? Why does he
grip the woman's dress? The answer lies amongst those moving
figures in the background. They have brought danger both to him
and to her. The interest of the thing fascinated me. I thought no
more of its relation to my own nerves, but I stared and stared as if
in a theatre. But I could get no further. The mist thinned. There
were tumultuous movements in which all the figures were vaguely
concerned. Then the mirror was clear once more.

The doctor says I must drop work for a day, and I can afford to do so, for I have made good progress lately. It is quite evident that the visions depend entirely upon my own nervous state, for I sat in front of the mirror for an hour tonight, with no result whatever. My soothing day has chased them away. I wonder whether I shall ever penetrate what they all mean? I examined the mirror this evening under a good light, and besides the mysterious inscription, 'Sanc. X. Pal.', I was able to discern some signs or heraldic marks, very faintly visible upon the silver. They must be very ancient, as they are almost obliterated. So far as I could make out, they were three spearheads, two above and one below. I will show them to the doctor when he calls tomorrow.

Jan. 14.—Feel perfectly well again, and I intend that nothing else shall stop me until my task is finished. The doctor was shown the marks on the mirror and agreed that they were armorial bearings. He is deeply interested in all that I have told him, and cross-questioned me closely on the details. It amuses me to notice how he is torn in two by conflicting desires—the one that his patient should lose his symptoms, the other that the medium—for so he regards me—should solve this mystery of the past. He advised continued rest, but did not oppose me too violently when I declared that such a thing was out of the question until the ten remaining ledgers have been checked.

Jan. 17.—For three nights I have had no experiences—my day of rest has borne fruit. Only a quarter of my task is left, but I must make a forced march, for the lawyers are clamouring for their material. I will give them enough and to spare. I have him fast on a hundred counts. When they realize what a slippery, cunning rascal he is I should gain some credit from the case. False trading accounts, false balance sheets, dividends drawn from capital, losses written down as profits, suppression of working expenses, manipulation of petty cash—it is a fine record!

Jan. 18.—Headaches, nervous twitches, mistiness, fullness of the temples—all the premonitions of trouble, and the trouble came sure enough. And yet my real sorrow is not so much that the vision should come as that it should cease before all is revealed.

But I saw more tonight. The crouching man was as visible as the lady whose gown he clutched. He is a little swarthy fellow, with a black pointed beard. He has a loose gown of damask trimmed with fur. The prevailing tints of his dress are red. What a fright the fellow is in, to be sure! He cowers and shivers and glares back over his shoulder. There is a small knife in his other hand, but he is far too tremulous and cowed to use it. Dimly now I begin to see the figures in the background. Fierce faces, bearded and dark, shape themselves out of the mist. There is one terrible creature, a skeleton of a man, with hollow cheeks and eyes sunk in his head. He also has a knife in his hand. On the right of the woman stands a tall man, very young, with flaxen hair, his face sullen and dour. The beautiful woman looks up at him in appeal. So does the man on the ground. This youth seems to be the arbiter of their fate. The crouching man draws closer and hides himself in the woman's skirts. The tall youth bends and tries to drag her away from him. So much I saw last night before the mirror cleared. Shall I never know what it leads to and whence it comes? It is not a mere imagination, of that I am very sure. Somewhere, some time, this scene has been acted, and this old mirror has reflected it. But when—where?

Jan. 20.—My work draws to a close, and it is time. I feel a tenseness within my brain, a sense of intolerable strain, which warns me that something must give. I have worked myself to the limit. But tonight should be the last night. With a supreme effort I should finish the final ledger and complete the case before I rise from my chair. I will do it. I will.

Feb. 7.—I did. My God, what an experience! I hardly know if I am strong enough yet to set it down.

Let me explain in the first instance that I am writing this in Dr Sinclair's private hospital some three weeks after the last entry in my diary. On the night of January 20th my nervous system finally gave way, and I remember nothing afterwards until I found myself three days ago in this home of rest. And I can rest with a good conscience. My work was done before I went under. My figures are in the solicitors' hands. The hunt is over.

And now I must describe that last night. I had sworn to finish my work, and so intently did I stick to it, though my head was bursting, that I would never look up until the last column had been added. And yet it was fine self-restraint, for all the time I knew that wonderful things were happening in the mirror. Every nerve in my body told me so. If I looked up there was an end of my work. So I did not look up till all was finished. Then, when at last with throbbing temples I threw down my pen and raised my eyes, what a sight was there!

The mirror in its silver frame was like a stage, brilliantly lit, in which a drama was in progress. There was no mist now. The oppression of my own nerves had wrought this amazing clarity. Every feature, every movement, was as clear-cut as in life. To think that I, a tired accountant, the most prosaic of mankind, with the account-books of a swindling bankrupt before me, should be chosen of all the human race to look upon such a scene!

It was the same scene and the same figures, but the drama had advanced a stage. The tall young man was holding the woman in his arms. She strained away from him and looked up at him with loathing in her face. They had torn the crouching man away from his hold upon the skirt of her dress. A dozen of them were round him—savage men, bearded men. They hacked at him with knives. All seemed to strike him together. Their arms rose and fell. The blood did not flow from him—it squirted. His red dress was dabbled in it. He threw himself this way and that, purple upon crimson, like an over-ripe plum. Still they hacked, and still the jets shot from him. It was horrible—horrible! They dragged him kicking to the door. The woman looked over her shoulder at him and her mouth gaped. I heard nothing, but I knew that she was screaming. And then, whether it was this nerve-racking vision before me, or whether, my task finished, all the overwork of the past weeks came in one crushing weight upon me, the room danced round me, the floor seemed to sink away beneath my feet, and I remembered no more. In the early morning my landlady found me stretched senseless before the silver mirror, but I knew nothing myself until three days ago I woke in the deep peace of the doctor's nursing home.

Feb. 9.—Only today have I told Dr Sinclair my full experience. He had not allowed me to speak of such matters before. He listened with an absorbed interest. 'You don't identify this with any well-known scene in history?' he asked, with suspicion in his eyes. I assured him that I knew nothing of history. 'Have you no idea whence that mirror came and to whom it once belonged?' he continued. 'Have you?' I asked, for he spoke with meaning. 'It's incredible,' said he, 'and yet how else can one explain it? The scenes which you described before suggested it, but now it has gone beyond all range of coincidence. I will bring you some notes in the evening.'

Later.—He has just left me. Let me set down his words as closely as I can recall them. He began by laying several musty volumes upon my bed.

'These you can consult at your leisure,' said he. 'I have some notes here which you can confirm. There is not a doubt that what you have seen is the murder of Rizzio by the Scottish nobles in the presence of Mary, which occurred in March 1566. Your description of the woman is accurate. The high forehead and heavy eyelids combined with great beauty could hardly apply to two women. The tall young man was her husband, Darnley. Rizzio, says the chronicle, "was dressed in a loose dressing gown of furred damask, with hose of russet velvet". With one hand he clutched Mary's gown, with the other he held a dagger. Your fierce, hollow-eyed man was Ruthven, who was new-risen from a bed of sickness. Every detail is exact.'

'But why to me?' I asked, in bewilderment. 'Why of all the human race to me?'

'Because you were in the fit mental state to receive the impression. Because you chanced to own the mirror which gave the impression.'

'The mirror! You think, then, that it was Mary's mirror—that it stood in the room where this deed was done?'

'I am convinced that it was Mary's mirror. She had been Queen of France. Her personal property would be stamped with the Royal arms. What you took to be three spearheads were really the lilies of France.'

'And the inscription?'

'"Sanc. X. Pal." You can expand it into Sanctæ Crucis Palatium. Someone has made a note upon the mirror as to whence it came. It was the Palace of the Holy Cross.'

'Holyrood!' I cried.

'Exactly. Your mirror came from Holyrood. You have had one very singular experience, and have escaped. I trust that you will never put yourself into the way of having such another.'

The Haunted House

E. Nesbit

IT was by the merest accident that Desmond ever went to the Haunted House. He had been away from England for six years, and the nine months' leave taught him how easily one drops out of one's place.

He had taken rooms at the Greyhound before he found that there was no reason why he should stay in Elmstead rather than in any other of London's dismal outposts. He wrote to all the friends whose addresses he could remember, and settled himself to await their answers.

He wanted someone to talk to, and there was no one. Meantime he lounged on the horsehair sofa with the advertisements, and his pleasant grey eyes followed line after line with intolerable boredom. Then, suddenly, 'Halloa!' he said, and sat up. This is what he read:

A HAUNTED HOUSE.—Advertiser is anxious to have phenomena investigated. Any properly accredited investigator will be given full facilities. Address, by letter only, Wildon Prior, 237, Museum Street, London.

'That's rum!' he said. Wildon Prior had been the best wicket-keeper in his club. It wasn't a common name. Anyway, it was worth trying, so he sent off a telegram.

'Wildon Prior, 237, Museum Street, London. May I come to you for a day or two and see the ghost?—WILLIAM DESMOND.'

On returning next day from a stroll there was an orange envelope on the wide Pembroke table in his parlour.

'Delighted—expect you today. Book to Crittenden from Charing Cross. Wire train.—WILDON PRIOR, Ormehurst Rectory, Kent.'

'So that's all right,' said Desmond, and went off to pack his bag and ask in the bar for a timetable. 'Good old Wildon; it will be ripping, seeing him again.'

A curious little omnibus, rather like a bathing-machine, was waiting outside Crittenden Station, and its driver, a swarthy, blunt-faced little man, with liquid eyes, said, 'You a friend of Mr Prior, sir?' shut him up in the bathing-machine, and banged the door on him. It was a very long drive, and less pleasant than it would have been in an open carriage.

The last part of the journey was through a wood; then came a churchyard and a church, and the bathing-machine turned in at a gate under heavy trees and drew up in front of a white house with bare, gaunt windows.

'Cheerful place, upon my soul!' Desmond told himself, as he tumbled out of the back of the bathing-machine.

The driver set his bag on the discoloured doorstep and drove off. Desmond pulled a rusty chain, and a big-throated bell jangled above his head.

Nobody came to the door, and he rang again. Still nobody came, but he heard a window thrown open above the porch. He stepped back on to the gravel and looked up.

A young man with rough hair and pale eyes was looking out. Not Wildon, nothing like Wildon. He did not speak, but he seemed to be making signs; and the signs seemed to mean, 'Go away!'

'I came to see Mr Prior,' said Desmond. Instantly and softly the window closed.

'Is it a lunatic asylum I've come to by chance?' Desmond asked himself, and pulled again at the rusty chain.

Steps sounded inside the house, the sound of boots on stone. Bolts were shot back, the door opened, and Desmond, rather hot and a little annoyed, found himself looking into a pair of very dark, friendly eyes, and a very pleasant voice said:

'Mr Desmond, I presume? Do come in and let me apologize.'

The speaker shook him warmly by the hand, and he found himself following down a flagged passage a man of more than mature age, well-dressed, handsome, with an air of competence and alertness which we associate with what is called 'a man of the world'. He opened a door and led the way into a shabby, bookish, leathery room.

'Do sit down, Mr Desmond.'

'This must be the uncle, I suppose,' Desmond thought, as he fitted himself into the shabby, perfect curves of the armchair. 'How's Wildon?' he asked, aloud. 'All right, I hope?'

The other looked at him. 'I beg your pardon,' he said, doubtfully.

'I was asking how Wildon is?'

'I am quite well, I thank you,' said the other man, with some formality.

'I beg your pardon'—it was now Desmond's turn to say it—'I did not realize that your name might be Wildon, too. I meant Wildon Prior.'

'I am Wildon Prior,' said the other, 'and you, I presume, are the expert from the Psychical Society?'

'Good Lord, no!' said Desmond. 'I'm Wildon Prior's friend, and, of course, there must be two Wildon Priors.'

'You sent the telegram? You are Mr Desmond? The Psychical Society were to send an expert, and I thought——'

'I see,' said Desmond; 'and I thought you were Wildon Prior, an old friend of mine—a young man,' he said, and half rose.

'Now, don't,' said Wildon Prior. 'No doubt it is my nephew who is your friend. Did he know you were coming? But of course he didn't. I am wandering. But I'm exceedingly glad to see you. You will stay, will you not? If you can endure to be the guest of an old man. And I will write to Will tonight and ask him to join us.'

'That's most awfully good of you,' Desmond assured him. 'I shall be glad to stay. I was awfully pleased when I saw Wildon's name in the paper, because——' And out came the tale of Elmstead, its loneliness and disappointment.

Mr Prior listened with the kindest interest.

'And you have not found your friends? How sad! But they will write to you. Of course, you left your address?'

'I didn't, by Jove!' said Desmond. 'But I can write. Can I catch the post?'

'Easily,' the elder man assured him. 'Write your letters now. My man shall take them to the post, and then we will have dinner, and I will tell you about the ghost.'

Desmond wrote his letters quickly, Mr Prior just then reappearing.

'Now I'll take you to your room,' he said, gathering the letters in long, white hands. 'You'll like a rest. Dinner at eight.'

The bed-chamber, like the parlour, had a pleasant air of worn luxury and accustomed comfort.

'I hope you will be comfortable,' the host said, with courteous solicitude. And Desmond was quite sure that he would.

Three covers were laid, the swarthy man who had driven Desmond from the station stood behind the host's chair, and a figure came towards Desmond and his host from the shadows beyond the yellow circles of the silver-sticked candles.

'My assistant, Mr Verney,' said the host, and Desmond surrendered his hand to the limp, damp touch of the man who had seemed to say to him, from the window above the porch, 'Go away!' Was Mr Prior perhaps a doctor who received 'paying guests', persons who were, in Desmond's phrase, 'a bit barmy'? But he had said 'assistant'.

'I thought,' said Desmond, hastily, 'you would be a clergyman. The Rectory, you know—I thought Wildon, my friend Wildon, was staying with an uncle who was a clergyman.'

'Oh, no,' said Mr Prior. 'I rent the Rectory. The rector thinks it is damp. The church is disused, too. It is not considered safe, and they can't afford to restore it. Claret to Mr Desmond, Lopez.' And the swarthy, blunt-faced man filled his glass.

'I find this place very convenient for my experiments. I dabble a little in chemistry, Mr Desmond, and Verney here assists me.'

Verney murmured something that sounded like 'only too proud', and subsided.

'We all have our hobbies, and chemistry is mine,' Mr Prior went on. 'Fortunately, I have a little income which enables me to indulge it. Wildon, my nephew, you know, laughs at me, and calls it the science of smells. But it's absorbing, very absorbing.'

After dinner Verney faded away, and Desmond and his host stretched their feet to what Mr Prior called a 'handful of fire', for the evening had grown chill.

'And now,' Desmond said, 'won't you tell me the ghost story?'

The other glanced round the room.

'There isn't really a ghost story at all. It's only that—well, it's never happened to me personally, but it happened to Verney, poor lad, and he's never been quite his own self since.'

Desmond flattered himself on his insight.

'Is mine the haunted room?' he asked.

'It doesn't come to any particular room,' said the other, slowly, 'nor to any particular person.'

'Anyone may happen to see it?'

'No one sees it. It isn't the kind of ghost that's seen or heard.'

'I'm afraid I'm rather stupid, but I don't understand,' said Desmond, roundly. 'How can it be a ghost, if you neither hear it nor see it?'

'I did not say it was a ghost,' Mr Prior corrected. 'I only say that there is something about this house which is not ordinary. Several of my assistants have had to leave; the thing got on their nerves.'

'What became of the assistants?' asked Desmond.

'Oh, they left, you know; they left,' Prior answered, vaguely. 'One couldn't expect them to sacrifice their health. I sometimes think—village gossip is a deadly thing, Mr Desmond—that perhaps they were prepared to be frightened; that they fancy things. I hope the Psychical Society's expert won't be a neurotic. But even without being a neurotic one might—but you don't believe in ghosts, Mr Desmond. Your Anglo-Saxon common sense forbids it.'

'I'm afraid I'm not exactly Anglo-Saxon,' said Desmond. 'On my father's side I'm pure Celt; though I know I don't do credit to the race.'

'And on your mother's side?' Mr Prior asked, with extraordinary eagerness; an eagerness so sudden and disproportioned to the question that Desmond stared. A faint touch of resentment as suddenly stirred in him, the first spark of antagonism to his host.

'Oh,' he said, lightly, 'I think I must have Chinese blood, I get on so well with the natives in Shanghai, and they tell me I owe my nose to a Red Indian great grandmother.'

'No negro blood, I suppose?' the host asked, with almost discourteous insistence.

'Oh, I wouldn't say that,' Desmond answered. He meant to say it laughing, but he didn't. 'My hair, you know—it's a very stiff curl it's got, and my mother's people were in the West Indies a few generations ago. You're interested in distinctions of race, I take it?'

'Not at all, not at all,' Mr Prior surprisingly assured him; 'but, of course, any details of your family are necessarily interesting to me. I feel,' he added, with another of his winning smiles, 'that you and I are already friends.'

Desmond could not have reasoningly defended the faint quality of dislike that had begun to tinge his first pleasant sense of being welcomed and wished for as a guest.

'You're very kind,' he said; 'it's jolly of you to take in a stranger like this.'

Mr Prior smiled, handed the cigar-box, mixed whisky and soda, and began to talk about the history of the house.

'The foundations are almost certainly thirteenth century. It was a priory, you know. There's a curious tale, by the way, about the man Henry gave it to when he smashed up the monasteries. There was a curse; there seems always to have been a curse——'

The gentle, pleasant, high-bred voice went on. Desmond thought he was listening, but presently he roused himself and dragged his attention back to the words that were being spoken.

'——that made the fifth death. . . . There is one every hundred years, and always in the same mysterious way.'

Then he found himself on his feet, incredibly sleepy, and heard himself say:

'These old stories are tremendously interesting. Thank you very much. I hope you won't think me very uncivil, but I think I'd rather like to turn in; I feel a bit tired, somehow.'

'But of course, my dear chap.'

Mr Prior saw Desmond to his room.

'Got everything you want? Right. Lock the door if you should feel nervous. Of course, a lock can't keep ghosts out, but I always feel as if it could,' and with another of those pleasant, friendly laughs he was gone.

William Desmond went to bed a strong young man, sleepy indeed beyond his experience of sleepiness, but well and comfortable. He awoke faint and trembling, lying deep in the billows of the feather bed; and lukewarm waves of exhaustion swept through him. Where was he? What had happened? His brain, dizzy and weak at first, refused him any answer. When he remembered, the abrupt spasm of repulsion which he had felt so suddenly and unreasonably the night before came back to him in a hot, breathless flush. He had been drugged, he had been poisoned!

'I must get out of this,' he told himself, and blundered out of bed towards the silken bell-pull that he had noticed the night before hanging near the door.

As he pulled it, the bed and the wardrobe and the room rose up round him and fell on him, and he fainted.

When he next knew anything someone was putting brandy to his lips. He saw Prior, the kindest concern in his face. The assistant, pale and watery-eyed. The swarthy manservant, stolid, silent, and expressionless. He heard Verney say to Prior:

'You see it was too much—I told you——'

'Hush,' said Prior, 'he's coming to.'

Four days later Desmond, lying on a wicker chair on the lawn, was a little disinclined for exertion, but no longer ill. Nourishing foods and drinks, beef-tea, stimulants, and constant care—these had brought him back to something like his normal state. He wondered at the vague suspicions, vaguely remembered, of that first night; they had all been proved absurd by the unwavering care and kindness of everyone in the Haunted House.

'But what caused it?' he asked his host, for the fiftieth time. 'What made me make such a fool of myself?' And this time Mr Prior did not put him off, as he had always done before by begging him to wait till he was stronger.

'I am afraid, you know,' he said, 'that the ghost really did come to you. I am inclined to revise my opinion of the ghost.'

'But why didn't it come again?'

'I have been with you every night, you know,' his host reminded him. And, indeed, the sufferer had never been left alone since the ringing of his bell on that terrible first morning.

'And now,' Mr Prior went on, 'if you will not think me inhospitable, I think you will be better away from here. You ought to go to the seaside.'

'There haven't been any letters for me, I suppose?' Desmond said, a little wistfully.

'Not one. I suppose you gave the right address? Ormehurst Rectory, Crittenden, Kent?'

'I don't think I put Crittenden,' said Desmond. 'I copied the address from your telegram.' He pulled the pink paper from his pocket.

'Ah, that would account,' said the other.

'You've been most awfully kind all through,' said Desmond, abruptly.

'Nonsense, my boy,' said the elder man, benevolently. 'I only wish Willie had been able to come. He's never written, the rascal! Nothing but the telegram to say he could not come and was writing.'

'I suppose he's having a jolly time somewhere,' said Desmond, enviously; 'but look here—do tell me about the ghost, if there's anything to tell. I'm almost quite well now, and I *should* like to know what it was that made a fool of me like that.'

'Well'—Mr Prior looked round him at the gold and red of dahlias and sunflowers, gay in the September sunshine—'here, and now, I don't know that it could do any harm. You remember that story of the man who got this place from Henry VIII, and the curse? That man's wife is buried in a vault under the church. Well, there were legends, and I confess I was curious to see her tomb. There are iron gates to the vault. Locked, they were. I opened them with an old key—and I couldn't get them to shut again.'

'Yes?' Desmond said.

'You think I might have sent for a locksmith; but the fact is, there is a small crypt to the church, and I have used that crypt as a supplementary laboratory. If I had called anyone in to see to the lock they would have gossiped. I should have been turned out of my laboratory—perhaps out of my house.'

'I see.'

'Now, the curious thing is,' Mr Prior went on, lowering his voice, 'that it is only since that grating was opened that this house has been what they call "haunted". It is since then that all the things have happened.'

'What things?'

'People staying here, suddenly ill—just as you were. And the attacks always seem to indicate loss of blood. And——' He hesitated a moment. 'That wound in your throat. I told you you had hurt yourself falling when you rang the bell. But that was not true. What *is* true is that you had on your throat just the same little white wound that all the others have had. I wish'—he frowned—'that I could get that vault gate shut again. The key won't turn.'

'I wonder if I could do anything?' Desmond asked, secretly convinced that he *had* hurt his throat in falling, and that his host's story was, as he put it, 'all moonshine'. Still, to put a lock right was but a slight return for all the care and kindness. 'I'm an engineer, you know,' he added, awkwardly, and rose. 'Probably a little oil. Let's have a look at this same lock.'

He followed Mr Prior through the house to the church. A bright, smooth old key turned readily, and they passed into the building, musty and damp, where ivy crawled through the broken windows, and the blue sky seemed to be laid close against the holes in the roof. Another key clicked in the lock of a low door beside what had once been the Lady Chapel, a thick oak door grated back, and Mr Prior stopped a moment to light a candle that waited in its rough iron candlestick on a ledge of the stonework. Then down narrow stairs, chipped a little at the edges and soft with dust. The crypt was Norman, very simply beautiful. At the end of it was a recess, masked with a grating of rusty ironwork.

'They used to think,' said Mr Prior, 'that iron kept off witchcraft. This is the lock,' he went on, holding the candle against the gate, which was ajar.

They went through the gate, because the lock was on the other side. Desmond worked a minute or two with the oil and feather that he had brought. Then with a little wrench the key turned and re-turned.

'I think that's all right,' he said, looking up, kneeling on one knee, with the key still in the lock and his hand on it.

'May I try it?'

Mr Prior took Desmond's place, turned the key, pulled it out, and stood up. Then the key and the candlestick fell rattling on the stone floor, and the old man sprang upon Desmond.

'Now I've got you,' he growled, in the darkness, and Desmond says that his spring and his clutch and his voice were like the spring and the clutch and the growl of a strong savage beast.

Desmond's little strength snapped like a twig at his first bracing of it to resistance. The old man held him as a vice holds. He had got a rope from somewhere. He was tying Desmond's arms.

Desmond hates to know that there in the dark he screamed like a caught hare. Then he remembered that he was a man, and shouted, 'Help! Here! Help!'

But a hand was on his mouth, and now a handkerchief was being knotted at the back of his head. He was on the floor, leaning against something. Prior's hands had left him.

'Now,' said Prior's voice, a little breathless, and the match he struck showed Desmond the stone shelves with long things on them—coffins he supposed. 'Now, I'm sorry I had to do it, but science before friendship, my dear Desmond,' he went on, quite courteous and friendly. 'I will explain to you, and you will see that a man of honour could not act otherwise. Of course, you having no friends who know where you are is most convenient. I saw that from the first. Now I'll explain. I didn't expect you to understand by instinct. But no matter. I am, I say it without vanity, the greatest discoverer since Newton. I know how to modify men's natures. I can make men what I choose. It's all done by transfusion of blood. Lopez—you know, my man Lopez—I've pumped the blood of dogs into his veins, and he's my slave—like a dog. Verney, he's my slave, too—part dog's blood and partly the blood of people who've come from time to time to investigate the ghost, and partly my own, because I wanted him to be clever enough to help me. And there's a bigger thing behind all this. You'll understand me when I say'—here he became very technical indeed, and used many words that meant nothing to Desmond, whose thoughts dwelt more and more on his small chance of escape.

To die like a rat in a hole, a rat in a hole! If he could only loosen the handkerchief and shout again!

'Attend, can't you?' said Prior, savagely, and kicked him. 'I beg your pardon, my dear chap,' he went on, suavely, 'but this is important. So you see the elixir of life is really the blood. The blood is the life, you know, and my great discovery is that to make a man immortal, and restore his youth, one only needs blood from the veins of a man who unites in himself blood of the four great races— the four colours, black, white, red, and yellow. Your blood unites these four. I took as much as I dared from you that night. I was the vampire, you know.' He laughed pleasantly. 'But your blood didn't act. The drug I had to give you to induce sleep probably destroyed the vital germs. And, besides, there wasn't enough of it. Now there is going to be enough!'

Desmond had been working his head against the thing behind him, easing the knot of the handkerchief down till it slipped from head to neck. Now he got his mouth free, and said, quickly:

'That was not true what I said about the Chinamen and that. I was joking. My mother's people were all Devon.'

'I don't blame you in the least,' said Prior, quietly. 'I should lie myself in your place.'

And he put back the handkerchief. The candle was now burning clearly from the place where it stood—on a stone coffin. Desmond could see that the long things on the shelves *were* coffins, not all of stone. He wondered what this madman would do with his body when everything was over. The little wound in his throat had broken out again. He could feel the slow trickle of warmth on his neck. He wondered whether he would faint. It felt like it.

'I wish I'd brought you here the first day—it was Verney's doing, my tinkering about with pints and half-pints. Sheer waste—sheer wanton waste!'

Prior stopped and stood looking at him.

Desmond, despairingly conscious of growing physical weakness, caught himself in a real wonder as to whether this might not be a dream—a horrible, insane dream—and he could not wholly dismiss the wonder, because incredible things seemed to be adding themselves to the real horrors of the situation, just as they do in dreams. There seemed to be something stirring in the place— something that wasn't Prior. No—nor Prior's shadow, either. That was black and sprawled big across the arched roof. This was white, and very small and thin. But it stirred, it grew—now it was no longer just a line of white, but a long, narrow, white wedge—and it showed between the coffin on the shelf opposite him and that coffin's lid.

And still Prior stood very still looking down on his prey. All emotion but a dull wonder was now dead in Desmond's weakened senses. In dreams—if one called out, one awoke—but he could not call out. Perhaps if one moved—— But before he could bring his enfeebled will to the decision of movement—something else moved. The black lid of the coffin opposite rose slowly—and then suddenly fell, clattering and echoing, and from the coffin rose a form, horribly white and shrouded, and fell on Prior and rolled with him on the floor of the vault in a silent, whirling struggle. The last thing Desmond heard before he fainted in good earnest was the scream Prior uttered as he turned at the crash and saw the white-shrouded body leaping towards him.

'It's all right,' he heard next. And Verney was bending over him with brandy. 'You're quite safe. He's tied up and locked in the laboratory. No. That's all right, too.' For Desmond's eyes had turned towards the lidless coffin. 'That was only me. It was the only way I could think of, to save you. Can you walk now? Let me help you, so. I've opened the grating. Come.'

Desmond blinked in the sunlight he had never thought to see again. Here he was, back in his wicker chair. He looked at the sundial on the house. The whole thing had taken less than fifty minutes.

'Tell me,' said he. And Verney told him in short sentences with pauses between.

'I tried to warn you,' he said, 'you remember, in the window. I really believed in his experiments at first—and—he'd found out something about me—and not told. It was when I was very young. God knows I've paid for it. And when you came I'd only just found out what really had happened to the other chaps. That beast Lopez let it out when he was drunk. Inhuman brute! And I had a row with Prior that first night, and he promised me he wouldn't touch you. And then he did.'

'You might have told me.'

'You were in a nice state to be told anything, weren't you? He promised me he'd send you off as soon as you were well enough. And he *had* been good to me. But when I heard him begin about the grating and the key I *knew*—so I just got a sheet and——'

'But why didn't you come out before?'

'I didn't dare. He could have tackled me easily if he had known what he was tackling. He kept moving about. It had to be done suddenly. I counted on just that moment of weakness when he really thought a dead body had come to life to defend you. Now I'm going to harness the horse and drive you to the police station at Crittenden. And they'll send and lock him up. Everyone knew he was as mad as a hatter, but somebody had to be nearly killed before anyone would lock him up. The law's like that, you know.'

'But you—the police—won't they——'

'It's quite safe,' said Verney, dully. 'Nobody knows but the old man, and now nobody will believe anything he says. No, he never posted your letters, of course, and he never wrote to your friend, and he put off the Psychical man. No, I can't find Lopez; he must know that something's up. He's bolted.'

But he had not. They found him, stubbornly dumb, but moaning a little, crouched against the locked grating of the vault when they came, a prudent half-dozen of them, to take the old man away from the Haunted House. The master was dumb as the man. He would not speak. He has never spoken since.

How It Happened

Arthur Conan Doyle

S HE was a writing medium. This is what she wrote:

I can remember some things upon that evening most distinctly, and
others are like some vague, broken dreams. That is what makes it
so difficult to tell a connected story. I have no idea now what it was
that had taken me to London and brought me back so late. It just
merges into all my other visits to London. But from the time that I
got out at the little country station everything is extraordinarily
clear. I can live it again—every instant of it.

I remember so well walking down the platform and looking at the
illuminated clock at the end which told me that it was half-past
eleven. I remember also my wondering whether I could get home
before midnight. Then I remember the big motor, with its glaring
headlights and glitter of polished brass, waiting for me outside. It
was my new thirty-horse-power Robur, which had only been
delivered that day. I remember also asking Perkins, my chauffeur,
how she had gone, and his saying that he thought she was excellent.

'I'll try her myself,' said I, and I climbed into the driver's seat.

'The gears are not the same,' said he. 'Perhaps, sir, I had better
drive.'

'No; I should like to try her,' said I.

And so we started on the five-mile drive for home.

My old car had the gears as they used always to be in notches on
a bar. In this car you passed the gear-lever through a gate to get on
the higher ones. It was not difficult to master, and soon I thought
that I understood it. It was foolish, no doubt, to begin to learn a

new system in the dark, but one often does foolish things, and one has not always to pay the full price for them. I got along very well until I came to Claystall Hill. It is one of the worst hills in England, a mile and a half long and one in six in places, with three fairly sharp curves. My park gates stand at the very foot of it upon the main London road.

We were just over the brow of this hill, where the grade is steepest, when the trouble began. I had been on the top speed, and wanted to get her on the free; but she stuck between gears, and I had to get her back on the top again. By this time she was going at a great rate, so I clapped on both brakes, and one after the other they gave way. I didn't mind so much when I felt my foot-brake snap, but when I put all my weight on my side-brake, and the lever clanged to its full limit without a catch, it brought a cold sweat out of me. By this time we were fairly tearing down the slope. The lights were brilliant, and I brought her round the first curve all right. Then we did the second one, though it was a close shave for the ditch. There was a mile of straight then with the third curve beneath it, and after that the gate of the park. If I could shoot into that harbour all would be well, for the slope up to the house would bring her to a stand.

Perkins behaved splendidly. I should like that to be known. He was perfectly cool and alert. I had thought at the very beginning of taking the bank, and he read my intention.

'I wouldn't do it, sir,' said he. 'At this pace it must go over and we should have it on the top of us.'

Of course he was right. He got to the electric switch and had it off, so we were in the free; but we were still running at a fearful pace. He laid his hands on the wheel.

'I'll keep her steady,' said he, 'if you care to jump and chance it. We can never get round that curve. Better jump, sir.'

'No,' said I; 'I'll stick it out. You can jump if you like.'

'I'll stick it with you, sir,' said he.

If it had been the old car I should have jammed the gear-lever into the reverse, and seen what would happen. I expect she would have stripped her gears or smashed up somehow, but it would have been a chance. As it was, I was helpless. Perkins tried to climb across, but you couldn't do it going at that pace. The wheels were whirring like a high wind and the big body creaking and groaning with the strain. But the lights were brilliant, and one could steer to an inch. I remember thinking what an awful and yet majestic sight we should appear to anyone who met us. It was a narrow road, and we were just a great, roaring, golden death to anyone who came in our path.

We got round the corner with one wheel three feet high upon the bank. I thought we were surely over, but after staggering for a moment she righted and darted onwards. That was the third corner and the last one. There was only the park gate now. It was facing us, but, as luck would have it, not facing us directly. It was about twenty yards to the left up the main road into which we ran. Perhaps I could have done it, but I expect that the steering-gear had been jarred when we ran on the bank. The wheel did not turn easily. We shot out of the lane. I saw the open gate on the left. I whirled round my wheel with all the strength of my wrists. Perkins and I threw our bodies across, and then the next instant, going at fifty miles an hour, my right front wheel struck full on the right-hand pillar of my own gate. I heard the crash. I was conscious of flying through the air, and then—and then——!

When I became aware of my own existence once more I was among some brushwood in the shadow of the oaks upon the lodge side of the drive. A man was standing beside me. I imagined at first that it was Perkins, but when I looked again I saw that it was Stanley, a man whom I had known at college some years before, and for whom I had a really genuine affection. There was always something peculiarly sympathetic to me in Stanley's personality, and I was proud to think that I had some similar influence upon him. At the present moment I was surprised to see him, but I was like a man in a dream, giddy and shaken and quite prepared to take things as I found them without questioning them.

'What a smash!' I said. 'Good Lord, what an awful smash!'

He nodded his head, and even in the gloom I could see that he was smiling the gentle, wistful smile which I connected with him.

I was quite unable to move. Indeed, I had not any desire to try to move. But my senses were exceedingly alert. I saw the wreck of the motor lit up by the moving lanterns. I saw the little group of people and heard the hushed voices. There were the lodge-keeper and his wife, and one or two more. They were taking no notice of me, but were very busy round the car. Then suddenly I heard a cry of pain.

'The weight is on him. Lift it easy,' cried a voice.

'It's only my leg,' said another one, which I recognized as Perkins's. 'Where's master?' he cried.

'Here I am,' I answered, but they did not seem to hear me. They were all bending over something which lay in front of the car.

Stanley laid his hand upon my shoulder, and his touch was inexpressibly soothing. I felt light and happy, in spite of all.

'No pain, of course?' said he.

'None,' said I.

'There never is,' said he.

And then suddenly a wave of amazement passed over me. Stanley! Stanley! Why, Stanley had surely died of enteric at Bloemfontein in the Boer War!

'Stanley!' I cried, and the words seemed to choke my throat—'Stanley, you are dead.'

He looked at me with the same old gentle, wistful smile.

'So are you,' he answered.

The Power of Darkness

E. Nesbit

IT was an enthusiastic send-off. Half the students from her atelier were there, and twice as many more from other studios. She had been the belle of the Artists' Quarter in Montparnasse for three golden months. Now she was off to the Riviera to meet her people, and everyone she knew was at the Gare de Lyon to catch the last glimpse of her. And, as had been more than once said late of an evening, 'to see her was to love her'. She was one of those agitating blondes, with the naturally rippled hair, the rounded rose-leaf cheeks, the large violet-blue eyes, that looked all things and meant Heaven alone knew how little. She held her court like a queen, leaning out of the carriage window and receiving bouquets, books, journals, long last words, and last longing looks. All eyes were on her, and her eyes were for all—and her smile. For all but one, that is. Not a single glance went Edward's way, and Edward—tall, lean, gaunt, with big eyes, straight nose, and the mouth somewhat too small, too beautiful—seemed to grow thinner and paler before one's eyes. One pair of eyes at least saw the miracle worked, the paling of what had seemed absolute pallor, the revelation of the bones of a face that seemed already covered but by the thinnest possible veil of flesh.

And the man whose eyes saw this rejoiced, for he loved her, like the rest, or not like the rest, and he had had Edward's face before him for the last month, in that secret shrine where we set the loved and the hated, the shrine that is lighted by a million lamps kindled at the soul's flame, the shrine that leaps into dazzling glow when the candles are out and one lies alone on hot pillows to outface the night and the light as best one may.

'Oh, goodbye; goodbye, all of you,' said Rose. 'I shall miss you. Oh, you don't know how I shall miss you all!'

She gathered the eyes of her friends and her worshippers in a glance, as one gathers jewels on a silken string. The eyes of Edward alone seemed to escape her.

'En voiture, messieurs et dames!'

Folk drew back from the train. There was a whistle.

And then at the very last little moment of all, as the train pulled itself together for the start, her eyes met Edward's eyes. And the other man saw the meeting, and he knew—which was more than Edward did.

So when, the light of life having been borne away in the retreating train, the broken-hearted group dispersed, the other man—whose name, by the way, was Vincent—linked his arm in Edward's and asked, cheerily:

'Whither away, sweet nymph?'

'I'm off home,' said Edward. 'The seven-twenty to Calais.'

'Sick of Paris?'

'One has to see one's people sometimes, don't you know, hang it all!' was Edward's way of expressing the longing that tore him for the old house among the brown woods of Kent.

'No attraction here now, eh?'

'The chief attraction has gone, certainly,' Edward made himself say.

'But there are as good fish in the sea——'

'Fishing isn't my trade,' said Edward.

'The beautiful Rose!' said Vincent.

Edward raised hurriedly the only shield he could find. It happened to be the truth as he saw it.

'Oh,' he said, 'of course, we're all in love with her—and all hopelessly.'

Vincent perceived that this was truth, as Edward saw it.

'What are you going to do till your train goes?' he asked.

'I don't know. Café, I suppose, and a vilely early dinner.'

'Let's look in at the Musée Grévin,' said Vincent.

The two were friends. They had been schoolfellows, and this is a link that survives many a strain too strong to be resisted by more intimate and vital bonds. And they were fellow-students, though that counts for little or much—as you take it. Besides, Vincent knew something about Edward that no one else of their age and standing even guessed. He knew that Edward was afraid of the dark, and why. He had found it out that Christmas which the two had spent at an English country house. The house was full; there was a dance. There were to be theatricals. Early in the new year the hostess meant to 'move house' to an old convent, built in Tudor times, a beautiful palace with terraces and clipped yew trees, castellated battlements, a moat, swans, and a ghost story.

'You boys,' she said, 'must put up with a shake-down in the new house. I hope the ghost won't worry you. She's an old lady in a figured satin dress. Comes and breathes softly on the back of your neck when you're shaving. Then you see her in the glass, and as often as not you cut your throat.' She laughed. So did Edward and Vincent and the other young men. There were seven or eight of them.

But that night, when sparse candles had lighted 'the boys' to their rooms, when the last pipe had been smoked, the last 'Goodnight' said, there came a fumbling with the handle of Vincent's door. Edward came in, an unwieldy figure, clasping pillows, trailing blankets.

'What the deuce?' queried Vincent, in natural amazement.

'I'll turn in here on the floor if you don't mind,' said Edward. 'I know it's beastly rot, but I can't stand it. The room they've put me into, it's an attic as big as a barn—and there's a great door at the end, eight feet high, and it leads into a sort of horror hole—bare beams and rafters, and black as night. I know I'm an abject duffer, but there it is—I can't face it.'

Vincent was sympathetic; though he had never known a night terror that could not be exorcized by pipe, book, and candle.

'I know, old chap. There's no reasoning about these things,' said he, and so on.

'You can't despise me more than I despise myself,' Edward said. 'I feel a crawling hound. But it is so. I had a scare when I was a kid, and it seems to have left a sort of brand on me. I'm branded "coward", old man, and the feel of it's not nice.'

Again Vincent was sympathetic, and the poor little tale came out. How Edward, eight years old, and greedy as became his little years, had sneaked down, night-clad, to pick among the outcomings of a dinner party, and how, in the hall, dark with the light of an 'artistic' coloured glass lantern, a white figure had suddenly faced him—

leaned towards him, it seemed, pointed lead-white hands at his heart. That next day, finding him weak from his fainting fit, had shown the horror to be but a statue, a new purchase of his father's, had mattered not one whit.

Edward shared Vincent's room, and Vincent, alone of all men, shared Edward's secret.

And now, in Paris, Rose speeding away towards Cannes, Vincent said:

'Let's look in at the Musée Grévin.'

The Musée Grévin is a waxwork show. Your mind, at the word, flies instantly to the excellent exhibition founded by the worthy Mme Tussaud. And you think you know what waxworks mean. But you are wrong. The Musée Grévin contains the work of artists for a nation of artists. Wax-modelled and retouched till it seems as near life as death is: this is what one sees at the Musée Grévin.

'Let's look in at the Musée Grévin,' said Vincent. He remembered the pleasant thrill the Musée had given him, and wondered what sort of a thrill it would give his friend.

'I hate museums,' said Edward.

'This isn't a museum,' Vincent said, and truly; 'it's just waxworks.'

'All right,' said Edward, indifferently. And they went.

They reached the doors of the Musée in the grey-brown dusk of a February evening.

One walks along a bare, narrow corridor, much like the entrance to the stalls of the Standard Theatre, and such daylight as there may be fades away behind one, and one finds oneself in a square hall, heavily decorated, and displaying with its electric lights Loie Fuller in her accordion-pleated skirts, and one or two other figures not designed to quicken the pulse.

'It's very like Mme Tussaud's,' said Edward.

'Yes,' Vincent said; 'isn't it?'

Then they passed through an arch, and beheld a long room with waxen groups life-like behind glass—the *coulisses* of the Opéra, Kitchener at Fashoda—this last with a desert background lit by something convincingly like desert sunlight.

'By Jove!' said Edward. 'That's jolly good.'

'Yes,' said Vincent again; 'isn't it?'

Edward's interest grew.

The things were so convincing, so very nearly alive. Given the right angle, their glass eyes met one's own, and seemed to exchange with one meaning glances.

Vincent led the way to an arched door labelled 'Galerie de la Révolution.'

There one saw—almost in the living, suffering body—poor Marie Antoinette in prison in the Temple, her little son on his couch of rags, the rats eating from his platter, the brutal Simon calling to him from the grated window. One almost heard the words: 'Holà, little Capet!—are you asleep?'

One saw Marat bleeding in his bath, the brave Charlotte eyeing him; the very tiles of the bathroom, the glass of the windows, with, outside, the very sunlight, as it seemed, of 1793, on that 'yellow July evening, the thirteenth of the month'.

The spectators did not move in a public place among waxwork figures. They peeped through open doors into rooms where history seemed to be relived. The rooms were lighted each by its own sun or lamp or candle. The spectators walked among shadows that might have oppressed a nervous person.

'Fine, eh?' said Vincent.

'Yes,' said Edward; 'it's wonderful.'

A turn of a corner brought them to a room. Marie Antoinette fainting, supported by her ladies; poor, fat Louis by the window looking literally sick.

'What's the matter with them all?' said Edward.

'Look at the window,' said Vincent.

There was a window to the room. Outside was sunshine—the sunshine of 1792—and gleaming in it, blonde hair flowing, red mouth half-open, what seemed the just-severed head of a beautiful woman. It was raised on a pike, so that it seemed to be looking in at the window.

'I say,' said Edward, and the head on the pike seemed to sway before his eyes.

'Mme de Lamballe. Good thing, isn't it?' said Vincent.

'It's altogether too much of a good thing,' said Edward. 'Look here—I've had enough of this.'

'Oh, you must just see the Catacombs,' said Vincent; 'nothing gruesome, you know. Only early Christians being married and baptized, and all that.'

He led the way down some clumsy steps to the cellars which the genius of a great artist has transformed into the exact semblance of the old Catacombs at Rome. The same rough hewing of rock, the same sacred tokens engraved strongly and simply; and among the arches of these subterranean burrowings the life of the early Christians, their sacraments, their joys, their sorrows—all expressed in groups of waxwork as like life as death is.

'But this is very fine, you know,' said Edward, getting his breath again after Mme de Lamballe, and his imagination loved the thought of the noble sufferings and refrainings of these first lovers of the crucified Christ.

'Yes,' said Vincent, for the third time; 'isn't it?'

They passed the baptism and the burying and the marriage. The tableaux were sufficiently lighted, but little light strayed to the narrow passage where the two men walked, and the darkness seemed to press, tangible as a bodily presence, against Edward's shoulder. He glanced backward.

'Come,' he said; 'I've had enough.'

'Come on, then,' said Vincent.

They turned the corner, and a blaze of Italian sunlight struck at their eyes with positive dazzlement. There lay the Coliseum—tier on tier of eager faces under the blue sky of Italy. They were level with the arena. In the arena were crosses; from them drooped bleeding figures. On the sand beasts prowled, bodies lay. They saw it all through bars. They seemed to be in the place where the chosen victims waited their turn, waited for the lions and the crosses, the palm and the crown. Close by Edward was a group—an old man, a woman, and children. He could have touched them with his hand. The woman and the man stared in an agony of terror straight in the eyes of a snarling tiger, ten feet long, that stood up on its hind feet and clawed through the bars at them. The youngest child only, unconscious of the horror, laughed in the very face of it. Roman soldiers, unmoved in military vigilance, guarded the group of martyrs. In a low cage to the left more wild beasts cringed and seemed to growl, unfed. Within the grating, on the wide circle of yellow sand, lions and tigers drank the blood of Christians. Close against the bars a great lion sucked the chest of a corpse, on whose bloodstained face the horror of the death-agony was printed plain.

'Good heavens!' said Edward. Vincent took his arm suddenly, and he started with what was almost a shriek.

'What a nervous chap you are!' said Vincent, complacently, as they regained the street where the lights were, and the sound of voices and the movement of live human beings—all that warms and awakens nerves almost paralysed by the life in death of waxen immobility.

'I don't know,' said Edward. 'Let's have a vermouth, shall we? There's something uncanny about those wax things. They're like life—but they're much more like death. Suppose they moved? I don't feel at all sure that they don't move, when the lights are all out and there's no one there.'

He laughed.

'I suppose you were never frightened, Vincent?'

'Yes, I was once,' said Vincent, sipping his absinthe. 'Three other men and I were taking turns by twos to watch by a dead man. It was a fancy of his mother's. Our time was up, and the other watch hadn't come. So my chap—the one who was watching with me, I mean—went to fetch them. I didn't think I should mind. But it was just like you say.'

'How?'

'Why, I kept thinking, "Suppose it should move." It was so like life. And if it did move, of course it would have been because it *was* alive, and I ought to have been glad, because the man was my friend. But all the same, if he had moved I should have gone mad.'

'Yes,' said Edward, 'that's just exactly it.'

Vincent called for a second absinthe.

'But a dead body's different to waxworks,' he said. 'I can't understand anyone being frightened of *them*.'

'Oh, can't you?' The contempt in the other's tone stung him. 'I bet you wouldn't spend a night alone in that place.'

'I bet you five pounds I do!'

'Done,' said Edward, briskly. 'At least, I would if you'd got five pounds.'

'But I have. I'm simply rolling. I've sold my Dejanira; didn't you know? I shall win your money though, anyway. But *you* couldn't do it, old man. I suppose you'll never outgrow that childish scare.'

'You might shut up about that,' said Edward, shortly.

'Oh, it's nothing to be ashamed of; some women are afraid of mice or spiders. I say, does Rose know you're a coward?'

'Vincent!'

'No offence, old boy. One may as well call a spade a spade. Of course, you've got tons of moral courage and all that. But you *are* afraid of the dark—and waxworks!'

'Are you trying to quarrel with me?'

'Heaven in its mercy forbid. But I bet *you* wouldn't spend a night in the Musée Grévin and keep your senses.'

'What's the stake?'

'Anything you like.'

'Make it that if I do you'll never speak to Rose again, and, what's more, that you'll never speak to me,' said Edward, white-hot, knocking down a chair as he rose.

'Done,' said Vincent. 'But you'll never do it. Keep your hair on. Besides, you're off home.'

'I shall be back in ten days. I'll do it then,' said Edward, and was off before the other could answer.

Then Vincent, left alone, sat still, and over his third absinthe remembered how, before she had known Edward, Rose had smiled on him more than the others, he thought. He thought of her wide, lovely eyes, her wild-rose cheeks, the scented curves of her hair, and then and there the devil entered into him.

In ten days Edward would undoubtedly try to win his wager. He would try to spend the night in the Musée Grévin. Perhaps something could be arranged before that. If one knew the place thoroughly! A little scare would serve Edward right for being the man to whom that last glance of Rose's had been given.

Vincent dined lightly, but with conscientious care—and as he dined he thought. Something might be done by tying a string to one of the figures and making it move when Edward was going through that impossible night among the effigies that are so like life—so like death. Something that was not the devil said:

'You may frighten him out of his wits.'

And the devil answered: 'Nonsense; do him good. He oughtn't to be such a schoolgirl.'

Anyway, the five pounds might as well be won tonight as any other night. He would take a greatcoat, sleep sound in the place of horrors, and the people who opened it in the morning to sweep and

dust would bear witness that he had passed the night there. He
thought he might trust to the French love of a sporting wager to
keep him from any bother with the authorities.

So he went in among the crowd, and looked about among the
waxworks for a place to hide in. He was not in the least afraid of
these lifeless images. He had always been able to control his nervous
tremors in his time. He was not even afraid of being frightened,
which, by the way, is the worst fear of all.

As one looks at the room of the poor little Dauphin one sees a
door to the left. It opens out of the room on to blackness. There
were few people in the gallery. Vincent watched, and, in a moment
when he was alone, stepped over the barrier and through this door.
A narrow passage ran round behind the wall of the room. Here he
hid, and when the gallery was deserted he looked out across the
body of little Capet to the gaoler at the window. There was a
soldier at the window too. Vincent amused himself with the fancy
that this soldier might walk round the passage at the back of the
room and tap him on the shoulder in the darkness. Only the head
and shoulders of the soldier and the gaoler showed, so, of course,
they could not walk, even if they were something that was not
waxwork.

Presently he himself went along the passage and round to the
window where they were. He found that they had legs. They
were full-sized figures, dressed completely in the costume of the
period.

'Thorough the beggars are, even the parts that don't show—
artists, upon my word,' said Vincent, and went back to his
doorway, thinking of the hidden carving behind the capitals of
Gothic cathedrals.

But the idea of the soldier who might come behind him in the
dark stuck in his mind. Though still a few visitors strolled through
the gallery, the closing hour was near. He supposed it would be
quite dark. Then—and now he had allowed himself to be amused
by the thought of something that should creep up behind him in the
dark—he might possibly be nervous in that passage round which, if
waxworks could move, the soldier might have come.

'By Jove!' he said; 'one might easily frighten oneself by just
fancying things. Suppose there were a back way from Marat's
bathroom, and instead of the soldier Marat came out of his bath

with his wet towels stained with blood and dabbed them against your neck!'

When next the gallery was deserted he crept out. Not because he was nervous, he told himself, but because one might be, and because the passage was draughty, and he meant to sleep.

He went down the steps into the Catacombs, and here he spoke the truth to himself.

'Hang it all,' he said, 'I *was* nervous. That fool Edward must have infected me. Mesmeric influences or something.'

'Chuck it and go home,' said common sense.

'I'm hanged if I do,' said Vincent.

There were a good many people in the Catacombs at the moment. Live people. He sucked confidence from their nearness, and went up and down looking for a hiding place.

Through rock-hewn arches he saw a burial scene—a corpse on a bier surrounded by mourners; a great pillar cut off half the still lying figure. It was all still and unemotional as a Sunday-school oleograph. He waited till no one was near, then slipped quickly through the mourning group and hid behind the pillar. Surprising— heartening, too, to find a plain rush-chair there, doubtless set for the resting of tired officials. He sat down in it, comforted his hand with the commonplace lines of its rungs and back. A shrouded waxen figure just behind him to the left of his pillar worried him a little, but the corpse left him unmoved as itself. A far better place, this, than that draughty passage where the soldier with legs kept intruding on the darkness that is always behind one.

Custodians went along the passages issuing orders. A stillness fell. Then, suddenly, all the lights went out.

'That's all right,' said Vincent, and composed himself to sleep.

But he seemed to have forgotten what sleep was like. He firmly fixed his thoughts on pleasant things—the sale of his picture, dances with Rose, merry evenings with Edward and the others. But the thoughts rushed by him like motes in sunbeams—he could not hold a single one of them, and presently it seemed that he had thought of every pleasant thing that had ever happened to him, and that now, if he thought at all, he must think of the things one wants most to forget. And there would be time in this long night to think much of many things. But now he found that he could no longer think.

The draped effigy just behind him worried him again. He had

been trying, at the back of his mind, behind the other thoughts, to strangle the thought of it. But it was there, very close to him. Suppose it put out its hand, its wax hand, and touched him? But it was of wax. It could not move. No, of course not. But suppose it *did*?

He laughed aloud, a short, dry laugh, that echoed through the vaults. The cheering effect of laughter has been overestimated perhaps. Anyhow, he did not laugh again.

The silence was intense, but it was a silence thick with rustlings and breathings, and movements that his ear, strained to the uttermost, could just not hear. Suppose, as Edward had said, when all the lights were out these things did move. A corpse was a thing that had moved, given a certain condition—life. What if there were a condition, given which these things could move? What if such conditions were present now? What if all of them—Napoleon, yellow-white from his death sleep; the beasts from the amphitheatre, gore dribbling from their jaws; that soldier with the legs—all were drawing near to him in this full silence? Those death masks of Robespierre and Mirabeau—they might float down through the darkness till they touched his face. That head of Mme de Lamballe on the pike might be thrust at him from behind the pillar. The silence throbbed with sounds that could not quite be heard.

'You fool,' he said to himself; 'your dinner has disagreed with you with a vengeance. Don't be an ass. The whole lot are only a set of big dolls.'

He felt for his matches and lighted a cigarette. The gleam of the match fell on the face of the corpse in front of him. The light was brief, and it seemed, somehow, impossible to look by its light in every corner where one would have wished to look. The match burnt his fingers as it went out. And there were only three more matches in the box.

It was dark again, and the image left on the darkness was that of the corpse in front of him. He thought of his dead friend. When the cigarette was smoked out he thought of him more and more, till it seemed that what lay on the bier was not wax. His hand reached forward and drew back more than once. But at last he made it touch the bier and through the blackness travel up along a lean, rigid arm to the wax face that lay there so still. The touch was not reassuring. Just so, and not otherwise, had his dead friend's face felt, to the last touch of his lips. Cold, firm, waxen. People always said the dead were 'waxen'. How true that was! He had never thought of it before. He thought of it now.

He sat still—so still that every muscle ached; because if you wish to hear the sounds that infest silence you must be very still indeed. He thought of Edward, and of the string he had meant to tie to one of the figures.

'That wouldn't be needed,' he told himself. And his ears ached with listening, listening for the sound that, it seemed, *must* break at last from that crowded silence.

He never knew how long he sat there. To move, to go up, to batter at the door and clamour to be let out—that one could have done if one had had a lantern or even a full matchbox. But in the dark, not knowing the turnings, to feel one's way among these things that were so like life and yet were not alive—to touch, perhaps, these faces that were not dead and yet felt like death! His heart beat heavily in his throat at the thought.

No; he must sit still till morning. He had been hypnotized into this state, he told himself, by Edward, no doubt; it was not natural to him.

Then, suddenly, the silence was shattered. In the dark something moved, and, after those sounds that the silence teemed with, the noise seemed to him thunder-loud. Yet it was only a very, very little sound, just the rustling of drapery, as though something had turned in its sleep. And there was a sigh—not far off.

Vincent's muscles and tendons tightened like fine-drawn wire. He listened. There was nothing more. Only the silence, the thick silence.

The sound had seemed to come from a part of the vault where long ago, when there was light, he had seen a grave being dug for the body of a young girl martyr.

'I will get up and go out,' said Vincent. 'I have three matches. I am off my head. I shall really be nervous presently if I don't look out.'

He got up and struck a match, refused his eyes the sight of the corpse whose waxen face he had felt in the blackness, and made his way through the crowd of figures. By the match's flicker they seemed to make way for him, to turn their heads to look after him. The match lasted till he got to a turn of the rock-hewn passage. His next match showed him the burial scene. The little, thin body of the martyr, palm in hand, lying on the rock-floor in patient waiting, the grave-digger, the mourners. Some standing, some kneeling, one crouched on the ground.

This was where that sound had come from, that rustle, that sigh. He had thought he was going away from it. Instead he had come straight to the spot where, if anywhere, his nerves might be expected to play him false.

'Bah!' he said, and he said it aloud. 'The silly things are only wax. Who's afraid?'

His voice sounded loud in the silence that lives with the wax people.

'They're only wax,' he said again, and touched with his foot contemptuously the crouching figure in the mantle.

And, as he touched it, it raised its head and looked vacantly at him, and its eyes were bright and alive. He staggered back against another figure and dropped the match. In the new darkness he heard the crouching figure move towards him. Then the darkness fitted in round him very closely.

'What was it exactly that sent poor Vincent mad—you've never told me?' Rose asked the question. She and Edward were looking out over the pines and tamarisks across the blue Mediterranean. They were very happy, because it was their honeymoon.

He told her about the Musée Grévin and the wager, but he did not state the terms of it.

'But why did he think you would be afraid?'

He told her why.

'And then what happened?'

'Why, I suppose he thought there was no time like the present—for his five pounds, you know—and he hid among the waxworks. And I missed my train, and, *I* thought, there was no time like the present. In fact, dear, I thought if I waited I should have time to make certain of funking it. So I hid there, too. And I put on my big black capuchon, and sat down right in one of the waxwork groups—they couldn't see me from the gallery where you walk. And after they put the lights out I simply went to sleep. And I woke up—and there was a light, and I heard someone say:

"They're only wax," and it was Vincent. He thought I was one of the wax people till I looked at him; and I expect he thought I was one of them even then, poor chap. And his match went out, and while I was trying to find my railway reading lamp that I'd got near me he began to scream. And the night-watchman came running. And now he thinks everyone in the asylum is made of wax, and he screams if they come near him. They have to put his food near him while he's asleep. It's horrible. I can't help feeling as if it were my fault somehow.'

'Of course it's not,' said Rose. 'Poor Vincent! Do you know, I never *really* liked him.'

There was a pause. Then she said:

'But how was it *you* weren't frightened?'

'I was,' he said, 'horribly frightened. It—it—sounds idiotic, but I was really. And yet I *had* to go through with it. And then I got among the figures of the people in the Catacombs, the people who died for—for things, don't you know, died in such horrible ways. And there they were, so calm—and believing it was all right. So I thought about what they'd gone through. It sounds awful rot, I know, dear, but I expect I was sleepy. Those wax people, they sort of seemed as if they were alive, and were telling me there wasn't anything to be frightened about. I felt as if I was one of them—and they were all my friends, and they'd wake me if anything went wrong. So I just went to sleep.'

'I think I understand,' she said. But she didn't.

'And the odd thing is,' he went on, 'I've never been afraid of the dark since. Perhaps his calling me a coward had something to do with it.'

'I don't think so,' said she. And she was right. But she would never have understood how, nor why.

The Horror of the Heights

Arthur Conan Doyle

THE idea that the extraordinary narrative which has been called the Joyce-Armstrong Fragment is an elaborate practical joke evolved by some unknown person, cursed by a perverted and sinister sense of humour, has now been abandoned by all who have examined the matter. The most macabre and imaginative of plotters would hesitate before linking his morbid fancies with the unquestioned and tragic facts which reinforce the statement. Though the assertions contained in it are amazing and even monstrous, it is none the less forcing itself upon the general intelligence that they are true, and that we must readjust our ideas to the new situation. This world of ours appears to be separated by a slight and precarious margin of safety from a most singular and unexpected danger. I will endeavour in this narrative, which reproduces the original document in its necessarily somewhat fragmentary form, to lay before the reader the whole of the facts up to date, prefacing my statement by saying that, if there be any who doubt the narrative of Joyce-Armstrong, there can be no question at all as to the facts concerning Lieutenant Myrtle, RN, and Mr Hay Connor, who undoubtedly met their end in the manner described.

The Joyce-Armstrong Fragment was found in the field which is called Lower Haycock, lying one mile to the westward of the village of Withyham, upon the Kent and Sussex border. It was on the fifteenth of September last that an agricultural labourer, James Flynn, in the employment of Matthew Dodd, farmer, of the Chauntry Farm, Withyham, perceived a briar pipe lying near the footpath which skirts the hedge in Lower Haycock. A few paces further on he picked up a pair of broken binocular glasses. Finally, among some nettles in the ditch, he caught sight of a flat, canvas-backed book, which proved to be a notebook with detachable leaves, some of which had come loose and were fluttering along the base of the hedge. These he collected, but some, including the first, were never recovered, and leave a deplorable hiatus in this all-important statement. The notebook was taken by the labourer to his master, who in turn showed it to Dr J. H. Atherton, of Hartfield. This gentleman at once recognized the need for an expert examination, and the manuscript was forwarded to the Aero Club in London, where it now lies.

The first two pages of the manuscript are missing. There is also one torn away at the end of the narrative, though none of these affect the general coherence of the story. It is conjectured that the missing opening is concerned with the record of Mr Joyce-Armstrong's qualifications as an aeronaut, which can be gathered from other sources and are admitted to be unsurpassed among the air-pilots of England. For many years he has been looked upon as among the most daring and the most intellectual of flying men, a combination which has enabled him to both invent and test several new devices, including the common gyroscopic attachment which is known by his name. The main body of the manuscript is written neatly in ink, but the last few lines are in pencil and are so ragged as to be hardly legible—exactly, in fact, as they might be expected to appear if they were scribbled off hurriedly from the seat of a moving aeroplane. There are, it may be added, several stains, both on the last page and on the outside cover, which have been pronounced by the Home Office experts to be blood—probably human and certainly mammalian. The fact that something closely resembling the organism of malaria was discovered in this blood, and that Joyce-Armstrong is known to have suffered from intermittent fever, is a remarkable example of the new weapons which modern science has placed in the hands of our detectives.

And now a word as to the personality of the author of this epoch-making statement. Joyce-Armstrong, according to the few friends who really knew something of the man, was a poet and a dreamer, as well as a mechanic and an inventor. He was a man of considerable wealth, much of which he had spent in the pursuit of his aeronautical hobby. He had four private aeroplanes in his hangars near

Devizes, and is said to have made no fewer than one hundred and seventy ascents in the course of last year. He was a retiring man with dark moods, in which he would avoid the society of his fellows. Captain Dangerfield, who knew him better than anyone, says that there were times when his eccentricity threatened to develop into something more serious. His habit of carrying a shotgun with him in his aeroplane was one manifestation of it.

Another was the morbid effect which the fall of Lieutenant Myrtle had upon his mind. Myrtle, who was attempting the height record, fell from an altitude of something over thirty thousand feet. Horrible to narrate, his head was entirely obliterated, though his body and limbs preserved their configuration. At every gathering of airmen, Joyce-Armstrong, according to Dangerfield, would ask, with an enigmatic smile: 'And where, pray, is Myrtle's head?'

On another occasion after dinner, at the mess of the Flying School on Salisbury Plain, he started a debate as to what will be the most permanent danger which airmen will have to encounter. Having listened to successive opinions as to air-pockets, faulty construction, and over-banking, he ended by shrugging his shoulders and refusing to put forward his own views, though he gave the impression that they differed from any advanced by his companions.

It is worth remarking that after his own complete disappearance it was found that his private affairs were arranged with a precision which may show that he had a strong premonition of disaster. With these essential explanations I will now give the narrative exactly as it stands, beginning at page three of the blood-soaked notebook:

'Nevertheless, when I dined at Rheims with Coselli and Gustav Raymond I found that neither of them was aware of any particular danger in the higher layers of the atmosphere. I did not actually say what was in my thoughts, but I got so near to it that if they had any corresponding idea they could not have failed to express it. But then they are two empty, vainglorious fellows with no thought beyond seeing their silly names in the newspaper. It is interesting to note that neither of them had ever been much beyond the twenty-thousand-foot level. Of course, men have been higher than this both in balloons and in the ascent of mountains. It must be well above that point that the aeroplane enters the danger zone—always presuming that my premonitions are correct.

'Aeroplaning has been with us now for more than twenty years, and one might well ask: Why should this peril be only revealing itself in our day? The answer is obvious. In the old days of weak engines, when a hundred horsepower Gnome or Green was considered ample for every need, the flights were very restricted. Now that three hundred horsepower is the rule rather than the exception, visits to the upper layers have become easier and more common. Some of us can remember how, in our youth, Garros made a world-wide reputation by attaining nineteen thousand feet, and it was considered a remarkable achievement to fly over the Alps. Our standard now has been immeasurably raised, and there are twenty high flights for one in former years. Many of them have been undertaken with impunity. The thirty-thousand-foot level has been reached time after time with no discomfort beyond cold and asthma. What does this prove? A visitor might descend upon this planet a thousand times and never see a tiger. Yet tigers exist, and if he chanced to come down into a jungle he might be devoured. There are jungles of the upper air, and there are worse things than tigers which inhabit them. I believe in time they will map these jungles accurately out. Even at the present moment I could name two of them. One of them lies over the Pau-Biarritz district of France. Another is just over my head as I write here in my house in Wiltshire. I rather think there is a third in the Homburg-Wiesbaden district.

'It was the disappearance of the airmen that first set me thinking. Of course, everyone said that they had fallen into the sea, but that did not satisfy me at all. First, there was Verrier in France; his machine was found near Bayonne, but they never got his body. There was the case of Baxter also, who vanished, though his engine and some of the iron fixings were found in a wood in Leicestershire. In that case, Dr Middleton, of Amesbury, who was watching the flight with a telescope, declares that just before the clouds obscured the view he saw the machine, which was at an enormous height, suddenly rise perpendicularly upwards in a succession of jerks in a manner that he would have thought to be impossible. That was the last seen of Baxter. There was a correspondence in the papers, but it never led to anything. There were several other similar cases, and then there was the death of Hay Connor. What a cackle there was about an unsolved mystery of the air, and what columns in the halfpenny papers, and yet how little was ever done to get at the bottom of the business! He came down in a tremendous vol-plané from an unknown height. He never got off his machine and died in his pilot's seat. Died of what? "Heart disease", said the doctors. Rubbish! Hay Connor's heart was as sound as mine is. What did Venables say? Venables was the only man who was at his side when he died. He said that he was shivering and looked like a man who had been badly scared. "Died of fright", said Venables, but could not imagine what he was frightened about. Only said one word to Venables, which sounded like "Monstrous". They could make nothing of that at the inquest. But I could make something of it. Monsters! That was the last word of poor Harry Hay Connor. And he *did* die of fright, just as Venables thought.

'And then there was Myrtle's head. Do you really believe—does anybody really believe—that a man's head could be driven clean into his body by the force of a fall? Well, perhaps it may be possible, but I, for one, have never believed that it was so with Myrtle. And the grease upon his clothes—"all slimy with grease", said somebody at the inquest. Queer that nobody got thinking after that! I did— but, then, I had been thinking for a good long time. I've made three ascents—how Dangerfield used to chaff me about my shotgun!— but I've never been high enough. Now, with this new light Paul Veroner machine and its one hundred and seventy-five Robur, I should easily touch the thirty thousand tomorrow. I'll have a shot at the record. Maybe I shall have a shot at something else as well. Of course, it's dangerous. If a fellow wants to avoid danger he had best keep out of flying altogether and subside finally into flannel slippers and a dressing-gown. But I'll visit the air-jungle tomorrow—and if there's anything there I shall know it. If I return, I'll find myself a bit of a celebrity. If I don't, this notebook may explain what I am trying to do, and how I lost my life in doing it. But no drivel about accidents or mysteries, if *you* please.

'I chose my Paul Veroner monoplane for the job. There's nothing like a monoplane when real work is to be done. Beaumont found that out in very early days. For one thing, it doesn't mind damp, and the weather looks as if we should be in the clouds all the time. It's a bonny little model and answers my hand like a tender-mouthed horse. The engine is a ten-cylinder rotary Robur working up to one hundred and seventy-five. It has all the modern improvements—enclosed fuselage, high-curved landing skids, brakes, gyroscopic steadiers, and three speeds, worked by an alteration of the angle of the planes upon the Venetian-blind principle. I took a shotgun with me and a dozen cartridges filled with buck-shot. You should have seen the face of Perkins, my old mechanic, when I directed him to put them in. I was dressed like an Arctic explorer, with two jerseys under my overalls, thick socks inside my padded boots, a storm-cap with flaps, and my talc goggles. It was stifling outside the hangars, but I was going for the summit of the Himalayas, and had to dress for the part. Perkins knew there was something on and implored me to take him with me. Perhaps I should if I were using the biplane, but a monoplane is a one-man show—if you want to get the last foot of lift out of it. Of course, I took an oxygen bag; the man who goes for the altitude record without one will either be frozen or smothered—or both.

'I had a good look at the planes, the rudder-bar, and the elevating lever before I got in. Everything was in order so far as I could see. Then I switched on my engine and found that she was running sweetly. When they let her go she rose almost at once upon the lowest speed. I circled my home field once or twice just to warm her up, and then, with a wave to Perkins and the others, I flattened out my planes and put her on her highest. She skimmed like a swallow down wind for eight or ten miles until I turned her nose up a little and she began to climb in a great spiral for the cloud-bank above me. It's all-important to rise slowly and adapt yourself to the pressure as you go.

'It was a close, warm day for an English September, and there was the hush and heaviness of impending rain. Now and then there came sudden puffs of wind from the south-west—one of them so gusty and unexpected that it caught me napping and turned me half-round for an instant. I remember the time when gusts and whirls and air-pockets used to be things of danger—before we learned to put an overmastering power into our engines. Just as I reached the cloud-banks, with the altimeter marking three thousand, down came the rain. My word, how it poured! It drummed upon my wings and lashed against my face, blurring my glasses so that I could hardly see. I got down on to a low speed, for it was painful to travel against it. As I got higher it became hail, and I had to turn tail to it. One of my cylinders was out of action—a dirty plug, I should imagine, but still I was rising steadily with plenty of power.

After a bit the trouble passed, whatever it was, and I heard the full, deep-throated purr—the ten singing as one. That's where the beauty of our modern silencers comes in. We can at last control our engines by ear. How they squeal and squeak and sob when they are in trouble! All those cries for help were wasted in the old days, when every sound was swallowed up by the monstrous racket of the machine. If only the early aviators could come back to see the beauty and perfection of the mechanisms which have been bought at the cost of their lives!

'About nine-thirty I was nearing the clouds. Down below me, all blurred and shadowed with rain, lay the vast expanse of Salisbury Plain. Half-a-dozen flying machines were doing hack-work at the thousand-foot level, looking like little black swallows against the green background. I dare say they were wondering what I was doing up in cloud-land. Suddenly a grey curtain drew across beneath me and the wet folds of vapour were swirling round my face. It was clammily cold and miserable. But I was above the hail-storm, and that was something gained. The cloud was as dark and thick as a London fog. In my anxiety to get clear, I cocked her nose up until the automatic alarm-bell rang and I actually began to slide backwards. My sopped and dripping wings had made me heavier than I thought, but presently I was in lighter cloud, and soon had cleared the first layer. There was a second—opal-coloured and fleecy—at a great height above my head, a white unbroken ceiling above, and a dark unbroken floor below, with the monoplane labouring upwards upon a vast spiral between them. It is deadly lonely in these cloud-spaces. Once a great flight of some small water-birds went past me, flying very fast to the westwards. The quick whirr of their wings and their musical cry were cheery to my ear. I fancy that they were teal, but I am a wretched zoologist. Now that we humans have become birds we must really learn to know our brethren by sight.

'The wind down beneath me whirled and swayed the broad cloud-plain. Once a great eddy formed in it, a whirlpool of vapour, and through it, as down a funnel, I caught sight of the distant world. A large white biplane was passing at a vast depth beneath me. I fancy it is the morning mail service betwixt Bristol and London. Then the drift swirled forwards again and the great solitude was unbroken.

'Just after ten I touched the lower edge of the upper cloud-stratum. It consisted of fine diaphanous vapour drifting swiftly from the westward. The wind had been steadily rising all this time and it was now blowing a sharp breeze—twenty-eight an hour by my gauge. Already it was very cold, though my altimeter only marked nine thousand. The engines were working beautifully, and we went droning steadily upwards. The cloud-bank was thicker than I had expected, but at last it thinned out into a golden mist before me, and then in an instant I had shot out from it, and there was an unclouded sky and a brilliant sun above my head—all blue and gold above, all shining silver below, one vast glimmering plain as far as my eyes could reach. It was a quarter past ten o'clock, and the barograph needle pointed to twelve thousand eight hundred. Up I went and up, my ears concentrated upon the deep purring of my motor, my eyes busy always with the watch, the revolution indicator, the petrol lever, and the oil pump. No wonder aviators are said to be a fearless race. With so many things to think of there is no time to trouble about oneself. About this time I noted how unreliable is the compass when above a certain height from earth. At fifteen thousand feet mine was pointing east and a point south. The sun and the wind gave me my true bearings.

'I had hoped to reach an eternal stillness in these high altitudes, but with every thousand feet of ascent the gale grew stronger. My machine groaned and trembled in every joint and rivet as she faced it, and swept away like a sheet of paper when I banked her on the turn, skimming down wind at a greater pace, perhaps, than ever mortal man has moved. Yet I had always to turn again and tack up in the wind's eye, for it was not merely a height record that I was after. By all my calculations it was above little Wiltshire that my air-jungle lay, and all my labour might be lost if I struck the outer layers at some farther point.

'When I reached the nineteen-thousand-foot level, which was about midday, the wind was so severe that I looked with some anxiety to the stays of my wings, expecting momentarily to see them snap or slacken. I even cast loose the parachute behind me, and fastened its hook into the ring of my leathern belt, so as to be ready for the worst. Now was the time when a bit of scamped work by the mechanic is paid for by the life of the aeronaut. But she held together bravely. Every cord and strut was humming and vibrating like so many harp-strings, but it was glorious to see how, for all the beating and the buffeting, she was still the conqueror of Nature and the mistress of the sky. There is surely something divine in man himself that he should rise so superior to the limitations which Creation seemed to impose—rise, too, by such unselfish, heroic devotion as this air-conquest has shown. Talk of human degeneration! When has such a story as this been written in the annals of our race?

'These were the thoughts in my head as I climbed that monstrous inclined plane with the wind sometimes beating in my face and sometimes whistling behind my ears, while the cloud-land beneath me fell away to such a distance that the folds and hummocks of silver had all smoothed out into one flat, shining plain. But suddenly I had a horrible and unprecedented experience. I have known before what it is to be in what our neighbours have called a *tourbillon*, but never on such a scale as this. That huge, sweeping river of wind of which I have spoken had, as it appears, whirlpools within it which were as monstrous as itself. Without a moment's warning I was dragged suddenly into the heart of one. I spun round for a minute or two with such velocity that I almost lost my senses, and then fell suddenly, left wing foremost, down the vacuum funnel in the centre. I dropped like a stone, and lost nearly a thousand feet. It was only my belt that kept me in my seat, and the shock and breathlessness left me hanging half-insensible over the side of the fuselage. But I am always capable of a supreme effort—it is my one great merit as an aviator. I was conscious that the descent was slower. The whirlpool was a cone rather than a funnel, and I had come to the apex. With a terrific wrench, throwing my weight all to one side, I levelled my planes and brought her head away from the wind. In an instant I had shot out of the eddies and was skimming down the sky. Then, shaken but victorious, I turned her nose up and began once more my steady grind on the upward spiral. I took a large sweep to avoid the danger-spot of the whirlpool, and soon I was safely above it. Just after one o'clock I was twenty-one thousand feet above the sea-level. To my great joy I had topped the gale, and with every hundred feet of ascent the air grew stiller. On the other hand, it was very cold, and I was conscious of that peculiar nausea which goes with rarefaction of the air. For the first time I unscrewed the mouth of my oxygen bag and took an occasional whiff of the glorious gas. I could feel it running like a cordial through my veins, and I was exhilarated almost to the point of drunkenness. I shouted and sang as I soared upwards into the cold, still outer world.

'It is very clear to me that the insensibility which came upon Glaisher, and in a lesser degree upon Coxwell, when, in 1862, they ascended in a balloon to the height of thirty thousand feet, was due to the extreme speed with which a perpendicular ascent is made. Doing it at an easy gradient and accustoming oneself to the lessened barometric pressure by slow degrees, there are no such dreadful symptoms. At the same great height I found that even without my oxygen inhaler I could breathe without undue distress. It was bitterly cold, however, and my thermometer was at zero Fahrenheit. At one-thirty I was nearly seven miles above the surface of the earth, and still ascending steadily. I found, however, that the rarefied air was giving markedly less support to my planes, and that my angle of ascent had to be considerably lowered in consequence. It was already clear that even with my light weight and strong engine-power there was a point in front of me where I should be held. To make matters worse, one of my sparking-plugs was in trouble again and there was intermittent missfiring in the engine. My heart was heavy with the fear of failure.

'It was about that time that I had a most extraordinary experience. Something whizzed past me in a trail of smoke and exploded with a loud, hissing sound, sending forth a cloud of steam. For the instant I could not imagine what had happened. Then I remembered that the earth is for ever being bombarded by meteor stones, and would be hardly inhabitable were they not in nearly every case turned to vapour in the outer layers of the atmosphere. Here is a new danger for the high-altitude man, for two others passed me when I was nearing the forty-thousand-foot mark. I cannot doubt that at the edge of the earth's envelope the risk would be a very real one.

'My barograph needle marked forty-one thousand three hundred when I became aware that I could go no further. Physically, the strain was not as yet greater than I could bear, but my machine had reached its limit. The attenuated air gave no firm support to the wings, and the least tilt developed into side-slip, while she seemed sluggish on her controls. Possibly, had the engine been at its best, another thousand feet might have been within our capacity, but it was still missfiring, and two out of the ten cylinders appeared to be out of action. If I had not already reached the zone for which I was searching then I should never see it upon this journey. But was it not possible that I had attained it? Soaring in circles like a monstrous hawk upon the forty-thousand-foot level I let the monoplane guide herself, and with my Mannheim glass I made a careful observation of my surroundings. The heavens were perfectly clear; there was no indication of those dangers which I had imagined.

'I have said that I was soaring in circles. It struck me suddenly that I would do well to take a wider sweep and open up a new air-tract. If the hunter entered an earth-jungle he would drive through it if he wished to find his game. My reasoning had led me to believe that the air-jungle which I had imagined lay somewhere over Wiltshire. This should be to the south and west of me. I took my bearings from the sun, for the compass was hopeless and no trace of earth was to be seen—nothing but the distant silver cloud-plain. However, I got my direction as best I might and kept her head straight to the mark. I reckoned that my petrol supply would not last for more than another hour or so, but I could afford to use it to the last drop, since a single magnificent vol-plané could at any time take me to the earth.

'Suddenly I was aware of something new. The air in front of me had lost its crystal clearness. It was full of long, ragged wisps of something which I can only compare to very fine cigarette-smoke. It hung about in wreaths and coils, turning and twisting slowly in the sunlight. As the monoplane shot through it, I was aware of a faint taste of oil upon my lips, and there was a greasy scum upon the woodwork of the machine. Some infinitely fine organic matter appeared to be suspended in the atmosphere. There was no life there. It was inchoate and diffuse, extending for many square acres and then fringing off into the void. No, it was not life. But might it not be the remains of life? Above all, might it not be the food of life, of monstrous life, even as the humble plankton of the ocean is the food for the mighty whale? The thought was in my mind when my eyes looked upwards and I saw the most wonderful vision that ever man has seen. Can I hope to convey it to you even as I saw it myself last Thursday?

'Conceive a jelly-fish such as sails in our summer seas, bell-shaped and of enormous size—far larger, I should judge, than the dome of St Paul's. It was of a light pink colour veined with a delicate green, but the whole huge fabric so tenuous that it was but a fairy outline against the dark blue sky. It pulsated with a delicate and regular rhythm. From it there depended two long, drooping green tentacles, which swayed slowly backwards and forwards. This gorgeous vision passed gently with noiseless dignity over my head, as light and fragile as a soap-bubble, and drifted upon its stately way.

'I had half-turned my monoplane, that I might look after this beautiful creature, when, in a moment, I found myself amidst a perfect fleet of them, of all sizes, but none so large as the first. Some were quite small, but the majority about as big as an average balloon, and with much the same curvature at the top. There was in them a delicacy of texture and colouring which reminded me of the finest Venetian glass. Pale shades of pink and green were the prevailing tints, but all had a lovely iridescence where the sun shimmered through their dainty forms. Some hundreds of them drifted past me, a wonderful fairy squadron of strange, unknown argosies of the sky—creatures whose forms and substance were so attuned to these pure heights that one could not conceive anything so delicate within actual sight or sound of earth.

'But soon my attention was drawn to a new phenomenon—the serpents of the outer air. These were long, thin, fantastic coils of vapour-like material, which turned and twisted with great speed, flying round and round at such a pace that the eyes could hardly follow them. Some of these ghost-like creatures were twenty or thirty feet long, but it was difficult to tell their girth, for their outline was so hazy that it seemed to fade away into the air around them. These air-snakes were of a very light grey or smoke colour, with some darker lines within, which gave the impression of a definite organism. One of them whisked past my very face, and I was conscious of a cold, clammy contact, but their composition was so unsubstantial that I could not connect them with any thought of physical danger, any more than the beautiful bell-like creatures which had preceded them. There was no more solidity in their frames than in the floating spume from a broken wave.

'But a more terrible experience was in store for me. Floating downwards from a great height there came a purplish patch of vapour, small as I saw it first, but rapidly enlarging as it approached me, until it appeared to be hundreds of square feet in size. Though

fashioned of some transparent, jelly-like substance, it was none the
less of much more definite outline and solid consistence than
anything which I had seen before. There were more traces, too, of
a physical organization, especially two vast shadowy, circular plates
upon either side, which may have been eyes, and a perfectly solid
white projection between them which was as curved and cruel as
the beak of a vulture.

'The whole aspect of this monster was formidable and threatening, and it kept changing its colour from a very light mauve to a
dark, angry purple so thick that it cast a shadow as it drifted
between my monoplane and the sun. On the upper curve of its huge
body there were three great projections which I can only describe
as enormous bubbles, and I was convinced as I looked at them that
they were charged with some extremely light gas which served to
buoy up the misshapen and semi-solid mass in the rarefied air. The
creature moved swiftly along, keeping pace easily with the monoplane, and for twenty miles or more it formed my horrible escort,
hovering over me like a bird of prey which is waiting to pounce. Its
method of progression—done so swiftly that it was not easy to
follow—was to throw out a long, glutinous streamer in front of it,
which in turn seemed to draw forward the rest of the writhing
body. So elastic and gelatinous was it that never for two successive
minutes was it the same shape, and yet each change made it more
threatening and loathsome than the last.

'I knew that it meant mischief. Every purple flush of its hideous
body told me so. The vague, goggling eyes which were turned
always upon me were cold and merciless in their viscid hatred. I
dipped the nose of my monoplane downwards to escape it. As I did
so, as quick as a flash there shot out a long tentacle from this mass
of floating blubber, and it fell as light and sinuous as a whip-lash
across the front of my machine. There was a loud hiss as it lay for a
moment across the hot engine, and it whisked itself into the air
again, while the huge flat body drew itself together as if in sudden
pain. I dipped to a vol-piqué, but again a tentacle fell over the
monoplane and was shorn off by the propeller as easily as it might
have cut through a smoke wreath. A long, gliding, sticky, serpent-
like coil came from behind and caught me round the waist, dragging
me out of the fuselage. I tore at it, my fingers sinking into the
smooth, glue-like surface, and for an instant I disengaged myself,

but only to be caught round the boot by another coil, which gave me a jerk that tilted me almost on to my back.

'As I fell over I blazed off both barrels of my gun, though, indeed, it was like attacking an elephant with a pea-shooter to imagine that any human weapon could cripple that mighty bulk. And yet I aimed better than I knew, for, with a loud report, one of the great blisters upon the creature's back exploded with the puncture of the buck-shot. It was very clear that my conjecture was right, and that these vast clear bladders were distended with some lifting gas, for in an instant the huge cloud-like body turned sideways, writhing desperately to find its balance, while the white beak snapped and gaped in horrible fury. But already I had shot away on the steepest glide that I dared to attempt, my engine still full on, the flying propeller and the force of gravity shooting me downwards like an aerolite. Far behind me I saw a dull, purplish smudge growing swiftly smaller and merging into the blue sky behind it. I was safe out of the deadly jungle of the outer air.

'Once out of danger I throttled my engine, for nothing tears a machine to pieces quicker than running on full power from a height. It was a glorious spiral vol-plané from nearly eight miles of altitude—first, to the level of the silver cloud-bank, then to that of the storm-cloud beneath it, and finally, in beating rain, to the surface of the earth. I saw the Bristol Channel beneath me as I broke from the clouds, but, having still some petrol in my tank, I got twenty miles inland before I found myself stranded in a field half a mile from the village of Ashcombe. There I got three tins of petrol from a passing motor-car, and at ten minutes past six that evening I alighted gently in my own home meadow at Devizes, after such a journey as no mortal upon earth has ever yet taken and lived to tell the tale. I have seen the beauty and I have seen the horror of the heights—and greater beauty or greater horror than that is not within the ken of man.

'And now it is my plan to go once again before I give my results to the world. My reason for this is that I must surely have something to show by way of proof before I lay such a tale before my fellow-men. It is true that others will soon follow and will confirm what I have said, and yet I should wish to carry conviction from the first. Those lovely iridescent bubbles of the air should not be hard to capture. They drift slowly upon their way, and the swift monoplane

could intercept their leisurely course. It is likely enough that they
would dissolve in the heavier layers of the atmosphere, and that
some small heap of amorphous jelly might be all that I should bring
to earth with me. And yet something there would surely be by
which I could substantiate my story. Yes, I will go, even if I run a
risk by doing so. These purple horrors would not seem to be
numerous. It is probable that I shall not see one. If I do I shall dive
at once. At the worst there is always the shotgun and my knowledge
of . . .'

Here a page of the manuscript is unfortunately missing. On the
next page is written, in large, straggling writing:

'Forty-three thousand feet. I shall never see earth again. They are
beneath me, three of them. God help me; it is a dreadful death to
die!'

Such in its entirety is the Joyce-Armstrong Statement. Of the
man nothing has since been seen. Pieces of his shattered monoplane
have been picked up in the preserves of Mr Budd-Lushington upon
the borders of Kent and Sussex, within a few miles of the spot
where the notebook was discovered. If the unfortunate aviator's
theory is correct that this air-jungle, as he called it, existed only
over the south-west of England, then it would seem that he had fled
from it at the full speed of his monoplane, but had been overtaken
and devoured by these horrible creatures at some spot in the outer
atmosphere above the place where the grim relics were found. The
picture of that monoplane skimming down the sky, with the
nameless terrors flying as swiftly beneath it and cutting it off always
from the earth while they gradually closed in upon their victim, is
one upon which a man who valued his sanity would prefer not to
dwell. There are many, as I am aware, who still jeer at the facts
which I have here set down, but even they must admit that Joyce-
Armstrong has disappeared, and I would commend to them his own
words: 'This notebook may explain what I am trying to do, and
how I lost my life in doing it. But no drivel about accidents or
mysteries, if *you* please.'

Sources

The stories in this collection originally appeared in the *Strand Magazine* as follows:

June 1891: Villiers de l'Isle-Adam, 'A Torture By Hope'

September 1892: H. Greenhough Smith, 'The Case of Roger Carboyne'

October 1894: L. T. Meade, 'A Horrible Fright'

December 1897: Grant Allen, 'The Thames Valley Catastrophe'

June 1898: C. J. Cutcliffe-Hyne, 'The Lizard' (*Atoms of Empire*, 1904)

March 1899: Henry A. Hering, 'Cavalanci's Curse'

December 1901: J. B. Harris-Burland, 'Lord Beden's Motor'

April 1905: E. Nesbit, 'The Power of Darkness'

August 1908: A. Conan Doyle, 'The Silver Mirror' (*The Last Galley*, 1911)

October 1908: Morley Roberts, 'The Fog' (*Midsummer Madness*, 1909)

September 1913: A. Conan Doyle, 'How It Happened' (*Danger!*, 1918)

November 1913: A. Conan Doyle, 'The Horror of the Heights' (*Danger!*, 1918)

December 1913: E. Nesbit, 'The Haunted House' (as by 'E. Bland')

August 1915: Rina Ramsay, 'Resurgam'

December 1917: L. G. Moberly, 'Inexplicable'

December 1918: Ianthe Jerrold, 'The Orchestra of Death'

April 1919: D. H. Lawrence, '"Tickets, Please!"' (*England, My England*, 1922: in a shortened form)

March 1920: Edgar Wallace, 'The Black Grippe' (*The Death Room*, 1986)

July 1922: W. L. George, 'Waxworks'

December 1922: W. W. Jacobs, 'His Brother's Keeper' (*Sea Whispers*, 1926)

February 1923: L. de Giberne Sieveking, 'The Prophetic Camera'

December 1923: Hugh Walpole, 'The Tarn' (*The Silver Thorn*, 1928)

August 1924: Martin Swayne, 'A Sense of the Future'

February 1926: Sapper, 'Touch and Go' (*When Carruthers Laughed*, 1934)

November 1931: F. Tennyson Jesse, 'The Railway Carriage'

March 1932: H. G. Wells, 'The Queer Story of Brownlow's Newspaper' (*The Soul of a Bishop*, 1933)

August 1946: Beverley Nichols, 'The Bell'

March 1947: Graham Greene, 'All But Empty' (*Nineteen Stories*, 1947, as 'A Little Place off the Edgeware Road')

January 1950: B. L. Jacot, 'White Spectre'

Acknowledgements

The editor and publishers gratefully acknowledge permission to reproduce copyright material in this book.

C. J. Cutcliffe-Hyne, 'The Lizard'. Copyright 1898 C. J. Cutcliffe-Hyne.

Graham Greene, 'All But Empty'. Copyright 1947 Graham Greene. Reprinted by permission of Laurence Pollinger Ltd., on behalf of the Estate of Graham Greene.

W. W. Jacobs, 'His Brother's Keeper'. Used by permission of The Society of Authors as the literary representative of the Estate of W. W. Jacobs.

B. L. Jacot, 'White Spectre'. Copyright 1950 B. L. Jacot.

Ianthe Jerrold, 'The Orchestra of Death'. Copyright 1917 Ianthe Jerrold.

F. Tennyson Jesse, 'The Railway Carriage'. Copyright F. Tennyson Jesse 1930. This story is to be included in a forthcoming collection entitled *The Adventures of Solange Fontaine*, published by Ferret Fantasy. Reproduced by permission of Joanna Colenbrander on behalf of The Public Trustees Harwood Will Trust.

D. H. Lawrence, 'Tickets, Please!'. Copyright 1922 by Thomas Seltzer, Inc., renewal copyright 1950 by Frieda Lawrence, from *Complete Short Stories of D. H. Lawrence*. Used by permission of Viking Penguin, a division of Penguin Books USA Inc.

Beverley Nichols, 'The Bell' (1946). Used by permission of Eric Glass Ltd. on behalf of the Beverley Nichols Estate.

Lance Sieveking, 'The Prophetic Camera'. Used by permission of Lemon Unna & Durbridge Ltd.

Martin Swayne, 'A Sense of the Future'. Copyright 1924 Martin Swayne.

Hugh Walpole, 'The Tarn'. Used by permission of Sir Rupert Hart-Davis.